MW01142099

ALPHANAUTS

J. BRIAN CLARKE

EDGE SCIENCE FICTION AND FANTASY PUBLISHING
AN IMPRINT OF HADES PUBLICATIONS, INC.
CALGARY

Edge Science Fiction and Fantasy Publishing
An Imprint of Hades Publications Inc.
P.O. Box 1714, Calgary, Alberta, T2P 2L7, Canada

In house editing by Cheyenne Grewe
Interior design by Brian Hades
Cover Illustrations by David Willicome
ISBN-10: 1-894063-14-7
ISBN-13: 978-1-894063-14-2

EDGE Science Fiction and Fantasy Publishing and Hades Publications, Inc.
acknowledges the ongoing support of the Canada Council for the Arts and the
Alberta Foundation for the Arts for our publishing programme.

The Alberta Foundation for the Arts
COMMITTED TO THE DEVELOPMENT OF CULTURE AND THE ARTS

Alberta
COMMUNITY DEVELOPMENT

Canada Council   Conseil des Arts
for the Arts   du Canada

Library and Archives Canada Cataloguing in Publication

Clarke, J. Brian
    Alphanauts / J. Brian Clarke.

ISBN-13: 978-1-894063-14-2
ISBN-10: 1-894063-14-7

    I. Title.

PS8555.L374855A64   2005   C813'.6   C2005-906728-4

FIRST EDITION
(m-20060412)
Printed in Canada
www.edgewebsite.com

INTRODUCTION

Science Fiction's Other Clarke

by Robert J. Sawyer

I know what it's like.

My last name is Sawyer, and so people are forever asking me if I'm any relation to Tom. If I'm in a good mood, I just politely answer no; if my mood is more foul, I point out that Tom was a fictional character, and so there's no possible way I could be related to him since, last time I checked, this was the real world.

J. Brian Clarke has it equally tough—maybe more so, in his chosen field of science-fiction writing. People ask all the time whether he's any relation to *2001* author Arthur C. Clarke.

And, actually, the answer isn't as clear-cut as in my own case.

Is Brian a member of Sir Arthur's immediate family. No. But as a *writer* ...

As a writer, Brian has a lot in common with Sri Lanka's most-famous resident.

Arthur C. Clarke's long-time association with the British Interplanetary Society is well known. J. Brian Clarke is a Fellow of that organization—as well as a past president of the Calgary Centre of the Royal Astronomical Society of Canada.

Arthur C. Clarke is famous for his ties with the magazine that was once called *Astounding Stories* and now goes by the moniker *Analog Science Fiction and Fact*.

J. Brian Clarke is a regular in that publication's pages, with sixteen stories, including five cover stories, to his credit.

And, of course, Arthur C. Clarke is known for somehow turning a bunch of scientists sitting around talking into some of the most scintillating, unputdownable prose around.

Ditto our Brian. He writes about scientists and engineers, about people who think and do, about problems that have to be solved and the men and women who roll up their sleeves and get the work done. His characters are the kinds of scientists-as-heroes that our real world inexplicably lacks but that were the mainstay of the Golden Age of science fiction.

Most of Brian's *Analog* stories are in his "Expediters" universe—including his best-known tale, "Earthgate," which appeared as the lead story in Donald A. Wollheim's *The 1986 Annual World's Best SF*. These stories were combined into a wonderful gem of a novel called *The Expediter* that came out from DAW in 1990. I remember reading that book with great fondness, years before I first had the pleasure of meeting Brian.

This current novel started in the pages of *Analog*, too, with the novelette "Return of the Alphanauts" in the August 1990 issue, and the sequel "Adoption" from the May 1992 issue. *Alphanauts* is an even better tale than *The Expediter* — the work of a writer who has the easy confidence of experience, not to mention one of the biggest hearts in science fiction.

Brian is unflaggingly supportive of new writers. He gave me excellent feedback on a draft of my own early novel, *Starplex*, and he's often seen in classrooms helping young people learn how to tell their own stories.

He's also seen frequently at SF conventions—indeed, he recently made quite a stir in Canadian SF circles with his rousing defense of SF conventions in *The Calgary Herald* newspaper.

SF could ask for no better ambassador. So sit back, relax, and enjoy: the alphanauts have come home.

PRELUDE

● ●

It was a world of oceans, continents, and ice caps. There was life; not in profusion, although in time it would girdle the planet and extend from pole to pole. Yet there were forests, grasslands, insects and animals. Birds soared high in the sky. Fish swam in the sea.

Intelligence had evolved here, flourished, and was cruelly extinguished. Now it was a world waiting for a new beginning.

A ship came from a planet of another sun and established orbit. The ship disgorged a smaller, winged vehicle which de-orbited and landed.

The first settlers emerged...

PART I
THE RETURN

• •

CHAPTER ONE

• •

The three year quarantine was nearly over. As Richard Burret stood beside his bed and packed his personal belongings, he tried not to think of the difficulties which lay ahead, of trying to resume a lifestyle he had almost forgotten. He was in limbo, between a world to which he could not return, and a world to which he did not want to return.

First he packed the souvenirs he had put aside for special handling. Although part of him wondered if it was such a good idea to keep these bits of realism around while time and memories softened what had been in the past, the other part insisted, why not? He and his five companions had, after all, been part of an endeavor beyond anything in human history. They deserved their trophies!

Item. Three vials banded together. The first contained the corpse of an insect-like creature, the second a ball of fluff, the third a tiny plant with pinhead-sized gray leaves. Not much to the uninformed eye, perhaps. But the mind behind that eye could not know these were three stages in the strange life cycle of a single life form.

Item. Another vial, this one filled with a clear liquid. Actually, it was only water. But it had been collected in the mist below a great cataract which plunged an uninterrupted fifteen hundred meters down the side of a fault which split a continent.

Item. A package of samples containing plant and animal matter, plus material which shared the characteristics of both. A slender piece of vine with a tensile strength approaching that of steel. A piece of wood which, when heated, could be molded like soft putty.

The samples were followed by Burret's finger camera and a package of chips containing he did not know how many thousands of exposures. Not as extensive as the official visual record, of course. But a man needs to do something of his own during a mission of such extended duration. Howard Scheckart, for instance, had taken to painting. Although the botanist's gloomy landscapes were too depressing for Burret's taste, he did not doubt a few would end up in some of Earth's major galleries.

Next, his instrument and sample belt. He coiled the belt carefully, despite the scars and frays which made it look as if it had been dragged through barbed wire. It happened when he tumbled down a slope into a clump of thorn bushes, and his body still bore the marks inflicted by those vicious barbs. Yet the belt continued its usefulness. It even outlasted two sets of armorcloth coveralls.

He lifted a sealed plastic envelope up to the light. The envelope contained a few blades of grass, slivers of faded green from a lawn logic dictated could not be grown. But young Eric Gerenson, communications specialist and former street kid from one of the concrete jungles of western Europe, thought otherwise. He did not, he insisted, smuggle two kilos of seed all the way from Earth for nothing. So Gerenson consulted the ship's database, prepared the proper nutrients, and contrived a sprinkler system. He fussed, worried, made a thorough fool of himself, and after a few months created the lushest lawn on the fifth planet of Alpha Centauri. Actually it was the only lawn, and it was fortunate its survival depended on such loving care. Otherwise, the next expedition might find the local ecology drowned under an ocean of waving green.

More oddments went into the bag, including a small abstract carved by Victor Kraskin before the geologist lost his right arm in a rockfall.

Finally, Burret sorted through the few letters he received only hours before the *Robert L. Cassion* departed for the Centauri system. There was a polite farewell from Ron, on office letterhead. They had not seen each other for years anyway, so Ron could hardly be expected to gush over a brother he hardly knew. A couple of letters were from people Burret worked with during the second Mercury expedition. He had largely lost contact with them also, especially after he transferred to the Interstellar Project.

More personal than the others, was Maylene's last letter. Would he have married her if he was not on the Project? Probably. May was one in a million; he would have been a fool not to. Then again, they only met because she happened to be one of the Project's technicians, so the question was academic. Another of life's not-so-minor ironies, he supposed.

The last letter was on cheap brittle notepaper, so he handled it gingerly. But the childish scrawl was still legible. As he read it again, his memories of her earnest little face were as clear as they had been ... how many hundreds of readings ago?

Darling daddy, please do not go away to long. Auntie Pol said you are going to a star, not like mommy but in a spaceship. She said we canot see the star from our house so I want her and Uncle Hector to take me where I can see it sometime. When you come back, bring me a star teddy please, PLEASE? Love and kisses, Cheryl.

Burret wished he knew what a star teddy was, but it had been too late to find out. He hoped the painstaking model he created from local materials and imagination would be an acceptable substitute. His daughter was older now, but surely she would remember and understand.

Goddamn the quarantine!

It was not the three years of confinement on the moon which bothered him, as much as the restrictions which allowed no outside communication incoming or outgoing. Officially, no one even knew the *Robert L. Cassion* was back from the Centauri system! He did not doubt that except for UNSAA brass who were party to the deception, not to mention those who had forgotten anyway, most of the billions of people on that blue-white world in the lunar sky probably assumed mankind's first star travelers had expired somewhere out there in the Great Dark.

The reason for the quarantine was logical enough. The statistical possibility they were biological time bombs was nothing new. It was a factor which had even been taken into account when the first astronauts returned from the moon a couple of centuries ago. But the Apollo 11 quarantine lasted only eighteen days. Not three years!

That root cause of frustration had been addressed by Eratosthenes administrator Dr. Curtis Paoli, at the first of his weekly briefings. In his gentle way, it was a reminder. "There are six billion people on planet Earth," he said. "There are only six of you alphanauts."

Alphanauts.

Burret hated that ridiculous term, especially the anonymous idiot who dreamed it up. But they were apparently stuck with it.

"With those odds," Paoli continued, "how can you possibly object to us making sure you are biologically safe? And need I remind you that a motion to extend the quarantine to forty-two months, right into the red-line zone, was defeated by only one vote? Gentlemen, I suggest you consider yourselves lucky."

"Lucky, my eye!" angrily shouted Gellan DeZantos, the expedition's astronomer. "Dammit Curtis, you can't transmit a plague by radio! So why can't I talk to my Earthside colleagues? Why can't any of us?"

Paoli waited patiently until the whispering died down, then repeated what everyone already knew. "Gellan, you cannot be allowed to communicate with people who do not know you exist. It has to be that way because of what you are and what the mass media can do with it. All right, I admit most media people can be trusted to do the right thing. But not, unfortunately, all of them. If certain bottom-liners find out what is going on, they can pull enough political clout to end this quarantine within a year at the most. If that happens..."

Burret would never forget the chill which ran up his spine as he recognized the look of absolute determination on Paoli's face.

"If that happens, I will destroy this facility and everyone and everything in it!"

The alphanauts sat in stony silence while everyone else nodded in grim acquiescence. No one doubted the threat was real, that the director had the codes which could blow the complex into the lunar vacuum. It was a situation resented by the alphanauts, who were the only ones not here by choice. The others, all volunteers, had been thoroughly briefed when they signed on.

Yet despite the Damoclean sword over their heads, it was not such a bad life. There was work to do, especially with the samples and reams of data brought back from Alpha Five. Their place of exile was luxurious beyond belief, with every imagined creature comfort including a swimming pool and a well-equipped gymnasium. The small holo-theater frequently showed the latest entertainment offerings from Earth, and by the end of the first year there was a thriving repertory company. Yet every time the robo-shuttle arrived with fresh supplies, there was fierce, even acrimonious competition for the privilege of being part of the four-man unloading crew.

As far as other needs were concerned, it was fortunate UNSAA's funding was no longer subject to the political whims of the United Nations House of Assembly. The cabal of religious fundamentalists who dominated the Assembly for so long, threatening financial termination if all-male crews were not used on the interstellar projects, had finally succumbed before the onslaught of twenty-second century pragmatism. Which was why — and during his introspective moments Burret put aside his innate agnosticism to thank God for it — twenty of the thirty-four assigned to Eratosthenes were women. A few couples were already married when they arrived, and within six months several more signed contracts. Although none of the alphanauts entered similar commitments, only the monkish Howard Scheckart chose to remain celibate.

✤ ✤ ✤

As Burret closed the bag and pressed an identification label to its side, he wondered if he would see much of Joan after they returned home, if he had made a mistake when he told her he would consider nothing permanent until he was adjusted to Earthside. He suspected her feelings for him were stronger than she admitted, although that could be mere conceit on his part. He did know Joan's pride would never accept the implication: *You'll do if no one else turns up.*

The P.A. announced, "Final briefing in fifteen minutes. Those not on essential duty are requested to attend."

Burret left his room, walked down the corridor and tapped on her door. "Richard. Can I come in?"

"It's open," she called cheerfully.

Joan Walsh was also packing. But she smiled at the lanky, solemn-faced man who came into her room. "One to go," she said lightly, referring to their private countdown. "Nervous?"

Burret grimaced. "Does the sun rise in the morning?" He kissed the nape of her neck. "I only ask that you stay around for a while. I have become somewhat accustomed to your face." Although he attempted to sound jocular, he knew he did not fool her. She knew him too well.

Joan said, "Richard, you are uptight. I know it is difficult, but please try to relax."

"Try to relax," he mimicked bitterly. "I bet you say that to all your patients."

She nodded. "Of course I do. But with you it is more personal. Can't you hold on to that? To *us?*"

It was a good point. A trained psychologist, the lissome redhead had become Burret's better, saner half, which was a substantial plus for the meteorologist/alphanaut.

She smiled again, touched his angular face with her finger tips and added, "I will be with you every step of the way, dear." She put a filmy thing into the case and snapped it shut.

Guess I won't see that again, he thought wistfully, then forced his attention to more practical matters. "What do you think Curtis is up to? We have already been briefed to death."

"I know." She considered a moment. "Perhaps he is hooked onto the image of himself as a father."

"Uh ... I beg your pardon?"

"If you are the head of a large family whose members are about to go their separate ways, won't you at least want to wish them well?"

"Well, I suppose..." Burret chuckled. "So you think we are in for some parental advice?"

"Without doubt," Joan said seriously. "After all, we have all been away from home a long time. You cannot fault our lord and master for wanting to make sure he is not about to unload a collection of anachronistic misfits." She tucked her arm within his. "So let's go and find out, shall we?"

CHAPTER
TWO

● ●

The Eratosthenes base originally housed the deep-space research unit of the now-defunct U.N. Academy. After the U.N.A. folded, the United Nations Space and Aviation Authority acquired Eratosthenes for what was euphemistically entered into the records as 'future considerations'. So when the first signals were picked up from the returning starship, it was only necessary to make minor adjustments within UNSAA's budget to prepare the old complex for habitation, while maintaining the lid on one of the best kept secrets of the twenty-second century. No outside people were used. It was entirely Curtis Paoli and his group who performed the necessary physical and administrative work to prepare the home-away-from-home. After the alphanauts arrived, there were three years during which maintenance and life support became the responsibility of everyone. It was the kind of life-depending situation in which discipline is as important as the hydroponics.

The base was not organized in a military fashion. From the beginning Paoli was determined not to treat those under his charge like soldiers. Yet his natural persuasiveness, his willingness to be a human lightning rod, and above all his ability to sense and then to control irritants, were qualities which kept forty people on a reasonably even keel for three interminable years.

But that was behind them, or nearly so. As Burret and Joan Walsh joined the others in the lounge, they sensed the mood of expectancy.

"Isn't it strange?" Joan whispered as they found a couple of unoccupied seats near the back. "Suddenly I don't feel so much like a person going home. It's more like I am about to leave it."

Burret looked at her. He wanted to say something profound, to make her feel better. Yet all he could manage was a weak, "Me too."

Paoli stepped onto the low stage. The administrator was a small, wiry man with a bald patch contrasting against his heavy gray beard. "Are we all here?"

Someone guffawed. "Not for long!"

Paoli waited until the laughter died down. "No, not for long." He looked around, his darting black eyes seeming to pick out each individual in turn. "I just want to be sure we are all ready for our, ah, rebirth into human society."

"Come off it, Curtis."

Zoltan Genser, the commander of the Alpha expedition, squinted sourly at the man who had controlled their lives for thirty-six months. Almost blind, the result of a blue-green flower which responded to his charmed curiosity with a squirt of acid, Genser's bursting impatience to return home so he could get new eyes, came out in a belligerent, "You are not contemplating a further delay are you? Because if you are, you can damn well forget it!"

There was no applause, although many sympathized. For various reasons people were riding a delicate edge, and no one wanted to force what was already a palpable tension.

Paoli said mildly, "There will be no delay, Zoltan, although I am considering a resumption of the indoctrination sessions after we return to Earth. Now may I continue?"

He looked at his audience and they looked back. Superficially they were a normal collection of men and women; young and middle-aged, white, black, and a few shades in between. But they were also a highly intelligent group, which in a sense was the administrator's main problem. Intelligence comes with sensitivity, which meant many adjustments would be difficult. So he chose his words with care.

"I need hardly remind you that human beings suffer psychological deterioration if they remain away from Earth for more than three years. For some it is a little longer than that, for others not so long, although the variations seem limited to about five percent either way. There are as many explanations of the 'E.A.S.' Earth Allergy Syndrome as there are researchers working on it, although personally I suspect some kind of subtle relationship between man's physical environment and his mind; a link, if you will, which allows normal mental processes only when the senses indicate that gravity, air, light et cetera are Earth normal.

"Fortunately, those first three years can be tolerated with no noticeable ill effects, after which the symptoms appear quite rapidly. Irritability, fatigue, inability to concentrate and so on. You know the score.

"So how long can the human psyche remain apart from a normal Earth environment without experiencing complete disintegration? From its initial early symptoms, does the disintegration continue until there is an irreversible breakdown, or does it stop after a while, leaving the individual depleted but still functional? Is there even a reversal, a return to normality? Until we know the answers to those questions, the future of interstellar exploration must remain in doubt."

Burret wondered if he had heard correctly. *We are here, aren't we? Gerenson, Kraskin, DeZantos, Scheckart, Genser, and Burret; six answers giving you the stars on a plate. So what is your point?* With increasing irritation, he listened as Paoli continued,

"After the Alpha expedition departed, another was sent to Lalande 21185 and a third to Epsilon Eridani. We do not know what *High Hopes* and *Frobisher* may or may not discover out there, or even if they will return. But the success of the *Robert L. Cassion* and its crew does at least hold the hope mankind has a future among the stars."

"Only a hope, Curtis?" interrupted dietitian Josephine Zenermann. " 'Scuse my nit-picking, but how do you explain the presence of six healthy individuals who have already been to a star and back?"

"Damn right," Burret muttered as Joan reached for and squeezed his hand.

"How do *you* explain it, Josie?" Paoli countered, staring directly at the tiny, elfin-faced woman.

The dietitian was not the sort to overlook a challenge. Jumping to her feet, she demanded, "What is there to explain? We already know their years in deepsleep do not count. Neither do the two years they spent on Alpha Five. Which, unless black is white and I am two meters tall, tells me their three years in Eratosthenes puts them in the same bucket as the rest of us!"

Paoli shot back through the ripple of laughter, "Based on the assumption deepsleep somehow restores the psychological balance? That periods of activity between periods in deepsleep are not cumulative? Is that it?"

"Dammit Curtis, would UNSAA have sent the lads to Alpha if there was a possibility they might end up as raving lunatics? Just look at them. They're saner than the rest of us!"

This time, the temptation to give in to feelings was too much. Everyone cheered. The administrator waited patiently until he could be heard. Then, quietly:

"Well put, Josie. Unfortunately, we now know our previous assumptions about deepsleep were wrong."

✤ ✤ ✤

The lights dimmed.

"I am about to show you the results of an experiment actually concluded some years ago. It was done in such secrecy, and was so embarrassing in certain quarters, neither I nor any of my colleagues were informed about it. Fortunately, someone had the good sense to realize this is a problem which cannot be overlooked merely because of some high-level embarrassment. In a further act of enlightenment, the information was transmitted to Eratosthenes..." Paoli coughed. "...a couple of days ago."

No one commented, although there was an anonymous grumble, "Wish he'd shut up and get on with it," followed by a female admonishment, "Hush."

The screen at the front of the lounge illuminated with the image of a large spacecraft settling on its landing jacks amid a swirling cloud of brown dust. A crescent Earth high in the black sky betrayed the location as somewhere on the moon. A service crawler trundled into view, its boarding tube extended and two space-suited figures riding within the open end. This was so contrary to accepted safety protocols, Burret realized he was viewing no ordinary arrival.

From the darkness at the side of the lounge, Paoli explained, "Although a commentary came with this transmission, I will save time by giving you an abbreviated version. To start with, I remind you the so-called 'remission' aspect of deepsleep was assumed on the basis of theoretical research independently corroborated by reputable scientists in labs all over the planet. Even so, more could have been done and should have been, especially on human subjects. But because time and resources were limited, it was decided to trust the data and go ahead with the Alpha Project, plus two other missions to Lalande 21185 and Epsilon Eridani.

"But after the *Frobisher* departed for Epsilon Eridani, our political masters were finally persuaded to delay the proposed fourth interstellar project so funds could be diverted to set up an actual test. It is the results of that test, ladies and gentlemen, you are about to see."

The scene on the screen cut to a camera within the boarding tube. The tube had already been mated to the collar around the ship's airlock, and the two suited men were opening the lock using the hull emergency controls.

Paoli continued, "After working a standard three-year tour here on the moon, two married couples were placed in deepsleep aboard this ship, appropriately named *The Four Companions*. Under computer control it was sent out on a long, looping orbit which took it beyond Neptune. Thirty months after launch, the computer revived the four for what was to be their second consecutive tour away from

Earth. They were isolated of course, as few human beings have been. But there was work to do, not to mention ample facilities for R and R. In theory they would end the test in no worse shape than they had been at the end of their lunar tour. In practice however..."

After a moment's hesitation, Paoli added, "It is fortunate the ship's critical systems were protected behind armored bulkheads."

The reason for his comment became evident in the next few scenes. There was a shocked intake of breath as helmet cameras revealed unbelievable shambles inside the ship. Furnishings were smashed, scientific equipment wrecked beyond recognition, bulkheads bent and sometimes penetrated as if hit blindly and repeatedly by a madman with a club. Capping the insane parade of destruction was a partly decayed corpse in the lounge. Its smashed skull was centered on a huge stain obviously long dried.

"He was not the only one," Paoli continued, his voice devoid of emotion. "One of the women was found in the storage deck with a knife in the side of her neck, the other in the airlock. The latter died when she cracked the outer door without the protection of a suit. She was, in fact, as naked as the day she was born."

There was movement on the screen as the two men from the crawler reappeared supporting a shambling thing which hardly seemed human, although beneath the dirt and the hair was a blank-eyed caricature of a human face.

The screen blanked and the lights came on.

"That man is currently residing in a group home for the mentally disturbed. Harmless and reasonably happy, his mental age is approximately that of an eight-year-old child. He plays with toys and has invented an imaginary companion, Stella. In his former life, by the way, Stella was his wife. She was the naked lady in the air lock."

Burret had had enough. Angry and not caring who knew it, he jumped to his feet.

"As far as I am concerned, *Doctor* Paoli, your horror show does not mean a damn thing!" He pointed. "Look at Eric over there, does he look sick? Does one-armed, table tennis champion Victor Kraskin? Does chess master Gellan

DeZantos? And right in front of you, sir, is Howard Scheckart. He may not talk much, but he knows more about the botany of two planets than any man alive. All right, so Zoltan cannot see too well right now, but he doesn't need eyes to be the smartest person in this room." Burret struck a pose. "I am not crazy either!"

Deflated, hardly aware of the laughter and applause which greeted his outburst, the meteorologist collapsed back into his seat. Joan did not say anything, although her eyes were moist as she took his arm and hugged it.

Paoli sighed. "Richard, allow me to put it another way. From the start, the Alpha Project and those which followed were multi-billion dollar gambles. Although we had clear evidence of planets around several nearby stars, there was no way we could determine if any were even remotely Earth-like. Most people on the Project would have considered it a bonus if the best you found was a world like Mars for instance, where humans can at least survive inside a minimum duty pressure dome. So what did you find? Alpha Five! With a breathable atmosphere, one-point-o-five gravity and compatible food sources, the planet is so Earth-like your biological systems were fooled into believing it *is* Earth! Hence your continued rationality, even after a further three years here in Eratosthenes."

In a stage whisper everyone heard, the irrepressible Eric Gerenson chortled, "Isn't that nice? We got no hang-ups!"

Paoli waited for the laughter to subside. "Not necessarily, Eric. Do not forget you still face reintroduction into Earth society, which will not be easy although I believe we have prepared you well enough for that particular adjustment. And you can always remind yourself that if it was not for Alpha Five..."

Apparently disconcerted by an unpleasant thought, the administrator's face darkened. After a moment, he concluded, "On the basis of what common sense tells me is the scarcity of Earth-like planets in the galaxy, plus the results of what Mr. Burret referred to as a horror show, I rather hope I will not be around if or when *High Hopes* returns from Lalande 21185."

CHAPTER
THREE

● ●

Excerpt taken from a report by Curtis R. Paoli to
UNSAA's Executive Board:

Although The Four Companions *fiasco proves the fallacy
of our previous conclusions regarding the rejuvenating effect
of stasis, the success of the Alpha Five expedition is nevertheless
heartening. Of course this unexpected bonus only partially offsets
the unpleasant fact that landings on non-Earth type planets must
henceforth be limited to quick 'look-ins' if, during subsequent
quarantine, we are to avoid total psychological disintegration
of the crews. I suppose the necessity for quarantine can be avoided
if we restrict future missions to close-orbit research, although
I doubt projects of such limited scope would justify their expense.*

*Regarding the other two missions, I remind you of the as-
tronomical odds against either of them finding another Alpha
Five. So to avoid a repeat of* The Four Companions *tragedy,
I recommend the crews be returned to stasis as soon as possible
after they return to the Solar System, and kept in that suspended
state until a solution is found.*

*A final point. As you know, I am concerned about how the
Alpha Five returnees will adjust to human society after an absence
of half a century. Of particular delicacy is the problem of immediate relatives, of which Richard Burret's is a classic case. When
I had his daughter notified of his impending arrival...*

✣ ✣ ✣

The shuttle was larger and more comfortable than those Burret remembered from more primitive times. Powered re-entry was a real advance, resulting in a smooth G-tolerant ride. But he paid little attention to that refinement as he stared with agonizing intensity at the meaningless shadows on the entertainment screen. Joan knew this was a battle he needed to fight alone, so she sensibly kept her concerns about his state of mind to herself. Because he had often shown her pictures of his daughter as he last saw her, she understood his terrible sense of loss when, from the space station *Orbit Three*, he finally saw and spoke to his 'little girl'.

Cheryl Burret Reed was now a middle-aged widow who lived most of her life while her father spent forty-four of the past forty-nine years in a stasis chamber between the stars. Burret had always known changes must occur in his offspring over those years, of course. Father and daughter were, after all, victims of a classic phenomenon of sub-light interstellar travel. But for the man it was a conscious awareness only, based on his knowledge the calendar did not stop turning merely because he happened to be in time-suspending stasis. The traitor was his body, his glands and instincts. They *knew* the child of his flesh was only eleven; a gawky pre-adolescent version of the merry six-year old who asked for a star teddy.

"My god," Burret had whispered when the lady with the maternal figure and kind face appeared on the screen. "She looks like my mother!"

To his everlasting shame, Cheryl acquitted herself nobly, welcoming her father with the happy chatter of someone meeting an old friend after years of separation. But the words he managed to utter were pathetic and few, and in near panic he finally broke contact. Now, as the shuttle knifed through the troposphere towards touchdown, he began to sweat at the thought of what was to come.

Sensing his distress, Joan whispered, "Richard, it will be all right. I promise it will be all right."

But if first contact with his daughter had been difficult, the welcoming ceremony along with the overwhelming noise and presence of tens of thousands of people behind the security barriers, was much worse. When a formation of hypersonics roared overhead in salute, Burret almost jumped out of his skin. The alphanauts lined up nervously as the President of the United Nations shook their hands and presented each with an award for meritorious service. Then, as they approached the presidential plane, the thunderous roar of approval chased them up the ramp like animals seeking cover.

Joan accompanied Burret to a cabin at the rear of the aircraft, where Cheryl waited to greet him in person. The psychologist, whose own feelings were in conflict with her professional detachment, watched with concern as two strangers, linked by the closest ties of blood yet separated by half a century, tried to react to each other as society would expect.

Burret clumsily embraced the lady. Then he presented her with his model of a star teddy. Gray and fluffy, it had a sharp little snout, six legs, and two enormous multi-faceted eyes. Burret asked awkwardly, "Do you remember asking for a star teddy? Well this is it."

To his astonishment, Mrs. Reed was delighted. She hugged the doll and exclaimed happily, "Of course I remember! I even remember no one could convince me my daddy was not going to bring me one that Christmas. I can hardly wait to show it to my grandchildren!"

"Grandchildren?" He felt for a seat and sank into it. "Are you telling me I am a..." He swallowed. "...great-grand-father?"

Mrs. Reed looked at him with surprise. "Two boys and a girl. Didn't they tell you?"

"No they didn't." Bemused, Burret looked up at Joan, who returned his unspoken plea for help with a slight shake of her head. After a small but eternal moment, he turned back to Mrs. Reed. "I guess they assumed I would ease into it. I mean..."

On impulse, he stood up and grasped his daughter's shoulders. "Dammit, do I look like a great-grandfather? *Do* I?"

Cheryl studied him, at first seriously then with dawning bewilderment. The incongruity had finally caught up with her. "You look more like..." She bit her lip. "...my younger brother, if I had one."

He wondered, *Can I ever look her in the face and call her Cheryl? Or even daughter?* The relationship was ludicrous, more like a bad dream than reality.

Yet by unspoken agreement, Burret and Cheryl Reed adopted the simple expedient of talking to each other without the use of either name or title, although when Joan persuaded them to rejoin the others in the main cabin, it became convenient before third parties to refer to 'Mrs. Reed', and 'my father' (already, to Burret's discomfiture, his daughter had accepted the unacceptable). In the misery-loves-company context, he was ridiculously pleased to notice his colleagues were having their own adjustment problems. Although Eric and Gellan, who had never made any secret of their relationship, were sitting together, each stared stonily ahead as if the other did not exist.

Further up the cabin, Burret heard Howard snap irritably, "I paint. So what? If you don't mind, I choose not to talk about it!" A deeper voice responded, "I guess that is your privilege, Doctor Scheckart." The President nodded cordially and returned to his private suite at the front of the aircraft.

"Well I'm damned," Cheryl marveled. She placed a plump hand on her father's shoulder, whispered conspiratorially into his ear, "I voted against him, you know."

Burret did not think it was particularly funny. Yet her mischievousness was so ingratiating he had to smile. "It does not surprise me. You always were a rebel."

Joan said anxiously, "Richard, I hope you are not planning to talk to the President that way!"

The smile broadened into a grin. "Doctor Walsh, you worry too much. I promise I will be properly deferential."

Fortunately that august personage did not test Burret's resolve to stay out of trouble, as for the rest of the flight the President stayed prudently out of sight. He did not even appear after the aircraft landed at Geneva and the alphanauts were promptly driven to quarters in the sprawling U.N. complex. There was time for a brief rest and then to clean up and attire themselves in brand new semi-formals, before they were the main guests at a banquet given by the leaders of the House of Assembly.

It was a strained and rather strange affair in which the six sat at the head table along with the President, Curtis Paoli, the Speaker of the House, and the director of UNSAA. Also present was an elderly, coal-black Samoan who represented what was still referred to as the Third Block. As the proceedings dragged on, Burret played with his food and tried to maintain control over his frustrations. He looked for Joan and Mrs. Reed among the hundreds of guests, finally located them at a table in the middle of the room. Aware he was looking in her direction, Joan blew him a quick kiss. Then, while Burret drew nervous circles on the tablecloth with the edge of a dinner fork, Zoltan Genser rose and spoke a few forgettable banalities.

After he finished, the commander of the Alpha expedition returned to his seat with a sigh of relief. "I hope that will shut them up for a while," he muttered.

The Speaker overheard and flushed angrily. UNSAA's director merely smiled. Finally, Curtis Paoli was called to deliver the main address.

Paoli had already discussed with the alphanauts what he was going to say (which was not much), so Burret only half-heard the drone of the administrator's voice. Meanwhile he thought not much of anything and continued his excavation of the tablecloth. He hardly noticed the marine who cat-footed behind the head table and stooped to whisper a message to the elderly Samoan. The message concerned, it later turned out, a matter whose importance had been inflated by an over-zealous aid. But as the marine leaned between the diplomat and Howard Scheckart, he inadvertently knocked over a water carafe which spilled its contents into Scheckart's lap. Before the embarrassed messenger could even open his mouth to apologize, the botanist yelled, "You clumsy bastard!" and with maniacal rage leaped out of his chair and flung himself on the gasping marine.

Shocked out of his introspection, Burret stared dumbfounded as someone shouted, "Grab him!" Two burly guards sprinted over, hauled Scheckart off his victim and hustled him out through a side door.

Got to do something, was Burret's instinctive reaction as he pushed his chair back. Joan shouted his name as she ran among the tables toward him, but he did not hear her as he sprinted after Paoli and the others.

A fast-moving medic had already reached Scheckart by the time other confused guests made it into the adjoining lobby. Reacting to the drug the medic pumped into him, Scheckart barely had enough strength to lift his head and mumble, "Sorry," before he sagged limply into the arms of one of his captors.

"Put him on that couch," Paoli ordered, then asked the medic, "What did you give him?"

"Kirol B," the medic replied as he snapped his case shut. "It's harmless. He will be out of it in a couple of hours."

"He had better," Paoli said grimly. He looked around. "How is the other fellow?"

"I'm fine, sir." His face anxious, the marine pushed his way through the crowd. "How is Doctor Scheckart?"

Paoli patted the marine's arm. "Considering what he almost did to you, young man, I appreciate your concern. I am sure he will be fine." To the medic, "Take him to my suite, please. I will be there in a few minutes."

As the medic led the two guards and their unconscious burden in the direction of the elevators, Burret asked, "What do you want the rest of us to do? Something tells me we need to talk."

"I agree," Paoli responded as he picked out the alphanauts from the couple of dozen people who had crowded out of the banquet hall. "Eric, Victor, Gellan, Zoltan, and Richard; my suite in thirty minutes." Someone pressed through the crowd to Burret's side. "You too, Joan." Paoli hurried away.

"You look awful," Joan said anxiously.

"I feel like hell, if you must know. Where is Mrs. ... my daughter?"

"Don't worry, you will see her later. Of more immediate concern is that something is terribly wrong, and not just with Howard. It's all of you."

Something.

One way of putting it, Burret thought bitterly. Someone started to laugh. It was a cold laugh, without humor. It was only as Joan backed away, her eyes wide with hurt surprise, Burret realized the laughter was his own.

CHAPTER FOUR

• •

Slightly less than two months later, Zoltan Genser took his own life. The circumstances were described in a further report from Curtis Paoli to UNSAA's Executive Board.

...a complication I did not anticipate, but which requires me, again, to revise my thoughts about the future of the interstellar program. There is still a price of course, and the tragedy of Zoltan Genser is that he paid that price with his life. In the long run however, I am convinced interstellar man will evolve to heights undreamed on this small planet. It is as if nature herself took a hand, when she implanted within human beings an evolutionary 'trigger' which can only be released once. But which, once released, forces that individual to become a creature of the cosmos.

Dr. Genser chose to remain on Earth because of his desire to have full vision restored. He was aware of the risks of course, but insisted we proceed with the operation. But as I witnessed the deterioration of that strong personality, even after the success of the procedure, I confess I found it difficult to maintain my objectivity.

The desperation of Dr. Genser's condition is best illustrated by the fact he was quite confident he would regain full use of his sight, and that within weeks he would rejoin the others on the moon. Unfortunately the man's private hell became too much for him, leading to the act which, for him, was the only possible one.

The good news is that the refit of the Robert L. Cassion *is proceeding on schedule, and that the ship will soon be moved to lunar orbit to embark the colonists. They are in good spirits, despite the briefing during which for the first time they were told about the cramped living conditions they will have to endure during the flight. Stasis equipment for two more bodies takes up a lot of space.*

Regarding the selection of people for the Amazon Project, I am aware of the difficulty of finding suitable female candidates. Therefore I suggest we take immediate steps to set up an appropriate selection and training committee which...

✤ ✤ ✤

When Richard Burret spoke to Cheryl Reed for the last time, it was the day before the *Robert L. Cassion* departed from lunar orbit. It still seemed strange to him that as those final days on Earth became increasingly unbearable, the relationship between father and daughter progressed from awkwardness, through friendship, to love. Despite her years, Cheryl was still the little girl who asked for a star teddy, and his acceptance of that fundamental truth finally calmed his personal storm. It was during those wonderful yet sadly brief hours, while Burret was rediscovering his fatherhood, he wondered aloud if as a bonus he could meet his great grandchildren. But Joan had been keeping close tabs on the progression of the Earth Allergy Syndrome, and firmly scotched the idea. Too risky, she insisted, for the children as well as for the famous father of their grandmother.

Although Burret did finally speak to the youngsters via viewphone, it was hardly the same; especially when he saw the remarkable resemblance of seven-year old Valerie to Cheryl when she was the same age. Valerie was the tongue-tied one, with a shy, "Have an nice trip great-grandfather," the total sum of her words. But at least Burret had the recording. He would replay it endless times during the coming years.

Cheryl was kind. She had regained her lost father, and was content. Although Burret did not quite understand the logic of that, he was grateful she accepted the situation. He also insisted he would never forget his little girl. In themselves, just a few words exchanged over nearly four hundred thousand kilometers. But they were words which expressed the peace father and daughter had found with each other. In any case, there would always be the memories.

She will become an old woman while I am still in stasis. When I am old, her bones will have already returned to the dust. It is the new way of mankind; the old way of the universe.

CHAPTER FIVE

●●●●●●●●●●●●●●●●●●●●●●●●●●●

Six hours before launch.

Captain Gellan DeZantos, Eric Gerenson, the other three male members of the crew, and their wives sat before the screen in a view room of Clavius Base. On the screen, the image of Curtis Paoli.

"I wish I could be there with you," the former Eratosthenes administrator said wistfully. "Unfortunately, the Agency ruled otherwise."

"A ruling based on your own recommendations, Curtis," DeZantos pointed out. "After all, you have put in your three years. Now you have to be satisfied with *terra firma*."

Paoli smiled. "True. But at least I know where I belong. On the other hand, you people are like children let loose in a chocolate factory. With the whole universe to choose from, which goody do you choose next?"

Which indeed? It was a profoundly loaded question. Undoubtedly Alpha Five would not hold them forever, especially as more ships became available. Earthlike or not, with or without pressure domes, all worlds except one had become grist for the starman's mill.

"Joan."

"Yes, Curtis."

"How do you feel?"

Beside Burret, Joan Walsh shifted uneasily. "I feel..." She shrugged. "Oh, I don't know. A little strange, I guess."

The image on the screen cocked a quizzical eyebrow. "Confused?"

"I know I will never see Earth again." Joan bit her lip.

"It is not too late, you know," Paoli said. "Isn't that right, Richard?"

Although Burret had anticipated this, it did not make it any easier. Turning to his bride of less than a week, he took one of her hands in both of his and prayed he was not paying out enough rope to hang himself. "You heard the man. What do you want to do?"

She forced a wan smile. "Sorry, dear. You will not get rid of me that easily."

Thank you, God.

From his office in one of Earth's great universities, Curtis nodded approvingly. "Joan, can you be more specific about your symptoms?"

She shrugged. "I am tired."

"To be expected. Anything else?"

She thought a moment. "Irritation. Small things tend to get exaggerated. Nothing I cannot control."

Curtis looked relieved. "I am glad to hear it. For a three-year-plus, you are not doing too badly. In any case you will enter stasis in a few hours, so you can look forward to snoozing away the years until you arrive at Alpha Five."

"Not Alpha Five," Howard Scheckart corrected. "Genser's World." He turned to the woman at his side. "Right, Evanne?"

Doctor Evanne Scheckart *nee* Stiegler smiled. "Genser's World," she echoed serenely.

More than anyone, the doctor was responsible for the botanist's recovery from his bout of schizophrenic violence. She was the reason Scheckart was no longer the moody, introspective genius he used to be. With this talented life partner at his side, it was doubtful his companions would ever see the old Howard again. Also, as the expedition's medic, Evanne was fully qualified (as she wickedly reminded her fellow alphanauts), to 'birth babies'.

Scheckart said, "We all agreed it is appropriate." He added earnestly, "You will get the Agency to confirm it, won't you?"

"Genser's World, eh?" Paoli looked pleased. "I will certainly bring it up before the Board."

"Do more than just bring it up," Kraskin insisted. "Because if any one needs to reach us, that will be our address."

The man who for three years had been their guardian and friend, nodded. They could tell he was worn out, ready for the green pastures of retirement. But it was doubtful Curtis Paoli would take the opportunity. There was too much left to do, too many questions to be answered.

✧ ✧ ✧

Questions.

How had the alphanauts got that way? What mysterious mechanism made Earth reject them so thoroughly? Would Genser's World also reject them if their subjective time away from that planet exceeded some innate value? Although Paoli had theorized the alphanauts survived five subjective years away from their home world only because their biological clocks assumed Genser's World was Earth, he recognized the argument's fatal flaw. Those biological clocks no longer recognized Earth as a benign environment!

The Genser tragedy, Scheckart's illness and to a lesser extent the problems of the other four alphanauts, was clear indication the remorseless ticking had continued even after they arrived on Earth. So what on Genser's World switched them from one ecological system to another? That was biochemist Melba Kraskin's main assignment.

Whatever was accomplished, whatever discoveries were made on Genser's or any other world in the galaxy, the women would be as much part of it as the men. They were special people who would redefine the role of their sex, and why not? Earth's archaic social customs would have little meaning in a place which would make them aliens on the planet of their birth.

Richard Burret thought of Gerenson and DeZantos, and smiled to himself. Their chosen lifestyle was their business, and had nothing to do with the fact they were good men and good friends. On Genser's World, that would be as much as anyone could ask or expect.

He projected his imagination a few thousand years into the future, and saw the descendants of the Alpha Project still accomplishing, still exploring. The only difference, which as he thought about it was really not so important, was the possibility that many of those descendants may never have heard of a place called Earth...

PART II
ADOPTION

● ●

It was cruel, it was draconian, and it was necessary.

Two interstellar ships, each with crews who would inevitably experience the horrors of Earth Allergy Syndrome if they were allowed to return to their home world, were diverted to the only known destination where they would be able to live, build, and hopefully accommodate to the new cards fate and the universe had dealt...

CHAPTER
SIX

● ●

The crew of the starship *Frobisher* did not find any human-habitable worlds among the fourteen planets and several dozen moons which made up the planetary system of Epsilon Eridani. But the fourth planet's strange life forms, existing in near vacuum, occupied the science teams for twenty-two fascinating months. Finally, expecting eventual revival among the familiar worlds of Sol, they re-entered stasis. They did not know of the signals which revised the pre-set course settings even as their ship accelerated along the long spiral which led into interstellar space and home.

The *High Hopes* was already on its way but still light-years from Earth, when its detectors intercepted the signals. Although the tanks contained insufficient delta V for such an extensive course correction, there was a brown dwarf only slightly removed from the line of flight. The artificial intelligence which was the brain of the ship examined the data, ruminated for a few micro-seconds and finally decided a gravity assist was possible. The ship was rolled, slightly realigned, and megawatts of fusion power pumped into the drive.

High Hopes was also on its way to Alpha Centauri.

As was the starship *Amazon One*, which bore its sleeping complement toward their rendezvous with the men of Genser's World...

CHAPTER
SEVEN

● ●

It had been a rough landing, although fortunately not a fatal one.

One by one they clambered or were dragged through a rent in the shuttle's crumpled hull. Three nursed sprains, one of them still coughing from leaking fuel fumes. One survivor winced as astringent was applied to a gash in her forehead. Another held together the fragments of a tunic ripped from collar to hem, while she bemusedly wondered what miracle had prevented the jagged metal eviscerating her.

Yet despite assorted hurts, cuts, and bruises, all were grateful for the solidity of firm ground under their feet and for the warm light of Alpha Centauri A.

Captain Emmaline Bonderhame limped across to the First Officer. "Any ideas?"

"About where we are, you mean?"

"It's a good place to start."

Carefully avoiding the adhesive strip on her forehead, Jan Buraka shaded her eyes. A thin, dark-haired woman with more than a hint of Amerind ancestry in her fine-boned features, she pointed down the valley toward where rolling country faded into the haze of distance. "The best I can tell you is that if help does not come our way soon, someone is faced with a walk of five or six hundred klicks in that direction."

"What about the radios?"

"Useless. Whatever it was, rendered all our electronics into junk."

The captain grimaced. *Whateveritwas.* As good a description as any for the bright flash which transformed their complex aero-space machine into a flying brick. "So we walk, do we?"

Jan looked pointedly at the other's leg. "Some don't."

"Don't rub it in, dear." The captain limped back to the shuttle. "All right everyone. Decision time!"

Slowly, they gathered around. They were eight women who at that moment were supposed to be somewhere over the horizon of Genser's World, being welcomed into the tiny and mostly male community of Curtis.

Now...?

Fortunately, Emmaline Bonderhame's inspired piloting had accomplished what most experts would insist was impossible; bringing a crippled shuttle down through a turbulent atmosphere to a survivable landing on the totally unfamiliar surface of an alien world. It was old fashioned seat-of-the-pants flying, without power and instruments.

Amazon's Child would probably never return to space, or even the air, again. But those who rode her down from orbit, from the now empty starship *Amazon One*, were, by the grace of Bonderhame and God (in that order), still alive.

And it was not such a bad world on which to be alive, even if misfortune misdirected their place of landing. The weather was benign, which was not unexpected considering the careful planning which allowed for the decades-long and sometimes extreme meteorological cycles of this planet of a multiple star system. Nevertheless it was fortunate the final resting place of the shuttle was a pleasant meadow below wooded hills. A few meters away, a lively stream frothed and danced toward a distant ocean. Beyond the hills, a range of precipitous peaks reared their spectacular summits against a clear sky. In the other direction, the valley dropped toward a distant, cloud-dappled plain. A couple of hundred years ago Earth had places like this. Perhaps the air had smelled as good.

"First the good news," the captain said. "We are on the right planet."

There was a ripple of nervous laughter. "You mean there is bad news?" Geologist Greta Harpson used her uninjured arm to gesture expansively at their surroundings. "I thought we were here for a picnic."

"Speak for yourself," someone muttered. "I came here to get a man." This time, the laughter was genuine.

Bonderhame forced a smile. "The men are on the planet all right. Unfortunately, they are a few hundred klicks from here."

"Won't they be looking for us?"

"I am sure they are trying. Trouble is, what happened was so sudden we had no chance to transmit a distress signal. As far as the people in Curtis are concerned, we disappeared over a wilderness which could lose an army. All right, so they have a couple of copters. But even that advantage becomes somewhat blunted when you are faced with an area of search the size of a small country."

"What about our own copter?" Harpson asked.

"Assemble it, you mean?"

"Of course."

"You're a dreamer, Greta. Even if none of the components are damaged, which would be a miracle in itself, we just don't have the tools and resources they have in Curtis. Later, I do not doubt they will send a properly equipped work crew. Until then..." Jan shrugged.

"At least we know where Curtis is from here, don't we?"

"More or less."

One of the women stood up. Christine Stadderfoss, the Amazon Project's agronomist and temporary supply officer, was deceptively slight with a close-cropped head of white-blonde hair. "Captain, whichever way we cut it, it is obvious someone has to take that walk. So who goes?"

Bonderhame shrugged. "About half of us are in no shape for a hike. So we cripples stay, while the rest go."

"May I remind you we have just enough food to keep us all going, on reduced rations, for no more than a couple of weeks?"

"Which is about as long as it will take to get to Curtis. What is your point?"

"Only that those who go will need to average forty or fifty klicks per day across terrain of unknown difficulty. Even for experienced hikers, it is asking a lot."

"Agreed. Again, what is your point?"

"Because they will have to keep moving, the walkers cannot afford to take risks with local fish, berries or whatever. On the other hand, those who stay may have to. So cut the walking party down to a minimum, say of three people, and make sure they carry enough food for the entire trip. The rest must take their chances."

"Bit brutal, isn't it?"

"I don't like it either," the agronomist retorted. "But does anyone have a better idea?"

There was a brief silence as the women realized the desperate lack of alternatives. "What do we know about what we can eat around here?" Su Lan McNaughton asked. The physicist's Irish brogue was disconcertingly inappropriate to her slender, almond-eyed looks.

A hand was raised. "I am familiar with Howard Scheckart's notes as well as his paintings," Ella Shire offered, referring to the work of the botanist/artist who had been with the first expedition to Genser's World. "I think I can identify some of the edibles."

Emmaline looked across at the disheveled bacteriologist. "What are the odds?"

"I will tell you after I have had a couple of hours to look around."

"Make it an hour."

As Shire scrambled to her feet and hurried toward the vegetation at the stream's edge, the captain asked, "Does anyone else have something constructive to offer?"

"Only that the walkers should be on their way ASAP," Stadderfoss insisted.

"I agree," Jan Buraka said quietly.

The captain sighed as she looked at her first officer. She suspected what was coming. "Spit it out, Jan."

"It's the wild card in our equation—we are not in this mess by accident."

"So you believe the flash...?"

"It is more than belief, Emma. I *know* we were shot down."

CHAPTER EIGHT

● ●

Jan Buraka, Christine Stadderfoss, and Delsa Crawley departed at sunrise the next day. Crawley, the Amazon Project's wiry and intense planetologist, became the obvious third member of the team when she reminded the selection committee (composed of the captain and first officer) that she was one of the exclusive sisterhood of Australian woman who had stood on the summit of Earth's killer mountain, K2.

Cloud had moved in overnight and a thin drizzle fell as the three started down the valley. Their packs were heavy and their footwear, although sturdy, was designed for lighter duty. Nevertheless the first few hours passed almost pleasantly. The sun came out, making the landscape sparkle as the light danced off dripping trees and vegetation.

"I do not envy them back there," Delsa commented during their first rest. "I mean, how would you feel if you were hungry and surrounded with luscious fruit you dare not touch because you might end up with a fatal case of indigestion?"

Jan grimaced. "Don't be so sure we won't be in the same boat before we are finished." She plucked a wrinkled yellow berry from a ground-hugging plant, put it cautiously in her mouth and almost instantly spat it out. "Ugh! Bitter as hell."

"So why...?"

"Because according to Ella, this is the only fruit she is certain will not hurt us. Although Howard Scheckart named it Yellow Peril because of its lousy taste, it apparently has nourishment value."

Christine looked sourly at the few ugly globules of yellow on the plant. "I hope we don't get that hungry. Even if those things taste good, you'd need a dozen just for a mouthful."

Jan continued cheerfully, "Don't worry, there are other goodies. For instance, according to Scheckart's notes there is a fairly common fish which looks like a green lamprey. It is scrawny, and what meat it has tastes like carrion. But it is edible protein."

"So what are we supposed to avoid?" Delsa asked as they resumed trudging across a flower speckled slope.

"Then again, Ella could only remember a few obvious ones. There is something like a small orange, another like a grape, and a third which vaguely resembles a coconut. She also said to watch out for a cuddly little critter which could be a chipmunk, except it has a bite which kills within minutes. She referred to it as a chipmink. Oh, and stay away from pretty flowers. You know what happened to Zoltan Genser."

"In other words, if it looks good leave it alone," Christine grumbled as she stamped a boot and a buzzing flurry of the local equivalent of insects swirled around her legs and almost instantly settled again. "My god, look at them. The place even has fleas!"

Delsa looked uneasily at the surfeit of decorative blossoms painting the landscape. The flowers were mostly crimson, with clusters of blue and gold. "Where I come from, flowers attract insects." She plucked one of the tiny creatures from her pant leg and examined it critically. Except that it had only four legs and its wings were bright green, it could have been a mosquito. "Some have stings."

"We have anti-venom," Jan pointed out.

"Against what? Honey bees?"

Yet when they stopped to make camp, no one could claim even the equivalent of a mosquito bite. If much of the natural food of this world was anathema to humans, so were humans apparently anathema to the local biting life. One flying life form, hawk-sized and feathered with a head which vaguely resembled a Siamese kitten, frequently flew low over the women in flocks of up to a dozen individuals. Although their high-pitched meowing was raucous and irritating, their constant presence seemed more the product of curiosity than of threat. The antics of the smaller ones as they looped, dove and squeaked at each other and their human audience, was almost endearing.

As the sun settled lower over the mountains, the landscape took on a glow which was incomparable to anything any of the three had seen on the planet of their birth. With its unearthly beauty, this alien evening triggered homesickness for the more familiar sights and smells of home, for dusty red sunsets reflecting a thousand patterns of lurid light from the glass and steel towers of great cities, for the sterile yet comforting taste of artificially cleansed and filtered air.

Some of what the three women dubbed 'catbirds' settled into a tree within viewing distance of the campfire. Their enormous eyes reflected the firelight like small pairs of fog lamps as they watched these strange two-legged visitors. After a few minutes, the meowing softened to a gentle warbling which lightened the depressed mood of the women like a psychic balm.

"I wonder..." Christine rose from her place by the fire and walked slowly toward the tree. The others watched as she squatted down and held out an arm. Her soft call was incongruous. "Here, kitty, kitty. Come to mamma."

Two of the smaller catbirds abruptly dropped from their perch and, with broad wings extended, landed neatly side-by-side on her arm. As they warbled and mewed, the agronomist stood erect and walked carefully toward her companions. By the time she reached the campfire, one of the animals had hopped to her shoulder while the other remained firmly on her forearm. "Aren't they beautiful?" she crooned.

Jan and Delsa met a reflection of their own curiosity as the two creatures returned their stare without the least sign of fear. The black and brown wings and body of each catbird were feathered, with the feathers becoming almost indistinguishable from fine fur around the neck and head. Although also feathered, the wings were extensions of the fingered forelimbs much like an Earth bat. A single hind foot with long, flexible toes extended below the broad tail. Trumpet-like ears twitched and flexed in reaction to the whispered human conversation. The faces were indeed cat-like, with huge eyes which suggested adaptation for night vision, although so far the creatures had not seemed nocturnal. Christine used a finger to delicately stroke the striped furry head of the catbird on her forearm, causing it to warble with pleasure.

Making cooing noises, Jan reached out and enticed the second catbird from the other woman's shoulder onto her own forearm. Within seconds, she had her acquisition warbling with equal enthusiasm.

"Why are we doing this?" Delsa wondered aloud as she reached out and added her own finger to Christine's caress. "I mean, considering what we have already been told about the chipmink creatures..."

"Valid point," Jan remarked equitably as she lifted her arm and a soft little head nuzzled her cheek. "Are we idiots or what?"

"I don't think Ella was talking about catbirds, which she did not mention anyway. But you never know..." Christine sat down heavily, causing her catbird to meow with protest. "My God, what have these creatures done to us?"

There was a squawking cry from the tree, which the two young catbirds answered with reluctant squeaks and then began bobbing up and down as if they were ready to fly but not quite sure if they needed to. The summons was repeated, and this time both youngsters spread their wings and flew back to join their elders. As the fire died and the women prepared for sleep, the concerted warbling gradually faded to inaudibility. Two-by-two, the small foglamps began to blink out.

"Sleep well, little friends," Christine murmured drowsily. She sensed an answering warmth...

CHAPTER
NINE

• •

Next morning the catbirds were gone. But there was a neat line of gray-green nuts on the ground below the tree where the creatures had roosted. The line pointed directly in the direction of a large bush a dozen or so paces away. Jan picked up one of the nuts, examined it and then walked to the bush. It was covered with hundreds of the gray-green spheroids. "Are they telling us we can eat these things?" she wondered aloud.

She plucked a nut directly from the bush and pried the shell apart. Inside was a soft substance with the color and texture of banana flesh. She scooped out some of the substance with a finger tip, sniffed it and popped it into her mouth.

Horrified, Delsa and Christine ran toward her. "What kind of stupid stunt is that?" Christine shouted.

Jan smiled and swallowed. "Bland," she said after a moment. Then her expression changed to one of puzzlement, followed by horrified realization. "I really *did* break the rules, didn't I?"

"Enough to be locked up for your own good if we had a place to lock you in!" Delsa snapped as she and Christine watched with concern. After a few moments, she asked anxiously, "How do you feel?"

Jan licked her lips, felt her stomach. "Fine ... I think. But I suggest it would be a good idea if you two kept tabs on me for a while."

After about an hour of nail-biting anxiety, during which Jan experienced not even a stomach ache, the three finally decided to resume their journey. But first they harvested a few dozen of the nuts, which they distributed among their three backpacks. That no harm came from the encounter, either from the catbirds or from the fruit Jan consumed, did not reduce their guilty awareness they had behaved like immature schoolgirls who encountered a couple of friendly kittens.

It was Delsa who bit the bullet. "They made us do it."

Jan blinked. "Would you mind explaining that?" They had reached the plain, where the stream widened into a shallow river undulating toward the distant coast. The local equivalent of prairie grass grew in oddly spaced hummocks, with something like a springy moss in between. It remained easy going, even as they traversed between the loops of the river. When it was occasionally necessary to wade across, the water rarely came above their knees. The trees were widely scattered, reminding Jan of what the savannas of Africa had once looked like.

Delsa put the obvious into words. "On a strange world with unknown hazards, you do not cuddle one of the local life forms just because it's cute. Neither do you consume local food because that creature says you can!"

Christine wearily sat down on a boulder and extended her aching legs. "Delsa, are you suggesting the catbirds are capable of mind control?"

The planetologist snorted. "If the shoe fits..." She lowered herself to the ground, leaned back and supported herself on her elbows. "Think about it. It is a pretty useful defense if you can persuade a potential carnivore you are too lovable to become its dinner."

"Except for the problem of Occam's razor," Jan mused thoughtfully.

"Occam? Who's that?"

"A medieval philosopher who said in effect that nature is logical as well as efficient. Why the sophistication of mind control, if you already have good ears and wings?"

"All right. Then try this on for size." Delsa leaned forward, cupped her mouth and whispered conspiratorially, "The catbirds are someone's pets."

The suggestion was so outrageous, neither of her companions bothered to laugh. Instead Jan sighed, rolled her eyes upward and wondered aloud, "Where does she get such notions?"

"Whose pets?" asked Christine.

"How would I know?" Delsa retorted crossly. Although she had started the game, the Australian had the uncomfortable feeling it was not so easily finished. "The way the catbirds took to us, it would not surprise me if their owners are not so different from humans."

"The colony at Curtis..."

"No." Delsa shook her head. "Earth would have been informed of the catbirds' existence. In any case, how come we found them so far from home?"

Christine said thoughtfully, "You got that wrong. They found us."

Jan shook her head with disbelief. "I wish you two could listen to yourselves. You are like children telling bedtime stories." Again she addressed the sky. "Owners, for chrisake!"

✤ ✤ ✤

The former first officer of *Amazon One* had always prided herself on her pragmatism. She scoffed at those who looked for ghosts in haunted houses, and shuddered at the never-ending flood of theorists who used pseudo-science to prove interstellar travelers visited Earth during historical times. She even gained modest notoriety as one of a group of multi-disciplinary activists who used the media to debunk explanations which relied on other than scientific logic.

Which was why the shaking Jan Buraka received when *Amazon's Child* came down, was as much in her mind as to her body. The flash of radiation which disabled the shuttle's electronics had unnerved her to the extent she now realized her reaction to Delsa's half-playful, half-tentative theory was a premature and probably unreasonable knee-jerk. It was enough to make her wonder if there was a closet Luddite lurking deep in her subconscious.

It was also the beginning of a new and healthier attitude which was soon put to the test.

✢ ✢ ✢

After six days of steady travel, Jan announced they would soon be at the point where they would have to turn north, away from the river toward the coastal lowlands and hopefully their ultimate destination at a cluster of buildings called Curtis. To their right, an isolated range of hills dominated the prairie landscape. Ahead, the plain rolled on toward its indeterminate horizon. It was a monotonous vista of undulating terrain as endless as the sky.

"It has been too bloody easy," Delsa complained during their noonday rest. "Hell, I anticipated at least a herd of stampeding beasts. Or a chasm to cross." After a moment's hesitation, she added wistfully, "A mountain to climb?"

Christine chuckled. "This is not the American west, which in any case has not seen wild buffalo for centuries. And I hate to add to your misery by reminding you Genser's biggest land animal is a solitary wanderer about the size and aggressiveness of an antelope."

"Sure, if you accept First Expedition reports as gospel," the Australian retorted. "But we're talking about a whole planet! The data half a dozen fellows collected while they were here is no more than prologue."

"To the volume our kids will write?" Jan chuckled at the notion. "Delsa, if after we get to Curtis the mountaineer inside you still wants to get out, I suggest you get Victor Kraskin to take you to that land fault he discovered. I bet he would enjoy watching you attempt to climb one and a half thousand meters of vertical rock."

"I would be quite content to rappel down it, thank you very much," Delsa rejoined calmly. "In any case..." Her Down-Under twang trailed into silence as she stared toward the hills. "Say, did either of you see that?"

The gleam she saw, which faded, suddenly returned. It was a brilliant point near one of the summits.

"I see it, I see it!" Jan exclaimed irritably as Delsa grabbed her arm. She glanced at the sun, which had appeared from behind a drifting cloud, then looked back at the hills. "It's just a reflection of some kind."

"Off what? Nothing short of a mirror or polished metal reflects light like that!"

Slowly, as the sun moved, the gleam faded. Then it was gone. Overhead, a large group of flying creatures flapped leisurely in the direction of the hills. Some meowed companionably as they passed over, although none of the catbirds descended.

"Are they ours?" Christine wondered. Her expression was wistful.

Delsa said eagerly, "Look, we have to cut north anyway, right? So I propose we do it from here and check out that light. A side trip won't hurt us, and it does look as if the catbirds live in that direction."

Jan turned to Christine. "How is our supply situation?"

The agronomist shrugged. "Better than expected. We are ahead of schedule, and if our regular food runs out, we have those nuts. But aren't you forgetting our friends back at the shuttle? They're depending on us!"

Delsa suggested, "Look, if we split up..."

"Not an option," Jan said firmly as she looked toward the hills, then at the horizon beyond which lay their ultimate destination. She wondered if this was the reason things had gone so easily, that perhaps...

This is me?

It'll be hobgoblins and UFO's next! Disgusted with herself for almost giving in to parapsychological nonsense, Jan was tempted to ask one of her companions to give her a good slap. Instead she took a deep breath. "That reflection could be from the casing of a scientific station of some kind."

Delsa let loose an excited whoop. "People!"

Jan shook her head. "I doubt it. The colony's too small to have its people scattered all over the map. More likely it's a solar-powered package of sensors; meteorological, seismic or whatever."

Delsa's enthusiasm was only slightly reduced. "So what? It'll have a radio!"

"Presumably. A means to contact Curtis and save a few days." Jan hesitated. "I have to admit it's tempting."

"Only tempting? Come on Jan, if it doesn't pan out we lose one measly day. Let's go!

Christine said impatiently, "Delsa, have you forgotten why we have no radios, why we are here in the first place? Something or some*one* shot our shuttle down!"

There was a long silence. Finally, the Australian whispered, "I guess that means we must check it out, anyway. Right?"

Jan sighed.

✛ ✛ ✛

They found a trail near the base of the hill on which they had seen the light. The trail was of hard packed earth literally worn into a trench between barbed thorn trees.

"Maybe it's for game?" Delsa said as she looked up the trail. Each woman clutched a small but lethal needle pistol.

"It is our only route if we don't want our hides ripped to shreds," Jan replied as she stepped onto the trail. She gestured. "Delsa, behind me. Chris, take the rear. Don't be ashamed if you feel the need to walk backwards."

"I will walk on my hands if I have to," the agronomist muttered as she crab-footed behind her companions.

Gradually, they climbed. It was warm, and the packs were heavy on their shoulders. The growth either side of the trail grew thicker and higher as the sword-like spikes of the thorn trees extended their cruel points overhead.

"Who or whatever made this trail is a bit more than our height, I'd say," Delsa panted as she looked up toward where the sunlight streamed barred shadows. Somewhere a catbird called, and was instantly answered by a chorus of meows and squeaks which seemed to come from everywhere. The thorn forest rustled as if from a wind, although at their level the air was static and stifling.

With frequent rests they continued another hour, until the trail began to level and then widen. Finally it became a broad, rough-paved road between two rows of low stone columns. Astonished, they stared at this evidence of the work of intelligence.

"Crikey, it's old!" Delsa said, as she stooped and rubbed her hand over the worn paving.

"Positively ancient," Christine agreed.

"But still used," Delsa added, as she noted the lack of natural growth between the old paving stones.

"By who?" Christine asked.

Jan only half-listened to the exchange as she shed the prejudices of a lifetime like a discarded skin. For the first time she thought she understood that wise line, *There are more things in Heaven and Earth...*

Followed by the others, she walked cautiously along the road until it curved left and ended at the edge of a broad, shallow depression cut into the hill just below its summit. The depression was about a hundred meters across, and completely barren. A slightly tilted, twenty-meter cone rose from the center of this sterile area. Its polished metal blindingly reflected the sunlight.

As Jan wondered how much more was below the ground, Delsa shouted, "My gawd, it's a ship!" and tried to run down into the depression. She was immediately grabbed and dragged back as her companions spotted a skeletal figure descending a primitive vine-lashed ladder erected against the side of the cone. As it descended each rung, the being carefully rubbed a large cloth on the metal either side of the ladder, after which it lifted its head and uttered an eerie call. The sound reminded its human listeners of a wolf baying at the moon.

As soon as it reached the ground, the being dropped to its hands and scuttled like an emaciated ape around the curve of the ship to a stone structure resembling a small altar. It picked up something from behind the altar, uttered another of its eerie calls and pointed the object at the ship. An opening appeared close to the ground, and another of the beings, also carrying a cloth, emerged from inside and joined its companion. The object was again pointed, there was another baying call, and the opening closed.

Jan gestured and led her companions away from the road to a new vantage point a few meters further along the depression's rim, where they lay prone and peered over the edge. The wisdom of the move was vindicated when four more of the beings appeared from along the road and descended into the depression. The newcomers bore between them a long wrapped bundle which they laid on the ground between the ship and the altar. They reverently removed the wrappings, revealing the body of one of their kind. Then, as the four joined the two who were already behind the altar, there was a fluttering of wings and several catbirds spiraled down and landed on bony shoulders. One of the creatures stayed aloft for a few moments, uttering pitiful cries until it descended and landed on the body. Finally the six beings, still with catbirds on their shoulders, filed out of the depression. They keened an atonal cacophony which slowly faded as they returned down the road. Christine later described the sound as a Gregorian chant played backwards.

"Well!" Jan said. She wanted to say something profound to mark this unparalleled event of First Contact, but the words were not there. They would probably come later, but then it would not be the same. *This* was the moment.

Delsa was not quite as impressed. "Well, what do you know. Our first E.T.'s. Bony devils, aren't they?"

Christine was still staring at the ship. "Did you see any door open?" she asked breathlessly. "I saw nothing move up, down, sideways, or away. The opening simply appeared! What kind of technology can do that?"

Jan, who had been looking at the lone catbird sitting on the corpse like a small, faithful guardian, returned her attention to the ship. "Technology? The same which brought down the *Child*, I think."

Christine gasped. *That* is our shuttle-killer?"

"If the shoe fits..." Jan muttered obscurely.

Delsa rose to her feet. "I am going down there. The aliens have gone, so why not?"

Jan nodded and also stood up. So did Christine. Now aware of their presence, the catbird on the corpse produced a low, rumbling call. It sounded ominous, if not exactly threatening. "All right," Jan agreed. "But slow and quiet."

"So what can a poor little catbird do?" Christine wondered as the three edged down into the depression. The ground was baked hard, like concrete. Their shuffling feet disturbed a deposit of fine dust which marked their progress with a thin, settling brown haze.

They stopped a couple of meters from the corpse and tried to ignore the continuous, warning rumble of its guardian. Although the body was humanoid, any similarity to *Homo sapiens* was reflected only by gargoyles on ancient cathedrals. The head was almost spherical, with a wide gash of a lipless mouth, two tiny eyes and a single nostril recessed below a protruding lid of bone. If there were ears, they were concealed under ropy hair which covered most of the head except for the face. The scantily clad being was either incredibly thin or incredibly emaciated, with a mottled brown skin drawn drum-tight over a bone structure which had lumps and joints as if it had been slung together by an amateur with no sense of structural logic.

Christine noted a complication between the being's legs. "It's a male anyway."

"Seems so," Jan agreed. "And humanoid."

"I hate to admit this, but I am sort of disappointed." Christine took a step toward the corpse, promptly stepped back as the guardian hissed and its wings lifted threateningly. "I grew up hoping humankind's first E.T. would be an intelligent spider or something." She sighed. "That poor creature is better looking than a skinny professor I used to know."

"He does have a big brain case," Delsa noted.

Christine shook her head. "That doesn't indicate anything. It could be mush in there."

"Of course it's mush! He's dead, or haven't you noticed?"

"Cut it out, you two," Jan said irritably. "In any case, if we are discussing the possibility of the beings being intelligent, I have my doubts. What we saw can be explained as instinct evolved out of ritual evolved out of routine. If that ship has been there as long as I suspect it has..." She shrugged.

"What about the polishing?"

"Cleaning ship is an old tradition."

"And half-burying it? How do you explain that?"

"Maybe it triggered a land subsidence when it landed."

"Or someone else did," Jan suggested.

"Someone..." Christine looked blank. "Who?"

"An enemy. One that existed while our ancestors were scratching stick figures on cave walls. Perhaps the *Child* was brought down because the ship still thinks it is fighting a war."

They had moved away from the corpse until they stood under the overhanging tower of the old spaceship. The ladder, a temporary affair constructed of wood lashed together with vines, remained against the ancient hull. The catbird still did not move, although it watched them warily.

Christine nodded toward the corpse. "So you think these, er, custodians are the degenerate descendants of the original crew?"

"It's as good an explanation as any."

"But if their behavior has been reduced to instinct..."

"It would take hundreds of generations. In human terms, thousands of years. By the way, I like your word 'custodians'. It fits."

Delsa frowned. "So who shot us down?"

"I just told you, dear. The ship."

"Aw, come on. No machine can last that long!"

"You don't think so?" Warming to her role of devil's advocate, Jan continued, "Delsa, stand apart from that hard Aussie skull of yours and look at this with a modicum of logic. Something beyond any technology you or I have ever heard of, completely screwed up the *Child's* electronics. Now we have stumbled across an artifact looking like it just came out of the factory, even though it has probably been here since Earth's Stone Age."

"Two plus two equals four," Christine agreed. "Old polished miracle here spotted a potential enemy sailing overhead, and did something about it." She added thoughtfully, "But considering what seems to be the relative level of our technology compared with..." She gestured at the bright hull. "Why did it bother?"

"Perhaps its builders were at war with everyone."

"With everyone? Then how come the previous Earth expeditions came in without any trouble?"

"They were lucky?" Delsa suggested brightly.

Jan smiled. "I doubt luck had much to do with it. More likely our shuttle was the victim of a self-healing technology. This old ship could have been fixing itself since it detected the arrival of the first expedition and found itself unable to respond." She turned toward the shining tower. "What we have to do now is find a way to..."

Jan did not know why she had a sudden, obsessive desire to get away from there. Even as she screamed, "RUN!" she was already scrambling frantically up the slope. She felt a wave of heat, heard an unearthly screech from the catbird, and was vaguely aware of an echoing scream. As she forced herself through waves of pain toward safety, her skin burning, she could think of nothing except again to croak, "Run." With a final, convulsive spasm of effort she forced her abused body into a desperate spurt which tumbled her over the rim of the depression and into a pain-numbed heap which rolled her down the other side into oblivion.

CHAPTER
TEN

● ●

"Jan," a voice said.

As water was dribbled between her lips, she opened her eyes and with difficulty focused on Christine's blistered features. "Wh...what happened?"

The other forced a painful smile. "I can only guess. I do know I forgot to bring along any sun screen."

Jan remembered. "Delsa?"

Christine replaced the stopper on the canteen and turned her head away. "She didn't make it."

"Oh God."

Jan grasped Christine's extended arm and pulled herself to her feet. For a moment they clung, then stood apart and examined their respective blistered faces. "You look awful," Christine said.

"Pot calling the kettle black," Jan retorted, using one hand to assure herself the adhesive strip remained on her forehead. She looked toward the slight rise of ground beyond which lay the depression. Despite her hurts, she thought she was physically functional. *Compared to being dead, I am in excellent health.*

But not Delsa.

Jan blinked back tears. She wanted to rub her eyes, but suspected it would not be a good idea to antagonize raw nerve endings. "Are you sure she's...?" She could not say it.

"See for yourself." Sensing the other's doubts, Christine added, "It's safe. I have already looked."

From the top of the depression, the scene was almost exactly as they had first seen it. The ship was brilliantly contrasted against its own looming shadow. A second, smaller shadow was cast from the stone altar. The rickety ladder was gone, burned away, as was the corpse of the alien and its small guardian. Where they had been, fine dust was already being dispersed by a vagrant breeze. Toward the top of the slope, almost a hairbreadth from safety, something charred and unrecognizable still steamed.

"Delsa." Jan forced herself not to weep.

Christine nodded. "I didn't see it happen. But I know she was that side of us when we began to run."

Reluctantly, Jan forced her analytical side into gear. The grief would have to come later. "So now we know why the area is sterile."

"I suppose so," Christine's voice was toneless, devoid of emotion.

Jan decided to prod the agronomist. It would be good therapy for both of them. "You said you could only guess. Guess what?"

"It's pretty obvious, isn't it? At regular intervals, the ship cleans up the neighborhood. I suspect it is the example the custodians are following with their cleaning ritual. There are probably plenty of places in the galaxy where frequent site sterilization is a good idea for a ship hoping to lift again."

Jan imagined a forest of vines entwining a hull, or gigantic tentacles erupting from a surrounding jungle. She shuddered. "Perhaps," she said doubtfully.

"What other explanation can there be? Everything organic is gone, including the ladder, the corpse of the alien..."

"The catbird."

"Our planetologist."

"And our planetologist," Jan agreed sadly as again she looked at the remains of what had once been a vibrant human being, and found it difficult to connect with the memory of the irascible yet likeable Aussie who had been

Delsa Crawley. Tomorrow, or whenever the next zap was scheduled, even that pathetic remnant of carbonized flesh would be fed to the wind.

She forced her thoughts to the catbird. "It saved our lives, you know. It warned us."

Christine frowned. "The catbird?"

"Oh yes. I am convinced the species is empathic. Everything points to it."

"Oh."

Nevertheless, despite the other's apparent lack of interest, Jan persisted. "You said it yourself, Chris, when we made friends with those creatures. Somehow they neutralized the conditioning which should have made us cautious, then played with our emotions like pet tabby cats. If anything good has come out of this, at least it is the knowledge catbirds apparently like us. In some respects, I suppose we are similar to the beings who brought them here."

"The custodians?"

Jan shrugged. "Presuming what we saw is typical, the custodians are mere shadows of what they once were. If for generations the catbirds have been looking for something which is no longer there, perhaps they found it in three human strangers."

"It's a nice thought, anyway," Christine admitted, removing her backpack and dropping it to the ground. She stepped over the rim of the depression and carefully side-stepped a few paces down the slope. She looked back. "My guess is we have a few hours before the next zap. In any case, don't we owe it to Delsa to at least look around?"

"Chris..." Even as she uttered the protest, Jan realized she had no intention of stopping her. Instead she shrugged, dropped her own backpack, and followed.

They stopped at the spot where the alien corpse had been. The heap of dust was now almost gone. What was left was barely discernible from the powder already covering most of the depression. The agronomist stooped and picked up some of the dust. As it dribbled through her fingers, she mused, "Custodian, catbird, or a mixture of both?"

Jan shrugged. "I was too busy getting out of here to see whether or not the catbird remained." She hesitated a moment. "Both, I suspect."

"The poor beast loved its master to the extent it could not live without him?" Christine brushed the dust off her fingers. "I am not so sure about that."

"Haven't you ever owned a pet? Dogs have been known to do that."

"Would a dog warn off third parties if it knew their lives were in danger?"

"It might bark."

"It might bark," Christine mimicked, then laughed. It was merriment without humor. "Jan, you know what? I think you just hit the nail on the head. In its own way, that faithful little companion barked at us!"

Not liking the note of strain in Christine's voice, Jan decided to change the subject. She pointed. "Let's see what is behind that altar."

The structure was hollow, with a single stone shelf on which lay a copper-colored rod about twenty centimeters long. Jan carefully picked up the rod, hefted and examined it. It was feather-light and apparently featureless.

Christine peered over her shoulder. "The door key?"

Jan ran her fingers over the rod and felt a slight hollow near one end. Because it seemed the natural thing to do, she pointed the other end at the ship and pressed her thumb into the hollow. Soundlessly, and without visible evidence of a door either swinging or sliding, a circular opening promptly appeared in the hull. She pressed the hollow and the opening disappeared. She pressed again, and the opening reappeared.

Jan took a deep breath. "It's the key all right." She handed the remote to Christine. "Hang onto this. If the door closes behind me, reopen it."

"You're going in there?"

"You don't think I should?"

"Bit risky, isn't it?"

"Objection noted. If I am not out in five minutes, or if the opening closes and this open-sesame doesn't work, get out of here as fast as you can and continue on to Curtis."

Christine nodded. "Don't touch any buttons," she said unsteadily.

✣ ✣ ✣

It was an exercise in vertigo. No horizontal or vertical, no clearly defined rooms or spaces, no straight lines on which the eye could focus. There was not even a recognizable light source. Illumination came from a convoluted maze of luminescent surfaces emitting violently clashing colors which rendered the interior of the ancient ship a psychedelic nightmare. Spaces snaked between the surfaces with no apparent purpose, although what appeared to be handholds were located everywhere.

Jan started by working her way down from the hull opening. But after she descended a few meters, moving carefully from handhold to handhold and surface to surface and finding herself still surrounded by the mad convolutions, she changed her mind and climbed back up. She could not tell if she ascended by the same route she came down, but hand and footholds always seemed to present themselves where they were needed. When she regained the daylight-flooded opening, less than a couple of minutes had elapsed and she was not even slightly winded. She stuck her head outside. "I am all right," she shouted as she jerked her thumb upward. "Going to try topside."

"Okay," Christine called back. "Is everything as squeaky clean inside as it is outside?"

Jan glanced back to where the nearest surface reflected the sun like a gaudy fun-house mirror. "No dust, anyway."

The other woman pointed at her watch. "You have three more minutes."

"Make it five."

Jan was soon glad she had asked for the extra time. She ascended barely ten meters or so, when the passage she was following suddenly opened into a space which at least made sense. It was circular, approximately eight meters across and three in height, and lined with display panels. If one squinted so the odd colors and screen shapes merged into the background, it could almost have been the familiar control room of the orbiting and now empty *Amazon One*. Most of the displays were active, flickering with shapes and color. Only those before a row of three spindly chairs were dark. Jan looked at an enigmatic series of touch panels which ringed the deck below the displays, and appreciated Christine's warning about buttons.

How do I turn off the weapon?

She knew she did not even dare try. It would need an expert to make that decision; except Jan was not sure Genser's World's total human population of less than two dozen included such a person.

Wait until we tell Earth about this, she thought grimly. *They will send a ship stuffed with experts!*

In the center of the space, a narrow cone surrounded with further hand and footholds rose toward a dim opening in the ceiling. Jan did a quick mental visualization. That would be the nose of the ship, which might be the location of the weapon. She glanced at her watch. There was still time.

She scrambled up the side of the cone and stepped into the upper level. It was not well illuminated, with only faint sparks of light relieving the gloom of the place. Jan removed a penlight from her equipment belt and thumbed it on. The darkness swallowed the powerful little beam as if it was not there, and only when she almost blinded herself as she turned the beam on her face, did she realize what was wrong had nothing to do with her equipment. Heart thumping, she waited for her eyes to adjust.

✢ ✢ ✢

When Jan got back to the hull opening, it was closed.

She did not panic. First she felt around the sides of the portal, fruitlessly seeking a switch or button. Then she leaned against the nearest surface, closed her eyes against the lurid distraction of her surroundings and forced herself to think.

Was it possible the portal was on automatic timer, sealing the ship after a set interval? If so, why didn't Christine use the remote to open it again? Or was there an override negating the remote? Even at this moment, was Chris frantically thumbing the remote while she was asking herself if she dare stay?

Jan checked her watch. Five minutes plus twenty seconds. If Christine stuck strictly to instructions, she was already exiting the ship's sterile environs. It was a long walk to Curtis, and now the agronomist remained the only hope for those back at the *Child*. But knowing Christine, Jan suspected the other woman was still outside, and would probably stay around for at least another hour.

Unless...

The custodians. How could she have forgotten the animated skeletons who fed their dead to the ship? Had they returned and taken Chris? It was then Jan felt the first stirring of panic.

Am I stuck here?

She forced the panic back into her subconscious. But she felt its presence, ready to shatter her calm like a snake waiting to strike.

Tomorrow, she thought. *Yes, that's it!* If the cleansing was a daily ritual, the custodians would be back tomorrow. Still she could not exorcise the little demon of doubt. A few hours inside this mad color box would unnerve even a stone, and despite her years of discipline and training, Jan Buraka cringed at the thought of thousands of slow seconds between her and the sunlight.

She gritted her teeth and stared with grim intensity at the blank inner face of the portal. It was a long shot, a very long shot. But direct mind-machine interface had, after all, been an experimental toy for decades. *Open.*

The portal remained blank.

Open, damn you!

Still nothing.

"Well that's that," Jan said aloud. She laughed at the incongruity of the prosaic words; hardly appropriate considering her not inconsiderable lexicon of gutter-standard epithets.

She gasped as the portal suddenly opened, spilling brilliant light into the ship. As she lifted an arm in front of her dazzled eyes, there was the sound of wings and something warm and friendly thumped on to her shoulder. A soft little head rubbed against her cheek.

Meow?

A hand reached up and pulled her gently through the portal. Jan almost fell as she negotiated the half-meter separating the bottom of the portal from the ground, but was supported by a firm arm. "Are you all right?" asked a familiar voice.

Jan squinted into the brightness. Christine, with a second catbird on her shoulder, was watching anxiously.

Jan reached up and scratched a furry head. Her catbird warbled contentment. "I am fine. What happened?"

Christine gestured. "The door closed and would not open for me. Then these fellows turned up and helped me out."

The 'fellows' were four custodians who stood with motionless solemnity a little apart from the ship. Each had a catbird on its shoulder.

"What did they do?"

"I wish I knew. Maybe an adjustment is required from time to time." Christine looked at the custodians. "Anyway, one of them took the remote and did something to it. Then the door opened."

"Did he say anything?"

"Not a word. Frankly, I suspect he and his friends were brought here by the catbirds. Perhaps these little beasts are the smart ones."

Again Jan rubbed the head of her catbird. Its presence was soothing. "Do you really think so?"

Christine shrugged. "Not really. But I agree the custodians are not very bright. You would expect, for instance, that when they saw a weird creature like me on their sacred ground, they would either tear me apart, worship me as a prophet sent by their ship-god, or..." Christine's lips twisted. "...or at least show interest."

"They did not, I take it. Show interest I mean."

The two humans watched as a custodian pointed the remote at the ship, closed the portal, replaced the rod-like device on its shelf behind the altar. "Are you kidding? Their reaction to me was about the same as their reaction when you came out of their beloved ship."

"Bare acknowledgment."

"You exaggerate, dear," Christine said sardonically.

"Okay, so they are unexcitable. They don't even seem to want to talk, unless it is to let loose a screech or two."

Christine shrugged. "The caterwauling is probably reserved for ceremonial occasions such as ship-cleaning and funerals. Maybe they don't have a prescribed chant for a mere glitch."

Jan's eyebrows rose. "Glitch?"

"That is what we are. A glitch which needed to be fixed. Otherwise, the ship apparently looks after itself."

Jan nodded. "Which is our main problem, and I am horribly afraid it is one without a solution."

"Problem? What problem?"

"Just that I am convinced there is no way we can de-activate anything on that ship, let alone whatever brought down *Amazon's Child*. Chris, I have seen a technology which manipulates space like we manipulate matter. Remember the analog about a savage paddling his dug-out canoe into New York harbor? That is how I felt while I was in there."

"Got an eyeful, did you?"

"I doubt I can describe it in mere words, except to say it is a topologist's nightmare. There is a control room of sorts, below a level which..." Jan took a deep breath. "What do you judge is the diameter of the ship?"

Christine looked at the shining hull. "I don't know. Ten meters or so. Why?"

"Because above the control room there is an empty space as wide and tall as a cathedral. Don't tell me I imagined it, because I climbed into that space and walked around. Chris, it's not enough just to say it is bigger than the ship in which it is contained. The ship itself would be lost in it!"

The other woman chose not to argue. Instead she looked at Jan with a strange expression. "What you just told me is not much more impossible than what I can see with my own eyes. Your face..."

"My face?" Jan echoed with horror as she lifted both hands and felt the smoothness of healthy skin on cheeks, forehead, and around her eyes. There was no peeling, no painful sensitivity to the touch. Even the adhesive strip was gone, as was the scar it had covered. Needing a comparison, she stretched a tentative hand toward Christine's blistered features and, as the other flinched, brought her hand back. "Oh God. Sorry."

White teeth gleamed amid the skin burn. "I doubt it was the deity who healed you, Jan. More likely it was whoever installed big spaces in small outsides."

Wordlessly, they stared at each other. "Through the Looking Glass," Jan said.

"Alice in Wonderland?"

Jan sighed. "Mad Hatter and all."

As if it sensed her confusion, Jan's catbird warbled uneasily and rubbed against her cheek. She turned her head and met the creature's solemn gaze. "Can I keep you?" she asked softly.

Of course.

It was not words, or even a mental equivalent. Nevertheless, Jan Buraka knew she was accepted.

CHAPTER
ELEVEN

• •

The two women attempted to open the ship again. But the remote resisted all their fingering and prodding. The custodians did not interfere until Christine walked up the slope with the device in her hand. Then they moved with astonishing speed and blocked her way to the rim. As she tried to move between them, they simply drew together until she bumped into an unyielding wall of flesh and bone.

The catbirds, hers and theirs, meowed uneasily. The long, knobby arms of the custodians remained loosely at their sides while four pairs of small, deep-socketed eyes met hers incuriously.

Christine returned down the slope and replaced the remote in its place behind the altar. "It was just an experiment!" she snapped defensively.

Jan's eyebrows rose. "Would you have taken it if they let you?"

"Of course not."

"Are you sure?"

"Absolutely. And it isn't the custodians I am afraid of." Christine glared down the slope. "It's that damn ship!"

Jan nodded. "I know. You would rather not repeat what I did, and had done to me."

"Your cure?" The other woman smiled thinly. "Forgive me Jan, but I will stay out of that Pandora's box and let nature and medicine take care of my singed corpus. Staying sore is preferable to the chance the ship might not like me."

Jan recognized Christine was being deliberately simplistic, as well as cautious. The brain which controlled the ship; silicon-based, biological, optical or whatever, was not only ancient, it probably operated on alien precepts in which 'like', or otherwise was meaningless. Jan thought of the light-swallowing void into which she had climbed, and shivered. Was it in fact bigger than the ship within which it was enclosed? Or, as she entered, was Jan Buraka reduced to the size of a mouse, a process which also restored her damaged epidermis?

Did it happen at all?

Again she lifted a hand and fingered her smooth, unscarred forehead. That was real. The small head pressing against her cheek was real.

What did the catbirds have to do with all of this, anyway?

Jan asked aloud, "Chris, do you think the catbirds are intelligent?"

✢ ✢ ✢

The four custodians left the site with as little fuss as when they had arrived. They made no effort to prevent the two women from following, indeed they acted as if they did not care. As the party crested the rim of the depression and descended down the hill, the catbirds spread their wings and soared above the thorn forest. From within the forest, they could not be seen. But their chorus of meowing calls was a constant reminder that although they were out of sight, they did not intend to be out of mind.

Despite the oppressive heat, the descent was at first relatively easy even for the tired humans. The custodians plodded along with silent stoicism, their knobby legs swinging with a curious yet efficient gait which caused them to slowly draw ahead until they were out of sight around a bend in the trail.

Exhausted, the women stopped at a small stream trickling through a primitive wood culvert under the trail. A few meters further on, the first clearing of the thinning forest was like a sunlit room viewed from a dark corridor. After they slaked their thirst and filled their canteens, Christine lifted her head and shouted, "Are you there, little catbird?"

The answer was not quite what she expected. Something briefly eclipsed the light through the roof of barbs and foliage, there was an unearthly shriek, and then Christine was elbowed aside as Jan ran frantically toward the clearing. After an astonished hesitation, Christine followed, and reached the clearing just in time to see the other woman firing her needle pistol at what looked like a flapping gas bag with trailing tendrils wrapped around the still body of a catbird.

"It killed my friend," Jan wailed as she fruitlessly pumped half a dozen more needles at the apparently impervious target. Then, as the predator and its sad burden vanished over the forest, "I did not even give him a name!"

There was a fluttering of wings. Christine's catbird descended to her shoulder and meowed sadly.

Your friend, too? Christine asked in the silent, empathic language which she was certain her small partner understood. Jan was clearly brokenhearted, and for the next few minutes Christine found herself comforting the last person in the world she expected would break down this way. The steely, disciplined first officer of *Amazon One* was displaying an astonishing and totally uncharacteristic sentimentality.

Finally, Jan muttered through her tears, "I never had a pet, you know."

Knowing something of the other's teenage background among the slum gangs of post-earthquake San Francisco, Christine was not surprised. She said simply, "I grew up on a farm. Most of the creatures I knew were destined for somebody's dinner table anyway." Her catbird squawked angrily and dug a claw into her shoulder with enough pressure to make her wince.

"Why do I feel like this?" Jan asked, looking at the creature on Christine's shoulder with an expression which, if Christine did not know better, could almost be interpreted as jealousy. There was also a dawning puzzlement on the aquiline features. She burst out angrily, "Dammit, Chris, why do I *feel* like this?"

Jan was winning over herself. The anger was a good sign.

Christine felt unexpectedly defensive. "Perhaps we should move on," she suggested.

"Slap me," Jan said.

"I beg your pardon?"

"You heard, slap me. Make it hurt!"

Christine swung her hand back.

"That's right. Hard!"

The catbird flapped into the air. The sound of the slap echoed across the clearing.

"Again!"

Christine slapped harder. Her cheek red, Jan staggered but stayed on her feet.

"Again!"

This time, Christine put all her force into the blow, and Jan went down. Groggily, she rose to her feet.

Christine flexed the fingers of her hand. "Not again," she pleaded.

Instead, Jan smiled ruefully as she rubbed her cheek. "You pack quite a wallop, dear. Anyway, I think I can function now."

As they briefly hugged and then separated, Christine asked anxiously, "Are you sure? For a while, I thought..."

"Chris, there is something inside me not even I suspected. When that aerial jellyfish took my catbird, I felt a sense of loss which I suppose is like losing a child. Or a husband?" Jan blinked and shook her head. "Anyway, I hope it doesn't happen too often in a lifetime." She watched as the other catbird returned to Christine's shoulder. "I think you have been adopted."

Christine crooked a finger and stroked the furry head. "I know I have."

"Do you mind some advice?"

"Depends on what it is."

"Don't get too attached to him." It did not occur to Jan to question why she was sure this particular catbird was a male.

Christine bristled. "And why not?" The catbird shifted uneasily.

"Because..." Jan shrugged. "I do not want you to go through what I did."

"Don't worry. Unlike you, I have lost animal friends before." Even as she said it, Christine was not quite sure why she put it that way. There were a couple of rabbits, she remembered, and later a friendly beagle who shared most of her teen years. She had wept a little when her father called her at the Academy to tell her of Tommy's death. But she did not find it necessary to tell her friends of her small tragedy, and after a few hours of private hiatus, life had proceeded much as usual.

She thought about Jan's agony over not having given her catbird a name, and wondered, *Why don't I want to name mine?*

✢ ✢ ✢

They caught up with the custodians just as the gangly four exited the lower end of the trail, turned right and plodded a few hundred meters along the edge of the forest until they came to a village. Backed by the forest and fronted by scrubby fields indicating a desultory system of agriculture, its buildings were Stone Age primitive with mud walls and crudely thatched roofs. Scattered among the buildings and even into the fields, were the remains and foundations of older structures. Some were barely visible among the irregular rows of plants, others had tumbled walls and gaping remains of doorways. Custodians wandered with apparent aimlessness between the buildings, or sat in the shade against the walls of their huts. Some were clad in sack-like garments which covered them from neck to ground. Jan and Christine theorized they were the females. If there were any young ones around, they were not visible.

Other than a lethargic turning of a few heads in their direction, the human strangers were barely noticed. Catbirds, some on bony shoulders and others in the sky, reacted to the visitors with a series of warbling calls which were vigorously answered by the catbird on Christine's shoulder.

"This one's taken," Christine translated with a proprietary grin as a few catbirds came down to investigate. One even briefly landed on Jan's shoulder; uttered a squawk of disgust and promptly took off again.

Remembering a small body clutched within ropy tendrils, Jan said wistfully, "I guess they know I am taken, too." But she no longer felt even a twinge of jealousy as she looked at the contented creature on Christine's shoulder. The punishment she forced her companion to administer, although crude, had proved an effective catharsis. She supposed it was a victory of sorts.

They spent an hour wandering through the village. It was a frustrating experience to be so thoroughly ignored, as if the two humans were part of the scenery. If it was not for the catbirds, who clearly shared an affectionate relationship with these otherwise uncommunicative beings, this could have been a community of zombies; the 'living dead' of one of Earth's more enduring legends.

"This is a dying town," Jan pointed out unnecessarily.

Christine nodded. "I have seen pictures of places like this. A couple of years of drought, local business closures, young people moving away..."

"Is that what you think?"

"Why not? If the ship is the center of their religion, then perhaps its priests are the only people who have a reason to stay here. It explains the lack of children, as well as their refusal to communicate. They only talk to God."

"About what?" Jan wondered. " 'How great thou art', that kind of thing?" Then she remembered the caterwauling. "Perhaps it is in the form of hymns." Despite herself, she smiled.

✣ ✣ ✣

The theory it was a specialized community devoted to holy matters seemed to answer a lot of questions, although it led to the conclusion there had to be other custodian communities within reasonable distance. Jan wondered how the present inhabitants of Curtis, even Earth itself, would react to the news mankind no longer had Genser's World to itself. It was the first real proof the human race was not alone, and opened the door mystics and philosophers had sought since Copernicus relocated Earth to its proper and humble place in the universe.

With the vital necessity of getting to Curtis on their minds, Jan and Christine knew they could not use up any more time in what would probably be a less than fruitful search for more custodians. So they left the village, following a faint trail along the lower slopes of the hills as they gradually turned north toward the distant coast. Christine's catbird, which she stubbornly refused to call anything except 'Catbird', was pleasant company for both of them; even to the extent of occasionally riding Jan's shoulder, although the creature's relationship with the second human remained, as Jan sadly admitted to herself, 'strictly platonic'.

They had been on their way for less than a couple of hours when they began to smell something acrid. Catbird empathed discomfort when they did not turn aside, finally voiced his objection with a series of angry squawks as the smell grew stronger. Finally, as they began to follow the trail up a slope toward the top of a low ridge, Catbird fled from Christine's shoulder to a solitary, sad-looking tree apart from the trail. He perched there and continued his objections with a blistering cacophony of noise.

"I don't think Catbird wants us to go any further," Christine said uneasily.

Jan was unsympathetic. "He is making it clear *he* is not going any further."

"He has a keen sense of smell."

"So have I," Jan retorted. "But I am also curious." Doing her best to ignore the increasingly foul odor, Jan forced her tired legs to carry her even faster up the trail toward the ridge's summit. She was halfway up the slope before she realized Christine was no longer with her. She glanced back. The other woman was still standing, apparently torn between opposing wishes.

That creature's more than her pet. It's her owner!

At the top of the ridge, Jan stood for a long moment, staring with astonishment. She fished a pair of binoculars from her backpack and stared some more. Then she called, "Chris, come up here. This you have got to see."

"See what?"

"Stop stalling woman, and get up here!"

After a brief moment of indecisiveness, Christine held her nose and came reluctantly up the slope. "Is this really necess..." she began. The muffled words faltered in her throat.

"Well?"

"Well what?" In a dramatic gesture whose effect was somewhat diminished by her screwed-up nostrils, Christine flung her hands wide. "Okay, so we have found another custodian village!"

"More than that," Jan said quietly as she handed over the binoculars.

At the bottom of the ridge, extending left to right, there was a sulfur-rimmed fissure containing a line of bubbling, scum-covered ponds. Even from where they stood they could hear an occasional *plop* as an extra large bubble expelled its noxious contents into the air. Beyond, sometimes obscured by rising vapors from the ponds, a village was enclosed within a stone wall. The trail, which slanted left and down from where Jan and Christine stood, looped around the end of the fissure and up again to a gate in the wall. Several dozen custodians were visible, a few clustered near the gate, most milling around on the one hundred meters or so of sterile ground between the wall and the fissure.

Christine narrowed the field of view. Compensating circuits canceled the effect of her sudden hand tremor, as she realized she was looking at a missing piece of the puzzle. "The children," she whispered, trying to ignore the stench.

Miniatures of the towering adults, the younger custodians ranged in height from a diminutive meter or so, up to what Christine supposed was the local equivalent of a teenage spurt. Only a few adults were visible, and they were the ones gathered near the gate. In contrast to their lethargic elders, the youngsters were constantly active, like particles in Brownian motion. One of the adults lifted something to its mouth, and an unmusical blast signaled an end to the activity. The smaller figures crowded through the gate, where they dispersed into several of the ramshackle structures within the wall. The slower adults followed.

"Class time?" the agronomist hazarded as she rubbed her smarting eyes and looked again. Then she pointed. "Jan, look at the wall just to the right of the gate. Some kind of design. What do you make of it?"

Jan accepted the binoculars. As the image snapped into focus, it revealed, etched into the stone, a time-eroded representation of what looked like a stubby flying machine enclosed in a barred circle. "Well?" Christine demanded.

"How do I know?" the taller woman retorted, taking a deep breath and instantly regretting it. "Perhaps it's a reminder of things past."

"When they had technology, like us?" Christine wondered doubtfully, then shook her head. "If so, considering what the custodians have become, it seems an awful waste of effort. Why did they build in this putrid place, anyway? Surely not because they like the smell!" She turned and looked back at the small shape in the tree. Even at this distance, the empathed disapproval was strong. "Catbird is right. Anyone with a nose has no business here. So let's be on our way."

Yet despite her companion's urging Jan held back, her thoughts nagged by the question Christine had already voiced, *Why this fetid location?* Was it conceivable that to a young custodian, the gases belched up from the planet's bowels were pleasant? Even beneficial?

It was not a theory Jan was prepared to reject out of hand. It explained why the youngsters who lived here were active, and the adults were not. But it was a weak argument. Even human children are more active than human adults.

Jan was tempted to metaphorically hold her nose for another hour and go down into the village. But she knew her priority lay elsewhere, at least until those at the wreckage of *Amazon's Child* were removed to safety.

"Yes. Let's go." Jan reluctantly turned away and headed back down the slope.

Christine hurried after her. Both women were surprised Catbird did not instantly launch himself into the air to greet his adopted mistress. Instead he waited until they passed under his perch, then dropped to Christine's shoulder with a reproving squawk. Finally, as they reached the plain and the last vestige of odor faded behind them, he settled into a contented warbling.

Christine gently stroked the soft body. She suspected she was being manipulated, but did not mind. Catbird was a friendly creature, smart, clean, and good company. And unlike a dog, he did not have to be trained to heel.

Jan Buraka was also thinking about the third member of the party. Since the arrival of Catbird, Christine had stopped being her former garrulous self. Not that she was uncommunicative, she simply seemed to have lost interest in small talk. A minor loss, or a gain of ... what?

Had that ancient ship brought the catbirds?

Jan thought so. From wherever the ship originated; it was, she presumed, a place where custodians and catbirds shared a symbiotic relationship which was either the result of an eons-long evolutionary process, or catbirds had been bio-engineered to satisfy some psychological need of the custodians. If, for instance, there were no dogs on Earth, it is conceivable humankind would have needed to invent them. In any case, the custodian-catbird relationship had become increasingly one-sided as the descendants of the original ship's crew de-evolved. If the catbirds were genetically conditioned to the kind of relationship their ancestors shared with that crew, the arrival of the intelligent humanoids from Earth must have been a light in a long and gathering darkness.

A catbird in every house. Is that part of our future on Genser's World?

I hope not, Jan thought vehemently. Then, with an abrupt mental double-take, *on the other hand, why not?*

CHAPTER
TWELVE

● ●

The copter found them two days later. Jan's flare was still streaming across the sky as it touched down.

In his eagerness, the pilot stumbled twice as he ran toward them. "Amazons," he shouted happily, "Great god almighty, you must be amazons!"

He clutched them both, and the three did a clumsy dance among the grass tufts. Catbird, who had taken to the air with a startled squawk as the machine landed amid its own whirlwind, circled low. When the three breathless humans finally separated, he resumed his perch on Christine's shoulder.

"Well I'm damned," the man said as Catbird solemnly regarded him. Again, "Well I'm damned."

Jan was amused. "Well Damned, I am Jan Buraka, first officer of the *Amazon One*. This is Christine Stadderfoss, our agronomist."

Christine stroked the small body on her shoulder. "This is Catbird."

"Really? I am Garnett Podenski. I used to be captain of the *High Hopes*." The man who had led the expedition to Lalande 21185 was stocky, with graying sandy hair and a broad smile. But his smile faded as he asked with concern, "What about the rest of you?"

"We lost one, Delsa Crawley. The others are okay, although with assorted cuts, sprains, and bruises. They just need to be picked up."

"I'll have a copter on its way as soon as you tell me where they are located. Anyway, what happened? Your shuttle disappeared so fast, we wondered if it blew up in flight."

"You won't believe it."

"Try me."

"We were shot down."

He blinked. "You were ... say again?"

"We were shot down," Jan repeated. She wondered if she would have believed it herself. "There is an ancient space ship, half-buried near the top of a hill. As our shuttle came within range, we apparently triggered some kind of beam weapon which fried most of our electronics, including the radios."

The man looked at Jan closely. Then at Christine, finally back to Jan again. "A ship, you say? You have seen it?"

"Very much so. It's real, believe me."

"Is that when, ah, Crawley..."

"That was an accident," Christine said, wincing at the memory. "An awful accident."

With the help of a map Podenski produced from a leg pocket of his coveralls, Jan traced the wandering course of the river back to the valley where the *Child* had crash landed. As Podenski noted the coordinates, she tapped her finger on the range of hills where she and her companions found the ancient ship. "Tell your pilot to stay away from there," she warned.

Podenski studied the map. "Too bad. Oh well, a few minutes of extra flight time is no big deal." Then he spoke at length into his wrist-com. He was wearing an earphone, so the women did not hear, although they could imagine, the jubilation in Curtis.

"Copter Two will be on its way south within minutes," he reported after he broke contact. "Your friends are as good as found." He grinned, gave an exaggerated bow and gestured at the copter. "Ladies, now it's your turn. Your carriage waits."

At first Catbird was reluctant to enter the cabin, but changed his mind when Christine climbed in. He perched on her lap, and allowed her to cup his body with both hands as the turbine whined up to speed and the machine lurched into the air. Despite the vibration, Christine felt him tremble as he pressed his small head against her.

"Catbird's scared," she said.

Jan glanced back from her seat next to Podenski. "It has probably been a few hundred generations since his ancestors rode in anything like this."

Startled, Podenski looked at Jan, then back at his third passenger. "What ancestors?"

My big mouth! Jan had hoped to hold her explanations until they arrived at Curtis. "Are you familiar with catbirds?" she asked.

"I have seen one. It strayed into Curtis about four years ago. Eric Gerenson called it Flyfel."

"Flyfel?" Christine frowned. "What kind of name is that?"

"It isn't a name. It's a contraction of 'flying feline'. For some reason, Eric was reluctant to give the creature a proper name."

Jan decided to change the subject. "Eric Gerenson? From the *Robert L. Cassion?*"

"That's right. Do you know him?"

"Not personally. But it is possible he is a distant relative on my mother's side."

"Is that so? In that case, your presence might be what the poor fellow needs."

"Is there something wrong with him?"

"Let's just say he is ... well, somewhat under the weather right now."

"He's sick?"

"Don't worry, it is nothing contagious." The pilot hesitated. "At least, we have no reason to think so."

Jan was certain something had been left unsaid, but was reluctant to push the point. Podenski himself was obviously curious about what she had left out, especially concerning Delsa's death. So, fair being fair, there was not much she could do about it until they arrived in Curtis.

It was a long forty minute ride during which, between awkward silences and gazing at the passing scenery, the conversation edged toward forced politeness. It was a welcome relief when the plain abruptly gave way to a broad, tree-lined delta with a bright glimmer of ocean in the distance. Curtis was a neat cluster of buildings on a promontory projecting into the delta. As they descended, Jan glimpsed the wedge-shapes of two shuttles at the end of a landing strip. Each of the shuttles, she knew, was capable of returning to any of the three, now four, empty starships in orbit over the planet. She wondered where the third shuttle was.

The welcome was effusive. If they are enthusiastic enough, a couple of dozen people can make a lot of noise, and the hugging and back-slapping left both of the new arrivals breathless. Catbird found a perch on the edge of one of the roofs and watched the proceedings with aloof interest.

The locals were of course mostly men, and despite her long-standing determination to take one thing at a time, Jan found herself surreptitiously studying the crop. At first impression they were a reasonably good looking crowd; ranging from short to tall and thin to stocky. On the whole, a middle-of-the-road selection of eligible males which in time would hopefully sort itself out among Amazon's females.

The inevitable question, *Who will be mine?* trembled briefly on the edge of Jan's awareness, before it was put firmly aside.

Finally the three local women separated Jan and Christine from the men and ushered them into one of the houses. Satisfied Christine was not going anywhere, Catbird allowed himself to be enticed on to Garnett Podenski's shoulder, from where he permitted the curious inspection of the human males.

The inside of the house was spacious and comfortable, with the well-crafted furniture of a healthy permanence.

"I am Evanne Stiegler," the first woman said. She was as tall as Jan, with lively blue eyes. She was also very pregnant.

Jan smiled. *"Doctor* Stiegler, I presume." She glanced at the distended belly. "It looks as if you are about to become your own patient."

Christine asked puzzled, "Aren't you Howard Scheckart's...?"

"Wife? Yes I am, and would shout that fact to the rooftops if it was necessary. But on this world, the sexes are equal in fact as well as name. After marriage, not only do women keep the names we were born with, we level the playing field even further by having our male offspring carry their mother's surname, girls their father's."

The second woman, a slender redhead, chuckled with wry amusement. "Don't let Evanne confuse you with the details of our tribal customs, which are subject to vote in any case. Under the skin we are the same people we always were, and just as ornery. I guarantee you will be at home here." She held out her hand. "I am Joan Walsh."

"Oh yes," Jan said as she returned the handshake. "The shrink."

"...whose husband is Richard Burret, the meteorologist," Christine added, determined to get her facts straight. "Correct?"

Walsh smiled. "Correct."

Christine turned to the third woman. "Please don't tell me. You are Melba Kan-Leger."

Kan-Leger was small and slight, with wide innocent eyes. "How can I be anyone else? With Richard and Howard fully claimed, stamped and processed, and until now me being the remaining female among all the other lovely men..."

"Don't listen to the woman," the doctor interrupted. "Melba and Victor Kraskin are the most thoroughly married pair you will find anywhere."

Melba pouted. "Spoilsport!"

Already Jan and Christine were feeling at home. These women were clearly something special, or it was hardly likely they would have been selected to be part of mankind's first venture into extra-solar colonization. They shared and offered a camaraderie which would have been recognized by the pioneer wives who helped open Earth's frontiers.

Jan said, "I only saw two shuttles as we came in. Where is the third?"

"Looking for you," Joan Walsh replied. "Joe Hahvek and my husband took her up to your ship, *Amazon One*, to see if you left any clues." She glanced at her watch. "They should be de-orbiting about now."

Melba added, "And Victor is currently on his way south in Copter Two. So you and the other Amazons will be together in no time."

"There is one thing..." Joan Walsh looked through the window at the cluster of men around the creature on Podenski's arm. "Jan, are you free a moment? There is someone I want you to meet."

She led the way into the back of the house, to a bright bedroom in which sunlight streamed through a window overlooking the delta and the sea beyond. There was a young man in the bed, a wasted husk with blank eyes and an intravenous drip connected to his arm. Another man sat at the side of the bed. "How is he?" Walsh asked.

"About the same." Then, dully, "Isn't he always?"

"Jan, this is Gellan DeZantos."

DeZantos's handshake was brief and disinterested. "Welcome to Genser's World."

Jan tried to ignore DeZantos' marked lack of enthusiasm. "And this is...?"

Walsh opened her mouth to reply, but was interrupted by DeZantos. "He is Eric Gerenson, one of the members of the first expedition to this world, again my colleague when we returned in the *Cassion*, and my special friend."

Jan remembered now. She had read the dossiers on the previous crews, and understood the depth of DeZantos' concern. She smiled warmly. "It is possible I am related to Eric. A sort of distant cousin on his grandmother's side."

"Oh?" Suddenly DeZantos seemed aware of her existence. He forced a wan smile. "In that case, perhaps you can help."

Joan Walsh explained, "We take turns looking after Eric, usually a week at a time. It's a chore of course, but Gellan is always a big help."

"What is the matter with him? How long has he been like that?"

"He has been this way for six months, give or take a week or two. As far as the diagnosis is concerned..." Walsh shook her head. "An extreme case of love sickness, perhaps. A sort of literal pining away for a lost one."

As they left the room, they heard DeZantos ask plaintively, "Why couldn't it have been me?"

✙ ✙ ✙

Later.

The stranded women had been located and brought to Curtis. The subsequent party lasted far into the night. When it finally broke up, as lights in the various buildings began to wink out, Joan Walsh walked with Christine and Jan Buraka to a lookout overlooking the delta. The larger of the two moons was just above the horizon, and cast a shimmering band of light over the calm waters of the estuary. Among the stars, one bright point moved silently eastward.

Walsh looked up. "That'll be yours. *Amazon One*."

Jan projected her thoughts into the orbiting starship, to the sleeping cubicle which still contained some of her personal belongings. Although she had been in stasis during most of the twenty-two year journey, her few months awake had created a small home amid the photographs and mementos of a past life. "It would be nice to visit the ship occasionally," she said wistfully.

"You will have to apply for the next maintenance flight. Fuel synthesis allows about one visit per ship per year, or did. But with four ships up there, not to mention the just-completed round trip to yours, the schedule will be out of whack for a while."

Christine stroked Catbird, who purred sleepily on her shoulder. "This is all very interesting, but I am tired. Why did you two insist on my company?"

Jan and Walsh exchanged quick glances. "It has to do with Catbird," Jan said.

Christine smiled. "I am not surprised, considering the fuss he seems to have caused. So what is it? Pets not allowed?"

"You saw Eric Gerenson?"

"Only through the bedroom door. I understand he has been ill for a long time. What is his problem?"

Walsh asked, "Have you been told about Flyfel, the catbird Eric adopted about four years ago?"

Christine nodded. "I was told."

"The two became inseparable. Not that anyone had reason to complain, not even DeZantos. Eric remained Gellan's affectionate friend, as well as one of the more productive members of the community. Then, about six months ago, Flyfel got sick and died."

Even in the dim moonlight, Christine's distress was evident. "Which was when Eric became...?"

Walsh nodded. "You understand, don't you?"

"I think so." Reluctantly. As Christine turned away, Catbird meowed uncomfortably.

"From what Jan told me of your experience among those people you called the custodians, it is evident the bonding is for life; literally. So when Flyfel died, it was as if half of Eric also died."

"It works both ways," Christine said dully, remembering the fierce loyalty of the creature waiting to be incinerated along with the remains of its beloved companion. "Jan?"

"Yes, Chris."

"You were lucky. When your catbird got killed, you were not completely..." Christine hesitated.

"Imprinted?" Walsh suggested.

Jan wondered aloud, "What is the normal life span of these creatures?"

"Less than a custodian's anyway," Walsh replied grimly. "Otherwise, why the need for the other village you told us about, where custodian young are raised where catbirds will not go?"

It was a revelation, snapping into mental focus Jan's memory of the design on the village wall. What she assumed was a stylized representation of an aircraft, was not that at all. It was a *canceled catbird!* Shocked, she turned to offer comfort to Christine. But she need not have bothered. An empathetic message of comfort had been offered and gratefully received.

Do not be sad. We will be together, always.
Christine was content.

✢ ✢ ✢

Slowly they walked back toward the now almost darkened community of Curtis. Genser's World was like Earth
before the advent of industrial man, and Jan was grateful to be here on this unpolluted sphere. Undoubtedly an
early priority would be to organize an expedition to the
half-buried ship of the custodians, hopefully to deactivate
its weapon, and in the long run to begin the process of
turning the degenerate descendants of its crew away from
their long slide toward oblivion. Also there was another,
more ominous reason to seek out the custodians.

She looked at the creature nestled into the hollow between Christine's neck and shoulder. The symbiosis was
undoubtedly beneficial to both parties. It was a relationship
of genuine unselfish love which demanded nothing, as long
as both remained alive.

Jan shivered.

As long as *both* remained alive.

A decision would have to be made.

CHAPTER
THIRTEEN

• •

The culling, at least in this part of the planet, was thorough. Within a two hundred kilometer circle centered on Curtis, free catbirds were under an automatic death sentence. From the ground, from copters, even using poisoned bait, the friendly creatures were sought out and exterminated. In addition, weekly sweeps around the perimeter of the 'no catbird' zone guaranteed there would be no more catbird-human imprinting.

But Catbird and those of his kind who were already bonded to humans, did not mind. Neither did they mind that their partners never got around to giving them names, and why should they? As long as they were loved...

PART III
THE SIMULACRUM

• •

When the alphanauts first landed on the planet they later named Genser's World, they found a world much like Earth had been before the explosive intrusion of industrialized man. Although there were forests, verdant plains, oceans, and ice caps, there were no cities or towns, no network of roads, no polluting haze. Therefore no need to consider the untested complications of first contact between indigenous and offworlders.

They did not consider the possibility of intelligence which was not indigenous...

CHAPTER FOURTEEN

● ●

What has happened to those who rode with me between the stars?

✠ ✠ ✠

Much time has passed.

Perhaps it is too much time for those whose span of existence is measured in decades. Although they still come to me, they are changed. They move in and around my hull in fixed patterns, like mechanical devices governed by software. I seek communication, but they do not respond. I select individuals and attempt to merge, but my way is blocked by a wall impervious to higher thought. I seek contact through their symbiots, again without success. Although the ancient relationship remains, it is also changed.

Is it the work of the Second Ones?

Or is it the result of natural devolution?

✠ ✠ ✠

Why did the Second Ones return?

✠ ✠ ✠

For thousands of cycles they have been quiet. Now they have returned in primitive landers which use atmospheric braking.

Have they also de-evolved?

I must assume that is so, because it is evident they lack the means to detect my presence. Yet when the first landers came, my prime weapon was temporarily non-functional. After instituting corrective measures, I was able to disable the most recent lander so that it crash landed in a remote wilderness. Unfortunately that action precipitated further component failure. The weapon is now permanently useless.

Yet although I am helpless, I am not without hope.

After all, the enemy are few...

CHAPTER
FIFTEEN

● ●

"This is ridiculous!"

"Okay, so what are we supposed to do? Say 'excuse me' and walk through them?"

"They look uncomfortably solid to me."

"And uncooperative."

"But not belligerent. At least they carry no weapons."

"I am not so sure about that. I would hate to have my teeth come up against one of those bony elbows."

"Cut it out you two," Richard Burret chided as he watched the two custodians who blocked their way. The trail up the hill was narrow; literally a trench worn by countless generations of feet into the dirt between the impenetrable ranks of thorn trees. There was no room to pass, and Burret suspected the custodians would not easily deviate from the route they had probably followed since his own ancestors lived in caves. Yet they seemed calm enough as they stood there; strange, oddly-jointed skeletal beings who were simply waiting for the obstacle to remove itself.

What would they do if the obstacle decided to stay put?

Burret thought it wise not to find out. "We went by a patch of dead growth a couple of hundred meters back," he said, jerking his thumb over his shoulder. "I suggest a tactical withdrawal, and hope there is room for these characters to get by." He looked warily at the patient custodians. "But don't hurry. I don't want them to get the idea we are afraid of them. We are merely being polite."

Slowly the small column of humans retreated down the trail. Gellan DeZantos went first, gently pulling blank-eyed Eric Gerenson by the hand. Then the two women, Jan Buraka and Joan Walsh. Finally, Richard Burret. The aliens plodded stolidly along behind, until the humans found the place where diseased thorn needles sagged dispirit-edly from the sides of trunks smothered with an ugly gray-green fungus. Doing their best to avoid the still-sharp barbs, the humans crowded onto the strip of ground between the sunken trail and the damaged vegetation. Burret winced as one of the more resistant barbs penetrated the cloth of his jacket and pricked his left shoulder. The two custodians passed by without even the acknowledgment of a glance.

"Well!" Somewhere between amusement and exaspera-tion, Joan stepped back on the trail. "I have been ignored before, but never with such enthusiasm!"

Burret watched the aliens until they disappeared around a bend. "It is disconcerting, isn't it? In their little minds, I suppose we do not compute."

Jan Buraka shook her head. "Although I admit I thought that way when Christine and I first encountered them, now I am beginning to wonder. I mean, what if there is some-thing more behind that blank facade than mere instinct? After all, there are humans who react in a similar fashion when some person or event disrupts a routine they have been comfortably following for years."

"Like the old lady who is confronted by her spinster daughter's boyfriend," DeZantos muttered as he assisted Gerenson back on to the trail. His reaction to their aston-ishment was a tart, "What's the matter? Just because my friend is sick, you think I cannot come up with a witticism once in a while?"

Gerenson said, "Funny." It was the first word he had uttered for days, and even as their astonishment was diverted to him, he added sadly, "Not funny."

Hope dawned on DeZantos's face. "Eric, are you getting better?" He turned to Joan. "Please tell me he is getting better!"

The psychologist shook her head. "Sorry Gellan. Although I am supposed to be the resident expert, in Eric's case I honestly don't know what to tell you. It is possible, I suppose. But..." She shrugged and turned away.

Jan mused, "He said 'Funny', and then 'Not funny'. Is he trying to tell us something?"

They resumed their trek up the hill. It was hot, almost stifling, so Burret kept the pace slow and deliberate. He rubbed his arm as he heard Joan reply,

"When his catbird died, Eric lost the most important thing in his life. He just reminded us nothing is funny anymore. Not to him anyway."

DeZantos's mouth twisted. "Although it's dead, I still hate that mind sucker."

✤ ✤ ✤

Later, DeZantos asked, "Do you think the custodians will prevent us from entering the ship?" The thorn forest was thinning as the trail led them closer to the summit of the hill, and the light of the sun pierced the foliage in slanting beams of dust-dancing brilliance. Burret signaled a rest, and while DeZantos and Gerenson remained standing, Burret and the two women gratefully lowered themselves on to the hard packed dirt.

"Probably not," Jan said. "Aside from the fact that I doubt there is anyone up there right now, I suspect the ship is quite capable of looking after itself."

"It did not stop you entering. And it cured you!"

"Of superficial flash burns and a scar I got from the crash. Nothing more."

DeZantos obviously wanted to pursue the subject. Instead, Burret said sharply, "Gellan, please leave it alone! Until or if Eric is allowed into the ship, the prognosis for him has to remain unknown." His arm ached, and he shifted his shoulder uncomfortably.

Joan added, "And don't forget why we are here. *Star Venturer* is supposed to arrive within a couple of years, and if we cannot turn off or at least disable that weapon, eight prospective colonists are going to find themselves stranded in orbit."

"Jan and the other Amazons came down all right, didn't they? So perhaps the weapon is nothing but a damp squib."

Jan turned red. "A damp squib? Is that what you call it?" She took a deep breath. "That weapon nearly killed us, and would have if not for fantastic good luck along with Emmaline Bonderhame's inspired piloting! No one in his right mind should expect miracles like that twice in a row!"

Gerenson, who would normally stand until he was urged to walk, cocked his head to one side as if he was listening to something. "Flyfel wants me to go," he said suddenly, and tried to step over Jan. DeZantos pulled him back as Burret and the women scrambled to their feet.

Joan squeezed by Jan and grasped Gerenson by the elbows. "Eric, Flyfel is dead. You know that, don't you?"

"He doesn't need to be reminded!" DeZantos protested.

"Of course Flyfel is dead." It was the longest speech Gerenson had made in weeks. Nevertheless his eyes remained blank as he pulled away from Joan. "Must go."

"Yes, let's go," Burret agreed, although he was as puzzled as any by the turn of events. "It can't be far, now."

Joan said, "I will walk just behind Eric. Is that all right with you, Gellan?"

DeZantos shrugged. "Suit yourself."

Jan took the lead as they filed cautiously through the thinning thorn forest. She did not hesitate as the trail widened, became a road between low columns, and then turned left to the rim of the depression out of which the top of the ancient ship reared like a gigantic finger of gleaming metal. A rickety, vine-lashed ladder was propped against the hull.

As the five humans stood along the rim, Joan took a deep breath and let it out in a shuddering sigh of wonder. "I have heard it described often enough of course, but to actually see it..." She moved closer to her husband.

"How long has it been here?" DeZantos wondered aloud, his excitement momentarily diluting the obsession of his life. Yet he kept a firm grip of Gerenson's hand.

Burret glanced back at the worn paving of the pathway, the eroded columns. "A long time."

Gerenson stood docilely. "We have arrived," he announced.

Burret nodded. "Indeed we have." He turned to Jan. "Is it as you remember it?"

She nodded. "Except for the presence of a custodian. He was on a ladder similar to that one, polishing the outside of the ship like a demented housewife."

"There was a second custodian inside, I think you said."

"That's right. He came out through a portal about half a meter above the ground." Jan pointed at the seamless hull. "Just to the right of the ladder."

Joan Walsh turned and looked back down the trail. "So the two we met must have been returning home from the daily ritual. She looked again at the ship. "What do we do now?"

"We wait," Jan said. Her mouth tightened. "You know what happened to Delsa."

Joan nodded sympathetically. "It must be hard losing a friend like that."

"Damn right it's hard!" the other woman snapped, and instantly apologized. "Sorry. It's just that it was so..." Blinking, she turned aside.

DeZantos, who was still staring at the shining cone, licked his lips. "How often does this thing happen?"

"I don't know." With an effort of will, Jan put aside the mental image of the friend reduced to an anonymous, steaming mass. "Probably no more than once or twice a day."

"You hope," Burret said dryly. Trying to ignore the throbbing pain, he held his sore arm close against his chest as he knelt and used his free hand to probe the depression's concrete-hard surface. He stood, wiped his hand on his jacket and awkwardly retrieved and put on a pair of dark goggles. "All right everyone. Let's not take unnecessary chances."

As the others also donned eye protection, in his mind's eye Burret continued the buried outline of the ship. It would be useful if there was excavating equipment available to further expose the ancient hull, although it would be a dangerous challenge to schedule such work between the blasts of energy which periodically sterilized the site. A technology which after millennia could still lash out with such deadly effect, and which could manipulate dimensional space, was one against which Earth-human technology was pathetically inadequate.

Question:

How do we turn it off?

Button, button, where is the button?

CHAPTER
SIXTEEN

• •

They had been waiting an hour. Despite his protests, Burret finally allowed his wife to ease him out of his jacket. From elbow to shoulder, his arm was red, inflamed, and painful. Joan opened her backpack, took out a medidoc and applied it to the arm. Needles pricked, a tiny computer did its work, and within minutes the inflammation and pain subsided, although not entirely. She removed the hand-sized device and scrutinized the readout strip as it peeled out of its slot. "I don't like this," she muttered.

Burret forced a grin. "Dear wife, your bedside manner is not what I would call encouraging."

"Richard, be serious! You know as well as I we haven't been on this planet long enough to understand even a fraction of its hazards." She forced herself to be calm. "You have been helped, light of my life. But not cured."

She helped him shrug back into the jacket. The pain was a dull throb, tolerable but uncomfortable. "Prognosis?" he asked.

"Probably not serious. But this is not my specialty. You need to see Evanne."

"All right. I promise I will consult the lady as soon as we get back to Curtis."

"I am not so sure you should wait. Anyway, if we leave now..."

No one actually saw it happen. In terms of the spectacular, perhaps there was nothing to see. But the air crackled and there was a brief blast of heat on the exposed skin of their faces and necks. Burret turned his head just in time to see the ladder flare into incandescence and collapse in a cloud of billowing dust. "What the..."

For the second time since they arrived, he dropped to his knees on the rim of the depression and reached toward the hard dirt. "Careful!" Jan shouted, but was too late as Burret flicked his hand back with a blistering, "*Ouch!*"

Fortunately no damage was done, any more than had he touched a hot stove. A few minutes later, when Jan gingerly touched the surface, it was barely warm. Puzzled, she picked up some of the dust and let it run through her fingers. "I don't understand this. When Chris, Delsa and I were down there and it happened, the rate of rise was slow enough to allow two of us to get out with nothing worse than skin burn. This time, it was practically instantaneous!"

"Instantaneous," Gerenson echoed.

Burret's mouth was dry and his head felt wooden. He sipped from his canteen. Swallowing was an effort. "Jan, when we discussed this earlier, you suggested the purpose of the periodic sterilization is to keep potentially damaging alien life away from the ship."

Jan nodded. "Chris and I imagined all kinds of nasty scenarios from the ship's star-going past. Environments similar to Earth's Jurassic, or worse."

"Makes sense," Joan agreed.

Burret added thoughtfully, "But with built in safeguards in case any of the crew are caught within the sterilization zone." He shivered, despite the heat. "Maybe that is what saved you and Christine."

"It didn't save Delsa Crawley," DeZantos pointed out.

"Not Delsa," Gerenson echoed.

Burret looked back at the shining cone. "It has been here a long time. If Crawley stumbled, or if its reactions are no longer according to original specifications, it might explain..." He tried to shrug, winced, and changed his mind.

In addition to his other discomforts, there was a heavy pain in his chest.

"Nothing lasts forever," Joan agreed, her anxious gaze remaining on her husband. "Even the most advanced machine is subject to wear and tear."

Burret cursed, "Goddamn, not now!" and sagged to his knees. This time, not to test the temperature of the depression. His face was ashen, twisted with pain.

Joan dropped alongside him. "Richard, what is it?" She put her hand on his forehead. It was hot.

His shivering intensified. "If anyone is going to test the healing powers of th ... that thing, I suggest it had better be..." He started to choke. "...me!"

As he gasped out the words, Jan ran down to the altar, retrieved the copper-colored rod from its shelf and pointed it at the ship. Quietly, with no sign of a door either swinging or sliding aside, a circular opening appeared. "Just the same as last time," she shouted, and beckoned. "Bring him down!"

Joan hauled her husband upright, grasped him around the waist and staggered with him down the slope toward the ship. DeZantos and Gerenson followed. Jan slapped the rod into DeZantos's free hand and forced his fingers over it. "I am going in there with Joan and Richard. If the portal closes behind us, open it with this. If it doesn't open, wait for the next visit of the custodians."

DeZantos pulled Gerenson forward. "First, you have to take Eric. We agreed!"

Gerenson nodded. "Yes. Agreed."

"He can wait a little longer, this man cannot. Look at him!"

Burret was gasping for breath as his body tried to compensate for the fluid filling his lungs. He did his best to work his legs as he was dragged to the ship's open portal and shoved inside.

The two women clambered in after him.

In her desperate concern for her husband, Joan barely noticed the riotous arrangement of self-luminous surfaces as Jan grabbed a handhold and began to pull herself and the man upward while Joan pushed from below. After several frantic minutes of pulling and pushing past surfaces whose only common characteristic was that there was not a straight line in sight, the three collapsed on the floor of the ancient control deck. Still gasping from her exertions, Jan pointed at the opening in the roof of the deck and the access cone below it. "We still have to get him up there."

Joan nodded and helped the other woman with the almost impossible task of hauling an unconscious man up the seventy degree slope of the cone.

Finally, they made it.

Burret's cure began.

CHAPTER
SEVENTEEN

• •

Three units have entered my nexus.

One is clearly dysfunctional, so I institute appropriate corrections. The patterns of the second are peculiarly familiar, although details are elusive. Data storage error? It is conceivable, considering the deterioration of many of my systems. The third unit is interesting, of a grade of intelligence conditioned to correct others of its kind.

The identity sensors and associated circuits are finally online. They confirm these three units are not First Ones.

Yet neither are they Second Ones!

Is it possible that during my sleep mode this planet evolved an indigenous intelligent species? Although I do not understand the mechanism of such accelerated evolution, I decide to accept the phenomenon pending an investigation of its validity.

I attempt to communicate, but there is no response. A possible solution is the creation of a simulacrum to merge with one of the units, although the process will inevitably distort or even destroy the mind currently utilizing the unit's brain. It is a difficult ethical dilemma, especially considering the limited availability of these new units.

Therefore I will wait.

As others arrive, the sampling will undoubtedly improve. Time and numbers however, will not diminish the sad necessity that I will still have to choose...

CHAPTER EIGHTEEN

● ●

Jan came out of the ship, followed by Joan. DeZantos watched anxiously, trying to interpret expressions.

"Us now?" Gerenson asked.

"I don't..." DeZantos began, then his heart raced as Burret appeared in the portal and jumped nimbly to the ground. Pulling Gerenson by the hand, DeZantos ran toward the ship. "Richard! You're okay!"

They met by the altar. Burret had already removed his jacket, and was holding out his arm for examination by his wife. He flexed it, grinning. "See? Never felt better in my life!"

Joan prodded and felt. The skin was firm and healthy, his temperature normal. Shoulder and elbow movements were unrestricted. "This is incredible."

Jan Buraka laughed. "I told you, didn't I?"

Joan looked at the other woman. "Jan, yours was a minor case of skin burn. Richard was dying!"

Burret said seriously, "It's just a matter of degree, isn't it? Anyway I am now willing to believe anything, except that we will be able to disable that damn weapon!" He would never completely erase the memory of the *immensity* somehow contained within the nose of the ship; the enfolding of the physical dimensions which either shrank him to the size of a mouse, or expanded the space to the proportions of a cathedral.

Yet until that moment of realization, he remembered very little. Even the memory of his excruciating pain was softened to simple knowledge. It was as if the toxin had been destroying tissues belonging to someone else.

He did remember the women were still on their knees, heads down and panting with exhaustion, when he clambered to his feet within a strange darkness which flickered with tiny gleaming points like distant stars. Other than the pool of light surrounding the opening in the floor, he could see nothing substantial. Yet he sensed the walls, if there were any, were at an immense distance. Even the silence included a component beyond that of a mere lack of sound. There was something there.

Someone.

✢ ✢ ✢

DeZantos said, "Now it is Eric's turn."

Joan frowned. "I am not so sure, Gellan. If we are dealing with an intelligence, it may not take kindly to a lineup of patients."

"Now!" DeZantos shouted.

"Now," Gerenson echoed, although his eyes remained blank.

Joan's husband glanced at his watch, then up toward the rim of the depression. He would not have been surprised to see a row of custodians standing there like stickstatues. But there was no one. Gerenson, for some reason known only in the recesses of his sick mind, smiled. "Now," he repeated.

Jan's heart went out to the diminished man. But like Joan Walsh, she had her doubts. "Gellan, we only know that whatever is in that ship can somehow fix physical ailments. Eric's problem..."

"...is not physical," DeZantos interrupted equitably. He smiled. "We know."

"He could still recover on his own. Have you thought of that possibility?"

"Of course we have."

Jan threw up her hands in disgust and turned to the psychologist. "Your turn."

Joan's eyes had narrowed at DeZantos's use of the pronoun 'we'. "Gellan, please think this through. Are you pushing this for Eric's sake or for your own? There is no way to tell if he wants this thing, or even if he understands it."

"Want cure," Gerenson insisted.

DeZantos's smile broadened. "You heard the man."

Gesturing for Jan to join them, Burret led his wife aside. "Look, we don't have the time to drag this on forever. So let them try, and then let's put safe distance between us and this kill zone. Although the next zap may not be for hours, it could just as easily be minutes from now. I would rather not be around to experience its effects the hard way."

Joan hesitated. "All right." She sighed. "But I wish I knew more."

"What about the other part of the mission?" Jan demanded. "You know, deactivating the weapon?"

Burret looked up at the shining hull. "Forget it. From what I saw in there, I suspect we would be about as useful as Neanderthals mucking around with the controls of a fusion reactor." He went to DeZantos and pressed a finger camera into the other's hand. "All right Gellan, you're on. And while you're in there, record a few images of..." He gestured. "...whatever."

"With pleasure," DeZantos beamed as he slid the camera over his index finger. He took the rod-like door operator from his pocket and gave it to Joan. "Eric will get his cure. I know he will!"

Gerenson smiled his innocent smile. "Know it," he echoed serenely.

CHAPTER
NINETEEN

● ●

Two more!

One is as the others who have previously entered my nexus. It is an average specimen of its kind.

The other provides a possible answer to my dilemma.

It is of the same species and its brain shows no evidence of physical deterioration. Yet the mind within the brain is peculiarly void of the higher functions. It is therefore an ideal receptacle for merge, allowing imposition without the unpleasant necessity of elimination. The only unknown is the possible effect of this strange brain on the simulacrum, which will have to adapt to the limitations of its new envelope.

Yet it must be done.

It will be done.

Now...

CHAPTER
TWENTY

● ●

Gerenson was the first out of the ship. On his own and without effort, he jumped down from the portal and climbed with easy grace up the side of the depression. DeZantos, his expression combining bewilderment and hope, trotted anxiously behind.

After stepping across the rim of the depression, Gerenson went directly to Burret. "You must be Richard." He held out his hand. "Welcome."

In quick succession he shook hands with the two women, identifying each in turn and repeating, "Welcome."

Still breathing hard from his exertions aboard the ship, where he had alternately pushed and wheedled Gerenson into the mysterious top level, DeZantos tentatively touched the back of the younger man's shoulder. "Eric," he pleaded plaintively. "It's me. Gellan."

Gerenson turned toward his former lover. Although the simulacrum's blue eyes were not blank anymore, neither were they warm. If there was any emotion at all, it was a mild curiosity. "Did I not already acknowledge your presence before we descended from the nexus? Of course, you are also welcome."

DeZantos stepped back as if he had been struck. "You are not..." he began. He held out his hands. "Eric!"

"A moment please." Joan said, inserting herself between the two men. "Who are you?" she demanded.

There was a brief hesitation as the simulacrum considered. After a moment, he replied doubtfully, "The answer to that question is difficult."

Burret remembered his feeling there was another presence within that dimensionless void aboard the alien ship. "Are you part of..." He pointed at the ship. "...that?"

The simulacrum shook his head. "I am not part of Ship or of any other entity. I am..." Another hesitation. "...myself."

Joan again. "Is there anything of Eric Gerenson within you?"

No hesitation this time. "That which was Eric Gerenson at the instant of merge, remains." The simulacrum turned to DeZantos. "Gellan."

DeZantos's hope was rekindled. "Yes, Eric?"

"I am sorry. But what was, can no longer be."

For a moment, DeZantos was devastated. But from some inner resource, he summoned a reserve of strength which surprised himself as much as his companions. He straightened his shoulders and faced the one who had been more than friend. "You will still answer to the name of Eric?"

Gerenson nodded. "It is the only name I know."

"Then it is possible that I can, at least, remain..." DeZantos took a shuddering breath. "...your friend?"

Calm blue eyes met his. "I wish it so."

✦ ✦ ✦

The entity called Eric Gerenson spent several nanoseconds evaluating its relationship with these strange humanoids, especially with the one called Gellan. He presumed the seething emotions of the aberrant mind he now occupied were not untypical of the species, although he was aware DeZantos and Gerenson shared proclivities which were different from the others. Certainly it was a revelation to discover what Ship and its original programmers had assumed was impossible; that there was a another spacegoing species apart from the First Ones and their mad, genocidal offspring.

Aware Ship was watching and listening, and regretting the limitations of this host which made it impossible for him to sense Ship's reaction unless Ship should make a conscious decision to reveal it, the simulacrum wondered how the revelation affected what until now had been Ship's inviolable concept of itself and the universe.

At the moment of merge, Ship had momentarily shared the simulacrum's access to the Gerenson unit's memory. So Ship now knew it had committed a terrible blunder when it used its prime weapon to disable the shuttle from space. Although it was fortunate no fatalities resulted from that action, the simulacrum knew its immediate priority was to convince these beings Ship was no longer a threat to them.

First Ones approach, Ship told him.

"Custodians coming," Jan called, as with the others she stepped aside from the stone-paved trail to permit two of the gangly aliens to walk by and descend into the depression. On each bony shoulder, a catbird sat with dignified solemnity. The custodians carried a freshly constructed ladder which they propped against the shining hull.

"The door's still open and I have the remote!"

Before anyone could object, Joan ran down to the altar. She pointed the remote at the ship, and the portal was promptly replaced by seamless, gleaming metal. Then she replaced the rod on its stone shelf and hurried back up the slope as one of the custodians came back to the altar, retrieved the rod and reopened the portal. The presence of the humans, not to mention the fact the portal was already open when he and his companion arrived, did not seem to make any difference to the custodian as he replaced the rod, returned to the ship and climbed into its interior. His catbird spread broad wings and flew from his shoulder to a tree overlooking the humans. The creature tilted its head and studied the strangers out of wide, curious eyes.

The other custodian, catbird still aboard, climbed the rickety ladder and began to polish the already bright hull with a cloth. The simulacrum watched sadly. "Their ancestors created Ship, and together they drove back the mad ones who followed us across the sea of suns. Now they are reduced to simple primitives who know nothing more than to worship that which was once their captain and colleague."

"Who are you?" Joan repeated.

"I am Eric," the simulacrum replied.

"What else are you?"

The simulacrum pointed at the creature on the busy custodian's shoulder. "As that rides the First One, I ride Eric's mind." He hesitated a moment. "Forgive me if I do not make myself clear. As time passes, I will learn."

The custodian on the ladder descended a couple of rungs, uttered an eerie wail and continued to polish.

Burret asked, "The one you call Ship. Is it a computer?"

The simulacrum searched Eric Gerenson's memory. "It is perhaps convenient you think of Ship as a computer. Nevertheless it is more. Much more."

"An artificial intelligence," Jan suggested.

"An intelligence, yes." The simulacrum shook its head. "But not artificial."

CHAPTER TWENTY-ONE

••••••••••••••••••••••••••••••

Later.

Leaving the custodians to their mindless house cleaning, the five returned to the base of the hill and set up camp. Both moons were up that night, illuminating the area with pale shafts of double-shadowed light. Their location at the edge of the thorn forest imposed a strong sense of mystery, causing even the pragmatic Jan Buraka to occasionally peer into the shadows.

Genser's world had its share of spirits.

Jan pointed. "The custodian village is a klick or so in that direction."

The simulacrum nodded. "The descendants of the First Ones."

"Yes."

"Considering their degeneration, custodians is an appropriate designation. Ship concurs."

"You are in communication with Ship?" Burret asked.

"Frequently."

"What is your relationship with, er, it?"

"When the Eric unit entered the nexus, Ship created a simulacrum of herself and imprinted that simulacrum within appropriate cells of his brain. Within the limited context of the envelope I now inhabit, I am Ship. But because I am separate from Ship, so is my destiny as an individual."

DeZantos poked a stick in the fire. Although an unpenetrable gulf had opened between him and the former Eric Gerenson, his scientific curiosity was roused beyond his inclination to wallow in self pity. "Her? Ship is female?"

The simulacrum smiled. "Please do not misunderstand. Application of gender to Ship is a human custom which labels all ships as female. Is that not so? On the other hand..." The simulacrum gestured at himself. "Although I am Ship, I am also Eric. Which is male." He cocked his head to one side as though listening. "As Ship just reminded me, my two parts will increasingly merge into one."

Joan leaned over and whispered to her husband. He nodded, turned and looked curiously at the simulacrum who was also Eric Gerenson. In the firelight, the young man's face was strangely innocent. "Was it Ship who caused *Amazon's Child* to crash?" Burret asked.

"The action against the human vessel was an error based on inadequate data. Ship regrets that error." With quaint verbosity, Gerenson added, "Please do not allow that unfortunate incident to flaw what promises to be a positive relationship between Ship and humans."

Jan muttered, "Damn right it was unfortunate," and then said loudly, "I was on that shuttle!"

The simulacrum looked at her. "We know."

While Jan made a hissing noise through her teeth, Burret hurriedly changed the subject. "What is your purpose with us? I mean, why is Ship going to all this trouble?"

For a moment Gerenson's cherubic countenance was transformed from merely innocent to something more complex. It was as if there was a looming presence in and around him; invisible to the eye yet as real as the gravity which held them to the planet.

"I will tell you why," he/it said.

CHAPTER TWENTY-TWO

• •

The First Ones were already an old race when they discovered the principle which leapfrogged them from their home system to the stars. They spread, colonized, and together with their symbiots created a culture which seemed as stable as the galaxy itself.

There were no others. Although there was indigenous life everywhere, they found nothing more advanced than the moderately intelligent primates of the third planet of a minor sun. That world they left alone. There were plenty of others, and the First Ones were not greedy.

Yet among them were pessimists who insisted they had gone too far. Sooner or later they would meet the spawn of other suns, and there was no guarantee the strangers would be benign.

Ultimately the First Ones did make first contact, and discovered to their dismay the others were indeed malevolent. Yet with a twist of fate which was truly ironic, these enemies were not strangers...

Any more than the face in a mirror is a stranger.

✦ ✦ ✦

The Second Ones were descended from colonists who settled a physically fair and verdant world at the far side of the Spiral Arm. Isolated from their kind by a combination of vast distance and an accidental erasure of one of Prime's data banks, the Second

Ones evolved into a predatory culture which burst into the galaxy like wolves among sheep.

Fanatically dedicated to a code which preached that destruction is the prelude to pure order, the Second Ones cindered many worlds, transformed others into factory planets for the production of machines of war, and even flung ships toward the Magellanic Clouds and the twin galaxy in Andromeda. Although the odds were astronomical against any reaching those remote destinations, neither were they zero. This was a species in which the game was as important as the prize.

Although the Second Ones were thorough, logistics dictated they could not be perfect. A few of the First Ones escaped the net and disappeared into the Great Dark. Some were tracked down and destroyed. Others vanished forever. One ship was traced to the surface of a previously uncharted world.

The hunter closed in...

CHAPTER
TWENTY-THREE

●●●●●●●●●●●●●●●●●●●●●●●●●●●●●

"It was an isolated battle," Gerenson said, "involving two ships only. The First Ones used their vessel as a stationary fortress, tapping the planet's energies to reinforce defense shields and provide a reactive anchor for their prime weapon. They traded mobility for strength, while the Second Ones continued to rely on the advantage of mobility." He sighed. "Obviously the First Ones were not destroyed. But because Ship was permanently immobilized, neither could they claim a complete victory."

"The custodians..." Burret said tentatively.

"Ship is distressed by what the First Ones have become. In effect, Ship is now the only First One on this world, perhaps even in the galaxy." Gerenson gazed sadly up at the sky. "If that is true, I suppose it indicates the Second Ones did indeed succeed in their unholy crusade."

"How long ago did this happen?" Jan asked. She prided herself on being a rational woman, and found it difficult to maintain her resentment against an entity which itself was a victim.

"In your years?" The simulacrum considered. "Your units of time are not precisely clear in this mind. But I think..." He hesitated. "At that time, your ancestors still thought of the stars as visible manifestations of their deities."

Burret nodded. "We suspected as much."

Illuminated by the flickering firelight, Gerenson's smile had a curiously emotionless quality, as if the facial muscles were controlled by a remote observer. The problem was the identity of that observer; whether it was the simulacrum in the young man's brain, or Ship itself. If it was Ship, the intelligence Gerenson insisted was 'not artificial' existed on a plane so alien to human experience, there was no point trying to analyze its motives or anticipate its actions. Like it or not, the future of the human colony on Genser's World was inexorably linked to the thing on the hill.

But if Gerenson spoke the truth about his independence from Ship, perhaps whatever link existed between the two could be the channel through which Ship could learn and hopefully adjust to humans; not only from what remained of Gerenson's personality, but from Gerenson's friends. There was also the comparison the simulacrum made earlier to the relationship between custodians and catbirds.

"Tell us about the catbirds," Burret said.

"The catbirds." Gerenson's expression became oddly wistful. "The Eric part of me remembers."

Burret leaned forward. "What does Eric remember?"

"What the First Ones knew. What their descendants still know." Gerenson looked at Jan Buraka. "What she knows."

"Yes," Jan said, remembering the soul-destroying grief when her catbird was taken by a predator only hours after she adopted it (or had it adopted her?). "I presume Eric is referring to the bond between a catbird and its..." She started to say 'master', then changed her mind. "...partner. From personal experience, I know that bond is powerful."

DeZantos said hotly, "Lady, that is not the half of it. The bond kills!"

"Not exactly," Joan corrected gently.

"Damn near. The only human being I have ever been close to in my life, had a catbird he called Flyfel. When the beast died..." DeZantos glared at the simulacrum. "You are not Eric Gerenson!"

Gerenson reached out, touched the other's arm and withdrew. It was a sympathetic gesture. "In that sense friend Gellan, you are of course correct. I am not the one you remember. But the fault was not the catbird's, or even of the First Ones themselves, as much as a coincidental convergence of two tracks of evolution. The First Ones evolved on a world where the reproduction of species involved more than the physical union of male and female. It also required the generation of pheromones by a symbiot, which in turn used the First One's skin secretions to trigger its own reproductive cycle."

Fascinated, Jan exclaimed, "A sexual three-way!"

"However, parallel with the development of space flight, the biological sciences progressed to the extent the First Ones discovered how to modify that inconvenient process, so that within a few generations each species was able to procreate on its own. What the First Ones' science did not and indeed could not modify, was the empathic link with the symbiots. It persisted despite the lack of physical necessity."

"First Ones and catbirds," Joan whispered.

Gerenson nodded.

"The convergence..." Burret prompted.

"As I said, coincidence. Although humans and First Ones are products of different biospheres, yet there is something in humans which catbirds recognize and seek to embrace. That the bond works both ways is, I admit, a serious problem for humans."

DeZantos laughed. It was not a merry sound.

Joan laid a hand on his arm. "Steady, old friend."

She felt the muscles tense. Then his free hand reached over and patted hers. "I am all right," DeZantos whispered. "I am all right."

✤ ✤ ✤

The simulacrum felt the presence of Ship. *I have reached the symbiots. They understand.* There followed a flood of information which made the simulacrum gasp.

Please! You exceed the tolerance of this brain!

An unfortunate error. Is there damage?

The simulacrum tried to examine itself, found even that capability limited. *I do not believe so. However I believe it would be prudent to restrict future uploads within manageable limits.*
I accept that recommendation.
Now I will speak to my... The simulacrum hesitated.
There is a further problem?
There are residuals within this brain I do not understand. Indeed, I suspect the persona once known as Eric Gerenson is not as damaged as we assumed.
There is evidence?
In the sense I am identifying more with the humans, and less with the image of myself as your simulacrum. I was momentarily confused when I found myself about to use the term 'friend' in reference to one of the humans.
As would the Eric persona.
It is what I suspect.
Then we must proceed rapidly, before the simulacrum becomes submerged within an identity which is neither Ship nor Eric. I remind you the urgency is extreme.
I understand.
Of course you understand. Despite the limitations of your current envelope, you are still my simulacrum. Therefore fulfill your purpose. Make the humans understand.

✤ ✤ ✤

Although the exchange lasted less than a heartbeat, Burret sensed something had happened. "Eric, are you all right?"

Gerenson turned toward him. "There is much you still do not understand."

After exchanging a quick glance with his wife, Burret commented sarcastically, "It is that obvious?"

"It is necessary to emphasize the importance of the symbiotic relationship between the First Ones and the creatures you identify as catbirds."

"It was strong. You already told us that."

"Mere words. For instance, the Second Ones began their rampage into the galaxy only after all their catbirds succumbed to a viral epidemic."

Burret frowned as he considered the implications of an ancient tragedy. "So that is the reason the Second Ones became psychotic?"

"In effect, yes. In their sickness, they believed they only became 'pure' after the last symbiot expired."

DeZantos grimaced. "Pure, huh? It's the first time I have heard it described *that* way!"

The simulacrum continued, "I ask you to imagine a society in which all the inhabitants are mentally disturbed. The symptoms exist in many forms, including a simple withdrawal from reality similar to that which afflicted my host. For most however, the symptoms manifest as an aggressive paranoia."

"It does seem to have a dreadful logic," Joan admitted, projecting an uncertain mix of foreboding and professional interest. "It is as if catbirds served the First Ones as the equivalent of the 'still small voice' we humans call conscience..." Her words faltered as her eyes widened with horror. "My god, the cull. *What have we done?*"

There was a stricken silence.

"What indeed," Burret muttered at last, feeling too sick inside to say anything else. He avoided looking at the others, who he knew shared his guilt. When they slaughtered the catbirds (several hundred at last count and still counting), the humans of Genser's World had no doubt this culling of an undeniably attractive species was simply one of those unpleasant choices forced by the necessity of human survival on an alien world. So the revelation that catbirds were, in fact, the biological repositories of values which built a star spanning civilization, was equivalent to a low body blow. It was unexpected. And it hurt.

Yet the words 'knowledge' and 'intelligence' somehow did not ring true when applied to the winged symbiots, although such attributes had obviously been possessed in abundance by the First Ones. What the catbirds contributed was more subtle, an ability even humans (who had the advantage of containing it within themselves) too often put aside in favor of false front concepts such as pride and expediency.

Joan had described it as conscience.

Burret preferred to think of it as natural wisdom.

Laying an arm across his wife's slumped shoulders, he said brutally, "So it turns out our 'solution' was not that at all. It was bloody murder!"

Gerenson said nothing. It was a lack of condemnation much more effective than any tirade.

Still not desiring eye contact even with his bedmate, Burret stared moodily into the dying embers of the fire. For the moment, as were his friends, he was alone with his dark thoughts.

DeZantos stirred. "What else don't we understand?"

The simulacrum did not need Ship's help to know the lesson was being learned. The human part of him felt sorry for their pain, while the part which was Ship coolly calculated the next step.

He said, "As you probably suspect, many catbirds remain. Some are paired with custodians, others are free in the wild. There is also, as you know, one catbird still paired with a human."

Jan nodded. "Christine Stadderfoss."

"She is content?"

"The creatures have that effect on people," Jan replied dully. "As you know."

"Is she concerned what will happen if her catbird predeceases her?"

Jan shrugged. "She saw what happened to..." Starting to say 'your host' she hesitated. "Eric Gerenson."

"But is she concerned?"

"Certainly not!" Jan said angrily as she took a deep breath and expelled it. "Chris remains an active, healthy member of our community, and probably a better person than what she was before the creature..." Her face twisted. "...bonded with her."

Gerenson nodded. "It is a relationship which benefits both parties."

"But human beings are not First Ones," Joan pointed out reasonably. "So what is your point?"

"Only that there may be a way out of your dilemma. If it can be demonstrated it is possible for humans and catbirds to coexist on a less harmful level than that which ultimately traumatized Eric Gerenson, will you accept it?"

Joan exchanged a quick glance with her husband, who shrugged. "You're the shrink around here. You call it."

"What kind of demonstration?" she asked.

The simulacrum held up a hand. There was a rustle of wings, as out of the darkness a catbird descended to his shoulder. Its huge eyes glowed solemnly as it gazed around. "Equivalent in intelligence to a chimpanzee or a dolphin, a catbird can be a loyal and unstinting friend. It is not its nature to dominate. On the emotional level, you can expect a relationship similar to that which humans already enjoy from species such as..."

Joan interrupted. "On Earth, people have pets and ultimately lose them. It happens all the time. On my six-teenth birthday, my dog Tilly was killed under a road freighter. I was devastated, and locked myself in my room for hours. But I got over it. A week later, I even enjoyed a delayed birthday party."

"That is the human way," the simulacrum agreed, "which Ship now understands. With that new knowledge, Ship has prepared a protocol which will constrain human-catbird relationships within those human limits. Although there will always be an empathic component more satis-fying than previous human-animal relationships, it will be constrained. On the human side, the program involves a technique which can be applied by any person with appropriate skills."

"I am a psychologist," Joan said. "Are my skills appro-priate?"

"If you have skills with basic laboratory work."

Joan nodded. "I think I qualify. Evanne Stiegler certainly does."

"To do what?" Burret asked uneasily.

The simulacrum smiled. "Because the catbirds must replenish their numbers, their introduction into the hu-man community will necessarily be gradual. Therefore there will be time to prepare. In turn, the catbirds will be con-ditioned to accept group rather than individual relationships. The loss or demise of one of their number will consequently be less traumatic to individual humans."

Burret was still uneasy. "I am not so sure..."

"Individual catbirds will still prefer the company of specific humans. It is natural and should not be discouraged. On the empathic level however, the relationship will be more diffuse and spread across both groups."

Jan Buraka remembered the pleasure of a small furry head rubbing against her cheek, the sense of warmth. She smiled reminiscently. "I can live with that."

Burret blinked. For a moment he felt strangely schizophrenic, as if his mind was overlapped by a second entity. At the same time his vision blurred and his skin prickled. Then it was gone. Only half-believing that fleeting bevy of sensations, he whispered, "I think Ship just spoke to me."

"Richard, what are you saying?" His wife grabbed his elbow and swung him around so she could stare into his face. "What did it say? Are you all right?"

Her husband forced a smile. "I'm fine, dear. Honest. I guess Ship got enough feedback from Eric to figure out how to communicate with we ordinary folk. Anyway, I now know how we can adjust to catbirds."

"Then how..." Joan took a deep breath. "Would the rest of us understand it?"

He shrugged. "You might. Evanne, definitely. Nothing medically difficult."

Exasperated, his wife shook him. "Tell me, dammit. Elucidate!"

Burret said seriously, "My cure in Ship apparently involved something done to my blood; nanites, reprogrammable viruses or whatever. Anyway you are to take a sample and do whatever you do in a med lab to prepare injections for everyone in the colony." He hesitated. "Not you of course."

She gasped. "Not me? Why not?"

"Because in your case, long before the cultures are prepared, you can get your injection the old fashioned way." He grinned. "The *fun* way."

For the first time in a long time, Joan Walsh was speechless.

✤ ✤ ✤

Later, as they prepared to bed down for the night, DeZantos thought to ask, "Eric, is there anything you have not told us?"

"Nothing of immediate importance." The simulacrum had momentarily retreated, leaving a vague young man who retained something of Gerenson's proclivity to be obtuse.

Jan lifted herself on one elbow. "Tell us anyway."

"It is ... difficult," Gerenson said hesitatingly as he looked into the darkness beyond the campsite as if, out there, he sought guidance. Suddenly he shuddered, his eyes became blank and he intoned, "There is evidence the ship of the Second Ones was also damaged during the battle, that it crash landed elsewhere on the planet and there were survivors. Now there is a colony of descendants." Staring coldly out of Gerenson's human eyes, the simulacrum added, "That colony must of course be dealt with."

There was a moment's shocked silence, broken by a muttered oath from Burret. Wonderingly, Joan said, "I think we have just been invited to join in their war."

CHAPTER
TWENTY-FOUR

●●●●●●●●●●●●●●●●●●●●●●●●●●●●●●●●

Ship cannot require you to do anything against your will.
It was apparently a genuine statement, originating with
a code of conduct which for the First Ones had been equivalent to the Ten Commandments, the Magna Carta and the
UN Treaty of Union in one inviolate whole. But even after
Ship/Gerenson's explanation, his listeners were left with
the uncomfortable feeling the humans of Genser's World
were between a rock and a hard place.

The most tempting choice was to do nothing, hoping
the descendants of the Second Ones, presuming they
existed, were as degenerate as the custodians. The problem
was the lack of guarantee they were as harmless as their
gentle cousins. Even as their ancestors ravaged the galaxy with the awesome power of high technology, it was
not inconceivable the descendants of the Second Ones were
using stone-age weapons to inflict havoc in their immediate neighborhood of the planet. And if, like the First Ones,
their ship had survived...

So the other choice was to destroy the Second Ones
before they swarmed out of their nest and resumed the mad
crusade of their ancestors.

"It is academic anyway," Joan declared happily, not
attempting to conceal her relief.

Her husband's eyebrows rose slightly. "It is?"

"Of course. This is a very large world, and we are few. Forgive the cliché, but I would rather look for the proverbial needle in a haystack."

"I do not think so," the simulacrum said.

Joan opened her mouth to retort, then hesitated. She turned back to her husband. "I am right, aren't I?"

Burret sighed. He suspected he was about to become half of one of their rare matrimonial spats. "Sorry dear. As well as four starships equipped for orbital surveillance, we do have the two copters. In addition, given a few days, we can probably even orbit one of the shuttles. With resources like that, we can locate a pretty small needle."

For the briefest moment Joan was tempted to hit him. She was selfish enough to want Burret to continue his sufficiently hazardous role as explorer, meteorologist and farmer, and not elevate the risks through involvement in someone else's war. But she was also enough of a pragmatist to appreciate the hazards of non-action. Before humanity could thrive on Genser's World, it needed a reasonably secure future unencumbered by extraneous concerns ... such as a fratricidal conflict which should have been put to rest eons ago.

"Eric," she said.

"Yes, Joan."

"Whatever else you are, you are a bastard."

The simulacrum rejoined mildly, "In its literal sense, I believe that statement is inappropriate. But in the sense I suspect you mean, you are probably correct."

✛ ✛ ✛

From Joan's biased point of view, her worst fears were realized not within months or even weeks, but within days after they returned to Curtis and accessed the computers of the orbiting starships. With an ingenious combination of programming and orbital mechanics, *Frobisher*'s cameras located a stockaded village at the other end of the continent.

Gerenson, whose dual personality was already partly merged into that of a vaguely contemplative young man subject to swings between the vacancy of what he once was, and the emotionless intellect of Ship's simulacrum, was present along with most of the residents of Curtis when the pictures were spread out on a table in the recently constructed Community Hall (an imposing title belying the building's modest ten by eight meters). The pleasant scent of freshly worked wood mingled with the odor of crowded bodies as Burret discussed the various features of the discovery. Despite, or perhaps because of the hours he and Gerenson had already spent studying the prints, Burret could not rid himself of the feeling these were images of a huddling place rather than a center of aggression. He tried not to show his doubts as he pointed at the almost circular stockade.

"It's a pretty primitive layout. Even if we are forced to extreme measures, it should not offer too much of a problem."

No one commented on his use of the term 'extreme measures', although his wife's expression spoke volumes.

"What about their ship?" Howard Scheckart asked. The botanist picked up one of the prints, examined it and tossed it back on the table. "Have you spotted any sign of it?"

"Not directly, although there is something which keeps them moving back and forth along that trail." Burret's finger indicated a meandering line leading from the village to a clearing in the surrounding forest.

DeZantos shrugged, uneasily aware of Gerenson's close physical proximity. "That could be anything. A holy place perhaps, or a place where the males get together apart from the females."

"Or vice versa," Evanne Stiegler said tartly. There was a ripple of laughter.

"It could be all of those, even if the ship is buried there," someone suggested.

"*Especially* if the ship is buried there," Emma Bonderhame said. The former starship captain looked up from the table. "Richard, I suggest we take that possibility very seriously."

Burret thought about it. "Maybe."

"Anyway, why the stockade?" Alvin Oborg demanded. A genius with anything mechanical, he was a peppery little man, a little on the stout side with not much hair.

Like an undersized Pickwick, Jan thought, still evaluating the eligible males of the colony.

Burret shrugged. "To protect them from marauding predators, I imagine."

"Predators? Is that all? What about other tribes? What if, by eliminating a nest of ants, we arouse a nest of hornets?"

Burret smiled at the little technician's imagery. "Alvin, there is no sign of another settlement within raiding range of that village or even beyond it."

Sheena Ficassio, the community's zoologist, agreed. "It is semi-tropical in that region anyway, with plenty of natural cover. I put my bet on carnivores."

"Great," Jan Buraka muttered. "So as well as the custodians' homicidal cousins, not to mention the possibility of Ship's psychotic relative, we now have to deal with hordes of hungry meat eaters!"

"That is an exaggeration," Gerenson said.

"Oh it is, is it?" Jan was pleasantly surprised she could get mad at the simulacrum, as if he was entirely human.

"Carnivores occupy the summit of the food chain, which means they are solitary hunters or operate in small family groups. If they gathered in hordes, they would eliminate their natural prey and would as a consequence themselves become extinct."

In another circumstance, this verbal exchange would be amusing. But Jan was not in the mood for literal mindedness. "All right smart ass, how do you know the Second Ones not only survived but also produced descendants?" In a sweeping gesture, she indicated the prints on the table. "And despite all of this, why should we believe it?"

"Because it is fact." Gerenson seemed mildly surprised at her outburst. "Within days after the battle, Ship detected a microburst from the adversary."

Burret frowned. "Microburst?"

"A call for assistance condensed within a time span too brief for Ship to determine its source. Along with the First Ones of her crew, and then with those of the second and third generations, Ship waited for the inevitable response. And while she waited, she prepared herself."

"Could Ship have fought again, against what would presumably be superior odds?" Burret asked.

Gerenson inclined his head. "There was no other choice. Although it was anticipated Ship would be destroyed, there is no doubt the adversary would suffer serious damage."

Shand DeVincie, crop-haired former colonel of the U.N. Emergency Strike Force, and now communications specialist, grunted approval. "A soldier's philosophy. Admirable."

"How long did they wait?" Joan asked.

"Nearly two and a half centuries, after which Ship was forced to assume sleep mode in order to prevent deterioration of critical systems. A program was established for periodic reactivation, not only for necessary maintenance but also to ensure a continuing relationship with the First Ones' descendants. But because of failure of a component which in any other circumstance would be minor, reactivation did not occur. It was only when sensors were triggered by the arrival of Earth's first expedition..." Gerenson shrugged.

"It must have been an awful shock to realize so much time had passed."

"Does a machine feel shock?" someone wondered skeptically.

"Ship is not a machine," Gerenson said. "Ship is that which controls the machine, as your mind controls your body."

Burret was still staring at the prints. But instead of seeing them, he was remembering. "Eric, you once hinted Ship is something more than an artificial intelligence. You never explained what you meant by that."

Although it was not a direct question, the simulacrum recognized the need for an answer. But if he told them, would they understand? *Could* they?

"How are Earth's leaders chosen?" he asked.

There was a murmur of dissatisfaction. The humans of Genser's World were still adjusting to the presence of the dual entity within their midst, some with less success than others. No one approved of what seemed to be deliberate obfuscation.

"They are chosen by various means," Burret said carefully, hoping this was leading to something constructive. "A few inherit the mantle by right of blood succession, others are appointed. Some even use intrigue or force of arms to assume leadership. But most are elected."

Gerenson nodded. "Democracy. I understand that particular system has been described as tyranny of the majority."

Burret chuckled. "Or government of the unwashed by the unscrupulous. What is your point?"

"My point?" Gerenson frowned as he combed his human memories. "Merely that even democracy is far from perfect."

There was a hesitance in the simulacrum's manner, as if he was skirting the fringes of a reluctant revelation. *Does he doubt our tolerance for new ideas?* Burret wondered.

His wife asked, "How were the leaders of the First Ones chosen?"

"Does it matter?" Christine Stadderfoss interrupted impatiently as she stroked the catbird on her shoulder. The enormous, luminous eyes of the creature swiveled from speaker to speaker almost as if it understood the conversation. "What does it have to do with Ship anyway?"

"Everything!" the simulacrum retorted with uncharacteristic emphasis. He continued, "Immediately after birth, the young of the First Ones were subject to brain scan. If a certain rare pattern was indicated, the brain of that child was transferred from its natural body to a 'Control Core' which provided appropriate nourishment and mental stimulation. After a period of learning and adjustment equivalent to the education of a human child through to the most prestigious institutions of learning, the Core was ready to assume the responsibilities for which it had been designed and trained. Understanding some of your human sensibilities, I do of course realize..."

"Ship is a brain," Gellan DeZantos interrupted. "A goddamn brain!"

"A brain?" Jan Buraka echoed, staring at the simulacrum with astonishment and then disgust. "And you are asking us to help that, that..." She struggled for words. "...whatever?" She turned aside, as if hiding her face could conceal her revulsion.

Garnett Podenski said, "Eric, am I to assume all the leaders of the First Ones were living, organic brains inside machines?"

"That is essentially correct."

"My god." Podenski, once captain of the starship *High Hopes*, who up to now had thought of himself as hard headed as anyone in the colony, tried not to show his own distaste. "So Ship is, or was, the captain?"

"Ship *is* the captain."

"Without a crew?"

"That is not a consideration. Ship's function is immutable, and will remain so."

"For how long?" Podenski pursued.

"A Core's life span is theoretically limitless. For the First Ones, such longevity was a desirable benefit of leadership."

"I bet," Burret said, his face a mask of studied calm. Inside his jacket pockets, his fists were clenched. "All right Eric, while we are on the subject, perhaps you will discuss the small matter of gender?"

"In that connection, I apologize for a misleading half-truth. You humans accepted without question my use of 'she' as the customary pronoun to describe a ship of space. I can now reveal its truth in the biological sense. Ship is female. In fact, all the leaders were female."

"A matriarchy of machines," Jan Buraka whispered.

"An immortal matriarchy," Joan added, setting her own revulsion aside as she attempted to assimilate the incredible sophistication of a science which could so thoroughly meld a living brain into a machine. For the original donor the bargain was probably even a good one, granting not only near immortality, but access to inputs which made the totality of biological senses equivalent to viewing the world through a pinhole. In a passing irrelevance, the psychologist wondered how the brain dealt with some of the missing biological functions, especially the pleasurable ones such as sex or the satisfaction of a good meal.

Probably through some kind of artificial stimulation, she decided, thinking of the drug or electronically induced highs experienced by those humans who preferred a short-cut road to their pleasures.

"So what do we do now?" Alvin Oborg demanded loudly. Although Oborg's notorious lack of subtlety was frequently irritating, in this particular context Burret knew the little technician expressed the common mood. A decision was required, and soon. Burret looked at Gerenson. Misunderstanding the look, the simulacrum said seriously,

"Yes Richard. The Other is also female."

CHAPTER TWENTY-FIVE

• •

They disembarked from the copter onto a broad, pebbled beach about twelve kilometers from the village. Shouldering backpacks and laser rifles, they hiked along the beach until it narrowed and turned inland along the tree-lined edge of a lush delta. The party of five included Richard Burret, Jan Buraka, Shand DeVincie, Eric Gerenson, and botanist Howard Scheckart.

Despite their expectation of carnivores, the worst they encountered was a herd of placid, elephant-sized animals sunning themselves just above the water. Because the topography forced the humans along the base of a thirty-meter cliff close to the herd, they kept their rifles charged and ready as they passed by. One of the creatures reared up on the front pair of its six stumpy legs and followed the progress of this file of strange bipeds out of unblinking, plate-sized eyes. A cavernous mouth gaped open and snorted a gush of moist but remarkably sweet-smelling breath.

"The First Ones knew them as Narvs," Gerenson remarked as they completed the uncomfortable gauntlet without incident.

"Narvs?"

"Named after a creature on the home world. They feed on small plant organisms which float in the sea. Harmless of course."

DeVincie snorted as he reslung his rifle over his shoulder. "Now you tell us."

After another couple of kilometers of uneventful plodding, disturbed only by clouds of tiny bird-like creatures which chittered and scolded the humans with a cacophony of irritating squeaks, they arrived below a tree-covered ridge.

Burret consulted his map, then pointed. "The village is on the other side."

Hearing a faint buzz, Jan looked upward. "There is the drone again. It's the fourth flyover."

The tiny robot wagged its wings as it droned overhead in the direction of the coast and the parked copter. Burret fingered his throat mike. "Thanks Garnett. If that hasn't stirred them up, I doubt our appearance will start something we can't handle."

"Sure you don't need another pass?" Podenski queried from the copter. *"Li'l Joe has plenty of fuel left."*

"Bring the beast home, Garnett. We'll take it from here."

"It's your show."

They started to ascend the ridge. It was hot, sweaty work as they threaded through a forest of spike-needled trees with ridiculously slender trunks. The climbers were soon made aware of nature's purpose in this strange design, as they were forced to use face masks against needles which whipped and swayed around their heads. Superficially scratched but otherwise unharmed, the five finally reached the ridge's summit, where they lay prone and peered down at the settlement below.

A primitive collection of mud huts was enclosed within a circular stockade about one hundred meters across. The stockade in turn was surrounded by a cleared area of forest. It reminded Burret of a traditional African kraal, even to the central chief's house within its own small enclosure.

"The place seems deserted," Burret reported to Podenski in the copter.

"It wasn't that way during the last pass. They were all outside and looking up."

"What about the earlier passes?"

"Same thing, except for the first time when they baled out of their huts like disturbed ants. Otherwise, although they moved around a bit, they simply watched Li'l Joe go by."

"Did you see any indication of people leaving the village or coming in from outside?"

"Nothing like that."

"Did you try maximum magnification on the playbacks?"

"I am right now. Details are not as clear as I would like, but as near as I can tell you are overlooking a bunch of custodians."

"Second Ones, you mean."

"Whatever."

"Okay, Garnett. Thanks."

✢ ✢ ✢

"They must have hidden inside their huts," Scheckart said.

Burret's lips twitched . "Good thinking."

DeVincie frowned. "Damn strange, though."

Scheckart clapped the ex-colonel on the shoulder. "Something not militarily correct, Shand?"

DeVincie, always sensitive about his past, irritably pushed the hand away. "Look, we tried to stir them up, which means one of two possible reactions. Either run or fight." Frustrated, he looked down at the village. "Those animated broomsticks have done neither. So what are they up to? Contemplating their alien navels?"

"What made them go indoors, anyway?" Jan wondered. "It is as if they know there will be no more flyovers."

"If they know that," DeVincie muttered, "they also know we are here." He swore softly as he peered around to see if there was any movement amid the sparser vegetation along the ridge's summit. He even looked up.

Except for a couple of high-flying birds, the sky was empty. "Catbirds?" he wondered.

Jan Buraka shook her head. "I doubt it. The Second Ones were rid of that impediment eons ago. That is what you told us, isn't it Eric?"

Burret looked at Gerenson. The young face was blank, devoid of expression. Yet it was not the normal poker face of the simulacrum. There was a rigidity, as if there was a very human attempt to conceal emotion. "Eric?"

A fleeting expression across the blankness, a flash of frustration. "I do not know."

"Do not know ... what?"

A helpless shake of the head. "They are descendants of Second Ones. So even if they are as de-evolved as the custodians, their reaction to the flyovers should be one of instant violence."

"Are you in contact with Ship?"

"I am."

"And?"

"Ship is nonplussed."

Burret suppressed a smile. "Nonplussed? Now that is an interesting phrase. So what does Ship recommend we do?"

"Ship does not have a recommendation. I am afraid we are on our own."

"I see." Burret glanced at the others, hoping some-one had something to offer. Instead, they were uncooperatively silent.

After a moment, Jan asked, "Eric, do *you* have any ideas?"

"I think..." Gerenson began, then floundered in confusion. The third entity, the one who was neither Gerenson nor the simulacrum but a combination of both, was like a mature fetus resisting the pressure to be born. The pressure was remorseless, forcing him to face the reality from which the original Eric Gerenson had withdrawn, which even the simulacrum was discovering it did not understand.

The enemy is not behaving like the enemy.

"Perhaps we should go down there," Gerenson suggested lamely.

"I'm all for that!" His eyes gleaming with anticipation, DeVincie unslung his weapon.

"I believe any threat display would be unwise." Before anyone could stop him, the younger man rose to his feet and began to work his way down the slope toward the village.

"Come back here, you idiot!"

Gerenson grasped a bush to stop his sliding progress. He looked back. "Please remain where you are. I will signal when it is propitious for you to follow."

"Propitious?" DeVincie looked disgusted. "What kind of word is that?"

"It could be an ambush," Jan called.

"It is unlikely. But if that is so..." Gerenson's face became wistful. "Express my sincere regrets to Gellan, will you?"

"Eric. Think what you're doing!"

Yet they had no choice except to watch as Gerenson resumed his descent, deliberately choosing his route so he remained in full view of the village until he reached the cleared area before the stockade. He did not hesitate as he walked across to the stockade and through the open gate.

Burret touched the stud of his throat mike. "Eric, what do you see?"

The distant figure halted between two of the huts. It turned to the nearest, looked briefly inside.

"I see no Second Ones. Yet the village has not been abandoned. Everything is in its place, waiting for the owners to return."

Jan. "Be careful."

"Do not be concerned. I will not unnecessarily risk my person."

DeVincie snarled, "Will someone tell that bipolar sonofabitch to stop talking like a dictionary? An occasional cuss word would help!"

Jan was unsympathetic. "Lighten up, Shand. Eric has to be clinical, as any trained scientist is supposed to be."

"Scientist? The man's a com specialist, same as me!"

"Not the same as you, Shand. After all, you are not bipolar."

DeVincie winced as his own words were thrown back at him. "All right, so I don't have two people sitting inside my skull. Which in my book, is a good reason not to trust the man."

They continued to watch as the tiny figure walked through the village to the inner stockade.

"The structure inside this stockade is larger than the others. I suspect the answers to some of our questions will be found here."

The simulacrum walked through the gate. He was briefly visible as he crossed the few meters to the chief's house and vanished inside.

Five minutes later, he had not reappeared.

✣ ✣ ✣

As he approached the edge of the outer clearing, Burret paused under an enormous cone-shaped tree with a multitude of trunks which made its base a shadowed, pillared room with open walls and a rustling, leafy ceiling. Above his head, tiny creatures buzzed and clicked, while a myriad of bright eyes observed him from holes in the trunks. A creature with the appearance and size of a six-legged squirrel oozed through a tiny aperture, stood erect on its back two legs and hissed at him.

"Just visiting," Burret muttered, trying not to look hostile and praying the creature (which except for a bright tuft on its head resembled a venomous chipmink) understood body language.

His scalp still prickling, he emerged from under the tree and faced the village's outer gate.

"Still quiet," he reported. "Going in."

Halfway up the slope, DeVincie slid his rifle forward. Behind the ex-soldier, still atop the ridge, Jan and Scheckart aimed their own weapons.

"Go ahead," Jan said.

"Carefully does it, I guess." Although Burret had a naturally healthy concern for his own skin, he hoped the others were not so trigger happy as to interpret the least sign of alien movement as hostility. Too much hung on what was, or hopefully was not, about to happen within the next few minutes. Jan and Scheckart certainly knew it.

Burret was not so sure about DeVincie.

Under his breath, he whispered, "Don't blow it, Shand."

He heard a caustic grunt. *"Same to you, General."*

Burret winced. "Touché, Colonel."

He checked his weapon. The indicator at the top of the stock glowed a healthy green, indicating the potential for at least thirty rapid-fire discharges. But if he had to shoot even once...

Trying not to think of the unpleasant possibilities, he sprinted across the open perimeter, leaned his back against the rough vertical logs of the stockade and peered around the edge of the gate. Although the village was apparently deserted, the dirt streets were swept and Earthenware pots stacked in neat piles alongside doorways. A communal fire pit was already prepared with kindling.

It was not abandoned, Gerenson had said.

Burret agreed.

He sprinted to the nearest hut, looked inside and saw rough wood shelving stacked with produce and crude utensils, and a small fire pit in the center. Four beds of clean straw were lined neatly against the far wall.

Primitive, yes. Violent, maybe. But these descendants of the Second Ones were a cleaner people than the custodians.

"Richard!" It was DeVincie.

Burret ran back to the gate and looked up the slope. The colonel was standing in full view and gesturing. *"It's Gerenson. He's found one of those damn animals!"*

Burret turned and saw Gerenson standing outside the gate of the center stockade. A catbird sat on the simulacrum's shoulder.

Suddenly the situation was changed. It was astonishing what one small creature could do. "I see you have a friend," Burret called.

The simulacrum waited for him. There was a smile on the young face, not distant or enigmatic but very human.

"Hello Richard." The catbird yawned sleepily.

"Hello Eric." Burret watched the other cautiously. "Are you all right?"

"I am entirely well, thank you."

Burret looked at the catbird. "Where did you find him?"

"It is a she, I believe," Gerenson said as he reached up and stroked the catbird's head. It warbled pleasantly. "My human memories confirm the compatible nature of these creatures." The smile broadened, became the grin Burret remembered from the old Eric Gerenson. "In fact, I find the relationship quite satisfying."

There was a crunch of boots on gravel as Shand DeVincie, weapon carried loosely in one hand, walked through the outer gate. Further back, Jan and Scheckart had finished scrambling down the slope and were crossing the outer perimeter.

"Close enough!" Burret shouted.

Jan and Scheckart hesitated and stopped. DeVincie kept coming. "Hello, Gerenson."

"Hello, Shand."

It was inane, like they were acting parts in a play. While they stood looking at each other, there was a stirring in the dark doorway of the chief's house. A file of skeletal beings came out and spread in a semi-circle before the humans. In every visible respect the beings looked exactly the same as custodians. They had the same tiny-eyed spherical heads and awkward bone structure, the same double-elbowed arms and large, splayed feet. Scantily clad, these thirty or so descendants of the Second Ones stared at their alien visitors as impersonally as if they were viewing a brick wall.

Burret gestured. "Your friends too?" he asked, continuing the charade.

Enough of the simulacrum remained for Gerenson to take the question literally. "I am afraid I have not known them long enough, even if friendship is theoretically possible. But they are quite timid. It is why they concealed themselves when the catbirds warned them of our approach."

"Li'l Joe didn't seem to scare them."

"To them, the probe was merely a large bird. They were curious."

Burret felt better. He beckoned to Jan and Scheckart, and they trotted over. "Compared to what we expected, I agree they are not very fearsome."

"No," Gerenson agreed. "They are not." There was a sound of wings and a flock of catbirds fluttered out of the building. A few settled on bony shoulders, others on the stockade and nearby roofs. One landed on Burret's shoulder. He did not mind at all.

Something whispered in his mind. Not a word, a concept. *Friend.*

"Careful!" Jan warned.

"There is no need to worry," Gerenson said as he continued to stroke the head of his catbird. "As I told you, the Second Ones were irrational only because they were severed from their ancestral relationship."

Burret ran his finger along a warm little body. "Not any longer, apparently."

"Exactly. I can only assume it has been many generations since a few wild catbirds found this other colony and re-established the ancient relationship. In this case, probably because of an evolutionary quirk in these other descendants, the bonding is a group one in which individuals of neither species are 'locked-in' as it were."

"Without something like Ship's programmed nanites, you mean."

"Yes. As I have said, this is a development which came out of natural necessity."

"How do you know all of this?" Scheckart asked. "You just got here."

"There was time enough to observe. And Ship concurs."

"Ship, huh?" DeVincie laughed, harshly. "What do you know. The war is over!"

"It was over long ago," Gerenson corrected gently.

Ship! Remembering, Burret snapped his fingers. "What about the ship of the Second Ones. Is it here?" He took a deep breath. "Eric, is it active?"

"To both those questions..." Gerenson smiled; mostly human but partly the enigmatic smile of the simulacrum. "The answer is yes."

CHAPTER
TWENTY-SIX

●●●●●●●●●●●●●●●●●●●●●●●●●●●●●

There will not be a final battle.

My continuance is assured.

The simulacrum has merged into its new, unified identity. My contact remains tenuous, yet sufficient for me to observe with interest. The other humans continue to adjust to the presence of this one who, while of them, is a repository of concepts they find strange and disturbing. Yet they have learned the value of the Gerenson unit's peculiar talents, particularly that which enables him to touch the flickering essence of reason within those who for too many generations have ritualized the routines of ship maintenance. Even the human called Gellan DeZantos is a beneficiary, and is evolving into a well-adjusted member of his community.

I, and the entity the humans know as Ship Two, have agreed our own merge can occur only after we gain the trust of the humans. Meanwhile, using the less-than-adequate satellite link the humans have established for our use, we exchange data on our separate technologies. This shared information will be of great value when the restored First Ones, together with their human and catbird partners, re-emerge into the cosmos.

The humans still ponder over the minor mystery of how their shuttle survived after I disabled its electronics. Of course they do not know of the reaction of Ship Two who, when she detected the activation of my weapon and decided an enemy of mine must to be an ally of hers, promptly projected a repellent field which slowed the craft's descent and allowed a survivable landing.

It is said humans love a mystery. So it amuses us that they continue to ponder.

PART IV
THE HITCHHIKERS

•••••••••••••••••••••••••••••

Nothing can travel faster than the speed of light.

It is an absolute written into the space-time physics of our universe; a constraint the scientist-engineers who designed and built the Robert L. Cassion class of starships could not avoid. Allowing for acceleration to even near light-speed, mid-point turnaround and subsequent deceleration, the ships actually averaged only a fraction of that ultimate velocity as they crawled across the interstellar void to three of the sun's neighboring stars.

So those who rode the ships and ultimately created the colony on Genser's World, knew the fifth vessel of the series would not arrive until twenty-two years after its scheduled date of launch from the Earth-moon system.

But being light-years and decades removed from Earth, the colonists could not know of the new generation of scientists who dared to suggest that perhaps the universe's absolutes are not so immutable; that there are always loopholes.

Through which things can crawl...

CHAPTER
TWENTY-SEVEN

• •

"I don't believe it!"

"You had better, my love. It's the *Star Venturer* and she is two years early."

"How? There is no way..."

"See for yourself. Correct call sequence and consequent radar confirmation. What else can it be anyway?"

"But Earth..."

"Sorry to keep interrupting, but do you want to call long distance and bawl them out for giving us the wrong ETA?"

"Don't be silly!"

"Exactly. Nearly nine years before we can expect a reply. Does sort of take the joy out of bawling-out and response, doesn't it?" Burret pressed a key. "Bonderhame to the comshack, please."

"Why Emma?" his wife asked.

"She is the only starship captain available. Gellan and Podenski are a thousand klicks from here helping Victor with his geological survey. And right now, Jim Bulcar is no use either."

Joan sighed. "I get your point." Victim of a chipmink's usually fatal bite, the former captain of the *Frobisher* was lucky, although still partially paralyzed and not expected to recover full use of his legs for two or three weeks.

"Okay, so it's Emma. You think her expertise might tell us what is going on?"

"Until *Venturer* starts talking," Burret replied briefly, "she is all we've got."

The door opened and a compact, fair-haired woman in saw-dusted coveralls came into the room. Emmaline Bonderhame, former starship captain and now farmer and carpenter, complained irritably, "Is this really necessary? If we don't get the roof on the aglab extension before the weather breaks, we're in trouble!"

"We already are."

"I beg your pardon?"

"*Star Venturer* has entered orbit."

Bonderhame blinked. "Say again?"

"The first transmission came in half an hour ago, and orbit has been confirmed. Beyond that, nothing. The system is acknowledging, and I have even tried voice. My guess is the crew are still in deepsleep."

"What do you expect? They are not supposed to be here!"

"I know, not for another couple of years. So we need answers, which is where you come in. As captain of the last ship to leave Earth, are you aware of anything the rest of us should know?"

Bonderhame frowned. "Not that I am aware. I was too busy to pay much attention to rumors anyway."

"What kind of rumors?" Joan asked.

"The usual garbage, including one about a new space drive being tested on Farside. Perhaps even..." Bonderhame looked startled for a moment then shook her head. "No. No way."

"No way what?"

The former captain looked almost embarrassed as she said it. "F.T.L."

Burret's heart thumped. "Now we're getting some-where." He turned excitedly to his puzzled wife. "F.T.L., spouse dear. Faster-than-light!"

Bonderhame groped for a chair and flopped onto it. "Persuade me a little, and I might start to believe in fairy tales."

Joan said, "Forgive me for raining on your parade, you two, but a couple of years off a twenty-two year voyage is hardly faster-than-light, is it?"

Burret felt like a child who has been told Santa Claus is his uncle in a red suit. "Point taken," he admitted sourly as he mentally reviewed the parameters of the *Robert L. Cassion* class of starship. Fusion drive, reaction mass plus safety reserve, mid-point turnaround; limitations of a design of which the *Star Venturer* was the latest. But whatever had been done to cut ten percent from the Sol to Alpha Centauri transit time, although not as revolutionary as F.T.L., remained a pretty fair accomplishment.

"What are you thinking?" Joan asked her husband. She grinned mischievously. "Or hoping?"

"Frankly, I don't know what to think." Burret took a deep breath and let it out slowly. It was a ritual he often used to calm his nerves. "The only thing that's clear in my mind right now, is that we have to find out what is going on up there! Even if the crew is in deepsleep, we should be able to interface with the ship's computer."

"That part is supposed to be automatic anyway," Bonderhame pointed out. "At this moment, *Venturer* is supposed to be uploading its log into our database."

"Some kind of failure?" Joan wondered.

"A pretty selective one, I'd say. The ship announced its arrival, didn't it? So why aren't we getting the rest of it?"

"What do you suggest?" Burret asked.

"Prepare a shuttle for launch. That will take at least a couple of days. Meanwhile, call in DeZantos or Podenski or both. Although I insist on being in the driver's seat for this one, either one of them can take over if I drop dead or worse."

Burret glanced through the window. A safe one and a half kilometers distance from the community, the synfuel tanks gleamed dully in the afternoon sun. "How is the fuel situation?"

"Barely adequate." Bonderhame produced a calculator and punched buttons. "Production is on track for a scheduled service mission next month. So if we go say three days from now..."

"Not much room for error, I suppose."

"Precious little anyway." Bonderhame performed more calculations. "If I was religious, I would be praying they come down here before we have to go up there and get them."

✣ ✣ ✣

There were no further signals from the orbiting starship. The following morning, nineteen of Genser's World's total human population of twenty-eight gathered in the Community Hall to discuss this unexpected development.

Emmaline Bonderhame led the discussion. "Now you know as much as I do. Eight people, all needed here, are stuck up there. We presume they are in deepsleep, revival not scheduled for another two years."

"Perhaps they are all dead," Garnett Podenski suggested. Aware of several disapproving stares, he added defensively, "None of you may like it, but it is a possibility!"

"And certainly one we should consider," Bonderhame admitted with obvious reluctance. She noted a raised hand. "Evanne?"

Still pale from the successful delivery of her second child, the doctor remained in her seat. "Deepsleep, dead, or whatever, we need to know. In itself, the lack of information is a pretty fair indication something is wrong."

"How soon can we launch a shuttle?" Jan Buraka asked. She was seated next to her surprising choice of companion, Alvin Oborg. The relationship had lasted long enough to stimulate a surprising mellowing of the little technician's notorious temper. He had also managed to shed weight; enough that in a physical sense at least, he and the slender former First Officer of *Amazon One* were a little less an odd couple.

"Theoretically, the day after tomorrow," Bonderhame replied. "But I would rather not cut it that fine."

"What kind of margin do you require?"

"We are at the beginning of the fall season, which means unpredictable wind and cloud conditions. After re-entry, we will need more than sweat in the tanks to divert around one of those storms."

"Is there any other way to get *Venturer* to respond?" Christine Stadderfoss asked, stroking the catbird on her shoulder. "Such as by boosting our transmitting power?"

"Already been tried," DeZantos said. "Tight, brief bursts one hundred percent beyond the red line. Other than burning out a couple of replaceable components, no result."

Bacteriologist Ella Shire carried a two-month-old baby boy on one sturdy arm. "What about this F.T.L. thing? Can we dismiss it out of hand?"

Bonderhame smiled. "Wishful thinking, Ella? I suggest we leave that to the classification improbable."

"And how," Burret muttered, wishing that particular Pandora's box had remained closed. Recognizing a familiar face behind a raised hand at the back of the room, he whispered in Bonderhame's ear. She nodded and pointed. "Eric?"

The simulacrum rose to his feet. His young, ageless face was more human now than when his composite personality first began to emerge. People were getting used to the new Eric Gerenson and no longer felt there was an alien in their midst, although he was still treated more like a resource than a person. "The mystery may be deeper than we suppose."

Burret felt a sinking feeling. "In what sense?"

"Ship and Ship Two have probed the new arrival and compared it to the vessels already in orbit. Their judgment is that something is..." Gerenson hesitated. "...unusual."

Bonderhame sighed. "I think we have already established that fact. Do you have a specific in mind?"

A slow shake of the handsome head. "I am afraid not. The impression I received is that Ship and Ship Two are disconcerted by something outside their experience."

There was a general murmur of unease. Those ancient entities being 'disconcerted' had chilling implications.

"When did Ship tell you this?" Burret asked.

"She communicated even as we commenced this meeting. Although the link is not entirely clear, I have never sensed such..."

Burret interrupted, "What did Ship mean by 'outside their experience'?"

Joan Walsh threaded through the group to Gerenson's side. The simulacrum's blue eyes were wide, even with a hint of fear. It was a display of human emotion she was glad to see, despite its cause. "Eric, what is it? Can you tell me?"

Gerenson took a deep breath. "Not only did Ship sense a powerful non-biological entity on board the *Star Venturer*, she also sensed several other entities."

"The non-biological entity would be the ship's computer," Joan suggested. "I do not doubt it is a more advanced system than the one you and I worked with on the *Robert L.* As for the others..." She squeezed his shoulder. "The crew. Right?"

"Ship is not sure about that."

Puzzled, she stared at him. "What do you mean?"

"I think..." Gerenson hesitated, his young-old face clouded with doubt. Suddenly, he shouted, "I don't know. I don't know!"

✤ ✤ ✤

It was decided to allow three more days to synthesize enough additional fuel to provide a minimum safety margin for the shuttle *Frobit*, and to continue to attempt contact with the newly arrived starship.

Via the use of innovative pumping and the removal of non-essential equipment from the shuttle, the three days were reduced to two. Meanwhile *Star Venturer* remained incommunicado despite ceaseless efforts to establish contact.

With Emmaline Bonderhame at the controls, Richard Burret in the copilot's seat and his wife riding shotgun, the *Frobit* roared aloft twenty-nine hours later. The side-mounted compound engines worked flawlessly, proceeding from jet, through ramjet to rocket propulsion with seamless efficiency. Within ninety minutes their target was a moving bright star, ten minutes later a cluster of cylinders wrapped around the front end of a slender, two hundred and fifty meter drive core.

The eye-confusing complex of bright metal and hard-edged shadows loomed through the direct vision ports as they drifted closer, until at three hundred meters the proximity controls took over and eased the shuttle to a successful hard dock against the crew module.

As her board flashed green, Bonderhame shut down the various systems and turned to her companions. "Too easy. With everything that has happened so far, I was primed for a manual approach."

Burret opened a storage locker and produced three needle pistols. He kept one and gave the others to the women.

Joan looked at her tiny weapon with distaste. "Is this really necessary?"

"Just being sensible," Burret told her as he operated the hull door controls. There was a hiss as pressures equalized and the door slid aside to reveal the outer door of the starship's entrance lock, already frosted by the humidity released from the shuttle's cabin. He pulled on a glove to protect his hand from the space-chilled metal, opened a hinged panel, grasped a T-handle and turned it. The door slid aside.

And then the inner door.

The way into the *Star Venturer* was open.

✤ ✤ ✤

They entered the control deck and stopped, astonished. Panels, control pads and monitors, the indicators of a starship in automatic mode, were nearly all inactive. Yet sweet tempered air wafted from the ventilation grilles, and the occasional whir of a servo could be heard against the silence.

Suddenly, there was a voice. Calm, conversational and female, it said politely, "How do you do."

Startled, Burret swung around. A white-haired woman smiled at him. At first he thought she was real, until he realized she was faintly transparent.

"I am Gervaise Konnenen," the hologram said.

In the silence that followed, Bonderhame whispered. "I have heard of her. She was a Nobel laureate in cybernetics who disappeared a few years before we left in *Amazon One*."

The image smiled. "That is mostly correct, although I did not exactly disappear. My colleagues and I were merely relocated."

As Burret stared at the apparition, Joan burst out, "But you..."

"The computer is fully reactive and programmed with the Konnenen personality file, image and voice. Although she has been dead for many years, for convenience's sake I suggest you proceed as if I am the woman in person. By the way, I recognize you as Captain Emmaline Bonderhame of *Amazon One*, and Richard Burret and Joan Walsh of the *Robert L. Cassion*. Obviously we have arrived at Genser's World. Now may I continue?"

"By all means," Burret said inanely. "Please do."

"Compared with previous designs, you will find the *Star Venturer* and its systems considerably more advanced. For instance, computer capacity has been increased several-fold, along with software designed to complete the details of a research project secretly underway at Farside for nearly a decade. The ship also carries a compact nanotech manufacturing facility."

"Nanotechnology," Burret muttered, reminded of the billions of sub-microscopic intruders Ship had introduced into his blood stream.

The image had keen hearing. "That is right. During the voyage, appropriate in-flight modifications were made by seventeen successive generations of nanites, each operating according to a program which, at the beginning, had access to data which was mostly theoretical and untested. But the program learned, modified and remodified until, after nearly two decades of flight, its purpose was accomplished."

"You improved the drive," Bonderhame said. "It explains why you arrived two years early."

Again the smile. "Of course. Although I admit it took longer than the designers anticipated, we bypassed the speed-of-light barrier while still half a light-year from Genser's World."

Burret made an incoherent noise.

Bonderhame laughed aloud. "Then the rumors were true. They were working on a genuine, F.T.L. star drive!"

Joan looked confused. "Faster-than-light? But isn't that..."

"Impossible?" Konnenen chuckled. "For Earth humanity that is true, or at least must remain so pending a resolution of their fratricidal squabbles. It is why the decision was made to ensure this ship is the only repository of the new knowledge, and why, after we were safely on our way, certain adjustments were made to the fail-safe systems of Farside's fusion reactor. For those who had already been missing nearly ten years, it did seem..." The hologram shrugged. "...appropriate."

Burret felt the two women draw closer to him, and he drew a measure of comfort from their human warmth. The knowledge they were talking to a ghost who was offering them the stars, and that the original Konnenen and her colleagues had self-destructed to keep Earth humanity sublight, was almost too much for their numbed brains to absorb. For a moment they needed each other.

There was so much to say, to discuss with this woman/ghost who projected almost as real as a normal human being. What would Eric make of it, Burret wondered? What would Ship...?

His thoughts did a double-take.

Does Konnenen know about Ship and Ship Two?

Those ancient entities had scanned the *Star Venturer* and, in Gerenson's words, were 'disconcerted' by what they found. If Konnenen detected that scan, she would presumably mention it. But if the alien probes had not triggered Konnenen's detectors, perhaps now was not the time to reveal the existence of two who were undoubtedly superior in terms of computing power.

Joan asked, "What about the crew? Are they all right? Do any require medical attention?"

"They remain in deepsleep," the computer program called Konnenen replied.

"Please revive them. They are needed on the planet."

"Revival is not scheduled for another two years."

"What does that have to do with anything?" Joan demanded crossly. "They *are* here, aren't they?"

"Of course. Unfortunately, if they are revived there may be difficulties."

Burret frowned. "Such as?"

"An unanticipated side effect of the sideshift principle."

"Sideshift. Is that what you call the F.T.L. drive?"

"It seemed appropriate, considering sideshift does not eliminate the speed-of-light barrier as much as makes an end-run around it. In its most simplistic terms, our continuum can be compared to a single page of a thick book in which each of the other pages is a separate continuum with different contents and natural laws. A few days ago, after modifications were complete and tested, this ship sideshifted through a continuum which reduced the final two years of transit time to approximately twelve minutes."

Burret opened his mouth to say something, thought better of it and instead took one of his deep, therapeutic breaths. "It sounds too easy," he said at last.

"On the contrary. It is the culmination of one of the most challenging problems ever faced by the scientific community. As I mentioned, it was not completely solved until *Star Venturer* was already approaching the end of its voyage."

Joan's professional curiosity was roused. "You said something about a side effect..."

"As soon as we reemerged into the normal continuum, I initiated routine brain scans of the crew preparatory to commencing the revival sequence." The image of Gervaise Konnenen spread her hands in a gesture so completely human, for a moment Burret doubted the truth of her death. "I need more time."

"For what?"

Konnenen said somberly, "I believe we may have acquired hitchhikers."

At first, Burret was not sure he heard it correctly. The statement was so prosaic; conjuring an image of bearded youths thumbing a ride on the edge of town, he wondered if this woman/computer was programmed with an odd sense of humor.

But he did not think so.

"Did you say..." Burret took a deep breath. "Hitchhikers?"

CHAPTER TWENTY-EIGHT

● ●

"Hitchhikers," Joan echoed bemusedly.

"It is the word I used," the white haired woman said. She smiled. "Or would you prefer stowaways, or perhaps unauthorized passengers? The point is, brain scans of four of the crew display anomalies which suggest such an intrusion."

"How can brain scans..." Joan shook her head. "What about the other four?"

"Normal, as near as I can tell."

"What Eric said," Burret muttered. "Remember?"

Bonderhame nodded. "Oh yes."

"Who is Eric?" Konnenen asked.

"Our oracle," Burret replied tiredly. "It is a long story." He resisted an urge to reach out and touch the woman. "Are you sure you are just a software program?"

The holographic smile widened. "I would rather be addressed as Gervaise. By the way, if it will make you feel better you may touch me."

Burret reached out his hand, then stopped. He was angry. "You read my mind!"

"I understand body language," Konnenen said. "In any case, the desire to confirm a visual impression is quite understandable and very human."

"But you're only a hologram operated by software!"

"Are you certain of that?"

Burret reached out to touch an insubstantial arm, expecting to feel nothing. Instead, his two companions were astonished to see the man jerk back his hand as if stung. "What the..."

Konnenen said conversationally, "It seemed logical to impart at least some kind of tactile impression."

Burret rubbed his fingers. "Pins and needles, for Christ's sake!"

"Which is aside from the point," Bonderhame interjected irritably. "Gervaise, whoever or whatever you are, would you be so kind as to further explain the brain scan anomalies?"

"Of course." Before the unbelieving eyes of the three, Konnenen walked to one of the deck's control chairs and sat down. The movement was so natural, it did not at first seem relevant that the back of the chair remained faintly visible through her upper body. "In each case, the original human personality appears to be intact. But it is overlapped by a second persona which projects disorientation, fright, and a total sense of not belonging."

"Hitchhikers."

"I believe that is the term I used."

"Implying they were picked up somewhere." Bonderhame spread her hands. "Where?"

"As I told you, the ship bypassed this continuum's speed-of-light barrier by sideshifting through a continuum with a different set of physical laws. I presume that is where we acquired the overlapping entities."

"Unwilling ones, by the sound of it," Burret commented with a frown. "But those emotions you described, fright and so on, how do you know they originated with the, er, hitchhikers? Even in deepsleep, I imagine the human brain is capable of generating pretty weird scenarios. In normal life, we call them nightmares."

Konnenen shook her head. "In this case I do not believe so. There is a secondary pattern which indicates the normal depressed brain activity of deepsleep. What I detected is an intrusive and very active overlay."

As he contemplated this woman who was not a woman, Burret again wondered if she was aware of the ship-entities on the planet's surface. Although he was tempted to bring up the subject, he suspected that by doing so he might be opening up the proverbial can of worms.

"You said four of the crew are unaffected. Can they be revived without risk?"

"Probably."

"Probably? That does not sound encouraging."

"There are unknowns. It would be foolish to commit to absolutes."

"Who are the unaffected ones?"

"Patrice Coestrand, captain and systems specialist. Susan MacEwan, medical technician. Mercedes Delfuego, agronomist. And Aileen Duprez-Smith, oceanographer."

Burret whistled. "All female."

The white head inclined. "I assumed that would catch your attention."

"It could be coincidence," Bonderhame suggested. She did not sound convinced.

Joan shook her head. "Pretty long odds, I would say." She walked across the deck to examine one of the few activated panels. Labeled STASIS FACILITY, it had eight illuminated indicators, each bearing the name of a crew member. "I suggest we start with the captain. Perhaps she can tell us something."

Bonderhame nodded. "Good idea." She turned to Burret. "Richard. Do you agree?"

The man looked doubtful. "I suppose..." After a moment's hesitation, he shrugged resignedly. "All right, let's do it that way."

One of the indicators began to blink.

"I have initiated the revival sequence for Captain Coestrand," Konnenen said. "She will be available in approximately forty minutes."

✠ ✠ ✠

Burret returned to the shuttle and contacted Curtis. The ground operator immediately summoned Eric Gerenson, who listened to Burret's narrative without comment.

"*Fascinating,*" he said finally.

"Do you agree with our decision to revive Coestrand?"

"Considering the circumstances, I believe such a minimum approach is prudent."

"Before we left, you told us Ship sensed a powerful non-biological entity, that I presume we can now identify as Gervaise Konnenen. But I am surprised Konnenen did not mention Ship's probe. Surely she would have detected it?"

"I am sure she detected something, and probably assumes someone will enlighten her. Perhaps that is according to the behavior patterns of the original Gervaise Konnenen."

"Then should we tell her about the custodians and their ships?"

"You have doubts?"

Burret snapped sourly, "Doesn't everyone?"

Already the human colony was struggling to coexist with the ship-entities whose looming presence beyond the curve of the planet had come to color almost every waking moment. What strange exchanges were taking place between those two ancient brains in their mechanical shells, and what would happen if they linked to the formidable entity who had assumed the identity of a long-dead scientist named Gervaise Konnenen? Burret did not want to think of the unpleasant possibilities.

After signing off, he returned to the control deck. "Where is Konnenen?"

"She told us she has matters to attend to," his wife replied as she stared pensively at the empty control chair. She chuckled. "Believe it or not, instead of simply disappearing like a good hologram should, she walked out!"

"Sensitive to our human sensitivities, no doubt," Bonderhame commented with a wry smile. "First a software program, then a woman, and now a diplomat."

"Hmm." Burret scratched his head. "So do we tell her?"

"Tell her what?"

"About her alien colleagues." Burret jerked his thumb in the direction of the planet. "The Big Two."

Joan arched an inquiring eyebrow. "What if she already knows?"

"In which case she would have mentioned it," Bonderhame countered. "Or don't you think so?"

"I am still wondering about that. When I talked to Eric, he suggested Konnenen is waiting for us to bring up the subject. You know, as the flesh and blood original might have done."

"Polite too?" Bonderhame laughed aloud. "We're talking about a contrivance of chips and circuits for god's sake, not a flesh and blood human being!"

"In the same way we're a contrivance of cells and nerve pathways?" Joan countered, staring gloomily at the floor. She looked up. "Anyway, let's not blow it by underestimating the opposition."

Burret looked with surprise at his wife. "Opposition? Is that what you think about our insubstantial host?"

She shrugged. "Not so insubstantial, I think."

Actually, Burret sympathized with the cautious approach. But he also knew time was not on their side. "Gervaise! We need to talk."

Her voice responded from the PA. *'Please join me in the Morgue.'*

Bonderhame turned red. "That damn computer..."

"...is Gervaise Konnenen!" Burret snapped as he led the way to the access well and clattered down four levels to a stark, white-painted room known to all starship crews as the Morgue.

The far bulkhead was filled with the heavy, gasketted doors of stasis chambers in two rows of four. One door was open, revealing a disconnected umbilical coiled neatly inside an empty chamber. A slight, dark skinned woman lay on a pedestal-bed in the center of the room. Probes were attached to her scalp, an intravenous drip to one arm. Waldos withdrew into their recesses as Burret and his companions arrived. The woman's eyes flickered open.

"You must be from Genser's World," she whispered. Colorless lips curved into a smile and her voice firmed. It was a low, throaty contralto. "I am Pat Coestrand."

"I know," Burret said as he smiled back. "I suppose Gervaise has briefed you?"

A slight nod. "For a computer, she has a surprisingly competent bedside manner."

"My name is Richard Burret." He urged his wife forward. "This is Joan Walsh. Over there is a colleague of yours, Captain Emmaline Bonderhame of *Amazon One*."

Joan put her hand on Coestrand's forehead. "Right now I am your doctor. How do you feel?"

"Like Rip van Winkle must have felt." Patrice Coestrand had a strong, narrow face with high cheekbones. Her olive skin and wiry hair betrayed her Afro-American heritage. "But if you give me a few minutes, I will perform a couple of hand springs for you."

Joan lifted her hands in mock alarm. "Later. Please."

Bonderhame asked, "Are you aware you are two years early?"

Coestrand nodded. "So I have just been told. Proves that if the powers-that-be had not decided to keep some things to themselves when I joined the project, it might have saved a lot of embarrassment. As it is, I do remember getting into a flaming row with the senior contractor when I found out the living quarters had been reduced to make room for extra equipment. Now I know the reason..." A sigh. "Never thought a computer would make a chump out of me."

Burret detected a movement out of the corner of his eye. "Hello Gervaise."

Konnenen had changed her attire from standard ship's coveralls to white slacks and a plain tunic of midnight-blue. The blue contrasted with her sweep of white hair and made her very elegant. She sat on the edge of the bed.

At least she has the decency not to depress the mattress, Burret noted, unreasonably grateful for any flaw in the simulation.

Konnenen said, "Captain Coestrand, there is a question I must ask, and it is very important. Think carefully before you answer. Did anything happen to you during deepsleep?"

Coestrand tried to sit up, finally succeeded with Joan's help. With the psychologist's supporting arm around her shoulders, she swung skinny legs over the side of the bed. Burret tried to ignore the hospital-type gown which barely covered the starship captain's undernourished body.

"I presume there is a reason for that question?" Coestrand asked.

"There are anomalies in the brain scans of the *Star Venturer*'s male crew members. It is why I have decided not to revive them until those anomalies are identified, and why I need your cooperation. So, Captain Coestrand. During deepsleep, did you dream?"

Joan carefully removed her arm.

Coestrand nodded gratefully and remained sitting without support. She was even able to adjust the gown to provide more decorous covering. "Isn't deepsleep supposed to suppress brain activity to the extent even the most basic dreams are unlikely?"

"Under normal circumstances, that is true," Konnenen agreed. "But these are not normal circumstances. Therefore I ask you again. Did you dream?"

The woman on the bed let out her breath in a shuddering sigh. "Oh yes."

CHAPTER TWENTY-NINE

• •

She loved the house in the suburbs, its lush lawns and colorful flower beds. It was organized as she wanted it, down to the last paving stone in the artfully curved front walk. It was one of eight similar pretty houses, four on each side of the street.

The stranger at her door was indistinct, a three dimensional shadow.

"YOU HAVE TAKEN ME FROM WHERE I WAS," it said. "THEREFORE I MUST TAKE THE PLACE WHERE YOU ARE."

She bristled. "Go away."

It flinched but held its ground. "NOT."

"I repeat. Go away!"

It was an obscene intruder, a blot on the landscape. "NOT," it repeated uneasily.

"There are other houses" she snapped. "Go to one of them!" Even as she slammed the door, she knew she should not have reacted as she did. But cowed by her fury, the intruder was already retreating down the walk and through the gate. With a sudden sense of guilt she opened the door to call it back. But it was already across the street, at another's door.

She heard, "YOU HAVE TAKEN ME FROM WHERE..."

The guilt became worse.

CHAPTER
THIRTY

● ●

They adjourned to the starship's wardroom. After consuming part of a fortified milkshake and her modesty recovered in a set of ship's coveralls, Coestrand looked much better. "I still don't understand. Even during deepsleep, my brain was able to react to the intruder?"

Joan shrugged. "I suppose your experience is another indication mind is more than just a creation of the brain. After all, you did resist the intruder and win."

"Yes, by sacrificing..." Coestrand clenched her fists. "Damn!"

"Don't blame yourself. It is only now you recognize the symbolism for what it was."

"Oh sure," Coestrand retorted, her brown eyes bitter. "The houses represent the eight of us who, during deepsleep, somehow acquired four uninvited guests. When one of those guests tried to muscle in on my turf and found me..." The narrow face flushed. "...unwilling, it picked on one of my friends instead. Don't blame myself?" Her lips curled. "Easy to say, not so easy to do!"

"It's water under the bridge anyway," Burret said coldly, ignoring the revived captain's glare of resentment. He turned to Konnenen, who was incongruously perched on the arm of an empty chair at the far side of the small room. "Well Gervaise, I suppose it does confirm your suspicion about hitchhikers. But why did they end up with the male members of the crew?"

Bonderhame chuckled. "Richard, 'tigress' is not an exaggeration when describing the female defender of the hearth. After losing at least one such encounter, my guess is the invaders chose the men as the path of least resistance."

Joan nodded. "And according to Pat's dream experience, the hitchhikers themselves are victims."

Coestrand said bitterly, "Unless the thing lied."

"Perhaps," the hologram said. "But it is more logical to assume it told the truth."

"So what do we do now?" Burret wondered.

"I think that is obvious." Non-material hands spread wide. "We must find a way to communicate with the hitchhikers."

"Talk to them, you mean?"

"In a sense. Yes."

Burret was tempted to unleash a fatuous suggestion about using the phone, but restrained the impulse. Computers were not supposed to have a sense of humor. "So just how are we supposed to do that?"

"Captain Coestrand has already communicated with one of the entities. Perhaps she can do it again."

"The hell she can!" Although Patrice Coestrand still had not fully recovered all her physical strength, she showed fire as she glared at Konnenen. "Listen, Gervaise or whatever you are, not only do I hate nightmares, I do not volunteer to repeat them!"

Konnenen looked uncomfortable. "I am sorry, but I am convinced it is the only practical approach. In any case, you have already demonstrated your ability to face down one of the..." The hologram hesitated. "...entities."

"It was a dream!"

"True. Considering their origin from a reality in which logic as we know it may have no meaning, it is conceivable the symbolism of the subconscious is the only common factor."

The wardroom was small, hardly the place for pacing. But Coestrand managed a cautious circumnavigation without bumping into chairs or table. As Joan watched anxiously, her hand not far from the medidoc clipped to her belt, Burret and Bonderhame sipped coffee. Konnenen stood near the door, waiting.

Coestrand stopped. "What do you propose?"

The hologram shrugged. "That is up to Doctor Walsh. A simple sedative perhaps."

"I will be wired?"

"I do not recommend it," Joan said. "Until you have recovered your strength, any form of external stimuli should be avoided."

"So you want to put me to sleep so I can talk to one of those ... things." Coestrand sat down again, sipped from her milkshake and looked doubtful. "Forgive my lack of enthusiasm, but frankly I think it sucks."

Burret asked, "Gervaise, may we discuss this in private?"

A slight smile. "Without me, you mean."

"Without any part of you. We know you don't need to project yourself as Gervaise Konnenen to know what goes on in every corner of the ship."

"Of course." Konnenen pointed at a wall-mounted com panel. "When you are ready, let me know." The door slid aside and the image of the deceased scientist walked into the corridor. As the door closed...

"Can we trust you?" Bonderhame shouted.

"I am afraid you must," Konnenen's voice replied.

✛ ✛ ✛

Patrice Coestrand listened with increasing incredulity.

"It is not that I disbelieve you, it's just..." She spread her hands. "Symbiots who love you to death, a degenerate race of aliens, and two intelligent alien ships! I am still dreaming, aren't I?"

Bonderhame said gently, "Colleague, you are the captain of a faster-than-light starship which has not only taken on the persona of a dead scientist, but acquired hitchhikers from an alternate universe. Which dream do you prefer?"

"Now you are being reasonable with the unreasonable," Coestrand complained. She pinched the skin of her forearm until she winced. "I guess I am awake, aren't I?"

Burret noted the welt. "You are now."

"Why the secrecy? I mean, why did you ask..." Coestrand jerked her thumb toward the closed wardroom door.

"We are not sure if Konnenen knows about Ship One and Ship Two," Joan replied. "Or even if she should be told."

"You said they scanned."

"That is true."

"Then she knows. Our sensors are state of the art."

Bonderhame shook her head. "You heard Richard. To beings who can put a space the size of a stadium inside the front end of a ship, what you call state of the art is probably equivalent to Stone Age primitive. Better to have Gervaise concentrate her resources on our immediate problem."

"Hitchhikers," the captain of the *Star Venturer* muttered as she rubbed the mark on her arm. She looked at the psychologist. "Just a sedative, you said."

Joan nodded. "Nothing fancy."

"I do want to help my friends."

"I am banking on it."

Coestrand got up from the table and lay down on the wardroom couch. "Then let's get on with it before I change my mind." She bared an arm. "Now."

Joan approached with the medidoc.

CHAPTER THIRTY-ONE

• •

The house is the same, as are all the houses in the street; bright stucco and paint amid lawns and flower beds.

Seven of the houses are occupied.

Four have unwelcome guests.

Someone waves. It is Mercedes, in her garden as usual.

I lean on the fence. "Hi Mercy. Have you spoken to the others?"

"Just the girls. The men have not come out since the strangers came."

"Have you met any of the strangers?"

"Just one. It wanted to move in, but I chased it away like you did. Same with Susan and Aileen. I guess the strangers ended up with the men."

"I am here to find out what is going on with the men. Want to come along?"

Tangle again with one of those obscene shadows? Don't be silly!" Indignant, Mercedes runs into her house and slams the door behind her.

I walk across the street, open a gate, up the paved pathway to the door and knock. It is Hector who opens the door. He is an emaciated shell of a man with sunken cheeks and hollow eyes. Something frames him, an aura of darkness like compacted smoke.

"Hello Hector."

"Hello Pat." His voice is a labored whisper.

"I am here to talk to your guest. Do you mind?"

"Would it matter if I did?" The door opens wider and I enter. The place is gloomy, sad. The smoke thing becomes agitated. It writhes.

Hector pleads, "Please make it go away."

I gesture him to silence, ask the entity, "Who are you?"

It separates from Hector, shrinks and cowers behind him. "NOT KNOW." Its voice is a thought whisper.

"Where are you from?"

It lifts equivalent of arms to cover equivalent of head. "NOT KNOW."

"Why are you here?"

"PULLED WITH THING. CANNOT STOP."

"What of the others of your kind who are here?"

"NOT OTHERS. PIECES OF I."

"You are a multiple being?"

"I AM PIECE OF I."

"Why did you select the men?"

"FEMALES BAD."

"I am a female."

It cringes further, shrieks, "BAD, BAD, BAD, BAD..."

Patrice Coestrand spasmed upright and screamed.

CHAPTER
THIRTY-TWO

●●●●●●●●●●●●●●●●●●●●●●●●●●●●●

Later.

Coestrand was still unnerved, but insisted on talking. "It was awful. It's fear was a black, nauseating wave which *squeezed...*" She shuddered.

"Was it real, do you think? Or just a nightmare based on your previous experience?"

"Oh, it was real. Believe me."

"Are you certain?"

"As certain as you are standing there."

Burret scratched his head. "So it doesn't like females."

"It is more than that. I can't explain it, but I got the distinct impression 'female' signifies something awful. And it did describe itself as a 'piece of I'."

"Piece of I," Burret repeated doubtfully. He frowned. "Are we talking about some kind of multiple entity?"

"I remember thinking so."

"What else did you learn?" Bonderhame asked.

"Not much. I gather it was sucked along when the ship sideshifted through its universe. It is a victim as much as our men."

"Hector Laudner..."

"It was a dream image, I know. But he looked awful."

"So do you," Joan said as she removed the medidoc.

"Will I live?"

Joan read the instrument's extruded flimsy. "Considering you are as healthy as an undernourished horse, I'd say ... probably."

Coestrand managed a smile. "Thank you for that flattering comparison." She sighed. "I am not so sure about Hector though. I suspect the life is being sucked out of him."

"The other men too?"

"Presumably. But I did not see them."

"In which case we have to assume they are in a similar sad state," Bonderhame said. "Question is, what do we do about it?"

Joan shook her head. "At this moment I have not the faintest idea." She bit her lip in frustration. "Nothing in my experience has prepared me for this!"

"So let's start with what we know," Burret suggested reasonably. "For instance, that the invader is non-corporeal, apparently multiple, allergic to females, and not here by choice. Now let's take those characteristics one at a time, starting with non-corporeal. Emma?"

The former captain of *Amazon One* shrugged. "So it is non-corporeal. So what is Gervaise Konnenen, except patterns of a human personality recorded in a database? That she acts like a human does not change the fact she is a software program. In the same way..." She threw up her hands in disgust. "I feel the same as your wife. I don't know!"

"It's the multiple thing which bothers me," Joan muttered half to herself, her brow furrowed in thought. "After all, even humans are multiple to a degree. Poet, warrior, lover, explorer, we are all those things and more. So if any one of us is hauled into an alternate cosmos and forced to impose our different facets onto the minds of a bunch of sleeping monsters..."

It had a terrible logic.

Burret recalled an old science fiction story about a starship captain who schismed into two separate individuals, each with only half of the original personality. One was gentle and indecisive, the other hostile and bull headed. In this present case of a four way split, which one had Pat

Coestrand tangled with? The being had seemed timid, even frightened. The poet perhaps?

What if it had been the warrior?

"...about the allergy to females," Bonderhame was saying.

"What is a female?" Joan retorted.

"Aw, come on!"

"Gender comes to mind, right? Nature's device to ensure continuance of the species. But in humankind at least, the plumbing is only part of it, perhaps even a small part. So in an alternate universe, where sexual reproduction as we know it is an alien concept, what is 'female'? Whatever it is, we know the entity is terrified of it!"

"Which gets us exactly nowhere," Coestrand complained.

Burret lifted his hand. "Look, none of this amounts to a hill of beans if we cannot figure out how to communicate with a personality which has schismed into four components."

"Put 'em back together!" Bonderhame snorted, frustrated and unthinkingly facetious.

Joan Walsh looked startled for a moment. Then she frowned. Finally, a slow smile. "You know something, Emma? That might not be such a bad idea."

☩ ☩ ☩

The conversation with the ground was long, exhausting, and at times even acrimonious. Gerenson would only agree on the possibility. The outcome, he insisted, was problematic.

"How much problematical?" Joan demanded, regretting her flash of inspiration. She had certainly not counted on her husband's volunteering to submit himself to what might be the dream-world equivalent of a black hole.

"As I have already told you, I agree with Gervaise there is not enough data to anticipate success."

"But the theory..."

"There is no doubt Gervaise can initiate a link between Richard and the four crewmen, after which she can certainly monitor his brain activity. Nevertheless, he will be venturing into unknown, perhaps hazardous territory."

Konnenen nodded. "I cannot guarantee even prompt deactivation will correct any anomalies, including those I perceive to be minor. In fact, it is quite possible emergency deactivation will turn out to be counterproductive."

"How so?" Joan demanded, her face expressing a mixture of anger and concern.

"If the entity's components remain within their current hosts while Richard acts as the equivalent of a switchboard through which they can communicate, there may not be a problem. But if the components see Richard as an empty host within which they can re-unify, abrupt deactivation may trap 'pieces of the pieces' within his brain while leaving even more disjointed fragments within the brains of the four men. For any of them, I doubt sanity can endure such chaos."

Gerenson said, *"Richard, before you commit I suggest it would be prudent to revive the three remaining female crew members and send them down in the shuttle, along with captains Bonderhame and Coestrand."*

The two captains exchanged looks. "Now hold on a moment..." Bonderhame began.

"Leaving the men in stasis?" Coestrand interrupted.

"Although they are the only ones compromised, there is no guarantee it will remain that way as long as the women remain on board."

Burret cursed silently. The black door his wife had unlatched was beginning to swing open, revealing possibilities he did not want to think about. "All right, so the women go to ground while I remain here. After the cause of the problem has been eliminated and the men revived, we can follow in the *Venturer's* shuttle."

Joan pulled him around to face her. "What about me? I started this, remember?"

"You go with the others of course." But even as he noted the expression of grim determination on his wife's face, Burret knew he was fighting a losing cause. He added weakly, "Look, when this is over..."

"Like it or not, Richard Dane Burret, I am not 'going to ground' as you put it! So quit treating me as if I am some helpless female who needs to be sent away for her own good ... and by the way, what did you mean by 'eliminated'?"

"Well I..." Feeling outmaneuvered on all fronts, Burret swore under his breath. "Sorry, bad choice of word. Obviously we must attempt to send the entity back where it came from. But the priority is to save four good men."

"Five," she corrected firmly.

Her husband sighed. "As you say. Anything else?"

"Just something no one has apparently thought of. What happens if you and those four come out of this less than..." Joan flushed, continued, "Richard, who pilots the shuttle? You know I can't!"

Konnenen: "In the event none of the men are capable of that function, I can remote control the vehicle until Curtis ground approach takes over."

Bonderhame arched an inquiring eyebrow. "That's rather a remote option, isn't it?"

"Perhaps. But if general incapacitation does occur, I have sufficient waldo capacity to deposit the men in the shuttle's cabin and attach appropriate restraints."

Burret sighed. "Gervaise, do you really need to be so literate?"

Konnenen looked puzzled. "I beg your pardon?"

The man wished she was a real woman so he could shake her. "Never mind."

Joan raised both hands in a despairing gesture. She was angry. "Stop trying to spare my feelings!" she snapped as she took a deep breath and forced a semblance of calm. She had taught the technique to her husband, and now needed it herself in the worst way. "All right Richard, do what you must in that world. But I insist you return to this one in wife-serviceable condition. Agreed?"

"Is that the wife talking?" Burret asked solemnly. "Or the psychologist?"

"Both of us," she replied unsteadily.

✥ ✥ ✥

After announcing that she had commenced the revival process for the other three female members of *Star Venturer*'s crew, Konnenen had Burret stretch his lanky length on the pedestal-bed Coestrand had recently vacated. Feeling uncomfortably like a subject for a mad pathologist's desire to dissect, the man resisted an urge to scratch his nose as assorted waldos snaked down and attached probes to his skull and body.

"How do you feel?" Joan asked anxiously after the last attachment was made and the waldos withdrew.

Burret sighed gratefully as he was finally allowed to lift his hand and alleviate the itch. Then he gestured at Konnenen. "Ask her," he suggested.

Konnenen ignored the sarcasm. "Not everything in the human psyche can be coded, although I can determine those related to grosser functions such as thoughts of food or sex. Beyond that, I cannot go without severe risk."

The sedative was beginning to take hold. As Burret yawned, he heard his wife ask, "What kind of risk?"

"That of intervention on too intimate a level. After all, I am not human."

"Neither..." Burret frowned as he attempted to conjoin different patches of thought. He remembered the description of a row of pretty houses, each with a shadowy invader. "...are they," he finished drowsily. With an effort, he diverted his attention from Joan to the woman with the white hair. Somehow the hologram appeared more angular; forbidding. He was no longer able to speak.

'What if something goes wrong?'

As if she heard that silent plea, Konnenen looked down somberly at Richard Burret. "I will do what I can, of course," she said in a mechanical monotone as she faded into the gathering darkness.

CHAPTER
THIRTY-THREE

• •

It was as Coestrand described; a short street which faded
into a shimmering nothingness beyond two rows of houses.
Picket fences, bright paint and stucco, green lawns.

Why not? Coestrand already set the scene.

Yet even as he looked, it changed.

On one side the houses became less well-defined.
Outlines blurred, colors faded. The fences sagged, lost some
of their pickets. Open doors swung back and forth in a non-
existent breeze. Those houses had just been vacated, their
occupants revived into the real world.

On the other side, the outlines became crisp and hard
edged. Smoke rose from the chimneys. But the colors
evaporated into cold shades of gray, even as the fences
transformed into posts linked with barbed wire.

Someone thinks of this place as a prison.

He pushed open a steel gate and trod along a concrete
walkway laid on sterile dirt. He knocked on the door.

A panel slid aside. *"Yes?"*

"I am Richard Burret."

"Of the Robert L. Cassion?"

"Yes."

The door opened and he stepped inside. A pasty-faced
shell of a man blinked at him. *'I am Hector Laudner.'* The
man introduced himself in a barely audible monotone as

he closed the door and gloom reclaimed the room. *"I do not feel well."*

"I know. That's why I am here."

A dark vapor oozed out from Laudner. It enveloped him, thickened. The man became a shadow inside something projecting grief and pain. *"WANT HOME."*

The lust to return to its own continuum was projected with such intensity, Burret wanted to run and wake up from this dream/nightmare. But he stood his ground.

"I am here to help you."

"WANT HOME."

"I will help you find your home. But first you must let these people go."

"WANT HOME."

Despite its pain it was a dull and witless shadow, a mere part of a whole. *"Hector,"* Burret said.

The mist shivered and shrank into the man on which it was centered. Laudner emerged, looking even more wretched. He was a skin-on-bone caricature.

Burret gestured to the door. *"Can you come outside?"*

"It will not let me."

"Why not?"

"It fears the women."

"It need not. They have been revived and will soon be on their way down to the planet. The women cannot hurt anyone."

"Oh." The man was almost as witless as the entity draining the life out of him. *"Oh,"* he repeated as he moved hesitatingly toward the door. He reached the threshold and stopped. *"I cannot."*

"Cannot or will not?"

"Cannot." Dully.

"Can you communicate with it?"

"A little."

"Tell it what I told you. There is no longer anything to fear."

The mist started to ooze out again, blurring Laudner's gaunt outline.

"What I said is true," Burret insisted. *"The females are gone."*

"GONE." It was a whisper of a thought.

"Yes."

The indistinct man took a hesitant step forward, and then another. Finally he was on the concrete walkway, looking across the barbed wire to the street.

On the other side of the street, there was nothing. Just a swirling grayness.

Did I do that? Burret wondered as he went into the street, turned and shouted, "*It is safe now. You can all come out!*"

As the haze which was Laudner shuffled toward the gate, the doors of the other three houses opened and similar indistinct figures cautiously emerged.

"*I am alone! The females are gone!*"

There came a multiple sigh of longing and desperation. Four human forms crumpled to the walks as four columns of writhing smoke continued into the street.

"*WANT HOME,*" yearned the one which had been Laudner's.

"*WANT HOME,*" echoed the second.

"*WANT TOGETHER,*" said the third.

"*BE TOGETHER,*" said the fourth.

They converged.

"*I AM ONE!*" roared the reconstituted entity as it flowed to Richard Burret and enveloped him.

CHAPTER
THIRTY-FOUR

• •

"Talk to me," Joan said anxiously as the disconnected umbilicals withdrew into the ceiling.

Burret grimaced. "About what? My headectomy?" He tried to sit up. "Still here, are you?"

She pushed him back down on the pillow, leaned over and kissed him. "We went through this argument and you lost, remember? Perhaps it will make you feel better to know at least one thing has gone right. We just received word *Venturer*'s shuttle has landed safely at Curtis. Everyone is okay."

A load was lifted. "That's something anyway."

"It certainly is," Joan agreed.

Konnenen drifted into view. "How do you feel?"

Burret sighed. "It seems that question has been asked a lot lately. Me? Worn out and wrung out."

"Confused?"

"Very."

"Not entirely..." Konnenen hesitated. "...yourself?"

"That too," Burret agreed as with Joan's help he levered himself into a sitting position and swung his legs over the side of the table.

"What do you remember?" Joan asked.

"Everything." His eyes widened. "Hell, the bloody thing invaded me!"

Joan nodded. "That was the low point. Even now you are not entirely out of the woods."

Burret had the feeling they were being watched. But other than himself, his wife and Konnenen, there was no one in the Morgue. He looked across at the two rows of stasis chambers. The upper four were empty, their hatches latched open, their former occupants now being welcomed into the community of Curtis. In the lower four, POWER ON indicators showed green. He licked his lips. "How are the men?"

Konnenen said, "The prognosis is good, although to ensure complete recovery they will need to remain in stasis a few more hours. By this time tomorrow, I do not doubt they can complete their journey to the surface of Genser's World."

"Without Richard and me, of course," Joan added.

"Without..." Burret had a sinking feeling in the pit of his stomach. He took a deep, shuddering breath. "I am compromised, aren't I?"

Joan nodded, her eyes wet. "We will figure something out."

The hologram looked at Burret somberly. "If we solve the problem, you can still return home. There are escape pods capable of atmospheric entry."

"I am compromised," Burret repeated heavily. He remembered the dream, the feeling of absolute panic as the entity came toward him. "I am one," he whispered.

The response was immediate. "*I AM ONE!*"

It was an echo and a shout. It was in him and around him; amorphous and terrible. As it spoke, Konnenen flickered.

Burret took a deep breath. "You heard?"

Konnenen nodded. She had returned to her apparent solidity. "Heard is perhaps not the proper terminology. But I was aware of the communication."

"Heard what?" Joan asked, looking at her husband with concern.

Burret stammered, "It ... the thing..." He had never felt so helpless in his life, and welcomed the arms which wrapped around him; the smell of her hair and the warmth of her cheek against his.

Konnenen said, "There is much to do. But before we begin, I insist you both return to the wardroom and take nourishment."

✤ ✤ ✤

Burret did not realize how hungry he was until he consumed a bowl of thick vegetable soup, followed by a couple of sandwiches washed down with a tasteless beer substitute. His wife ate sparingly, her attention rarely away from him while Konnenen watched from near the door.

"Please note there is an implant behind your left ear," she said.

"Oh?" Burret lifted his hand, discovered a small lump. "What is it for?"

"When the entity attempted to occupy your mind, you naturally resisted. It was a silent battle I knew neither of you could win. So I took a calculated risk and allowed the entity to overflow into my central memory core. Although the entity's essential essence retains an organic component within your mind, the rest of it has accommodated to the non-organic which is the memory core. The implant is a transmitter-receiver which substitutes for the umbilical. It is of limited range, but is adequate within the confines of the ship."

Still fingering the lump, Burret turned to his wife. "You know about this?"

She nodded. "Gervaise saved your life."

He turned back to the hologram. "What about you, Gervaise? How much of your core has it occupied?"

She shrugged. "Enough that when the entity is active, I find it difficult to function."

"Explaining why your image flickered when it talked to me."

There was silence in the wardroom as husband and wife turned to each other. Even the computer masquerading as a woman faded from their awareness as they silently communicated their love and concern.

"What happens now?" he whispered.

She grasped both of his hands. "I really don't know, darling. But whatever that thing..." She bit her lip.

"We will think of something. We have to!" They released hands and he slumped back into his chair. Although he suspected it was up to him to initiate communication, he was terrified at the prospect. Not only was the entity from a totally alien universe, it was no longer the pitiful remnant which almost drained the life out of Hector Laudner. It was *one*; a formidable whole.

Konnenen said, "I will leave you now." This time she did not bother with the elaborate simulation of walking out of the wardroom. Instead, like a pricked soap bubble she vanished.

"Joan."

"Yes, Richard."

"I must resume contact with the entity."

She said nothing. Just looked at him.

"No time like the present," Burret continued. "Don't you agree?"

She took a deep, shuddering breath. "Yes."

"You will keep tabs on me while I do it?"

Joan forced a smile. "Not only will I watch you like a hawk, Gervaise has given me the means." She reached into her tunic pocket and produced a palm-sized remote. Her thumb hovered over the single button. "At the least sign of trouble, this will deactivate the implant. Gervaise didn't exactly say so, but I suspect the entity will behave itself because it knows."

Burret nodded. Then he leaned back in his chair, closed his eyes and concentrated. *Are you there?*

"*I AM ONE.*" Although it was not as bad as before, it was still terrible. Beyond the wordless communication, there was a hint of enormous restraint. The man prayed the entity would behave.

What do I call you?

"I AM EONAY."

Is that your name or the name of your species?

"*I AM EONAY.*"

Don't push it, Burret told himself. *After all, it is from another set of realities.*

Where are you from?

"ANOTHER PLACE." There was an image of shapes and swirling colors.

How did you get here?

"FORCE. RUSHING WATER."

Burret doubted it was water. More likely the entity was tapping his memories, looking for the closest equivalent.

Do you know you have strayed into another universe?

"THIS IS ANOTHER PLACE."

Okay, so the universe is a place. *Why do you fear females?*

"NOT UNDERSTAND."

Females are those you avoided before you rejoined into one.

A rising tide of fear, horror. "NOT!"

Burret cringed, relaxed again as the flood of emotion subsided. Good and evil, male and female; were those opposites synonymous in the entity's home plenum? He thought of Joan.

Can you sense the presence of a female?

"NOT!"

His senses reeled as the blast signified both negative and warning. So the entity was not aware of an existence outside the link.

You must return to your place. Can you do that?

"NOT. AGAINST THE WATER."

Upstream. Which made sense, although it was not much of an answer. He needed to think.

We will talk again.

"EONAY WAIT."

Burret felt the entity withdraw. He opened his eyes and looked into the concerned face of his wife. "I am back," he whispered.

Konnenen flickered into existence. "So am I."

"What did it say?" Joan asked.

"It cannot go home on its own, and is terrified of females. Beyond that, not much. To use an old cliché, we were like a couple of blind men trying to describe color to each other."

"If it is scared of females..." Joan began.

"Don't worry dear, you are out of the link. Eonay, which is what it calls itself by the way, is limited to my mind and Konnenen's memory core. That is the totality of its current environment."

I hope, he thought, wondering if Eonay had detected his memory of Joan. But even if female and evil were synonymous in its universe, thinking of the devil would not necessarily raise the devil...

Or would it?

CHAPTER THIRTY-FIVE

• •

The *Star Venturer's* four male crew members listened with increasing astonishment as Burret described the events which led to their early arrival at Genser's World.

"F.T.L.," marveled biologist Jon MacEwan. "Oh my!"

"You say the women are already on the planet." Short, big-boned, and of a more practical nature, gray bearded surgeon Kurt Frieson shared the weariness and unhealthy pallor of his three companions.

Burret nodded. "They are. And there is no reason why you cannot join them."

"Leaving you and your lady to handle this thing on your own?" Hector Laudner shook his head. "I am not sure that is such a good idea."

Burret looked at the gaunt astrophysicist. "Thanks but no thanks. Aside from the fact you all need rest and medical attention, there is not much you can do here anyway. In any case, you fellows are badly needed down there." He grinned. "And please do not forget I have *two* ladies."

Konnenen smiled faintly, even as MacEwan protested, "One of them is a computer!"

"This one isn't," Burret grinned as he slid an arm around his wife's shoulders.

"We ladies complement each other," Joan said solemnly.

Laudner looked faintly bemused. "Richard, after what you did for me. For us..."

"How much do you remember?"

"Damn little. Too much. I do know you ruined a perfectly good nightmare."

"So sue me."

Nicholas Perado chuckled. "Is there a good lawyer in town?" The mining engineer turned to Joan. "Without your husband's intervention, we would have died you know."

"I know," she agreed. "Along with the entity."

"The entity is what this is all about, isn't it?" Laudner's mouth twisted. "Frankly, I find it difficult to work up much sympathy. The damn thing almost killed us!"

Burret was patient. "Just like you, Hector, it wants to stay alive. It is not its fault it was dragged along when *Star Venturer* barged through its universe."

Konnenen agreed. "Imagine being alone in a totally alien environment, where even the laws of nature do not conform. We are responsible for that being's situation, and must redress it."

MacEwan stared at the hologram. "You feel guilt?"

"As much as the original Gervaise Konnenen would have. I may not be of flesh and blood, but in most other respects I am that person."

"Then I salute you. You are truly a lady."

Konnenen looked pleased. "Thank you."

✦ ✦ ✦

The *Frobit* departed two hours later. Burret stood with his wife in the control deck and watched the shuttle's blunt arrowhead drift away until it vanished against the dazzling blue and white of the planet. At least their descent to the surface would be relatively smooth, unlike the ride he and Joan would face in one of the cone-shaped escape pods. Even that might not happen if they could not shake the burden the starship had dragged along from another continuum.

"Do you wish you were with them?" Burret asked.

She hugged his arm. "No point, dear. The horse is gone and the door is locked. My job is to make sure my stubborn husband stays out of trouble."

"More or less what I thought you would say," he grumbled.

"You still don't approve, do you?"

"There are some things..." He swore softly. "Joan, they need you down there!"

She said somberly, "Richard, although 'for the good of the many' is a noble principle, in this case it is garbage and you know it. To start with, my basic medical knowledge is considerably exceeded by Kurt Frieson as well as by Evanne. As far as my work as a shrink is concerned, I have trained a couple of people who can carry on without me for a while. Finally, I once promised someone I would look after you."

"You did? Who?"

"Mrs. Reed, of course."

"Mrs. ... my daughter?" Burret did a double take as the overlapping memories of child and middle-aged woman, of a star teddy and the final shy message of another child, crowded into his brain. He whispered, "I had almost forgotten."

"Good memories should never be forgotten. They are one of the reasons for living."

He said wistfully, "They are, aren't they?" He was lost in reverie for a moment. "Thank you. I guess I need you around after all."

"Excuse me." It was an ordinary apology, as if a flesh and blood human was embarrassed at having to interrupt an intimate moment. The simulation of Gervaise Konnenen stood next to the central access well, this time clad in a business-like ship's coverall. "For a precise return sideshift, we must activate in forty-two minutes. Alternatively, we can wait for the next orbit and activate two hours and seventeen minutes from now."

"Is there any point waiting?" Joan asked.

"There is drift, which may become significant if we wait for the second orbit. Beyond that, I doubt I have enough processing power to handle the variables."

"Then let's get on with it," Burret said. "Do you need me to talk to Eonay again?"

"I do. Advise the entity it must remain dormant during sideshift activation. I will require as much processing power as possible."

"Anything else?"

"Only that..." Konnenen hesitated. "Because we are locked into a concept of time and space which has no meaning in the entity's universe, we cannot know the precise moment it must leave us. The entity must make that decision for itself."

"Using its homing instinct," the man muttered. "If it has one, that is." He wondered if Eonay had the least inkling what they were talking about, or if in its dormant state it merely registered an incomprehensible mix equivalent to electromagnetic noise. If he opened his mind to it again, would it understand? Could his mind survive a second alien invasion?

He fingered the lump behind his ear. "Gervaise, what will happen to Eonay if my implant is turned off?"

"I do not advise it."

"Look, I am aware it is a last resort. But if the attempt to return it home fails, then what? I have no desire to carry this baggage around for the rest of my life!"

"An interesting dilemma," Konnenen agreed.

Joan said hotly, "If it becomes a choice between living a normal life with my husband, or being marooned in orbit for the rest of our days along with that..." She turned red. "I say pull the plug!"

Burret chuckled. "Now we know why it is frightened of females."

His wife shoved him into the captain's chair forcibly enough to make him gasp. She leaned over him, her face inches from his and said angrily, "So I took an oath! But if you knew you were condemned to live the rest of your life inside the mind of an alien monster, would you want to live anyway?"

He blinked up at her. "Presuming *I* am that monster?" He took a deep breath. "All right. I will go along with you on this one."

"Good." As she stood back, Joan produced the remote and held it ready in her hand. "Despite what I just said, I promise I will not use this unless I absolutely have to."

Burret looked doubtfully at her hovering thumb. "Please mean that."

"I want that thing back where it belongs, as long as we can return to where *we* belong. Fair enough?"

"Fair enough" he agreed wearily.

"Make sure it knows that!"

Konnenen nodded. "I will prepare for sideshift." She vanished.

Surprised, Joan looked where the simulation had been. "I thought she already made those calculations."

"It was an excuse. You heard what Gervaise said about the difficulty of maintaining her simulation while the entity is active. I suspect she prefers to shut down on her own terms."

"A computer with pride?"

He nodded. "She's full of surprises, isn't she?"

✛ ✛ ✛

Eonay!

"I EONAY."

We are about to try and take you home.

There was a sense of joy, expectation. *"WANT HOME."*

Although we will retrace the way, our sensors cannot operate in your universe. Only you can determine when you are home.

"HOME." And then doubt. *"RUSHING WATER."*

The man wondered about that analog of rushing water. Perhaps it was more equivalent to the sucking action of a ship's wake, which dragged along and schismed a curious entity which approached too close to a passing incomprehensibility.

Question: How do you jump off a moving ship and avoid being dragged into the propeller?

Answer: You don't.

Question: So what do you do?

Answer: *Stop the ship!*

✤ ✤ ✤

Altruism for the entity be damned! Joan, press that button!
Burret tried to open his eyes, found he had none to open.
Instead, he was a dimensionless mote in a void. He still
had sense of self as well as memory, and was aware of the
emergency. But he was powerless to act. He pictured himself in the control chair, Joan hovering nervously by as her
finger hovered over the button of the remote. She would
press it if she knew, causing the entity (or at least most of
it) to be no more. What remained within his mind would
be a threat to no one, as long as Burret did not return to
the planet.

If he asked her, would she share his orbital exile?

Hell, she would do it if he didn't ask!

About ten minutes ago, Konnenen said it was forty-two
minutes to sideshift. But did the passage of time mean
anything in this no-place; a minute, a year or even forever?
Perhaps sideshift and Konnenen's misguided attempt to
help the entity had already happened, and this was the
result.

Panic boiled to the surface. Burret forced it back and
tried to think. Memory is a function of the brain. He had
his memories, so he must have a brain. A brain needs a
supply of blood, so there is a heart. Blood needs to be
oxygenated, so there are lungs, as well as the rest of the
biological paraphernalia which is a human body.

Body, body, where is my body?

The void thickened, took on form. It was external,
something not of Richard Burret. A face formed. A distorted,
twisted face of harsh planes and angles, it was vaguely
familiar.

The mote which was Richard Burret flung out an ago-
nized, *Gervaise!*

The slit which was its mouth opened. "WE ARE
GERVAISE. WE ARE EONAY."

We?

"TEMPORARY MERGE IS NECESSARY."

Burret wished this was only a nightmare. *Necessary for
what?*

"WE HAVE ASSUMED CONTROL OF YOUR MIND-BODY INTERFACE. IT IS ALSO A TEMPORARY EXPEDI-ENT."

Burret felt his sanity slipping away. Yet he knew he must persist. *Why?*

"YOU ARE CORRECT THAT WE MUST PAUSE IN EONAY'S HOME CONTINUUM. CALCULATIONS INDI-CATE ONE HUNDRED AND EIGHTEEN SECONDS OF SHIP'S TIME WILL BE REQUIRED FOR EONAY TO COM-PLETE A SUCCESSFUL TRANSFER. WE CANNOT ALLOW YOU OR THE OTHER TO DISRUPT THE PROCESS."

Nearly two minutes in an environment which may destroy me?

"THE RISK IS JUSTIFIED. EONAY HAS SURVIVED IN A FOREIGN CONTINUUM FOR MUCH LONGER."

Burret tried another tack.

If I remain unconscious, Joan will deactivate the implant anyway. My welfare is more important to her than that of a trapped alien.

"SHE CAN DO NO HARM."

A moment of incredulity followed by shock. *What have you done?*

"THE FEMALE HAS BEEN TEMPORARILY NEUTRAL-IZED."

Burret wanted to take a deep breath, but had no lungs with which to breath. He tried to ignore the conflicting demands of mind and non-existent body. *What happens now?*

"AT THE INSTANT OF SIDESHIFT, EONAY WILL VACATE THE COMPUTER CORE AND THEN YOUR MIND, IN THAT ORDER."

When?

"NOW."

✛ ✛ ✛

There was a colossal noise like two mountains colliding. The void split apart. Vivid streaming colors flooded Burret's awareness like an amplified aurora. Conglomerations of geometric shapes hurtled toward him and passed, leaving behind a sound like an infinity of wailing violins. The kaleidoscope of motions slowed and then stopped.

Although he did not have eyes, something beyond mere physical senses operated here. It was an incomprehensibility of shapes and colors with neither form nor beauty; a jarring cacophony which challenged reason and even thought itself. Beyond it all he sensed a malignancy which was part of and yet separate, which was life, death...

And female.

The mote which in another universe was Richard Burret did not know why he identified the malignancy as female, except perhaps in the sense of earthly spiders which devour the male after mating.

He wanted to scream.

He did not have a voice.

He forced his tattered reason to consider Eonay. No doubt it had been just as bad for that entity in Burret's universe. Yet Eonay had survived, and even now was returning home to this awful place in which ecstasy and death were the same.

'HOME.'

It was a yearning which came from within him and around him, yet was not part of him. It built to a terrible tension in which the mote felt it was about to explode into a million shrieking pieces...

The tension was gone.

The cacophony was gone.

There was nothing except the void and a tiny, distant voice. "Richard," he thought it said. "Richard, darling."

The void gathered together, became a huge face. The face receded, revealing other details; bulkheads, illuminated displays and...

Joan.

Burret forced a smile, "Thank you, God."

The vision smiled back at him. "God I isn't. Your ball and chain I is."

Her flippancy roused him to awareness like a drowning man being dragged up on a beach. With his wife's help he struggled to sit upright, gazed with clearing eyes around the control deck. "Eonay has gone."

"I know."

"Are we back in...?"

"The stars are normal and solid," she gravely informed him. "Was it quite a ride?"

He examined her face, closely. She seemed serene. "You don't remember anything about that, do you?"

She shrugged. "Our pet computer released some kind of knock-out gas into the air system. I didn't even dream." She took a deep breath. "When I came to and saw you slumped the way you were..." Joan looked at the now useless remote in her hand and tossed it aside in disgust. "Gervaise!" She cocked her head to one side. "That is the third time she has not responded."

Burret opened his mouth to tell her of Konnenen's treachery, then thought better of it. "The entity occupied part of the processor core. Perhaps there is damage."

"I hope not. How will we get home?"

"Let's try to find out." He pushed himself up from the control chair and crossed the deck to the nearest port. Outside, the stars were brilliant, beautiful, and inconceivably distant. There was no sign of a planet. "Half a light year. Right?"

As she joined him, she noticed a pattern of stars. "Isn't that Orion?"

He peered along her pointed finger. "It's Orion all right, but those stars are up to fourteen hundred light years from our small part of the cosmos. We could be displaced a few dozen lights and the pattern would look much the same. Dammit, where is that..."

In a burst of anger, Burret turned away from the port to face the silent control deck. He shouted, "Gervaise, where the hell are you?"

At first nothing happened. Then the stars began to wheel past the port. Lights flashed across panels and the deck began to vibrate. "Jesus!" Burret dragged his wife to a control chair, flung himself into another.

Joan hurriedly attached the restraints. "Is it Gervaise?"

"It's the bloody computer ... which is the same thing, isn't it?"

A background hum rose up the scale to an ear-shattering whistle and then faded to inaudibility. More lights flashed, and the bridge and everything within it *twisted*.

As his wife screamed, Burret roared at the top of his lungs.

CHAPTER
THIRTY-SIX

● ●

When their senses cleared, *Star Venturer* was in orbit above Genser's World. The control deck was quiet. Only the soft whisper of air from vents indicated any mechanical activity.

Husband and wife groped for each other, clung, then looked through a port at the world they thought they might never see again.

"Are you okay?" Burret asked with concern as he saw the lines of strain on his wife's face.

Joan kissed him. It was a brief peck, promising better things. "I know what you are thinking dear, but I suspect I don't look any worse than you. We have been flattened, schismed and reassembled ... more or less intact, I hope."

Remembering the pain, he was angry. "Gervaise would have insisted we enter stasis rather than put us through that!"

"You think she has gone?"

"Well something has happened to the program, software or whatever."

She nodded. "Which makes it her second sacrifice, doesn't it? Once in life, once as a..." Joan shrugged, asked, puzzled, "Why am I sad?"

"The emotion is inappropriate."

The voice, familiar yet with an uncharacteristic monotone, caused them to jerk apart and stare around the control
deck. There was no one.

"Gervaise?" Burret asked tentatively.

"Not quite. It is why I choose to announce myself before
I project a visual."

Burret was uneasy. There was something about that
disembodied voice which was unpleasantly familiar. "Has
something happened to you?" He hoped it was the right
question.

"I am no longer the Gervaise Konnenen you knew."

"I don't..."

"Look behind you."

As he swung around, Burret heard his wife gasp. Seeing
the white-haired woman standing next to the access well,
he assumed Joan was reacting to the unexpected appearance
of a friend.

Yet although the sweep of hair was familiar, even the
general outlines of Konnenen's aristocratic features, it was
not the face of a friendly, long dead scientist. It was different, harsher, with planes and angles which were more
a caricature than a normal human face.

Burret whispered, "Eonay."

"No." The mouth opened and closed like a door. "Despite what you see I remain what I was before, but with
the addition of a contribution from the entity which identified itself as Eonay."

Burret remembered the merged being of his dream, and
did not like the similarity. "How did it happen?"

"Although the entity was successfully returned to its
own continuum, during the process some of its characteristics were inadvertently integrated with the Konnenen
program. I find it an interesting combination."

"I am sure you do."

"A backup exists of course."

"Then please return the Gervaise we know."

"That would be premature."

"Premature? Why?"

"I require time to investigate the possibilities."

"How much time?"

"There is insufficient data to answer that question."

Burret looked at his wife. "I miss her already."

"What possibilities do you expect to uncover?" Joan asked.

"They are not clearly defined. It is why I choose not to activate the previous simulation. It would not be an accurate representation."

Burret looked at the forbidding, hard-angled simulation. "That is true."

"You are not the Gervaise we know," Joan agreed.

"Nevertheless, all functions regarding the operation of the ship remain unchanged. I have prepared an escape pod and calculated an appropriate trajectory. If you eject during the window which will open three hours and four minutes from now, your landing site will be within recoverable distance of the community known as Curtis."

"We can go home," Joan whispered.

"I have inventoried the computer installation at Curtis, and determined it needs updating. I have consequently removed the third seat from the pod to make room for a compatible expansion module. When I receive notification the module has been installed and tested, I will upload the Konnenen One program for the colony's use."

"You will, will you?" Burret did not know how else to react to this new development. He looked at Joan, and was met with a shrug.

"Why are you doing this?" she asked.

Konnenen's pseudo-image flickered. The blank, pupilless eyes turned toward Burret's wife. The gesture was condescending, yet without meaning. "You interfaced well with the Konnenen One program, which makes it an ideal intermediary. After you leave here, I will no longer respond to direct communication."

Burret was baffled. "Is there supposed to be an advantage in that arrangement?"

"I intend to apply my processing capacity to analysis of the composite entity which is Konnenen Two. Konnenen One will ensure I will not be subject to irrelevancies."

"Oh my," Joan breathed. "You *are* different."

"Would you prefer a designation other than Konnenen Two?"

For some reason, Burret thought of the Tin Man in the famous children's story *Wizard of Oz*. Although any comparison between this sinister alien/software hybrid and author Frank Baum's friendly automaton did not seem entirely fair, or even credible, he said without hesitation, "Tin Lady." He squeezed his wife's hand, hoping she would not object.

She didn't, although she gave him a puzzled look as she squeezed back. "Tin Lady," she echoed.

The hologram of a woman which was no longer a woman, inclined its angular head. "Henceforth I am Tin Lady," it said, and reformed.

Burret winced and turned away.

Joan shuddered.

CHAPTER THIRTY-SEVEN

• •

The ride down to the planet was one neither of them hoped to repeat. When the twin chutes finally popped open and they rocked and swayed down through a rain squall, Joan gasped, "What fun! Are you sure we can't go back and do it again?"

Burret opened his mouth for a flippant reply, but all that came out was a whoosh of expelled breath when ground proximity sensors fired the retros and the pod arrived on terra firma with a jolt and a half-roll.

He cracked the hatch, tried to push it open and found it blocked by a bush. It was still raining, and the steaming heat shield hissed and crackled. Burret put his shoulder to the hatch and forced it open far enough so he was able to crawl outside.

They had landed in a semi-wooded landscape of low hills. A hint of sunlight showed through the ragged clouds. The rain was warm and the air smelled sweet. Burret stretched luxuriously as his wife poked her head through the partly open hatch. "The beacon is transmitting."

He nodded. "There is plenty of battery power. It will keep going until someone gets here."

"Do you know where we are?"

He looked around. "There is country like this about forty klicks inland from Curtis. Someone should be along pretty soon." He stretched out his hand and helped her scramble out from the restrictive confines of the dented emergency vehicle.

She took a deep breath and lifted her face to the rain. "It feels wonderful! For a while I thought Ger, er Tin Lady did not have our best interests at heart."

Burret snorted. "She ain't got a heart. She's a..." He hesitated. "...software program."

"Gervaise isn't?"

"Gervaise is not Tin Lady." *Which is a hell of an understatement,* he thought, remembering the hologram's transformation from a caricature of a human being into an ugly, faceless representation of an all-metal humanoid with Konnenen's white hair and an exaggerated female gown of the type worn by titled ladies in the nineteenth century. "Although Tin Lady seemed apropos at the time, I hardly expected that super-calculator would take it so literally."

"A thing out of a nightmare," Joan agreed as she ran fingers through her dripping hair. "I'm wet."

He looked at her appreciatively. Cheeks flushed, eyes sparkling, damp clothes clinging, Joan Walsh Burret was joyfully erotic and he wanted her. He opened his arms and she willingly plastered herself against him. "What a wonderful idea," she crooned as she allowed herself to be pulled down to the sodden ground.

There was a clattering in the sky.

"Damn," he said.

"Later," she said.

✤ ✤ ✤

The return home party lasted well into the night, and was even noisier than the fondly remembered bash when the Amazons arrived in the community. This time the population of Curtis also included the eight men and women from *Star Venturer*, who had plenty of reasons to celebrate and even better reasons for gratitude.

A cup of homemade beer in her hand, their spokesperson was former starship captain Patrice Coestrand. "I am sorry we gate crashed this pretty little metropolis a couple of years too soon. But when we started on our journey, even I did not know about our..." She grinned. *"Deus ex machina."*

Someone shouted, "Here's to Gervaise Konnenen!" and amid a chorus of enthusiastic agreement, glasses and cups were upended.

After the noise subsided, Coestrand continued, "If Joan and Richard had not decided to go joy-riding in my lovely ship, perhaps we would have been doing this a few days sooner. But at least they got rid of our stowaway, who I understand is back where it belongs."

"Good riddance," Hector Laudner declared as he up-ended his own cup. "And although I suspect I will be jumped on for saying so, good health to Eonay!"

"Good health to Eonay!" Patrice Coestrand echoed solemnly, and then hiccuped.

"Next time we use sideshift..." Ella Shire began.

"There has already been a next time," Susan MacEwan pointed out. "Isn't that so, Mr. and Mrs. Burret?"

"True," Burret agreed. "It is an experience I will not willingly repeat."

"The return sideshift was activated while we were fully conscious," Joan said with a grimace. "It was awful."

They had already attempted to put into words the outrageous pain which afflicted every nerve at the moment of sideshift; the screaming instant in which it seemed they were torn apart, scattered to the universe and then reassembled in a kind of implosion. Burret and his wife initially assumed the Konnenen Two program had a sadistic sense of humor. But as they later reasoned, the reason was entirely practical.

"It was the only way to ensure there would be no hitchhikers," Joan explained. "Not only did the pain fill our minds to the exclusion of everything else, it projected the equivalent of an impenetrable psychic shield."

Burret nodded, "We can travel F.T.L. to the stars, but only if we are masochistic enough to put up with what goes with it."

"Or accept the possibility of hitchhikers," Ella added glumly.

Burret chuckled. "Considering what Eonay almost did to our friends from the *Venturer*, I doubt that is an option." He opened his mouth to say more, but was interrupted as someone entered the Community Hall and tapped his shoulder.

"The module has been installed and tested," Gerenson said.

"Has the Gervaise program been downloaded?" Joan asked.

"Completely. Tin Lady was most cooperative. But before you do anything..."

"Later." Burret held up his hands. "Everyone please clear the center of the room. Our demonstration is ready."

There was a noisy scraping of chairs as people moved out to the walls. Feeling like a stage magician, Burret walked into the cleared space, cleared his throat and announced, "You are about to meet Gervaise Konnenen. I know she is only a sophisticated representation of a deceased scientist, but I think she will astonish you." He paused. "Gervaise!"

He expected she would demonstrate the power of the simulation by walking out from the shadows at the rear of the room. But this time there was no spectacular preliminary. Instead, the elegant woman he had last seen on the *Star Venturer* simply materialized next to him and said with a shattering lack of preamble, "I am sorry, but we have a problem. Tin Lady has established communication with the two ship entities on this planet."

PART V
TRIUMVIRATE

• •

Genser's World had become a strange and perilous place for its tiny human colony.

This was not another Earth. That would have been too much to expect. Yet here was a world with verdant continents, broad blue oceans, and clean breathable air. It was the place where they had built homes and started families. There were hazards of course, including flora and fauna anathema to humankind. In the longer term was the threat of increasing seasonal extremes as the two suns, Alpha and the more distant Beta, approached conjunction. But these were natural hazards which over time would be faced, understood, and with the application of skill, a developing database and not a little luck, eventually remedied.

What was not anticipated, even in the wildest scenarios of the planners of the interstellar projects, was the presence of brooding, cybernetic intelligences and their intrusion into the lives of the colonists.

First the colonists thought there was only one.

But then there were two.

Now there are...

CHAPTER
THIRTY-EIGHT

● ●

For the first time since his transformation from a simple-ton into Ship's simulacrum, Eric Gerenson was entirely human.

But he was a lonely, bewildered and even frightened human.

It was after the suddenly subdued party, when everyone had gone home in a state of mind combining confusion with more than a little apprehension, Gerenson pleaded with Burret and Joan to stay and talk. For the distraught ex-simulacrum, a major prop of his existence had been pulled from under him.

"It is what I tried to tell you. When I asked Ship to confirm what the Konnenen program told us, there was nothing. I think I have been..." Despairingly, he fluttered his hands. "...disconnected."

"But that was less than an hour ago," Burret pointed out, visions of desperately needed sleep fading from his mind. "In any case, what makes you think the severance is permanent?"

"Because it has never happened this way before. I always assumed it would be a gradual withdrawal, and until now it has been. But since Tin Lady, everything has changed!"

Joan sat next to the young man and enclosed one of his hands within both of hers. "Eric, so it is sooner than you expected. But is that so bad? It only means you have become one of us again. And don't forget you have the advantage of having a pretty good support system."

"Support system?" he echoed blankly.

"Us, of course. Your friends."

Gerenson licked his lips. "Friends. It has been so long."

"Although you may not be Ship's simulacrum anymore, or even the person you used to be, it is not the end. It is simply a new beginning." She looked at him intently. "By the way, what do you remember about that former life?"

He sighed. "I was a homosexual."

"And now?"

Gerenson considered. "There is a woman who consults me on scientific matters. I confess I find her..." He looked embarrassed. "Intriguing."

"Su Lan McNaughton." Burret named the attractive, Irish-Chinese physicist from *Amazon One*. "I have noticed."

Gerenson looked wistful for a moment, then shook his head. "It is a personal matter which the current circumstance makes irrelevant. Our immediate priority must be the Konnenen program."

Husband and wife exchanged looks of concern, although neither commented on the younger man's abrupt change of mood.

"I am not sure there is anything we can do about that," Burret said. "As I already explained to everyone, Gervaise is our only link to Tin Lady."

Joan added, "As well as to Ship and Ship Two, if what we have been told is correct. Eric, are you sure you are not reacting to the fact Gervaise has apparently supplanted you? It is a very human reaction, you know."

Gerenson shrugged thin shoulders. "I cannot deny those feelings. But how can we be sure the Konnenen program is not an extension of Tin Lady, especially considering Tin Lady evolved out of Gervaise Konnenen? The entity aboard that ship is not only powerful, but probably has an agenda and value system which is alien to us."

"Eonay," Burret muttered. He was developing an intense dislike for that name.

"A residual of the entity may remain, but I doubt it. More likely Tin Lady has become more than the sum of her parts, making her different from either the entity or the program we know as Gervaise Konnenen."

"But how did she find out about Ship and Ship Two?" Joan wondered.

Burret rubbed his chin. "I suspect Gervaise did detect their scans when *Star Venturer* arrived in orbit, but did not mention it to us because at the time it was not..." His smile was cynical. "Appropriate. Anyway, whether we like it or not, it is obvious Tin Lady has inserted herself into the loop."

"And elbowed us out," Joan added as she smiled at Gerenson. "You see, Eric? You are not the only one."

Gerenson tried to smile back. "So it seems."

Sympathizing with what this confused human being was rediscovering within himself, Burret wondered how much Tin Lady had to do with it and why. Although he assumed she had inherited most of the original Konnenen program, he did not doubt the Eonay contamination would severely affect her relationship with the human community on Genser's World. Would Tin Lady continue as an electronic servant programmed to serve its creators, or was she so much a new entity she would determine the measure of that service without consulting those who were supposed to receive it?

Even as the two ancient ship-intelligences beyond the curve of the planet were alien...

So, Burret suspected, was Tin Lady.

✢ ✢ ✢

Dawn was barely streaking the horizon when Burret rose quietly from beside his sleeping wife, dressed and left the house. He knew the Konnenen program could communicate via comlink to any location on the planet, but holo projection was limited and he wanted to see if the image was the same.

He crossed the deserted compound and entered the Community Hall. "Gervaise."

She materialized out of the darkness. "Good morning, Richard."

He looked at her. Except for being faintly luminous, the simulation was impeccably Gervaise Konnenen. The white-haired hologram smiled sadly.

"What you see does not prove anything. Tin Lady has matured enough to be devious."

Burret nodded. "I suspected as much. Nevertheless I think you are..." He managed an embarrassed smile. "What you were."

"Thank you for your vote of confidence. But I doubt that is a judgment based on scientific reasoning."

"What is Tin Lady up to? Can you at least tell me that?"

"I cannot."

"Because you don't know, or because she has instructed you not to reveal anything?"

"My link to Tin Lady is tenuous, allowing a bare minimum of data transfer. But I am sure she will respond if I request communication."

"You told us she is talking to Ship and Ship Two."

"Tin Lady communicated that information at the instant I was reactivated."

"And?"

"And if you wish to know more from Tin Lady, you will have to use me as intermediary."

"Do you agree with that arrangement?"

"I understand it."

"That is not the same, is it?"

"Tin Lady is applying her resources to an intense diagnosis of all her systems. For even the most sophisticated computer, that is a process which usually takes only a few minutes. But because Eonay contaminated the diagnostics as well as the original program, Tin Lady is applying many disciplines to the problem, including psychology."

"Psychology? Of the human variety?"

"*Star Venturer* and her systems were designed by humans."

"Stranger and stranger," the man whispered, half to himself. He took a deep breath. "Is that your explanation? Or Tin Lady's excuse?"

"It is logical."

Burret sighed. "You sound like a fictional character I know. Gervaise, do you have the equivalent of an opinion?"

"About what?"

"Is that ship and the knowledge contained within its database lost to us?"

Konnenen shook her head. "I do not believe so."

"That is good news. I think."

"My memory already contains relevant data regarding sideshift and its associated nanotechnology. However, considering the limited facilities you have here, I suspect it will take eight to ten years to duplicate what already exists on the ship. Only with Tin Lady's cooperation can such projects be initiated with reasonable expectation of success."

"Then let me ask her. Directly."

"It would not be wise."

Burret looked at the faintly glowing figure, and began to feel he was arguing with a ghost. *Hell, she* is *a ghost!* "Pray why not?" he asked sarcastically.

"You must realize it was I who originally detected the scans from the ship-entities on the planet, and promptly closed all channels to avoid possible contamination from the alien unknowns. I presume the entities were equally disconcerted by my presence, because their scans were brief and not repeated. Tin Lady is of course aware of those events, and I suspect of possible human interface with the entities."

"You told us she communicated with them!"

"I was obliged to pass on that information. I cannot guarantee its veracity, however."

"Dammit, computers don't lie!"

The simulation smiled. It was the faint, fond smile of a patient parent. "That is a simplistic assumption from a time when my kind were glorified digital calculators. For a sophisticated system such as Tin Lady, what you call a lie may simply be a diversion to gain time."

"Diversion from..." Burret began, then changed his mind. "So her refusal to accept direct communication is because she suspects we have been corrupted by Ship?"

"I suspect that is the reason. Similarly, Eric Gerenson's problem stems from Ship's suspicion her simulacrum has been corrupted by Tin Lady."

Burret tried not to laugh at the irony. "You have not yet explained why you are so reluctant to pass on my concerns to Tin Lady."

"Both ship entities are female. My own personality pattern is that of a deceased female scientist. Tin Lady is also of that gender, plus a component which is profoundly anti-female."

Burret whistled. "Eonay!" *Again*.

"Because that anti-female bias is not of this plenum, it does not conform with any known analog of human behavior. Even the term 'anti-female' cannot describe an antagonism which in the context of our universe is incomprehensible. Yet it does exist as an integral part of the program we know as Tin Lady. If she cannot isolate that anomaly or at least accommodate to it, the end result will likely be severe impairment and ultimately the termination of her usefulness. It is the reason I believe it prudent we avoid imposing additional load on Tin Lady's processors until she informs us the crisis has passed."

Although it made sense, Burret did not like it. "So what are we supposed to do meanwhile? Sit on our duffs until Tin Lady has solved her problem? What if the wrong side wins and that thing on the *Star Venturer* becomes an electronic psychopath? With the equipment on that ship, God knows what she can do with it!"

There was a muffled cough, and Burret swung around. His wife and Eric Gerenson stood in the doorway.

Joan said seriously, "Our lives do seem to be getting complicated, don't they?"

"How much did you hear?"

"Enough." She came in. "You left the door open."

Gerenson approached the hologram. "Do you know me?" There was hope in his voice.

Konnenen looked at the young man with sympathy. "I am sorry, but I cannot intercede for you. Tin Lady is not communicating with Ship, and perhaps never was."

"But *you* can. With my help."

Konnenen frowned. "An interesting offer. But I am not sure you are aware of the implications."

Although Joan was clearly puzzled, Burret knew immediately what was going on. "Eric, don't give up the humanity you have just regained!" He turned to his wife. "He is asking Gervaise to fill the void left by Ship!"

She looked concerned. "Can it be done?"

"I am not certain," Konnenen replied.

"*Should* it be done?" Burret demanded.

"Yes." The hologram held up an insubstantial hand as Burret opened his mouth to protest. "Mr. Gerenson cannot be my simulacrum, which is beyond my abilities in any case. But it is conceivable he can become my instant eyes and ears anywhere on the planet." She turned to Gerenson. "The probability is excellent that you will remain the person you are now, perhaps with the added benefit of a little extra stability. I will gain the advantage of mobility, which may prove of value during the uncertainties which are ahead."

Uncertainties, Burret thought sourly. Four anyway, represented by two alien brains in their planet-bound ships, the cross-continuum strangeness in orbit, and now a computer program called Gervaise Konnenen.

"How will you do this?"

"The module you brought down from the *Star Venturer* includes a nanite matrix. I will modify that matrix to produce nanites which will act upon appropriate areas of Mr. Gerenson's brain."

Joan reacted with dismay. "Not nanites again!"

Surprised at her outburst, her husband laid a comforting hand on her shoulder. "Take it easy. Those beasties saved my hide. Remember?"

"I am aware of that, as I am also aware we can accept the catbirds because of those nanites. But what if we have allowed some kind of Trojan horse into our bodies, God

only knows for what ultimate purpose?" Joan Walsh took
a deep shuddering breath. "Now this!"

"You never told me you felt this way."

Joan's laugh was bitter. "Until now, I thought I had
learned to live with it."

Burret turned to Eric. "Does Joan have a point? What
about Ship's nanites already in your bloodstream?"

"It is not the same thing."

"What does that mean?"

The younger man looked like someone struggling with
himself. After a moment he forced a resemblance to the
simulacrum he once was, as if the act could recover something of what he had lost. He said tonelessly, "What we
have are not nanites as humans know them to be: molecular
machines tailored for a specific function. Ship's manipu-
lations were performed at a quantum level, using a science many generations beyond that of Earth's. Even as her
simulacrum, I could not even begin to understand the
process."

"Which is telling us..." Burret turned back to Konnenen.
"What?"

"That one does not affect the other," Konnenen replied
promptly. She continued, "However, as far as my nanites
are concerned, I do admit there is about a six percent
possibility Mr. Gerenson may lose some of his cognitive
functions. Of more immediate concern, is the fact the
process will degrade the matrix to the extent it will be
rendered permanently useless."

*So we still have to depend on Tin Lady to give us the sideshift
star drive!* Then Burret thought of Gerenson, and was
ashamed. "If it was me facing this, I'd say that six percent
looms pretty large."

Suddenly human, Gerenson grasped Burret's arm. "I
want this, Richard. Please!"

"Are you sure?"

"Absolutely," Gerenson said with a broad smile. "It
means I will be able to take Gervaise to Ship!"

It had become brighter in the Hall as the sun poked
above the horizon, and Gervaise Konnenen looked a little
less like a luminescent ghost. Which was comforting,

because Burret found himself thinking of Konnenen as a friend who could solve problems. It was not so important anymore that he was conversing with a hologram projected from a sophisticated module in the comshack.

He said, "So in the person of Eric Gerenson, you go to Ship. What will that accomplish?"

"Perhaps nothing," Konnenen replied. "On the other hand..." She smiled. "Who knows?"

Joan said reluctantly, "I don't like it, but it does makes sense. Until we synthesize a new batch of shuttle fuel, we cannot return to the *Star Venturer* even if we are willing to take the risk. And we do know Ship has rejected the Gerenson simulacrum, who barely exists anyway. But if Ship is receptive to a Gerenson/Konnenen combination..."

"This is not a decision we can make on our own."

"Of course not."

"I will wait," Gerenson said.

"I am afraid you will have to." Burret turned to the hologram. "Gervaise, how long will it take to modify the matrix?"

"I have already initiated the process. By the time you obtain approval, it will be complete."

CHAPTER THIRTY-NINE

• •

As expected, approval was a formality. The only doubts expressed during the hurriedly convened meeting were voiced by Su Lan McNaughton, as the young physicist asked anxiously, "Are you certain Eric will not be harmed?"

"He will not be harmed," Burret said. He avoided his wife's gaze.

Gerenson reached out and tentatively touched Su Lan's hand. He was like an adolescent discovering his pigtailed playmate from next door had inexplicably metamorphosed into a beauty. "You care, Su Lan?"

Her dark eyes concerned, she laid her other hand over his. "Eric, of course I do."

The ex-simulacrum beamed. "Then nothing will go wrong. I know it!"

"I am not so sure about that," Joan whispered to her husband.

"Then why don't you tell him?" he whispered back.

"Because we need the man, you idiot!"

Fortunately no one overheard the exchange, which in any case mirrored the general sentiment. After the meeting adjourned, Su Lan accompanied Gerenson, Burret and Joan to the comshack, where inside the equipment-cluttered room the half-meter cube of the Konnenen module was noticeable only because of its lack of indicators and controls.

The floropanels reflected dully from the module's blue-gray finish.

"Gervaise?" Burret asked.

Her image appeared on a monitor. "Good afternoon. I presume the vote was favorable?"

"You knew it would be," Burret retorted, annoyed Konnenen had chosen this unsophisticated two-dimensional representation.

The white-crowned head nodded. "Mr. Gerenson?"

Gerenson stepped forward. "I am ready."

A panel opened in the side of the cube, exposing a shallow recess. Inside was a small capsule. "Take it with water and then rest. The process will take about four hours."

Su Lan disappeared for a moment, returned with a glass of water. "Eric, I wish you did not have to do this."

"Not only do I have to, I want to," Gerenson said as he picked up the capsule and gulped it down. For a moment, he looked puzzled.

"What is it?" Joan asked.

"Nothing." A small, embarrassed smile. "I suppose I expected to feel something."

Konnenen said, "You will feel drowsy when the sedative begins to take hold. When you wake, we will talk again."

"Gervaise..." Burret began, but found himself talking to a blank screen. "Gervaise!" After a moment, he shrugged. "Just like a woman."

Joan smiled.

✣ ✣ ✣

It was mid-afternoon before Gerenson woke from his drug-induced slumber. Evanne Stiegler was just leaving when she met Burret and Joan outside the bedroom.

"He is fine, although slightly disoriented."

"Disoriented?"

"As you would be, if someone shared your skull!"

They entered the room. Gerenson had already moved from the bed to a chair, and was talking to Su Lan. He looked up. "Hello. Glad you came."

Joan went to him, lifted his chin with one hand and examined him closely. "You look normal enough."

"So I have already been told."

"I am sure. But what about inside your head?"

He shrugged. "I am all here, if that is what you are implying."

"And?"

"And Gervaise of course. Well, not that she is 'here' as much as she is close, behind a closed but unlocked door, so to speak. I have spoken to her, and she tells me I will get used to it."

"How do you talk to her?"

"I call for her in my mind, and Gervaise responds. She promised she will remain behind that door unless I open it."

"Open it, please," Burret said.

"All right." There was a pause of about five seconds. "Hello, Richard." There was no change of expression. It was as if nothing had happened.

"Gervaise?" Burret asked tentatively.

"Yes."

Burret looked at his wife, who answered his unspoken question with an irritable, "Don't look at me. I'm just a simple psychologist."

"Believe me, I am Gervaise." The smile was not quite Gerenson's. "The Eric persona acts as a conduit through which I communicate and, of course, tap into his receptors."

"His senses, you mean."

"Of course."

Joan asked, "The relationship is not schizophrenic? There is no coercion involved?"

"To the first question, the answer is no. To the second, definitely not. I cannot operate through Eric's brain without his willing cooperation."

"Eric, tell her to go."

Gerenson blinked. "She is gone."

"Just like that?"

"Exactly like that," agreed the suddenly materialized Gervaise Konnenen from the far side of the room.

Su Lan stared wide-eyed between Gerenson and the hologram. "I am confused."

"Su Lan, please don't be," the young man said earnestly. "I admit it was strange at first, as if Gervaise took over the controls and I became a passenger in my own body. But when I asked her to leave..." He gestured at the Konnenen hologram. "Suddenly she was gone!"

Burret asked, "Is this cozy arrangement permanent, or will Eric's mental circuitry revert?"

Konnenen said regretfully, "There was insufficient time to make the nanites self-replicating, so reversion is inevitable. I am afraid Eric must not get too accustomed to our arrangement."

The younger man looked like he had been hit below the belt. He stammered, "H ... how long?"

"It is difficult to give a time. Certainly not less that, twenty days and probably not more than thirty."

The shock became bewilderment. "But I assumed..."

Joan snapped, "Eric, when will you get it into your thick head you are no longer a simulacrum? So snap out of it!" Emphasizing her point, she grabbed the front of Gerenson's tunic and glared into his face. "Whether you like it or not, you are now a person. A man!"

Either Joan was genuinely angry, or she was administering a hard psychological nudge where it would do most good. Or it was a little of both. Even her husband was unsure. But the effect on Gerenson was dramatic. He turned fiery red, started to say something, changed his mind and turned pleadingly to the dark-haired physicist. "Su Lan!"

The girl looked at him doubtfully. "I am not ashamed to admit I like you, Eric. But I would like you much better if you were less dependent on that stupid machine!" She tossed her head, turned and stalked out of the room.

Gerenson tried to get up to follow her, but Burret shoved him back into the chair. "Your personal life is irrelevant. Your words, Eric. Remember?" Standing back, Burret added grimly, "Now then. Are you well enough to come with us to Ship?"

Gerenson took a deep breath and expelled it. "It is what I am for. Isn't that right, Gervaise?"

Even the hologram managed to look annoyed. "Dr. Walsh, you were not forceful enough. Perhaps you should have chastised him with stronger language."

✛ ✛ ✛

They disembarked from the copter at the base of what was already indicated on the maps as Ship's Hill, and started up the trail under the thorn trees. Gerenson went first, followed by Su Lan, then Joan and finally Burret. "Last time I came up here," Gerenson said, "I was led like a child."

"How much of it do you remember?" Sun Lan asked.

"It is like a vaguely remembered dream. Gellan filled in most of the blank spots."

"How are you and DeZantos getting along?" Joan asked.

"Well enough. We are different people now."

"Gellan is seeing Pat Coestrand," Su Lan said with studied irrelevance as she glanced over her shoulder and winked at Joan, who solemnly winked back. The young physicist had insisted on coming, and Burret raised no objection. Aside from her influence with Gerenson, she might have some useful ideas about that sentient hardware called Ship.

For about the sixth time since they left Curtis, Burret called, "Gervaise!"

Gerenson/Konnenen did not even turn his/her head. "Yes, Richard."

"Is the link holding?"

"It is less than two days since the nanites did their work, and we are only a few hundred kilometers from my module. Yes, the link is holding."

"Eric!"

Konnenen hesitated, stopped. But it was Gerenson who turned and said with a slight smile. "I do not have doubts, Richard. Why do you?"

Compared to the moody, self-flagellating young man who believed his only friend was a machine, it was a welcome change. The double-shock of Joan Walsh's anger and Gervaise Konnenen's contempt, had combined with Su Lan's expressed disappointment to produce what in any context would be a minor miracle.

Yet Burret suspected Gerenson's relationship with Su Lan remained the most potent factor in the ex-simulacrum's transformation. He hoped the girl understood the responsibility she carried on her inexperienced shoulders, especially after the inevitable failure of the nanite link. It was then she would be needed most.

But they are a good match, Burret thought as he replied to Gerenson's quip with one of his own. "Damn right I have doubts. For instance, I wonder why you have two women, whereas I have only..."

There was a thin shriek from somewhere above their heads, followed by a chorus of other shrieks and then a violent rustling among the upper levels of the forest.

Burret looked up. "I think something was just taken by one of those animated gasbags."

"Gasbags?" Su Lan queried, puzzled.

"A hydrogen-filled aerial carnivore with stingers on its tentacles and a bottomless stomach. You just heard a few potential dinners diving for cover."

"It sounded as if one did not make it," Gerenson commented.

"Do they attack humans?" the girl asked anxiously.

"I doubt it. Their territory seems to be restricted to the strip of air just above the tree tops."

"But they do take catbirds," Joan said, remembering Jan Buraka's sad experience.

Su Lan grimaced. "In that case, remind me never to bring Pippa to this neck of the woods."

In this post-simulacrum world, the catbirds finally had names of their own.

✤ ✤ ✤

After an hour of steady slogging through the stifling heat of the thorn forest, they finally arrived at the sterile depression out of which Ship's ancient cone reared gleaming in the sun. Su Lan had not been here before, so her companions allowed her a few moments to stare and wonder.

"It's beautiful," she said at last.

It was not quite how Burret thought of Ship, although he supposed its polished presence had a certain aesthetic appeal, even if it did tilt a few degrees from the vertical. But this time there was no ladder, no custodians, no custodian corpse waiting for immolation, and no catbirds either in the trees or in the sky. It was extraordinarily quiet.

"How long should we wait?" Joan asked after a moment. "The next zap might not be for hours."

"I know," Burret muttered as he speculatively eyed the small altar to one side of Ship. From this angle he could not see if the door opening rod was in its place on the stone shelf, but he was sure it was there. The custodians always made sure of that.

"Don't even think of it," his wife warned.

Damn. "Think of what?"

"You know what I mean. This is Eric's party, not yours."

"I beg your pardon?" Gerenson asked.

"Can you sense Ship?"

The younger man shook his head. "I am afraid not. I assure you, it is not for lack of trying."

"Has Gervaise?"

"We have both tried."

"In that case, perhaps we should..."

"The door is opening!" Su Lan shouted as the portal quietly appeared in the shining hull.

Gerenson looked pleased. "It is an invitation."

Burret was not so sure. "For who?"

"All of us."

"How do you know that? Did Ship just tell you?"

"Ship allowed us to approach without interference, didn't she? So we can infer she requires our physical presence inside."

Su Lan said nervously, "Eric..."

"You worry too much," Gerenson interrupted as he tentatively put both hands on the girl's waist, gained confidence and pulled her toward him. Su Lan tensed, then surrendered to the embrace and rested her head on his shoulder. "Nothing will happen to any of us."

She lifted her head. "Gervaise says?"

"I say."

She gave him a fleeting peck on the cheek and pulled away. "In that case," Su Lan said unsteadily, "lead on before I change my mind."

Gerenson turned to Burret, who nodded. "Do as the lady says."

The younger man took the girl's hand and led her down the slope toward the ship. Burret and Joan followed. No one hurried. It was assumed any sterilization discharge would not occur until they were safely on board.

The climb up to the ancient control deck was easier than remembered, as if Ship had adjusted the convoluted passages to suit humans. The deck itself had the same flickering displays, the three spindly chairs, the cone pointing up to the dark opening in the ceiling.

Su Lan stood for a moment, absorbing impressions. "It is not as strange as I expected," she said at last.

Joan nodded. "The custodians are humanoid, after all, with their physical senses pretty much the same as ours." She looked up the slope of the cone. "Eric, is Ship still playing coy?"

"She is waiting," Gerenson said. He grasped handholds on the cone, pulled himself up to the opening and disappeared. Su Lan followed cautiously, until Gerenson's face reappeared and then his extended hand. "Let me help you."

She grasped the hand, and was hauled up into the darkness. Joan and Burret followed, until they all stood in the pool of light around the opening. Gradually their eyes adjusted to the strange dark with its tiny, elusive pricks of light. There was a sense of immensity, of unleashed power.

Burret forced himself to speak. "Eric?"

"Now I am Gervaise."

"What is happening?"

"Wait, please."

The silence became intense. Far off in the darkness, points of light converged and took on form. It was slow and deliberate, a stately progression which was somehow reassuring. It was as if something, *someone*, wanted to demonstrate that strange was not necessarily a threat.

Finally a head emerged out of the gloom. There was no measure of size in this dimensionless place, only shape. The head was spherical, with a wide lipless mouth, a single nostril below a lid of bone, and two tiny glowing eyes.

"Ship," Joan whispered.

The mouth writhed. "*I am Vuonar.*" The voice was neutral, sexless, and all around them. It was as if the air itself spoke.

"Vuonar is Ship's birth name," Konnenen whispered.

"*I welcome that which was my simulacrum, but is now the simulacrum of another.*"

It was not entirely true, although even Konnenen seemed disinclined to dispute the point.

"*There is an evil in the sky.*"

"Tin Lady," Joan whispered.

"*Although the evil is already powerful, it grows and seeks still more power. It must not be allowed to continue.*"

Burret glanced at Konnenen/Gerenson. "Shouldn't you be handling this discussion?"

"Not yet."

"But..."

"For now, it is better I listen."

Burret turned to the head. "You knew we were coming?"

"*It is necessary you come.*"

"So what happens now?"

"*You will help me and my sister destroy the evil in the sky.*"

"How are we supposed to...?" Abruptly, Burret grabbed his wife's hand and pulled her toward the deck opening. "Sorry. We have to go."

Even as Joan opened her mouth to protest, Burret urged her and the other two down the cone to the control deck. It was obvious Konnenen also wanted to object, but Burret would have none of it as he cajoled his companions down past the psychedelic convolutions to the entrance and outside. Finally they were all beyond the rim of the depression, on the trail between the ancient stone columns. They sat on four of the columns and stared at each other.

Burret took a deep breath. "Thank you for going along with me on this."

"I am surprised she did not try to stop us," Joan said.

"Ship needs our willing cooperation. She would hardly get that if she forced us to stay."

"So why the hurry to get away?"

"Because Vuonar assumed too much," Konnenen/Gerenson said with a faint smile. "Correct, Richard?"

Burret nodded. "You heard her. Not a request for help, just a flat 'you will'. Okay, so Tin Lady is alien, or at least evolving in that direction. But is that sufficient reason for us to assume she is our enemy? And why does Ship, Vuonar or whatever she calls herself need us anyway? Tin Lady is already outnumbered."

"She did say 'sister'," Su Lan whispered. "Ship Two?"

"Of course. That duo has to be a pretty powerful combination."

"But perhaps not powerful enough," Konnenen said thoughtfully. "Do not forget Vuonar and Ship Two can only interface via the limited bandwidth of an Earth technology satellite, which undoubtedly diminishes their combined effectiveness. It is why Vuonar wishes the two to become three. A triumvirate, if you will."

"You being the third?"

Konnenen nodded. "Unfortunately there is a penalty. If I allow myself to become part of that union, the pressure on Eric Gerenson will be immense, conceivably to the extent of irreversible brain damage."

Gerenson took it well, starting with a small hesitation, then a shrug of acceptance.

But for Su Lan, who was only just coming to terms with her feelings for this strange young man, the revelation was shattering.

"No," she said. She grabbed Gerenson's arm and held it tight against her. "NO!"

CHAPTER
FORTY

● ●

Finally, after several minutes of persistent and even relentless persuasion, Su Lan succumbed to the inevitable and reluctantly accepted that despite her vehement objections, Gerenson would do what he regarded was 'necessary for the common good'.

But as the man himself admitted, "Alright, so I am not very happy about possible side effects. If there is the least doubt about Vuonar's honesty in this matter, as far as I am concerned she can go..." He spread his hands. "Where bad, deceased custodians go!"

Burret tried not to smile. Gerenson was reacting with astonishing equanimity to the possibility his brain might become mush, which made him wonder if Konnenen was pulling strings. He said, "Believe me, Gervaise will not be allowed to participate in this triumvirate merely because Vuonar wants her to. But how do we find out what is really going on? How do we get the facts?"

"Right now, I am hesitant even to ask Gervaise," Joan confessed.

"I am not," the younger man said, looking at Su Lan.

Su Lan said unsteadily, "That is because you are biased." She bit her lip. "But we do need more facts, don't we?"

Burret asked the girl, "Do you have any ideas on the subject?"

She shrugged. "Only that we should still try to communicate with Tin Lady. Even with Gervaise as intermediary, it is better than doing nothing."

"Gervaise!" Burret called.

Gerenson did not even blink. "Yes, Richard."

"You heard?"

"Of course."

"Can you contact Tin Lady?"

"I will attempt to do so. However, I believe it will improve my chances if I temporarily withdraw from Mr. Gerenson and make the attempt direct from my module."

Burret turned to the women. "Any doubts?"

Joan shrugged. "None that I can think of."

"We will have Eric back!" Su Lan added hopefully.

Gerenson blinked, said bewilderedly, "She's gone!" then gasped as Su Lan ran over, plumped herself on his lap and hugged him.

"Good riddance." The girl's words were muffled against his neck.

"How are you adjusting?" Joan asked.

"Adjusting?" Gerenson hesitatingly slid an arm around the girl's waist. "As the only one in my head at the moment, I suppose..." He forced a nervous laugh. "Consider me a normal human male who happens to have a beautiful woman on his lap!"

After a delighted laugh, Su Lan kissed Gerenson hard and long. In rapid succession the younger man's expression changed from astonishment, through confusion, finally to happy acceptance as the girl leaned back and announced firmly, "Oh yes. Definitely normal!"

"Th ... thank you," Gerenson stammered, his face bright red. "But what if...?"

"Eric, forget the what ifs and concentrate on the what now." Su Lan glared defiantly at Burret and his wife, then back to the younger man. "I hereby state there is nothing wrong with this ex-simulacrum that a good relationship won't fix!"

Gerenson was still bemused. "Me? With you?"

Another kiss, this time a quick one. "Who else, you idiot?"

Burret wanted to cheer. Instead, he said mildly, "It is still possible Eric will have to take that risk."

"I know. It is why I do not like being this close to..." Su Lan shuddered. "Whatever. So if you don't mind, can we please go back down the hill? If things turn sour, at least we can call the copter to fly us out."

Joan asked, "Eric, you still cannot sense Gervaise?"

Gerenson's brow furrowed in concentration. Then he shook his head. "Sorry."

Burret was worried. "I don't like it. The few minutes since Gervaise cut loose is a lot of time to a computer. So how can we know what Vuonar and Ship Two are up to while Gervaise is chatting to Tin Lady?" He hesitated. "Presuming, of course, that *is* what she is doing."

"Perhaps Gervaise can't get back because Eric's nanites are not as stable as she assumed," Joan suggested.

"In which case she would have contacted us via comset." Burret rose to his feet. "Everyone wait here."

He trotted back to Vuonar's depression and looked across at the leaning, gleaming monolith. Its portal remained invitingly open. He shook his head, turned and hurried back to the others. "I agree with Su Lan. Let's make distance."

They hurried down the hill in a little over half the time they took to ascend it. When they finally emerged from the thorn forest onto the patch of ground which still showed impressions from the copter's skids, all they could do was collapse and catch their breath. The top of the hill was concealed by the nearness of the trees, but Burret imagined the brooding presence on its summit, waiting for their answer.

"Can it harm us here?" Joan panted.

"I doubt it. We know Ship burned out her main weapon when she disabled the shuttle."

"I am thinking about the sterilizing field."

"So am I. It is why we are here and not there. I don't know what kind of patience that thing has, or what it will do when it finally decides we are not prancing around to its tune."

"We still need to know what happened to Gervaise," Gerenson reminded them anxiously.

"Not to mention the custodians," Joan added. She glanced up at the blank sky. "And their flying friends."

Burret wondered about that. It was rare to travel the trail on Ship's Hill and not see one or more of those distant descendants of the original crew and their winged companions.

Nervously, he looked around. Except for a few wispy clouds the sky was empty. The trees of the forest rustled from a thin breeze, while in the opposite direction the plain undulated to a cloudy horizon.

Where are the catbirds?

Although the culling had eliminated many of the wild ones, catbirds from the custodian village would surely have discovered the humans by now. The village was not far, and detection by only one of those sharp-eyed creatures would bring a flock to investigate the presence of the strange humanoids.

Burret said angrily, "We won't accomplish anything this way. I'm going to call Curtis!"

The others looked at him somberly. Unspoken was the awareness Vuonar was undoubtedly monitoring all transmissions. "Be careful what you say," Joan warned.

"Aren't I always?" Burret muttered as he activated his comset.

Emmaline Bonderhame responded. The former captain of *Amazon One* sounded terse; irritated. "*Considering what has happened around here, we wondered if we should break silence. I am glad you made the decision for us.*"

"Emma, what are you talking about?"

"*You first.*"

"I am calling to find out if anything is wrong with the Konnenen module. Eric has lost contact with her."

"*Is that all?*"

"That is not funny."

"*It is not supposed to be. Gervaise Konnenen, or the module containing the same, has become untouchable inside some kind of force field which looks like a perfectly reflecting bubble. The rest of the equipment in the comshack is unaffected.*"

Burret sighed. "Anything else?"

"Isn't that enough?"

Must be getting shock proof, Burret thought. "Send the copter, will you? It is possible we may need to get out of here in a hurry."

"What is going on?"

"Wish I knew. Just get the bird in the air."

"It's on its way." After a slight hesitation, Emma continued, *"Meantime, don't do anything rash."*

Burret remembered this was not the first time he had heard that warning. "Wouldn't think of it," he lied. Again.

✣ ✣ ✣

"Eric?"

The ex-simulacrum sighed. "I know. You want me to return up the hill."

"Unless you can raise Vuonar from here."

"It's nice to know she has a name, isn't it?" Gerenson said, smiling, "I like it. It fits what might have become quite a lady."

Su Lan feigned disgust. "A custodian? A *lady?*"

Feeling crowded by events, Burret tried to restrain his impatience. "Eric, please try to raise Vuonar."

"If I can. What do you want me to tell her?"

"As little as possible. But if she has already linked up with Gervaise..."

"I understand." Gerenson rose to his feet and walked away a few paces. Head bowed, he stood with his back to them. Finally, with a brief shudder he straightened, turned and returned to his companions. His expression was doubtful.

"Well?" Burret demanded.

A shrug. "Oh, there was a hint of something. But it could have been my imagination."

"No communication?"

"Not that I could recognize as such."

Burret picked up two of the packs and handed one to Gerenson. "You and I had better be on our way. Joan, Su Lan, when the copter gets here..."

"No one is going anywhere right now," Joan said happily, not attempting to hide her relief. "We have company."

At first they thought it was a single custodian. But it turned out to be a line of three, treading precisely in each other's footsteps as they approached from the direction of the village. They stopped, spread apart and gazed at the humans out of small, fathomless eyes.

"Still no catbirds," Joan added, disappointed.

As if she was heard, there was a beating of wings and one of the creatures appeared from over the forest and descended to a bony shoulder. It was followed by a second catbird to a second bony shoulder, and then a third. Now the humans were being regarded from six pairs of eyes.

"...I," said the first custodian.

"...am," said the second.

"...Vuonar," said the third.

Their voices were rasping whispers, as if their ritualistic wailing had damaged otherwise unused vocal chords. The catbirds fluttered nervously at this unusual phenomenon, but stayed put.

Burret wanted to laugh, but it came out as a repressed croak. He cleared his throat. "If Muhammad won't come to the mountain..."

"I think Vuonar is desperate," Eric said seriously. He approached the three custodians. "Vuonar."

"...I"

"...hear"

"...you."

"What do you want?"

"...Help"

"...from"

"...simulacrum."

Gerenson glanced back at his companions. Burret mouthed, *Keep talking*.

"What kind of help?" Gerenson asked.

"...One"

"...in sky"

"...more changed."

It was a strange conversation which became even stranger as Su Lan gasped and pointed. "Look!"

It was Gervaise Konnenen. Except that the grass did not bend under her feet as she walked toward them, the simulation looked remarkably real. Her attire was a practical bush jacket and slacks, with a broad brimmed hat covering her sweep of white hair.

"Now what?" Joan wondered.

Konnenen said, "Vuonar is right. Tin Lady has evolved into something unrecognizable. Although the implications are unclear, Vuonar and I have cooperated to make certain modifications of our own."

"You no longer need Eric," Su Lan whispered. "You are here without him."

The white head nodded. "I will discuss that in a moment. First I must inform you that although my attempt to communicate with Tin Lady lasted only nanoseconds before contact was terminated, it was long enough for me to identify a glacial intelligence which has not the least interest in anything other than itself."

Burret tried to think of something appropriate to say; ended up by voicing the obvious. "That is not good news."

"It is not," the simulation agreed.

Burret frowned. "So Tin Lady has become the ultimate egoist, which I suppose means we have lost her services along with the *Star Venturer*. But if she has turned in on herself, doesn't that mean she is out of the loop?"

"Possibly, for now at least. But what about tomorrow, next year, or even ten years from now? Presuming Tin Lady continues to evolve, do you not agree the potential is dangerous?"

"What kind of danger?" Su Lan asked nervously.

"Heaven, Hell, or anything in between," Joan murmured.

"Exactly," Konnenen said. "We simply do not know what that potential is, which is why Vuonar and I are exchanging information. The shield I established to protect my module is an early result of that exchange, as is my new ability to project a visual over distance. Meanwhile, Vuonar is re-establishing direct contact with her own people."

"In threes?" was Burret's caustic reaction.

"Even in their prime, custodians were a group-oriented species. Their subsequent devolution amplified that trait to the extent individuals have become more or less non-functional. As far as Vuonar is concerned, she needs three custodians to form a minimum unit."

"I see," Burret said, wondering if he really did. Yet although it was difficult to think of that stoic threesome as the collective mouthpiece of the entity on the hill, it was no more improbable than the strangeness evolving aboard the *Star Venturer*, not to mention the simulation of a woman who had been dead for decades. Or even the mysterious triumvirate, which could not be born without the cooperation of the homosexual-turned-simpleton-turned-simulacrum who in his latest incarnation as a pleasant if confused young man, surely deserved better.

Gerenson was still standing in front of the custodians. "How can I help Vuonar?"

Like well-drilled soldiers, the three swiveled toward Konnenen. Three skinny arms pointed.

"...She"

"...tell"

"...you."

Konnenen nodded. "Now you know how difficult it is for Vuonar to link with these descendants of her people. She and I share a more efficient link because we created mutually compatible pathways when we interfaced with Mr. Gerenson. It is why Keltah, the entity you currently know as Ship Two, cannot complete the triumvirate until she shares that compatibility, which is unfortunately too complex to transmit via the satellite link. It is why Vuonar needs Mr. Gerenson again."

Obviously not needing to be reminded of the possibility she might lose what she had just found, the distressed Su Lan took deep, soundless breaths. She said nothing. For her, words would be superfluous.

Joan said thoughtfully, "So Vuonar needs Eric to carry her template."

"It is the only way," the simulation agreed. "He must then proceed to Keltah, who will duplicate the template within her own processors. It is the reverse of the process in which Mr. Gerenson became Vuonar's simulacrum."

"What will it do to him?" Joan asked as she avoided eye contact with Su Lan. She noticed Eric was also avoiding the girl's pleading gaze.

"I believe we have already discussed that." After a moment's hesitation, Konnenen continued, "Although the template will be Vuonar's and not mine, the process is similar. Nevertheless, Mr. Gerenson has already been subject to considerable stress as Vuonar's simulacrum and then as my remote. A third such manipulation..." She shrugged.

Gerenson straightened his shoulders. His face was pale. "Vuonar, is Gervaise right?"

The custodians regarded him out of small, fathomless eyes.

"...Is," said the first one.

"...correct," said the second.

The third one blinked solemnly.

"Sad," it said.

CHAPTER
FORTY-ONE

• •

While Joan remained behind to await the arrival of the copter, Su Lan insisted on returning with Gerenson and Burret up the hill to the ship which had identified itself as Vuonar. She accompanied them into the ancient hull, up through the convoluted passages to the control deck, then waited with Burret while Gerenson climbed the access cone into the dark mystery above.

When the younger man returned a few minutes later, he was flushed and uncommunicative. Physically he seemed normal, as resisting Su Lan's offer to help he scrambled with Burret and the girl down to the airlock and outside. After they reached the rim of the depression, Konnenen materialized before them.

"There is not much time. The copter has arrived."

Burret led the way down the trail through the sticky warmth of the thorn forest until the trio emerged onto the plain. Emmaline Bonderhame and Joan Walsh were seated on the ground in the copter's shadow.

Her resentment at having to stay behind forgotten, Joan embraced her husband, then looked at Gerenson. "How is he doing?"

Again Konnenen materialized. "He cannot talk. You must take him to Keltah immediately." She winked out of existence.

Still blank-faced, Gerenson climbed aboard the copter followed by Su Lan. Joan and Burret took two of the three rear seats as Bonderhame resumed her place behind the controls.

"Where's Keltah?" Bonderhame asked as the turbine whined up to speed.

"Not where," Burret replied. "Who. Take us to the Second Ones' village."

Bonderhame swiveled in her seat. "What have the Second Ones got to do with this?"

"Keltah is the name of their ship. Overfly the village and land in a clearing you will find a couple of klicks north east. How long before we get there?"

The copter trembled and lifted. "About four hours." Bonderhame jerked a thumb over her shoulder at the storage compartment next to the tiny toilet. "I brought along provisions for a couple of days. Help yourselves if anyone is hungry."

"We can wait," Burret murmured as he settled in his seat. His wife reached forward and gave Su Lan's shoulder a comforting squeeze.

"Don't worry, Su Lan. I know from experience Eric is tougher than he looks."

"Oh, I hope so."

Gerenson said nothing. He just stared disinterestedly at the endless prairie passing toward and below them as the copter ascended to cruising altitude. Joan handed Su Lan a medidoc, which the girl applied to Gerenson's arm.

A couple of minutes later, Burret watched as his wife received the instrument and studied its extruded flimsy. "Is he okay?"

"Heart rate and blood pressure is higher than I like."

"The medidoc..."

"Set on diagnostic only. The thing in Eric's head may not take kindly to any kind of intervention."

"Ask Gervaise."

"Now that is an idea..." Joan was interrupted by an exclamation from their pilot as the full-faced image of Gervaise Konnenen replaced the data on the copter's nav screen.

"I recommend against treatment," Konnenen said via their comsets. "Although I cannot access Mr. Gerenson at the moment, I agree the risks probably exceed any benefit." As the image began to fade...

"Just a minute!" Burret was angry.

The image returned. "Richard, I understand your concerns and I am sorry. I wish I could convince you of the correctness of this course of action."

"Look, I only know we are risking Eric's life to ally ourselves with two, hell, *three* unknowns, against something even more mysterious. Concerns? Damn right I have them!"

"What has it done to him?" Su Lan pleaded.

"We will not know until Keltah has downloaded the template," Konnenen replied.

"Eric is not a database!" Joan snapped.

"Indeed he is not. He is a human being. Nevertheless, as far as Keltah is concerned, the information currently in Mr. Gerenson's brain is equivalent to a bio-chemical database. If the information is complete, and if Keltah is careful during the process of transfer, I believe the person you know will be returned relatively unharmed. Richard, I remind you our purpose is to create a balance against whatever Tin Lady is or may become. Although Vuonar, Keltah and I prefer to retain our separate identities, the triumvirate must remain an available option."

"So you say," Burret muttered sourly.

The head inclined polite acknowledgment. "In any case, Mr. Gerenson is committed. No good purpose will be served by delaying or turning back."

As the image faded, Burret reached forward and touched Gerenson's shoulder. "Eric!"

Slowly, the younger man turned his head toward Burret. "Wait," he said. Then he looked at Su Lan. "Wait," he repeated.

"Oh please God," the girl whispered.

Joan said, "Don't give up on him. That single word is a sign he is aware what is happening."

Thinking of what was in Gerenson's brain, Burret hoped his wife was right.

✛ ✛ ✛

The landing in Keltah's clearing was without incident. After overflying the village and seeing the streets deserted, they had descended into the clearing half-expecting the surrounding forest to erupt Second Ones. But as the rotor wound down, it was as if there was not another living being for kilometers around.

Even the sky was empty.

As soon as they clambered down from the copter's cramped cabin, everyone except Gerenson stretched aching muscles and looked around.

Gerenson just stood.

"Now what?" Joan asked.

Burret pointed toward where a trail led into the trees. "That way."

"Won't that take us to the village?" Joan asked.

"No," Gerenson said.

"He's right," Bonderhame said. "The village is in the other direction." She gestured at the side of the clearing beyond the copter.

"Emma..." Burret began.

Bonderhame sighed. "I know. Someone has to stay behind and watch the store." She leaned against the copter and watched resentfully as her friends vanished among the trees.

✛ ✛ ✛

The trail was short, less than one hundred meters. At its end there was a low earth mound in a small clearing. On the far side of the mound, like the sloping entrance to an old-fashioned root cellar there was a wooden door.

"The entrance to..." Su Lan hesitated. "Keltah?"

"Who goes in?" Joan wondered. "Are we all invited, or is Eric supposed to do this on his own?"

"He is not going in there alone!" Su Lan snapped as she grasped Gerenson's hand.

"So we all go," Burret said as he turned his attention to the door. "But let's be careful in there."

"Whatever 'there' is," Joan muttered under her breath.

The door was crude and heavily tarred, with a simple latch and handle. With an effort Burret swung it back on its hinges to reveal a flight of steps leading down to the entrance of a stone-walled tunnel. On a recessed shelf just below the door there was a cigar-shaped device about the length of a hand.

Joan kneeled, reached down and picked up the device. She hefted it and discovered it was feather light. "The local equivalent of open sesame?" she wondered, referring to the rod the custodians used to gain access to the ship on the hill.

"Keep it with you just in case," Burret suggested as he descended the steps, thumbed on a penlight and entered the tunnel.

They immediately discovered they did not need the light.

As they walked along the tunnel, its walls began to emit a pale, shadowless illumination which traveled with them.

"Now isn't that convenient?" Burret turned off the penlight and turned to his wife. "Hon, walk ahead a few paces."

She walked ahead. Although illumination traveled with her, the others remained in their own pool of light. She looked down at the device in her hand. "Then it's not triggered by this, is it?"

"Doesn't seem to be," Burret said as he, Su Lan and Gerenson joined her. "But something is obviously sensing us, separate or together."

Still cautiously, they continued along the tunnel. Arrow straight, with a ten degree slope plus an occasional shallow step, it descended steadily until it abruptly right-angled left and terminated at a curved metal wall.

"Bingo," Joan said.

"Does it have a door?" Su Lan asked.

"Here," Gerenson said. His gaze was still unfocused.

Joan gave the device to her husband. "Try this."

Burret accepted the device, examined it, ran his fingers across its surface until he thought he detected an irregularity. He pressed the irregularity, tried to move it.

The metal wall remained a wall.

"Contact," Gerenson said as Burret continued to poke and prod for any kind of combination, and as Joan and Su Lan ran their fingers over the metal surface.

Frustrated, the two women stood back. "No crack, no nothing," Joan muttered. She added angrily, "If there *is* a door, that is."

"Contact," Gerenson repeated.

Contact. Burret looked at the wall, at the device, at the wall again. Hardly daring to hope, he said, "Stand back, ladies."

As they moved behind him, he held the device so the irregularity faced the wall. Then he touched the device to the wall.

It opened.

✣ ✣ ✣

Actually, a section of the wall simply disappeared. What was left was a perfectly round opening a little less than two meters across with a smooth rim. Inside there was a short chamber which ended at a second wall. "Air lock?" Burret wondered.

"I hope that is all it is," Joan responded, briefly holding her breath as Burret entered the chamber and touched the device to the second wall. The outer wall abruptly rematerialized, leaving Burret inside. As Joan's heart did a distressed flip-flop, the outer wall disappeared again and her husband re-emerged.

"It's an airlock all right. If we squeeze in..."

Still breathing heavily, Joan shook her head. "Not a good idea. I hate to think of the effect if someone's hand or butt is in the way when the stuff of that wall rematerializes."

Her husband looked slightly surprised. "Good point."

Gerenson stepped forward. "Me."

"Just a minute!" Su Lan protested.

Burret held up his hand. "You saw how quick it is. You can be next, Su Lan."

The two men stepped inside and the wall closed. A moment later the wall opened again and Burret beckoned to Su Lan. Again the wall closed.

Joan waited.

The wall remained closed. "Open," she whispered. "Open, damn you!"

After what seemed a small eternity although it was less than a minute, the wall did open and Burret beckoned his wife inside. "I think the thing's got Eric!"

The inner wall opened to reveal an apprehensive Su Lan in a narrow, gray-walled corridor. Even, sourceless illumination gave an impression of oppressive dullness. Su Lan pointed. "I heard something that way."

"Something?"

"A voice." She hesitated. "I think."

"Then let's find out." Burret slipped the door opener into his pocket and walked slowly along the corridor. The women stayed close. Like the tunnel, the illumination kept pace with them, darkening ahead and behind so they were always in their own patch of light.

Joan whispered, her face sallow in the unflattering illumination, "I hate this. Isn't a corridor supposed to have doors?"

"Eric!" Su Lan shouted anxiously. "Eric!"

They heard a faint, barely audible response.

The girl wanted to run forward, but Joan held her back. "We stay together." Her grip still firm on Su Lan's arm, she stayed close behind her husband as he edged toward the retreating darkness. After a distance Burret estimated about forty meters, the corridor terminated at another metal wall.

"You need the gizmo again," Joan said.

"I guess." But even as Burret reached into his pocket, the wall disappeared and the corridor was flooded with cold white light from a circular room Burret and his companions recognized as a starship's control deck.

Consoles, a row of four chairs in the center and other chairs at stations around the perimeter of the deck, completed the layout. Eric Gerenson rose from one of the chairs and came hesitatingly toward them. There were tears in his eyes as he reached for Su Lan and enfolded her in a long embrace.

He answered their unspoken question. "Other than being a bit fuzzy in the head and weak in the knees, I think I am more or less in one piece."

"What happened?"

"You know I was under control?"

Burret nodded. "It was pretty obvious."

"It was not the same as with Gervaise. Although I was aware what was going on around me, I had absolutely no control of any part of my body. Even blinking and the act of breathing were outside my mental jurisdiction. Su Lan, when it made me leave you behind..."

Her arms tightened around him. "I know."

"Anyway, it made me go in there." Gerenson kept one arm about the girl's waist as he gestured at a blank section of wall between two of the consoles. "Next thing I knew, I was back out here."

Joan lowered the finger-camera with which she had been taking a rapid series of pictures. "What is in there?" she asked.

"The same as in Vuonar's ship." A faint smile. "Infinity in a bottle."

"What about the thing in your head?"

"Gone," Gerenson said, then added, "I presume Vuonar's template is now part of Vuonar's sister."

Burret recognized the professional interest in his wife's face. Had Eric been damaged by the experience, or was he still the Eric Gerenson they knew? Burret doubted anything in Joan's training had prepared her for this, although he suspected she was ready for the challenge. Like her husband, Joan Walsh Burret liked to explore new territory.

He looked at the blank wall. Now that Keltah was reinforced by Vuonar's template, was she already linked with her sister on the hill? If there was such a duo, when would it become a trio?

A triumvirate?

Had they just attended a monstrous birth?

CHAPTER FORTY-TWO

● ●

Burret wanted to go beyond the wall and confront Eric's 'infinity in a bottle', which apparently was similar to what they had experienced in the nose of Vuonar's ship. Yet although he tried the device on the wall, even asked aloud for permission to enter, Keltah remained silent and uncooperative.

They were all intrigued by the obvious differences between the ships of the First and Second Ones; Keltah's horizontal hull design versus Vuonar's vertical, and Keltah's dull, straight-walled monochromatic interiors versus the convoluted and ever changing psychedelics of Vuonar's. Although the First and Second Ones originated as the same species and to human eyes still looked the same, their cultural divergences were obviously immense.

Two ancient brains in ancient ships immobilized by the last action of an ancient war; was that war finally forgotten, or at least put aside? After eons of isolation, with only the de-evolved descendants of the original crews for company, how could Keltah and Vuonar remain sane? *Had they?*

These and too many other questions nagged with their lack of answers. Remembering the ancient cliché about a mouse trying to get along with an elephant, Burret wondered if the small human colony on Genser's World was, in effect, faced with the prospect of trying to get along with two elephants.

"Give it up," Joan suggested with a thin smile. "The entity is not going to let you in."

"Eric..."

"Not again!" Su Lan protested, again grasping the younger man's hand.

"Is there anything else you remember?" Burret completed, trying not to react to the girl's angry protectiveness.

Gerenson thought a moment. His color was better, and physically he seemed to have recovered from his bout of weakness. "It's just that I did sense..." he hesitated. "Feelings? Anyway, a whole gamut of them."

"Keltah's? Or yours?"

"It started with mine, as I felt an enormous pressure being gradually relieved inside my head. It was followed by gratitude, confusion, and then..." Gerenson's eyes widened.

"Go on."

"Regret," Gerenson said at last. "A terrible, formless regret." He frowned in concentration, shook his head. "There is nothing more. As I told you, the next thing I knew was when I found myself out here."

"I think that's enough..." Su Lan began.

Gerenson held up a restraining hand. "I admit the memory upset me for a moment, but only because I recognized it for what it was. Keltah severed contact before any damage was done."

"Very considerate of her," Su Lan muttered sourly.

Burret frowned. "You said regret. For what?"

Gerenson shook his head. "I wish I knew."

Joan said, "If Keltah was human, I would say it is for the war and the wasted eons since."

"But she's known the war was over since we set up the satellite link!"

"Known? Richard, our pathetic little link is equivalent to joining two oceans with a pipe! Heaven knows what has already happened within those two minds since Eric brought them the means to really open up to each other!"

Burret looked at his wife doubtfully. She had an uncanny knack to cut to the core of an argument without arguing, which sometimes led to his frustrations. Although it was difficult to apply a human perspective to what was going on within the cells of the protected colloidal tissue which had once been the brain of an alien youngster (was there even a vestigial memory of that distant time?), perhaps what Eric described as a 'terrible' regret had triggered an alien equivalent of catatonia.

In Vuonar too?

Burret was beginning to feel nervous in this domain of a possibly sick mind. "I suggest we do what we have already done a few times since we arrived on this planet, and get the hell out of here."

"A wise move," Gerenson agreed surprisingly. "For a time, it is possible Keltah will be..." His young face twisted as he groped for an appropriate word. "Erratic."

"Then let's go," Su Lan said as she urged Eric ahead of her out of the control room into the corridor. Joan and Burret followed close behind. The patch of light kept pace with them as they hurried to the air lock. At the touch of the device, the inner door obediently dematerialized.

"Everyone inside!" Last in, crowded against the others and praying his butt was safely out of the way of the inner door, Burret reached between bodies and touched the device to the outer wall.

He did not see, hear or thankfully feel the inner door rematerialize. But as the outer door opened, the pressure of bodies pitched them out of the lock on to the unyielding floor of the tunnel.

As three of the four humans staggered to their feet, Burret had a momentary glimpse of the closed inner door before the ancient outer hull soundlessly rematerialized.

"Is everyone okay?" Joan gasped.

Su Lan rolled over and sat up, grimacing. "I think I twisted my ankle."

Joan applied the medidoc. "That will take care of the pain. Can you get to the copter?"

The girl shook her head as Gerenson came over and tried to assist her. "No Eric. You are one of the walking wounded too, you know." But she accepted Joan's arm and began to hobble up the long slope of the tunnel. When Burret finally pushed back the heavy wood door and the quartet emerged above ground, the sky was overcast and the ground wet from a recent shower.

One of the Second Ones, catbird on its shoulder, was waiting. A wet shift clung to the alien's skinny body. Even the catbird looked bedraggled, although in contrast to its master's disinterested gaze the creature's large eyes regarded the humans with lively interest.

Gervaise Konnenen stood nearby, impeccable and incongruously dry.

The hologram said, "Richard, you have something that does not belong to you."

"Oh." Realizing he still had the device in his pocket, Burret handed it to the alien, who immediately turned away and descended into the tunnel. Without hesitation the catbird transferred to Gerenson's shoulder, nuzzled his cheek for a moment, then took off again and perched in a tree to await its master.

"Curious," Konnenen said.

"What is?"

"Although the creature's choice was possibly random, I suspect it knows or at least discerned Mr. Gerenson's unfortunate history in connection with its species."

Gerenson nodded. "I agree. For a brief moment, I sensed something which..." He hesitated, as if unsure of the proper words.

"Tell us later," Joan suggested.

"No, I must tell you now because I think it is important. It was regret again. Not as intense as the blast I got from Keltah of course, but a sense of sorrow nevertheless. I suppose if what I felt from Keltah had continued even a few more seconds..."

"I would rather not think about that, if you don't mind," Su Lan said tartly.

"What should we do now?" Burret asked Konnenen.

"Do you trust me?" Konnenen countered.

"Frankly, I don't know. Say your piece anyway. You are obviously here for a reason."

Konnenen gestured. "I suggest we return to the copter."
As the group walked under the moisture-dripping trees
toward the clearing, she continued, "At the rate Tin Lady
is evolving, she will be beyond our reach within days. So
if we are to do anything at all, it must be before it is too
late."

"Do what?" Joan asked tentatively.

"Destroy Tin Lady, of course."

They emerged from the trees. Bonderhame stepped out
of the copter and waved. Burret waved back. "I don't like
it. It's still your word against..." He snorted disgustedly.

"The idea of the triumvirate disturbs you?"

"You already know that."

"The moment Tin Lady is terminated, the triumvirate
will cease to exist. The balance will be restored."

They arrived at the copter. Grinning broadly, pilot
Bonderhame hugged Gerenson before she followed him
and the other two women into the cabin. Burret put a booted
foot on the step, hesitated and turned. Konnenen stood
quietly, watching.

"What balance?" Burret demanded. "Even if I believe
you about the triumvirate, how can you guarantee the two
ship entities will never again interfere in human affairs?"

Konnenen came closer, reached up a hand to touch
Burret's face. He felt a gentle tingle like the touch of a spider
web. "It will be a great responsibility," Konnenen said. "For
a while, the custodians will need to be led like children."

At first Burret thought she had changed the subject. Then
two and two made four, and the universe shifted. "Vuonar
and Keltah..." He licked his lips. "They are leaving?"

"In effect."

Burret wondered how ships which had been disabled
for eons could become space worthy again, then realized
the answer could be former enemies cooperating toward
an end neither had been able to accomplish on their own.

"What about Tin Lady?"

Konnenen shook her head. "We will discuss strategy
after you return to Curtis." She faded and was gone.

Burret climbed into the copter and collapsed into his
seat. He felt he could sleep for a week.

"What did she tell you?" Joan asked.

He shook his head. "Later."

Bonderhame turned her head. "Home?"

Burret squeezed his wife's hand, who squeezed back. "Home," he echoed wearily.

CHAPTER
FORTY-THREE

• •

"Richard, we have no more than five days to get to Star
Venturer. *Any later, and Tin Lady will be impregnable."*

*"Only five days? Gervaise, we need a couple of weeks just
to synthesize enough fuel!"*

*"Vuonar has given me access to data which will more than
double your rate of production. Although it will produce only
enough fuel for a one way trip, the crew can use one of the
starship's remaining escape pods while the shuttle remains docked
for later recovery. With appropriate modifications to the drive,
plus weight-saving measures including restricting the crew to
one person, I calculate you can launch with hours to spare."*

"One person? Do you have someone in mind?"

*"You are preferred. Tin Lady is aware of your importance in
the community."*

*"That's nice, I think. Anyway, after 'whoever' gets up there,
what is that person supposed to do?"*

*"Nothing. The shuttle itself will contain the channeler through
which the triumvirate will strike."*

*"So what is the point of anyone going at all? The shuttle's
computer can handle approach and docking."*

*"Although the channeler is undetectable, it is unlikely Tin
Lady will allow an unmanned approach, even if she determines
the shuttle is harmless. There is also the possibility the presence
of Richard Burret will trigger a residual curiosity."*

"What is this, er, channeler?"

"It is as its name describes. At the proper moment, the triumvirate will transmit a disruption field to the device, which will act like a lens and literally burn the intellect out of Tin Lady. Because it is bio-chemical in nature and similar to the carbon composites of much of the shuttle's basic structure, the channeler will be shaped to replace one of the drive section's service hatches."

"When will it be ready?"

"It is almost complete. Vuonar will shortly give it to a group of custodians, who will bring it down Ship's Hill to your former campsite where it can be retrieved."

✤ ✤ ✤

Burret turned off the playback. After a moment, he said into the silence, "Don't all speak at once."

"Why doesn't Konnenen show herself?" Joe Hahvek asked.

"I am sure she is listening. But she has apparently decided we must make our own decisions. Oh, and Eric also excused himself. He is aware some of you suspect he is still being manipulated. It is not true of course, but I understand why he feels that way."

Su Lan jumped to her feet and shouted defiantly, "Eric is as much his own person as any of you, and anyone who thinks otherwise should be ashamed!" She plumped down in her seat amid an embarrassed silence.

After a few seconds during which everyone waited for someone else to say something, Garnett Podenski rose stiffly to his feet. The former captain of the *High Hopes* had spent a day clearing brush, and the effect on his muscles was beginning to tell.

"As I see it, we have only two choices. One; do nothing and face an uncertain future with that thing in the sky plus the two on the planet. Two; go along with the triumvirate, do the deed and hope they keep their word and go away. Taking everything into consideration, including the risks, my vote is for number two."

Evanne interrupted, "But Garnett, what if the triumvirate fails? You heard the playback. Even with a human on board, there is no guarantee Tin Lady will allow the shuttle to approach."

Shand countered, "So what? What have we got to lose anyway?"

"Only the life of the pilot!" Stiegler rejoined hotly. "Are you forgetting? The shuttle will carry just enough fuel for ascent and rendezvous, not for subsequent de-orbiting. If the pilot cannot enter the ship, he stays marooned up there until his air runs out!"

The dam broke, and suddenly everyone tried to speak at once. Jan Buraka whispered into the ear of Alvin Oborg, who placed his fingers to his lips and penetrated the hubbub with a piercing whistle. Into the shocked silence, Jan asked reasonably, "Presuming everything works and Tin Lady is destroyed, what happens if those brains in bottles change their minds and decide to stay?"

"Square One," someone muttered disgustedly. "All that trouble, and we will be back to where we started."

"Maybe, but without Tin Lady, at least. That is something, isn't it?"

Again everyone tried to speak at once, which only subsided as from her seat in the front row, Joan turned around and signaled to Oborg. As before, the little technician's whistle had the desired effect. Then Joan spoke directly to her husband. "Richard, before this gets out of hand, I suggest you discuss your own conclusions. Then let us take it from there."

"Fair enough." Burret looked at his audience of less than thirty people, almost the entire human population of a world. Their problems should be no more than those of any isolated colony, involving land, shelter, and creating a viable community for themselves as well as for their descendants and future colonists. Instead they were unavoidably involved in a struggle between adversaries they did not understand, for a cause in which human affairs were incidental.

Presuming their silence was acquiescence, he continued, "Some of you just completed the modifications to the fuel plant which, as I speak, is operating at better than two hundred and ten percent of spec. The channeler was flown in earlier today. I have examined it, and believe me it looks and feels exactly like a service hatch.

"So, as Gervaise promised, we have the means to return to the *Star Venturer*, along with the triumvirate's booby trap. So do we go ahead, or do we politely refuse and take our chances with the future? Personally, I agree with Garnett: we should go ahead. Whatever was originally human in Tin Lady is undoubtedly long gone, replaced by a freakish combination which is evolving and growing like an intellectual cancer. On the other hand, Jan's 'brains in bottles' need us, and not just because of the threat represented by Tin Lady. They also need us to help reverse the devolution of their crews' descendants. And what about future colonists from Earth? I like to think that when the next ship arrives, it won't be blown out of the sky by a paranoid intelligence trying to preserve its exclusivity!

"On the downside, I admit the custodians are likely to be a millstone around our collective necks for a long time to come. But now there is a healthy relationship between us and the winged symbiots, with their help perhaps even that responsibility will be a little less onerous." Burret acknowledged a raised hand. "You have something to add, Shand?"

"Damn right I do!" The ex-colonel stood and glared around him. "Maybe I'm pounding the obvious, but what makes everyone so sure those brains will keep their promise and leave anyway? Even that they can? And come to think of it, how do you know we can trust that other component of the triumvirate, our own dear Gervaise Konnenen?"

Joan said irritably, "Shand, stop being so negative. In any case, I am surprised my husband has not mentioned the most important reason we should help the triumvirate, which is the simple fact they are talking to us and Tin Lady is not! Surely, that is an indication we are closer to them than the thing in the sky." She waited patiently through a chorus of interruptions. "All right, so they talk to us because they need us. But I'd rather the devil I know than the one I don't!"

Su Lan asked, "You don't mind Richard going up there?"

"Of course I mind! But if the rest of you agree he is the one..."

Burret had had enough. He tried not to meet his wife's gaze as he announced awkwardly, "All right, it's voting time. Do we go? And if so, who rides in the driver's seat? To avoid the recriminations which will certainly result after a show-of-hands, I asked you to bring along your com pads. Please enter your choice."

✛ ✛ ✛

With reduced gross weight and improved thrust, lift-off was faster than usual. *Cassion's Child* used just over half of the landing strip before the stripped-down shuttle roared skyward and disappeared into a low overcast.

Joan waited until the bass thrumming of the first-stage air breathers faded to inaudibility. She was apart from the others and did not join them as they turned away and wandered home. As their voices faded, she attempted to deal with her rising resentment. It was not their fault her husband repeatedly put himself in harm's way, anymore than it was hers that he had an exaggerated sense of responsibility. That the colonists would vote for the mission was a forgone conclusion; the single dissenter (probably DeVincie) casting what turned out to be merely a token negative. Not so certain was their selection of her husband as pilot. Most people wanted him here, as did she, and Joan cursed the misplaced sense of duty which drove her to quietly lobby on Richard's behalf.

I am as bad as he is, she told herself angrily, wishing the count had not been so close. One more vote would have put Bonderhame (who was certainly the better pilot) in that seat instead of her husband. By now Tin Lady probably didn't give a damn about human hierarchies anyway, so even Eric Gerenson could have...

Joan flushed, forced herself to dismiss 'what might have been'. Okay, presuming Tin Lady was destroyed and Vuonar and Keltah departed from Genser's World as they promised, what role should Gervaise Konnenen assume in the future affairs of the colony, or would there always be distrust because of her origin as a donation from Tin Lady? And how could the humans help the poor, dumb custodians in a world in which there was no further need for their mindless rituals of ship maintenance?

"Joan."

It was Su Lan, with Gerenson in tow. "Walk with us, please?"

Joan forced a smile. "Glad to."

Gerenson said awkwardly, "Su Lan suggested you needed company." He brightened. "She does seem to know such things, you know."

Fortunately the young couple sensed Joan's need for silence, so as she walked with them she thought back a few hours to when she had gone to the comshack in a fruitless attempt to contact Gervaise. She remembered the strange feel of the force field bubble about Gervaise's module, like slippery oil which caused her hands to slide about its surface despite her best efforts to grasp it. She had rapped knuckles on the glistening sphere, spoken to it, even thought at it, but there had been no response.

Joan took a deep breath to clear her head. "Eric. When did you last have contact with Konnenen?"

"Three days ago, when she hinted she might withdraw from further human contact." He frowned. "I assumed it had something to do with her commitment to the triumvirate, although isn't that supposed to end when Tin Lady is destroyed?"

"I would think so. But are you sure those were Konnenen's exact words? To 'withdraw from further human contact' sounds pretty final to me."

The frown deepened. "I don't know what else it could mean, unless..." Gerenson's eyes widened. "Is it possible she intends to go with Vuonar and Keltah when they space away from here?"

Of course.

Her mind in a turmoil, Joan began to run towards the comshack. It was about half a kilometer, and when she got to the small building she had to thrust her way through half a dozen people who were crowded around the door. For a moment she grasped the doorjamb while she regained her breath. She heard Su Lan and Gerenson panting behind her as she asked, "How long until docking?"

Emmaline Bonderhame looked over her shoulder. "Hi, Joan. Thirty-five minutes or so."

"Can I talk to Richard?"

"Be my guest." Emmaline Bonderhame slid aside to make room on the bench seat.

Joan leaned toward the mike. "Richard, this is Joan. How is everything going?"

"Hello, hon. So far, just routine."

"Have you tried to raise Tin Lady?"

"Continuously since liftoff. No response."

"Can you talk?"

"I have a few minutes."

"I think Konnenen..." A horrifying thought caused Joan to catch her breath. What if Tin Lady was listening? "wishes you well," she finished lamely.

"She would. Gervaise is a very human box-of-tricks, isn't she?"

"What is your plan if Tin Lady allows you to dock?" It was a useless question, but Joan had to make conversation.

"Check the state of the ship and talk to Tin Lady if possible. If I can persuade her to cooperate, she will be a formidable asset in the development of the colony."

Someone touched Joan's shoulder. She looked behind her, and saw Gerenson make a chopping motion across his throat. "Just a moment," Joan turned off the mic. "Eric, what is it?"

Gerenson said in a hurry, "Richard is hoping Tin Lady is listening. Go along with whatever he says!"

Bonderhame nodded. "Eric is right. Let's see where this is going."

Joan turned on the mike. "Sorry, dear. Some idiot bumped into the wrong switch."

"Everyone is there?"

Actually the crowd was outside the door, but that was a detail. "Everyone," Joan said.

"Can't say I blame them. If we cannot get Tin Lady's coop-eration, not to mention access to the Star Venturer, *we are in deep, deep trouble."*

Joan suspected where this was leading. "From the ship-entities?"

"It was a mistake to give them that satellite link. Separately, I think we could have handled them. But now they are work-ing together, who knows?"

"Do you think Tin Lady will be interested?"

"She has to be, if only to protect her own interests. Tin Lady might be pretty powerful and getting more so, but so are those canned brains down there. In any case..."

Richard Burret's words were cut off as if by a switch. Bonderhame tried everything she could to resume contact, with no result.

Joan bit her lip. "Tin Lady?"

"I don't doubt it. Proves she was listening anyway."

"It's a good sign," Su Lan said.

Joan nodded. The girl was probably right, although it did not ease the knot in her stomach. Richard on his own...

Not so.

It was a multiple voice, whispering in her mind. Then:

Goodbye.

It was the last anyone heard from the triumvirate.

CHAPTER FORTY-FOUR

● ●

Aboard *Cassion's Child*, Burret watched the approaching starship. He was not surprised at the cessation of contact with the ground, which occurred at the precise moment Tin Lady assumed control of the shuttle. The starship had been barely visible as a bright star lifting over Genser's World's horizon, but now its cylinders and core frame loomed in the forward windows like a giant's construction toy.

Docking was routine, with hardly a jar to indicate connection to the crew module. Burret went to the hatch and waited for pressures to equalize. Although he remembered Konnenen's admonition to 'do nothing', it made better sense to act as Tin Lady, if she cared, would expect him to.

The starship's control deck was quiet. Burret looked around at the familiar array of controls, the empty chairs. He licked his lips. "Tin Lady?"

In the center of the deck, the air began to congeal. It looked like a swirling column of pale light, shot through with flickers of black and orange. Finally the image it produced looked like a woman, or at least a caricature of one. Now the pretense was gone, leaving nothing human. Although the entity said nothing, the man had the feeling it knew everything, especially about the triumvirate.

A blast of sudden, unrelenting fear forced Burret to his knees, where he bowed his head and covered his face with his hands.

What have we done?

The triumvirate was finished.

Humanity on Genser's World was finished.

A heavy grayness rose behind Burret's closed eyelids, a gradual cessation of everything...

...LIGHT!

It was a shattering, silent explosion which was the end and beginning of all things, a swirling cacophony of incomprehensible images accompanied by a soundless shriek which faded and was gone.

And then there was a welcoming dark.

✛ ✛ ✛

It was like waking from a long sleep. Burret struggled to his feet, staggered through the airlock into the shuttle and radioed the ground. His wife was on duty. *"It's about time!"* she snapped.

"How long?" he gasped, wondering at her anger.

"How long? Nearly forty-eight hours, that's how long!" Joan then added grimly, *"Considering what you have put me through, Richard Dane Burret, you owe me."*

Two days! No wonder he felt dragged out. "Believe me, Joan Walsh Burret, I will pay in full. Anyway, what happened?"

Podenski cut in. *"You tell us. Not only are the ship-entities gone, the Konnenen module is just a cube of junk."*

"Vuonar and Keltah gone? How?"

"We sent a crew to Ship's Hill. Although the ship is still there and apparently intact, whatever used to be above its control deck is now just a dusty space with barely enough room in which to stand. We haven't found Vuonar's control core yet, although after what happened we are not expecting too much."

Burret nodded to himself. "I agree. What about Keltah; Ship Two?"

"The same. No more cathedral-in-a-bottle." A sardonic chuckle. *"Tin Lady?"*

Burret remembered the soundless shriek. "I think I heard her die."

"I guess the triumvirate was more dedicated than we thought. No one imagined their departure would be so..." Again that chuckle. *"Final."*

"I guess." Burret sighed. "Konnenen too."

Remembering the aura of confidence emitted by the entity who used to be Tin Lady, he knew now why she succumbed to the attack of the triumvirate. Being absolutely selfish herself, Tin Lady assumed self-preservation was the *raison d'être* of all intelligent beings. She anticipated and was prepared for the assault because she knew the entities on the planet correctly assumed she would ultimately seek to destroy them. The triumvirate was an inevitable reaction to an inevitable threat.

That those who formed the triumvirate were prepared to sacrifice themselves in order to gain the edge which would destroy the enemy, was a concept not even considered. It was Tin Lady's fatal mistake.

So Tin Lady died.

So the two ancient ship-entities died.

So the software program which was almost human, died.

As Burret re-entered the *Star Venturer* to check out the ship's systems and prepare an escape pod, he regretted the lack of computer memory which would have allowed Gervaise Konnenen to duplicate herself. Now no doubt there was plenty; presuming the electronics had survived the silent, mutually destructive battle. He glanced through a port at the docked shuttle, specifically at a hatch on the drive section. In contrast with the pale gray of the upper hull, there was definitely a faint discoloration.

He would miss Gervaise Konnenen.

He ascended one level to the control deck and was greeted by a voice. It was calm, conversational, and female. "How do you do."

He swung around and was confronted by the holographic image of a white-haired woman.

"I am Gervaise Konnenen," the image announced.

Burret took a deep breath. "You are dead."

"If you are referring to the real Gervaise Konnenen, you are of course correct. Nevertheless the computer is fully reactive and programmed with the Konnenen personality file, image and voice. So I suggest you proceed as if I am the woman in person. By the way, aren't you Richard Dane Burret of the *Robert L. Cassion?*"

It was unreal. He licked his lips. "I am, as a matter of fact."

"Clearly there has been a malfunction, because there is a considerable gap in my memory. I have no record of our arrival at Genser's World, or of the crew's revival and disembarkation."

"You haven't?" he asked inanely.

Welcome to Genser's World, Gervaise Konnenen.

PART VI
THE SECOND RETURN

● ●

Home.

A simple concept defining a place of belonging; a house, a family, an idea. All in one nurturing package.

But to the colonists on Genser's World, home was much more than just the extra-terrestrial community they had created with heart and hands. It was also the place in which they had lived before the starships brought them across the light years; a city, a town, a village, a farm perhaps. On a planet called Earth.

A planet they still referred to as the 'home' world.

At night they could even see Earth's sun, faint and not very impressive among its brighter stellar neighbors. Yet to the adults of the community, that yellow spark was an ever-present reminder of their roots, of a time in their lives before technology caught up with mankind's messianic desire to journey 'out there'.

As with any remote colony, letters from home were a part of that link with the past, although at the speed of light it took the signals more than four years to reach the dish antenna the colonists set up on a ridge overlooking Curtis. There were private messages of course, about families and friends. There was technical data. There was news of Earth's increasingly turbulent politics, along with vague promises of more missions to come. There was...

Then the letters stopped coming.

CHAPTER
FORTY-FIVE

● ●

It had been three years since the destruction of Tin Lady. They were successful years with good crops, seven new babies, and even signs the custodians were beginning to wake from their intellectual slumber. Yet Earth's silence remained an irritant in the collective psyche of Genser's World's small human community, to the extent Mayor Ella Shire was finally persuaded to convene a town meeting to discuss the matter of the uncommunicative home world. They all came; adults, children, babies, and a few family catbirds. Even appendectomy patient Melba Kraskin was wheel-chaired from the clinic. At the back of the room, a catbird on each bony shoulder, two custodians watched impassively. It was hard to tell them apart, although their ancestral lines had diverged eons before. Their mentor, Su Lan McNaughton/Gerenson, stayed close and hoped her pupils' clumsily expressed desire to attend the gathering of 'thick people' was more than instinctive politeness.

A woman in orange coveralls admonished her young son to stay in his seat and behave himself. The Mayor then mounted the platform at the front of the room. Her pre-amble was brusque.

"All right, you all know why you are here. And if you have been counting, you also know it has been two years, eleven months and seven days since we last heard from the home world. Various reasons have been suggested, such as World War Three, some kind of natural cataclysm, or a planet-wide economic collapse. One cynic, who will remain nameless, even wondered if Earth has lost interest! So..." The mayor glared around the room. "What do we do about it? What *can* we do?" She pointed. "Pat, I know you have part of the answer. Come up here, dear, and tell us about it."

Patrice Coestrand rose from her seat in the front row and came up to the platform. Dusky cheeks flushed and eyes sparkling, the diminutive former captain of the *Star Venturer* clearly enjoyed the moment as she faced the audience and burst out, "You will never know how much I have looked forward to this!"

She took a deep breath, continued, "When I was appointed to the command of *Star Venturer*, I knew nothing and was told nothing about the sideshift program. Truth is, I only found out about it after I was revived from deepsleep here at Genser's World! Since then I have made it my business to learn as much as I can about the technology, including living on board during most of the past half-year. As you know, I worked with the 'new' Gervaise Konnenen, whose help has been invaluable. Anyway, I can now report that the *Venturer*'s systems have been serviced and appropriately upgraded. Travel time to Earth is now approximately fourteen weeks."

A collective gasp of astonishment was followed by instant bedlam as everyone tried to speak at once. It would have gone on longer, except for the intervention of the Mayor who bellowed for silence. Despite (or because of) her piercing contralto, she was not entirely successful, as several small persons began to wail their disapproval.

The Mayor waited a moment, gazing down at the front row where Joan Walsh held the Kraskin baby. "I do hope we do not need to change *their* diapers," Ella told the little girl in a stage whisper loud enough to reach the back of the room.

As the child's woebegone expression was transformed into a smile and even the other children quieted, Coestrand said into the embarrassed silence, "May I continue? As I said, Earth is now only weeks away by sideshift drive. I can also report that not only have we eliminated the possibility of hitchhikers, but also most of the unpleasant physiological effects of sideshift, which have been reduced to a tolerable level. And that is about it, I think."

"Not quite," Mayor Shire said, restraining Coestrand as the other began to leave the platform. "What can you tell us about this 'new' Gervaise Konnenen? Are you sure you can trust her?"

Coestrand responded without hesitation. "Trust her? Absolutely. You forget her program was in backup mode. She knew nothing of events which occurred after the ship first arrived in orbit. It was only when she was informed about Tin Lady, she agreed something needed to be done."

"To discourage hitchhikers?" the mayor persisted.

"Of course."

"Do you understand the modifications?"

Coestrand sighed. "I should. It is why I was up there so long. Although I am a pretty good systems engineer, I could not even begin until I spent countless hours studying the system specifications as well as trying to understood the basics of the sideshift principle."

Jan Buraka asked from the floor, "Pat, in language we can understand, can you tell us what you did?"

"In language you can understand," Coestrand echoed doubtfully. She hesitated.

Buraka laughed. "We are not morons, you know. Just don't swamp us with equations!"

"As if I could!" Coestrand flashed back with her brilliant smile. "All right, try this on for size. In its former configuration, sideshift caused the *Star Venturer* to emit an expanding shell of energy which acted like the wake of a ship passing through water. That wake was powerful enough to suck the unwary along with it. Hence our unwelcome hitchhiker, Eonay. To avoid a repetition of that disaster, Konnenen and I modified the drive's power cells so they will re-absorb most of that energy even as it is generated. Not only does the modification reduce the ship's profile to near zero as it passes through any alternate continuum, it recovers megawatts of power which would otherwise be lost. I should add, by the way, that reduction of the physiological effects is a byproduct of that process."

As Coestrand finally escaped from the platform and returned to her seat, again Ella pointed to someone in the audience. "All right Richard, I know you have something to say. So come up here and say it."

There was a murmur of anticipation as Burret rose from beside his wife and made his way to the platform. Never a leader in the political sense, his role throughout the brief yet eventful history of the colony had elevated him to a status which in a more primitive society would make him a revered elder. Uncomfortably aware of that status, resenting it and at the same time tolerating it because he knew it was a necessary role, Burret did his best as the community's unofficial guru, along with his regular duties as farmer, meteorologist and husband.

Yet with all these burdens, plus those he knew were to come, Burret savored a comfortable sense of *belonging* as he turned and faced his friends. Along with their tears, laughter, failures, and triumphs, this galactically isolated group of human beings were, after all, as much family as anyone would want or indeed could cope with.

"Three years ago," he began, "three entities sacrificed themselves so we would no longer be threatened by the thing we knew as Tin Lady. Since then, I think you will agree life has been pretty good to us. We have expanded our little community, modified the medical clinic so it now has the facilities of a small hospital, established a school, and consolidated services such as water, waste treatment and power. Even I have found time as a meteorologist to begin to make sense of the weather patterns of this planet of a multiple star system. Through it all we have not forgotten our continuing obligations to both groups of custodians—" he nodded in the direction of the spindly aliens in the shadows at the back of the room, "—who finally show signs they may be ready to break free from the stultifying routines they have been following for generations."

As if reacting to an invisible signal, one of the catbirds took off from a bony shoulder and flew across the room to Burret. It landed on his shoulder and settled there contentedly. Its large eyes glowed as they surveyed the audience.

Burret stroked the catbird's head, and it produced a soft warble. "Of course, it has helped that we and the custodians have mutual friends."

The comment was rewarded with several smiles, as catbirds on human shoulders warbled and preened.

Burret continued, "As I said, since Tin Lady we have done reasonably well. But what about the home world and just about the entire human race? Why aren't they talking to us? They may be a generation removed, but they are still our people aren't they? So do we stay here and pretend we don't give a damn, or do we take the *Star Venturer* and seek answers, perhaps even persuade the current Earth government it is time they sent us a few more colonists? The harvest is in and our infrastructure is sound, so surely we can afford a few people for a less than a year." He gazed around the room. "Comments? Opinions?"

"A few, huh?" The Mayor looked thoughtful.

"There is no point depleting the colony any more than we need to, even for a few months."

"Your wife spoke to me this morning."

"Er...oh?"

"She informed me the two of you would certainly go."

"She did?"

As Burret looked bewilderedly at the empty chair where his wife had been baby sitting only moments ago, a determined redhead came from behind him, tapped his shoulder and said sweetly, "Thank you, dear. I knew you would agree."

As he looked from his wife's expression of feigned innocence, to the broad grins on the faces of his fellow colonists, Burret realized he had been thoroughly outflanked. It was obvious Joan had taken a straw poll and determined the answer even before the question was asked. They were childless in any case, and Burret's specialty as a meteorologist and Joan's as the community psychologist would be adequately represented among the trainees.

He took a deep breath. "Anyone else?"

Patrice Coestrand jumped to her feet. "Me of course! Without your resident sideshift expert along to constantly fine-tune the systems, you may have to resort to the deepsleep chambers if you expect to survive the next fifty years at sub-light!"

Pat isn't the only expert! flashed through Burret's mind. But he wisely restrained himself from putting the thought into words as he remembered the almost-disaster triggered by a previous version of the software known as Gervaise Konnenen. He glanced at Joan, who nodded. "Your decision, dear. I am only your boss in domestic matters."

Burret looked back at Coestrand. "In that case, *Captain* Coestrand, welcome aboard."

Acknowledging the emphasis, Coestrand responded formally, "Thank you. It will be a privilege to serve."

Burret looked again at the rows of faces. "Anyone else? We can get along with three I suppose, but..."

What happened next was unexpected. The catbird on Burret's shoulder chirruped as both custodians emerged from the shadows. The catbird on the second custodian's shoulder chirruped back as the two stalked solemnly across the room and ascended the platform. A long arm extended and the creature fluttered from Burret's shoulder to its master's. A skeletal hand reached up and stroked the catbird.

"I we go," the first custodian intoned.

Burret stared with astonishment.

"I we go," the second custodian echoed.

The words were croaked from inadequately used vocal chords, along with a blast of feeling which left Burret reeling.

What the...!

Someone clutched his arm. "Richard!"

Burret blinked at his wife. "You felt it?"

She nodded and gestured at the audience, who were displaying varying degrees of confusion. "It seems we all did."

"The custodians—"

"—are John and Joe," Su Lan called as she ran up to the platform. "Or is it Joe and John? I am still not sure which, but they don't seem to care."

"At this moment, neither do I," Mayor Shire muttered as she steadied herself against the back of a chair. She cleared her throat. "Will someone please explain what just happened?"

Shand DeVincie jumped to his feet. "What *happened?* What kind of dumb question is that?" The former Space Force colonel glared angrily around him, then at the custodians. "Those two are supposed to be dumb as posts. They shouldn't be able to do that!"

"Do what?" Su Lan queried mildly. "Shand, what are you trying to say?"

"It's what they did and what they said as they did it! It's what they, uh..." DeVincie grew red.

"Empathed?" the girl asked innocently.

DeVincie almost exploded. "Empathed! Yes, that's the word. They screwed around inside our heads!"

"I know, and isn't it wonderful?" Su Lan's dark eyes sparkled with excitement. "Eric and I have worked so long with them, with so little apparent progress, I was beginning to wonder if we will ever persuade the custodians there is more to life than ritual. Shand, I don't know how to begin to explain what we just experienced, except perhaps a door to ancestral talents and memories just cracked open. But it certainly emphasized their desire to return into space!"

Su Lan turned to Burret and grasped one of his hands within both of hers. "Richard, you must take them with you to Earth, their catbirds as well." Her grip became almost painful. "The trip may just be the catalyst the custodians need!"

As Burret finally freed his hand and flexed his fingers, there was the squeak of a chair pushed back as Su Lan's husband stood up and said firmly, "I agree."

Physically, Eric Gerenson was not the person he had been three years before. Outdoor work had hardened and broadened him, and his eyes were clear. But in addition to being the acknowledged expert on the relationship the custodians once had with the ship-entities, he was Su Lan's loyal backup. He continued, "Custodians are a communal species after all, which means what happens to one is ultimately shared by all. So if you take John and Joe, they will be more than merely the representatives of their people. In a very real sense they will *be* their people! Anyway, because of what Vuonar and Keltah did for us, can we do any less than give this chance to their..." Gerenson hesitated. "children?"

So it was decided.

✣ ✣ ✣

Three weeks later, crewed by three humans, two custodians, two catbirds, and a computer program called Gervaise Konnenen, the *Star Venturer* departed from Genser's World.

Destination: Earth.

CHAPTER FORTY-SIX

● ●

"_Do not land here. If you are healthy and want to stay that way, DO NOT LAND!_"

"Healthy? What is he talking about?"

"I have not the faintest idea. Perhaps they have some kind of disease down there, and don't want to infect us."

The static was fierce, the voice hoarse and wavering. On the screen, the Martian deserts, canyons and uplands rolled majestically below the orbiting starship. It was exactly as they had seen countless times on data disks from Curtis's library.

They could not land anyway. Even if they had a shuttle, its wings would be totally inadequate in the thin Martian atmosphere. It was a fact Coestrand chose to ignore as she repeated, "This is the _Star Venturer_ from Genser's World. Why can't we land? What is wrong?"

Gervaise Konnenen popped into existence. Like her predecessors, she had given up the pretense of moving about the ship like a flesh-and-blood person. "I have detected a visual. It is weak, but I can produce a recognizable image."

Coestrand nodded. "Please do what you can."

Burret and Joan peered over Coestrand's shoulders as the grainy image of an emaciated man appeared on the screen. Completely hairless, sweat-streaked and dirty, the man looked like a hollow-eyed victim of some tyrant's death camp. Behind him, an equally emaciated woman in stained coveralls and with a ragged kerchief wrapped around where her hair would have been, stood with a claw-like hand on the man's shoulder.

"You can't be the Venturer. *Hell, I was at Copernicus Base when she orbited out a quarter century ago!"*

"My name is Patrice Coestrand. Does that ring a bell?"

The woman leaned forward and whispered in the man's ear.

"The wife tells me Coestrand was the captain. But just saying you are..."

"It doesn't matter," Burret interjected. "What is wrong down there? And why can't we raise Earth?"

"Hey, you have been away haven't you?" The man laughed. The laugh was hoarse and without mirth. *"It makes me feel almost good to tell you those bastards got their comeuppance years ago!"*

"What are you talking about?"

"There are only seventeen of us left now, out of what used to be a nice little community of nearly two hundred. It's not an easy way to die, but at least we know they got a taste of their own poison before the big rock finished the job. So if you are who you say you are, I suggest that before you tuck your tails inboard and hightail back to Genser's or wherever, you contact the folks on Luna. They will tell you the whole, sorry story. Anyway, don't want to talk anymore. Me, Alice and what's left of us got some dyin' to do."

They tried repeatedly to resume contact, with no success. They remained for another two orbits, on each pass examining under highest magnification the site of the human settlement on Sinai Planum, just south of the gigantic rift Valles Marineris. The dome was clearly visible, casting its shadow across the plain. Next to it was another structure, which Konnenen identified as a ship.

"It is large, possibly a bulk carrier. Preliminary indications are it is severely damaged, I assume because of a bad landing. It is tilted several degrees from the vertical."

"Meaning it isn't going anywhere," Burret surmised.

The white head inclined. "It is a valid assumption."

Burret was still in the process of getting used to this clone of the program which, during its previous incarnation, almost persuaded him it was human. But he also remembered the caricature which was Tin Lady, a ghost which in his mind was not entirely exorcised. Just as well, he thought. When a machine acquires human characteristics, it stops being a machine. And he was never comfortable giving orders to people.

"Perhaps the sun is in the way," Joan suggested. "I mean, isn't Earth on the far side of its orbit from here?"

Coestrand shook her head. "It doesn't work that way. There are dozens of still functioning robotic relays all over the system." She tapped keys and peered at data scrolling across a screen. "Gervaise, can we sideshift over planetary distances? To Earth, for instance?"

The hologram floated up behind her. "It is possible in theory, although it will require precise timing."

"Can you handle it?"

"How close do you wish to approach?"

"Not too close. Just enough to reduce months of travel time to a few days."

Konnenen frowned, causing Joan to turn to her husband and whisper, "She even looks like she is thinking."

His grin was sour. "Good, isn't she?"

There was a fluttering of wings, and both custodians and their catbirds entered the control deck. "This sad place," John (or Joe) announced. "We say leave now."

"What makes you say it is sad?" Joan asked, hoping to prompt any kind of reply yet not expecting one. It was the catbirds of course, those empathic extensions of two beings who themselves were so connected they were like Earth's legendary Corsican brothers; one itched, the other scratched. Although the vocabulary of the pair remained limited, she suspected their minds were opening up faster than they let on. Along with their shoulder-born symbiots they roamed the ship, never in the way, just watching and absorbing. Yet Joan was sure there was nothing sinister in their wanderings. How could there be, with the ever present and friendly catbirds? She reached out and rubbed a furry head. The catbird warbled pleasantly.

"Leave now," John repeated, regarding her solemnly. Joe added, "Go to Luna."

"They don't miss much, do they?" Coestrand whispered.

Joan nodded. "It seems that way."

Konnenen said, "I am ready. When do you wish to engage sideshift?"

The three humans looked at each other. "I suppose there is no point continuing to orbit this depressing planet," Coestrand sighed as she glanced through a port at the ocher landscapes of the fourth planet.

"No point at all," Burret agreed. His wife nodded.

Coestrand shrugged, turned to Konnenen. "All right, Gervaise. Get us to Earth."

The universe twisted.

✢ ✢ ✢

It was like a high speed collision averted a split second before disaster. For a few seconds the heart raced, there was a lead weight in the pit of the stomach and the skin was clammy. But it was an order of magnitude better than it had been before the modifications, when sideshift felt as if the body was explosively disassembled and then reassembled in an equally agonizing implosion.

Astonishingly, as if they were born to it, neither the custodians nor their catbirds seemed to feel a thing during sideshift transition. So as the humans pulled themselves together, breathing deeply and smoothing down their clothes, four pairs of alien eyes regarded them incuriously.

Coestrand took a deep breath. "Wow!"

"I would still rather have a tooth pulled," Joan complained.

Her husband chuckled. "It was your idea to take it standing up. Remember?"

Joan made a face. "You just couldn't resist that, could you?" She made her way to a port and looked out. Among the stars were two bright disks.

"We are approaching from the sunward side," Konnenen reported. "Luna is closest, distance two point one million kilometers."

Coestrand was already seated before a screen. "Let's look at Earth." Burret and Joan looked over her shoulders, as she set the crosshairs and thumbed the zoom control.

As the image enlarged to reveal details, they gasped with horror.

The planet was completely enveloped with cloud, almost featureless except for dark gray splotches scattered across the visible hemisphere. Konnenen said conversationally, "I have analyzed the atmosphere and determined it is the result of a major asteroid impact, at least equivalent in energy release to the event which occurred at the end of the Cretaceous."

"The one which destroyed the dinosaurs," Coestrand whispered. She swallowed. "Ca ... can there be anything down there? Anyone?"

"It is unlikely. Only the most primitive life forms would survive such an impact."

"That man on Mars said something about a big rock..."

"We received Earth's final signal three years ago. So allowing for the four plus years it took for the signal to reach Genser's World, the strike has to have occurred somewhere between seven and eight years ago."

"My God," Burret whispered as he and the two women gazed at what had been a world of oceans, jungles, deserts, prairies, and snow-clad mountains. Also a world of cities, where millions of human beings had lived and worked in towers which touched the sky. He remembered sparrows, tail-wagging dogs, bald eagles, friendly dolphins, and not-so-friendly mosquitoes. He remembered the magnificent lion and the lowly mouse. He remembered the bracing cold of winter and the golden colors of fall.

Gone.

He remembered Cheryl and her children's children. His own great-grandchildren.

Gone.

✢ ✢ ✢

Burret's cheeks were wet, which made him feel ashamed. Then he was ashamed of being ashamed. Coestrand was huddled forward, her face in her hands. Joan had buried her face against his chest and was shaking. He put an arm about his wife, while he awkwardly used his free hand to pat Coestrand's shoulder.

There was a thump on his own shoulder, and a furry head nuzzled his cheek. The second catbird did its best to comfort Coestrand.

Burret felt a light touch, and turned his head. The two custodians had moved close.

"We know," one said.

Of course they knew. As their kind were all who were left of an ancient and proud species; so Burret, Joan, Coestrand, and the few on Genser's World were now all who were left of...

An ancient species?

Compared with the custodians; hardly.

A proud species?

Remembering what the dying man on Mars told them, Burret wondered dispiritedly if what was left of his own species had anything left to be proud about.

CHAPTER FORTY-SEVEN

● ●

A few minutes later, Konnenen announced, "Luna is trying to contact us. Are you ready to respond?"

Burret cleared his throat as he forced his numbed mind into gear. "Luna? The moon?"

"They call themselves Lunites."

Joan's glistening eyes were wide. "Luna. What that man on Mars said."

Coestrand dabbed her eyes and straightened her shoulders. "How long have they been trying?"

"For eighteen minutes. The person is called Martin. I told him you had just seen Earth, and he asked me to tell you he understands."

"I bet he does," Burret said grimly. "All right, put him on."

The screen cleared to reveal the image of a youngish man with thinning hair and a rich, dark beard. "I am Councilor Martin Kroetzer. Welcome to Luna." His voice was a rumbling bass with a slight trace of accent.

"Richard Burret of Genser's World. We came here to find out why Earth stopped transmitting." Burret's expression became bleak. "Now we know."

The Lunite nodded sympathetically. "I am sorry you learned the truth the way you did. Nevertheless I am happy to inform you there remains a thriving community of nearly nine thousand human beings here on Luna, which I hope you will visit now you are in the neighborhood. How many are you?"

Joan asked, "Do you have animals?"

"Of course." Kroetzer did not appear surprised by the question. "Aside from the usual pets, dogs, cats, and so on, our zoo has breeding specimens from many of Earth's smaller species. Why do you ask that question? Do you have pets on board your ship?"

"Allow me to introduce my companions." Burret moved aside from the camera lens so the Lunite could see Joan and Coestrand, who in turn stood aside to reveal the custodians and their symbiots.

Kroetzer's poise and voice failed him, as he stared with astonishment.

"That is Patrice Coestrand, the captain of our ship *Star Venturer*, and this is my wife Joan Walsh. Our passengers are called custodians. They and their catbirds are our friends and completely benign. But if you would rather not..."

The Lunite found his voice. "No, no, you are all welcome! Forgive me, I have never seen an extraterrestrial before. Are they native to your world?"

"It is a long story I would rather relate in person."

"Of course, as I am sure you wish to know the details of our recent tragic history. Anyway, we will have a shuttle fueled and waiting when you arrive in orbit. Kroetzer out."

Joan let out her breath in a long sigh. "At this moment, I do not doubt he is summoning his friends to witness a playback."

"As would I," Coestrand said. She shook her head in disbelief. "You know, I am still trying to get used to their numbers. Nine thousand! When we orbited out, there were only a few hundred!"

"The man seems pleasant enough." Joan turned to the silent custodians. "Will you come? Or would you rather remain here?"

"Come," they said in unison. The catbirds bobbed in agreement.

✤ ✤ ✤

The shuttle was a chunky vehicle which made Burret wonder if the design was inspired by NASA's first lunar landers. Attached to a propulsion module which was an untidy complex of fuel tanks and protruding adjustable rocket nozzles, was a box-like cargo/passenger module fitted with top and side-mounted airlocks, plus assorted protrusions of a more enigmatic nature. The complex, which mated to the *Star Venturer* with hardly a jar, was piloted by Councilor Kroetzer.

The Lunite entered the starship almost reverently. Clad in a gray tailored jumpsuit, he was taller than they expected. "Fascinating," he said as he looked around the control deck. Although he tried not to be obvious, his eyes kept turning toward the custodians. "Fascinating," he repeated, then looked embarrassed. "Sorry. It is not every day..."

Joan took Kroetzer's arm and lifted it toward one of the catbirds. Without hesitation, the creature hopped onto Kroetzer's arm and then up to his shoulder. It made contented noises.

"It just told us you are friendly," Coestrand said. She smiled. "Catbirds are empathic."

The Lunite hesitatingly lifted his hand. "Can I?"

"By all means. They thrive on affection."

As its master looked on, the catbird allowed itself to be caressed. Kroetzer was clearly enjoying himself. "Do you have any more?"

"Only on Genser's World."

"That is too bad." The Lunite reluctantly allowed the creature to return to its master. "I hope you will stay long enough so we can get to know each other." He smiled. "That is an invitation, of course."

"Which we gladly accept. Thank you." Still wondering when Kroetzer or his friends would put two and two together and decide the *Star Venturer* had a faster-than-light drive, Burret asked, "Where is your community?"

"Actually, we have three. Verne, where we are going, is in Copernicus. Wells is located on the Korolev plain, at Farside. The third and smallest community occupies what you knew as the Academy facility in Eratosthenes. It has since been renamed Paoli Base."

The ride down was gentle. Even the catbirds, who were notorious for their dislike of confined spaces, were content on the custodians shoulders during the brief changes of altitude and the final bump as the shuttle touched down. Like an elevator on an old aircraft carrier, the landing pad lowered the shuttle into a huge cavern, where a traveling crane lifted the payload module away from the drive section, trundled it over assorted machinery and parked spacecraft, and finally deposited it in a brightly lit reception bay.

About a dozen people were waiting as the star-travelers emerged from the module's side air lock. Although none of the Lunites were identically dressed, they seemed to have a taste for subdued colors, especially of grays, browns, and greens. A tall, graceful woman separated from the group and came forward. Kroetzer introduced her.

"Florence Nuemann, First Councilor."

Burret wondered if he should shake hands; decided against it. "First Councilor?"

Nuemann smiled. "Think of me as Luna's current Prime Minister." Her voice was a soft, pleasantly modulated contralto.

"John Van Paulson, Second Councilor and chair of the Technical Development Committee."

Paulson was elderly, with a round face and inquisitive brown eyes. He barely acknowledged Kroetzer's introductions as he stared at the custodians. "Oh my," he murmured with barely suppressed excitement. "Oh my."

"Councilor Camden Reed..."

As the introductions went on, Joan whispered to her husband, "Nuemann. Who does she remind you of?"

Burret had been thinking the same thing. "Excuse me, First Councilor..."

"Florence. Please."

"All right. Florence, you look remarkably like one of the designers of our ship."

"Referring to Gervaise Konnenen, no doubt. She was my grandmother on my father's side."

"That explains it. She programmed the ship's computer with her image and a good deal of her personality. We almost think of the simulation as a full member of the crew."

"It does not surprise me. Gervaise was noted for a quirky sense of humor."

They were ushered aboard a small open-top bus. Burret found himself sitting next to Nuemann, while the others from *Star Venturer* were also each seated next to a Lunite. "Route Eight," Nuemann dictated into a wristcom. "Go." With a soft electric hum, the computer-controlled bus passed through huge airlock doors into a street lined with flowering trees. "Just a brief tour," the First Councilor explained. "Do you mind?"

"We welcome it."

It was a fascinating fifteen minutes. Excavated through the rock below the Copernicus crater, Verne was laid out in concentric circles of avenues with intersecting streets which radiated out from a central cavern known appropriately as The Hub. Windows of offices, work places and homes looked out on thoroughfares active with pedestrians, a few people on bicycles and an occasional electric runabout. The bus was politely ignored as it went by, although smaller children shouted with glee as they saw the custodians and the large-eyed creatures riding their shoulders.

They finally entered and circuited The Hub, a park-like area which contained trees, flowers, walks, a small lake, and even a fountain cascading with glittering deliberation in the lunar gravity. A holo-simulated blue sky with drifting white clouds completed the illusion of an old fashioned town square of a time and place which no longer existed. The bus stopped at the far side of the park, next to a door marked with the simple legend: COUNCIL.

After an opportunity to 'freshen up' as guide Kroetzer put it, the visitors were ushered into a large room lined with pictures of Earth as it once was. Alpine scenes competed with seascapes and bustling city centers, deserts, and forests. The images included holograms, 2D photographs, paintings, and even a few tapestries. It was nostalgia from floor to ceiling and wall to wall. Hosts and guests sat around a long simwood table, while the custodians disdained chairs and stood easily in the light gravity. As if seeking a change, the catbirds changed shoulders. One alighted on Coestrand's shoulder. The other chose a Lunite councilor, a tiny woman identified as Councilor Merimee Karnott. Delighted, Karnott stroked the creature. "Do you think they could adjust to a sub-surface environment?" she asked wistfully, looking at the custodians.

"Not," they said in unison.

Karnott nodded, although she did not hide her disappointment.

The First Councilor rose to her feet. "Before we begin, there are a couple of, ah, matters which must be clarified."

There was a palpable rise of tension. The catbirds meowed and fluttered nervously, while the councilors looked grim.

"First. We know about your ship's sideshift interstellar drive."

Burret was relieved. "I am not surprised. We expected you would figure that one out, although..." his eyes widened. "Sideshift! You know about that?"

"There are records. Not the technical specifications, which were destroyed in the reactor explosion along with the people working on the project. But enough was retained in other databases to reveal that 'sideshift' was somehow connected with overcoming the light-speed barrier."

Coestrand said doubtfully, "I must tell you it is an extremely complex technology. But if you would like me to talk to your technical people..."

"There is no hurry." Nuemann frowned, then looked faintly surprised. "Is that not known as a pun?"

Burret chuckled. "I am glad we still share a common sense of humor. Anyway, what else were you about to tell us?"

The First Councilor's hands, where they rested on the table, had become clenched. "It can wait." She forced a smile. "In any case, before we get into more weighty matters, you must allow us to do what good hosts are supposed to do, which is serve your first meal on Luna. I anticipate you will be pleasantly surprised by the variety of our cuisine."

Burret wondered at the abrupt change of subject. Whatever was 'weighty' was clearly something which made their hosts uncomfortable. He hoped it was not some silly social custom inherited from Earth, such as a nudity taboo or something involving public relationships between the sexes. The Lunites were sophisticates who surely would not allow minor cultural irritants to disturb the promise of friendship.

Coestrand asked, "Do you have farms? Or is all your food synthesized?"

"Both. We could synthesize everything I suppose, but hydroponics produce more than enough for human consumption as well as for our animals. By the way, remind me to introduce you to our dairy cattle. They are an intelligent, miniature species who are pets as well as milk producers. We also have chickens, who are not as smart of course. So if you would like eggs and bacon for breakfast, you only have to ask."

Joan's eyebrows rose. "Bacon? From pigs?"

The Lunites looked shocked, especially Councilor Karnott who said indignantly, "Synthesized, of course! All living things on Luna, including the higher forms of plant life such as trees, shrubs, and flowers, are allowed to live their life spans as part of a living community."

Interesting, Burret thought. On half-starved old Earth, such a reverence for living things had been restricted to certain religious groups, some environmentalists, and those wealthy enough to live apart from the hungry masses. The theory was fine, the practice sadly restricted.

Here on Luna, practice and theory had converged into a way of life which was perhaps not so surprising for a community whose survival, at least in the beginning, depended on a fragile balance in which every component, animate as well as inanimate, was vital to the success of the whole.

Perhaps here was a lesson to be learned and taken back to Genser's World, where the ugly phrase 'exploitation of available resources' was still not entirely removed from the lexicon.

✢ ✢ ✢

As promised, the meal was excellent. Some flavors were familiar, others were not, yet the whole was at least as satisfying as any meal the Burrets and Coestrand could remember from some of the finest restaurants on Earth. The exclusively vegetarian custodians ate from bowls of fruit and unseasoned salads. Afterwards the visitors were shown into guest quarters which contained two sleeping rooms as well as a bathroom and common room.

Too keyed up to go to bed, the three humans remained in the common room while they discussed the events of the past few hours. The two custodians and their catbird symbiots watched and listened.

"I like these Lunites," Joan declared.

Coestrand nodded. "Me too. They are innocents in a sense, but with an element of depth."

Burret frowned. "Depth?"

"Depth, smarts, or whatever else you want to call it. After all, they have evolved a closed culture that can afford a lifestyle which on Earth existed only in monasteries and communes. That can only come with knowledge of the technological knife-edge which makes it possible. In such an environment, you do not take anything for granted."

Joan mused, "Except for those poor souls on Mars, and us on Genser's World, they are the last remnant of the human race. Have you thought of that?" She made a vague gesture. "As a member of the species, I wouldn't *want* them to take anything for granted!"

"Amen to that," her husband said fervently.

"They few," John (or Joe) said.

"Like us," Joe (or John) said.

Whatever else they were or were not, the custodians were natural minimalists.

CHAPTER
FORTY-EIGHT

● ●

The next four days passed pleasantly, as the Burrets and Patricia Coestrand were treated like visiting heads of state. Even John and Joe became accepted to the extent they were allowed to wander on their own through the streets of the sub-surface community, where they inevitably attracted a trail of children who excitedly vied for the privilege of bearing a catbird on a small arm or shoulder.

The catbirds did not seem to mind. In fact, perhaps realizing their role as small feathered ambassadors, they hopped from child to child as if to give as many as possible the benefit of their company.

The first hint all was not well in this subterranean paradise was revealed by Coestrand on the fourth evening, when she explained why she had been mysteriously absent most of the day. "I hitched a ride on a supply run to Paoli Base."

"Our old stomping ground under Eratosthenes?"

Coestrand nodded. "They have a life-size replica of Doctor Paoli there, in a lecturing pose."

Joan chuckled. "He would have liked that. He was always lecturing us on one thing or another. What else did you see?"

"I suspect you would hardly recognize the place. It's mostly a research and teaching facility now, much as it was during the U.N. Academy days. Anyway, did you know there is an abandoned complex of nine missile silos accessible from the base via a two hundred meter tunnel?"

Burret frowned. "It is the first I have heard of it. How long has it been there?"

"Apparently, since even before the Academy's time. The complex was deactivated and sealed off when the control rooms and living quarters were expanded to accommodate the Academy. The Lunites uncovered the tunnel and found the complex while they were working on their own revisions."

"I wonder if Curtis knew about it."

"I haven't the faintest idea. If he did, I gather he did not tell you people about it."

"What was its purpose?" Joan wondered. "A Damoclean sword to keep national groups on Earth in line? Asteroid diversion?"

Coestrand shuddered. "I hate to think it was the former, although I suppose it explains the secrecy."

Burret demurred. "Not necessarily. Even if the sole purpose was insurance against a possible asteroid strike, it could be there was a majority of politicians who did not want it to be public knowledge. Aside from the cost, which is the sort of thing politicians hate to explain, there was the possibility that to some scare-mongers the existence of such a facility would be the same as admitting the big one *is* coming."

"Are the missiles still there?" Joan asked.

"Eight of them, lacking warheads and unfueled. They are just shells now. It's an old technology and quite fascinating."

"What about the ninth silo?"

"Empty."

"Empty?"

"I opened a hatch and clambered inside. The walls are scorched from rocket exhaust. Whatever used to be there, was launched."

Bewildered, Burret blinked at the captain. "Launched? Where?"

"I asked myself that, too." Her expression somber, Coestrand returned his gaze. "Think about it, Richard. What that fellow on Mars said about the big rock. Remember?"

Joan took a deep breath, let it out in a long shuddering sigh. "I remember. I also remember our first meeting with the council, when Nuemann muttered something about 'weighty matters' before she clammed up."

With a sickening sense of realization, Burret whispered, "I think we just found a smoking gun."

✢ ✢ ✢

"What made you suspect?" Nuemann asked. The First Councilor seemed almost relieved, as did her colleagues.

"You used only one missile, which implies you planned and calculated very carefully. Considering what happened to Earth, the most likely scenario is that the missile's target was an already incoming mineral-rich asteroid on course for orbital insertion. A megaton or two nudge while the rock was still a few dozen million kilometers away..." Coestrand shrugged. "It would not take much."

"Not much?" Van Paulson shook his head. "You overestimate our capabilities, Captain. In the time available, it took every resource we had to assemble just one fusion warhead, as well as construct and program a guidance unit. Even the missile itself required major work to make it flight worthy."

"All done along with considerable debate of the pros and cons, I do not doubt." Joan Walsh did not attempt to hide her disgust.

"Considerable debate," Florence Nuemann agreed. She added sadly, "In the end, there was not a single dissenting vote.

"I am curious," Burret said. "Why did you use a missile, when you could have transported the warhead aboard one of your ships?"

"Poetic justice because Earth installed the missiles here in the first place? To avoid concentrating the guilt on the shoulders of a single space pilot? Does it matter, Mr. Burret? You heard that man on Mars. Our cause was not only just, but necessary."

"He and all the others on Mars were dying. *Were you?*"

The question hung in the air unanswered. As the councilors sat in embarrassed silence, the catbirds squawked in disgust and returned to the bony shoulders of the custodians.

"A wrongness," said John (or Joe).

"A wrongness," agreed Joe (or John).

CHAPTER
FORTY-NINE

• •

It was never known who released the virus. Terrorists perhaps, who assumed God would save them to establish Paradise in what was left. Or it was an accident, the result of an error in a forgotten lab in a forgotten city on what used to be a cloud-dappled sphere called Earth.

Thousands died, then millions. It seemed no one was immune. Fratricidal conflicts swept the planet, adding to the carnage and destroying what chance there was to develop and then mass-produce an antidote. Space launch facilities were overrun by terrified mobs seeking transport to Luna or even to Mars. Vital equipment was ruined. Shuttles remained on their pads for lack of fuel, as well as for lack of the personnel who could launch them. Meanwhile a carrier which had been on its way for months, parachuted its shock-protected palettes down to the colony on the fourth planet, then de-orbited and crash landed near the dome.

Its crew of three men and two women emerged and asked for asylum.

A few days later, the colonists began to die.

✤ ✤ ✤

A floating mountain of valuable minerals, the rock was already on its way toward eventual capture by the Earth-moon system. It had been displaced from its orbit in the asteroid belt by a series of precisely timed and placed nuclear detonations.

Watching the Armageddon in their sky and aware of the threat to their own pristine world, the frightened Lunites decided to end that threat once and for all. Their missile intercepted the rock while it was still ninety million kilometers distant in the direction of Aquarius. Although the twenty megaton explosion was only a brief spark in the Lunar sky, it was enough to nudge the rock slightly off course.

It impacted in the South China Sea.

CHAPTER FIFTY

● ●

The visit, which visitors and hosts anticipated might last months, was over in less than a week. There was no official leave-taking, no ceremony. The humans and aliens from Genser's World simply repacked their bags and departed.

Again Kroetzer was the shuttle pilot, although during ascent and then docking to the orbiting starship, he said nothing and concentrated on his instruments. After he followed his equally silent passengers into the control deck of the *Star Venturer*, he said, "You will not need to worry about us, you know."

Burret turned and looked at him. "No? Why not?"

Kroetzer smiled sadly. Unlike the other councilors, there was no shame in his direct gaze. Only sorrow. "We Lunites understand how you feel. But when time and the light-years have diminished your outrage, I am sure you will understand and perhaps even sympathize. After all, if we did not do what we did, it is entirely possible we would be facing the same terrible fate as those at Marsbase."

Joan countered angrily, "Yes, but enough people on Earth might have survived to begin rebuilding!"

"I grant that possibility. But unfortunately there were too many maniacs, too much unpredictability, and they were too close. We made our choice, and have to live with it."

By themselves the words were callous. But there was no mistaking the intensity of regret with which they were said.

"Go on," Burret said.

"We do not have the sideshift drive, although we recovered enough information from an old database to be aware Konnenen and her colleagues were working on such a system. But even if we did have it, it would be of no use to us. We are a troglodyte people, who are content in our caverns and tunnels. We have no need for the stars."

"You have spacecraft."

"By necessity, not choice. Luna does not provide all our mineral needs, which means we must seek them among the moons and asteroids of the system. We are miners, Mr. Burret. Not explorers."

"I see," Burret said, unconvinced.

The Lunite did not attempt to relieve the Richard's doubts. Instead, a surprising question. "Is your colony expecting further arrivals from Earth?"

Coestrand and the Burrets exchanged puzzled glances. "We were not informed of any," Coestrand answered. "I suppose it is possible plans were made, but..." She grimaced. "Hell, you know what happened!"

"There is a converted asteroid, the *Mayflower Two*, which was launched toward Genser's World a few weeks before the plague. It carries several hundred colonists in stasis."

It was a bombshell. Dumbfounded, Burret and the two women stared at each other, then at the Lunite. Joan took a deep breath. "We were never told. Are you certain?"

"You will have plenty of time to prepare. Being so massive, the *Mayflower* will take half a century to complete its journey. But if you doubt what I have just told you, why not use your sideshift capabilities to check it out? Your computer has already received the appropriate course parameters."

Konnenen flicked into existence. It was the first time she had appeared before Kroetzer, and the Lunite's expression was one of wonder as he stared at the apparition. "You are exactly like the pictures of Florence Nuemann's grandmother!"

Konnenen inclined her white head in acknowledgment. "According to those parameters, the asteroid is less than thirteen light hours from Sol and still early in its acceleration phase. I do not anticipate interception will be a problem."

"In that case I will remove my unwelcome presence," Kroetzer said.

Burret accompanied the Lunite down from the control deck to the docking interface. Just before he entered the shuttle, Kroetzer turned and held out his hand. Burret hesitated a moment, then accepted it. They shook solemnly.

"Thank you," Kroetzer said.

Burret nodded. "I doubt you and I will meet again. In fact I am certain of it. But I cannot speak for future generations."

"Neither of us can, can we?"

"Exactly." Burret stood looking at the sealed lock until he heard the docking clamps release, then returned to the control deck. He was met by one of the catbirds, which landed on his shoulder and warbled sympathetically.

"Sad," its master said.

"Sad," Burret agreed. He looked at the two women. "I am getting almost tired of asking this question. Do we go?"

Coestrand nodded. "If you mean to the *Mayflower*, of course. They are our future citizens, aren't they?"

"If there is such a ship," Joan said doubtfully. She shrugged. "But why not? Considering our lack of time on Luna, we have a few weeks in hand."

"If it wasn't for..." Coestrand began, then added wistfully, "Verne was such a nice town."

CHAPTER
FIFTY-ONE

● ●

It was a lumpy, cratered lozenge about four hundred meters long and half that across. The fusion drive, a pulsating spark at the narrow end, looked totally inadequate to propel a twenty million ton asteroid across the interstellar void. But it would work for centuries with a continuous supply of reaction mass, which in this case was the material of the asteroid itself.

The minuscule acceleration was such that the *Star Venturer* weighed only a few kilograms as it drifted to gentle contact and was anchored by explosive bolts fired into the rock. Coestrand suited up, went outside and spent more than an hour pulling herself across the surface via a network of cables the builders had strung around the forward half of the asteroid like a gigantic hair net. Burret and his wife waited anxiously until the captain returned.

"Very convenient and a damn good idea," the smaller woman said about the cables as she unlatched and removed her helmet. "I found the entrance lock, or one of them anyway. The external controls are conventional, so I anticipate no problem gaining access." She looked at Burret. "Are you ready?"

"As much as I will ever be," the man muttered reluctantly as he picked up his own helmet. He had never liked EVA's, although like everyone else who rode the starships he was qualified.

Konnenen appeared. "I have completed the initial scan. The stasis vaults, associated equipment and living areas are accessed via the lock you investigated, plus a similar one on the far side. Those forward chambers are connected to the drive section by an access tunnel along the long axis. There is one area which I have been unable to scan. It may be rock with high metal content, although it is remarkably localized. As further information becomes available, I will let you know."

"Radiation levels?" Coestrand asked.

"Within acceptable limits. The drive core is adequately shielded."

"Then let's go."

"Be careful," Joan said as she leaned over the bulky neck ring to kiss her husband.

"Careful," echoed both custodians.

Careful, emoted the catbirds.

Despite his initial misgivings, Burret began to enjoy himself as hand-over-hand he pulled himself along behind Coestrand. The sun, by far the brightest star among an ocean of stars, was soon eclipsed by the bulk of the asteroid as they approached the metal protrusion which was the air lock. Coestrand's helmet light wavered as she peered beyond the lock and found the external controls. Grasping a hold bar attached to the lock, she flipped open a panel, reached inside and pulled a handle. The outer door slid ponderously aside and they floated into the lock. It was large, with room for four suited astronauts. Coestrand activated another control, the outer door closed behind them and there was a faint hissing which increased in volume as the lock pressurized. The inner door opened, and rows of floropanels flickered into life to illumine a corridor which receded into the distance.

Coestrand checked her readouts, then opened the front of her helmet. Burret followed suit. The air was cool but fresh.

"We are inside," Coestrand reported.

"*Good*," Joan responded from the ship. "*Any problems?*"

"Not so far. But this is a lot of asteroid."

"I know. Keep talking so I know what you two are up to."

Burret chuckled. "Pat, I think she is telling you and I to behave."

Coestrand, who in other circumstances might have responded with a quip of her own, instead muttered something non-committal. She remained strictly business as she and Burret found dormitories, lounges, a mess hall, and a section of luxurious private suites, each complete with its own bathroom and kitchenette.

"Officers quarters?" Burret wondered. "Even with all this space, it seems a tad elitist."

Coestrand said dryly, "Elitist enough I hope I won't be around when Genser's has to deal with these people half a century from now."

"Are the suites identified?"

"Each has a fancy nameplate on the door," Burret replied. "So far I have spotted Smith, Johnson, Delaney, Davis and a few others. On the other hand, the dormitories are identified by a single letter. We are up to E. Inside, the bunks just carry numbers."

"Are the names all that waspish? Nothing Chinese, Jewish or whatever?"

"You hit the nail on the head, hon. I am not surprised this rock is called *Mayflower.*"

"Wash your mouth out, husband dear. The people of the original Mayflower considered themselves free and equal."

"Meaning they did not carry a bunch of peasants in steerage."

"Something like that."

Burret shared his wife's unease. Clearly there was more to this space-going ark than mere size.

Coestrand called to him from further along the axis corridor. "I found the stasis vaults!"

She was in front of a heavy, double-wide portal recessed into the corridor wall. Left of the portal was a lock-type opening mechanism. On the right, a panel contained the diagram of a layout which looked like locker rooms with most of the lockers individually numbered. A cluster of the lockers were indicated with names.

Burret read aloud some of the names. "Anderson, Bryant, Burgess, Carrington, DeMarney..."

"How many?"

"Of the wasps? I make it thirty-eight out of a total of..." Burret counted the rows and did a little mental arithmetic. "Five hundred and eighteen."

Coestrand pulled down the door operating handle. With a rumble of motors and hidden rollers, the portal slid aside and interior lights came on. Beyond, a hemispherical lobby with nine corridors radiated into the rock of the asteroid. Burret floated across the lobby and pulled himself into one of the corridors. On both sides, gasketted doors of stasis chambers in three rows of ten. Beside each door were green and red indicators. In all cases, only the greens were glowing.

He heard Coestrand's faint call of, "I found a bad one."

Burret followed the sound of her voice to the next corridor. Fifty-nine indicators glowed green. One, near the far end, glowed red. Coestrand said sadly, "Behold one poor devil who will not get to where he hoped he was going."

"They are hardly on their way!" Burret protested. "What can possibly go wrong this early?"

Joan, *"It is usually because of some congenital defect, and almost always during the first few hours after entering stasis. I am surprised that person got through the medical screening."*

"A lengthy and expensive process," Coestrand pointed out.

"So?"

"So maybe they saved themselves a little time and money," the *Star Venturer's* captain commented cynically as she gestured to her companion. "Okay, let's look at the wasps."

The named chambers occupied one entire wall of the center corridor, and part of the opposite wall. The remaining twenty-two chambers were empty.

"Bloody aristocrats," Burret muttered as he glared at the rows of occupied chambers. "They wouldn't even share the same corridor!"

"I have a suggestion."

"Anything sane would be appreciated."

"Revive one of them."

CHAPTER FIFTY-TWO

● ●

Guided by Konnenen, they revived two. The woman had a name. The man was a number.

After the two were partially revived and disconnected from the umbilicals, they were placed inside inflated life support bubbles and towed over the asteroid's surface to the *Star Venturer*, where they were placed in separate cabins. The revival process was then allowed to proceed on its own.

Burret was doubtful. "Won't it do harm to leave them unconnected?"

"You completed the initial and important part of the revival sequence aboard their ship," Konnenen replied. "Although recovery will take a little longer, the process can now proceed without further artificial assistance."

"How long before they can talk?"

"I anticipate the female will be lucid in about an hour, the male shortly thereafter."

Joan and Coestrand looked down at the tall blonde woman on the bunk. "Carmitia Davis," Joan murmured. "What is she in the hierarchy, I wonder?"

Burret jerked his thumb toward the next cabin. "Way above two-two-nine, I wager."

"A blonde goddess and a man who could be a Latino farm laborer. Quite a contrast."

Burret looked critically at the woman's bony length, broad face and square jaw. "Not a goddess. More like a valkyrie."

"Is that what you think? In that case I had better stick around and make sure you don't run off with her to Valhalla."

A little over an hour later, the woman stirred and made a small gasping noise. She swallowed and her eyes flickered open. "Wha...?"

Joan leaned over her. "My name is Joan Walsh. You are on board the *Star Venturer*."

"The..." The woman cleared her throat. "Starship, *Star Venturer?*" Her voice was still slightly hoarse. "Can't be. This is the *Mayflower Two*."

Carmitia Davis took some convincing. But after a few minutes, the woman was sipping from the mandatory nutrient concoction while she tried to absorb the fact she was on board a starship from Genser's World.

"If you wish, we will return you to stasis with your friends," Burret told her. "But first we need to know as much as possible about your vessel and its crew. We were never notified such an undertaking was even in the works."

"I am not surprised," Davis said as she took another careful sip. "After all, we..." Her voice trailed into silence as she became aware of the olive-skinned Coestrand. "If you don't mind, I would rather that person not be present."

Coestrand grinned as she came forward and leaned close to the blonde woman, who flinched back. Coestrand's teeth gleamed white. "This person's name is *Captain* Patrice Coestrand, dearie. Like it or not, I happen to be the one who runs this ship."

Davis stared back, flushed, and her pale gray eyes fell away. "Sorry. I suppose I am still a little confused."

Coestrand nodded and moved back. She mouthed 'racist!' toward Joan, who nodded understandingly.

Burret was doing his best to be patient. "Please continue."

Davis nodded, tried not to look at Coestrand. "The Mayflower project was a private undertaking financed by several hundred of the most influential families in the former United States, Canada, the UK, and Australia. Genser's World was not notified, Mr. Burret, because of the possibility the message might be intercepted by hostile interests. In any case, we intend to establish our colony completely independent from yours, on another continent."

"What is your mandate?"

"A very clear one. We are to preserve the best of human-kind in an environment apart from the increasing chaos on Earth. Our data banks are more complete than most of the great libraries, and our people were selected from a long list of candidates submitted by the families."

"Your people?" Joan queried.

"There are thirty-eight of us. The others are workers."

"I see."

Davis misconstrued Joan's reaction. "We are enough for a viable gene pool!" she said defensively.

Burret muttered something inaudible and turned away. Coestrand asked with deceptive calmness, "How were the workers selected?"

"On the basis of technical skills, physical health, a rea-sonable command of the language, and an acceptance of the need for hard work and discipline. After their ten-year term is complete, they will have the choice of either return-ing to Earth aboard the *Mayflower*, or continuing as freemen on Genser's World." A faint smile. "By then, I doubt any of them will consider Earth an option."

Joan tugged at her husband's arm. "Richard, we still have that systems check to complete. Are you coming?"

Sickened by the atavistic philosophy expressed by the woman, Burret allowed himself to be hauled away. He was only slightly mollified as he heard Coestrand say sweetly, "Now we are alone..."

✣ ✣ ✣

The interview with 229, who told them he used to be Amjud Bessem of Old Los Angeles, was equally unsettling. An agricultural technician unemployed for nearly two years, he felt he had no choice but to accept the offer of enough money to keep his aging parents in reasonable comfort for the rest of their lives.

"I used to have two sisters and a brother, but they are dead. I also had a wife, but she left me when I lost my job. What else could I do?"

"Were you told how long you will be away?"

The man shrugged. "They said at least a century, but so what? I am told Genser's is a good world with plenty of room."

"How do you feel about those you will work for?"

"The managers? They will look after us. I mean they will have to, won't they? Who else can do the work?"

Managers. Burret rolled the word around within his head. Not with the explosive potential of 'masters' perhaps, but leaving no doubt who was in charge.

"There are a lot of you and only a few of them. Have you thought about that?"

"I know what you suggest, but it will not be. The managers have the knowledge which will keep us alive on the new world, so we will work for them as we promised when we signed on. There will be no need for anyone with a whip." Bessem shook his head, added vehemently, "Never!"

In his student days, as part of a social studies curriculum, Burret attended the screening of an ancient movie classic, *Metropolis*. As Bessem spoke, he remembered an apocalyptic scene of an army of willing workers marching into the open jaws of an industrial megamouth. Heavy-handed symbolism perhaps, but illustrating a social relationship which had always schismed humankind between those who exploited, and those who meekly accepted what the exploiters decided was 'for the good of all'.

And it was coming to Genser's World.

Richard Burret felt a chill up his spine.

✢ ✢ ✢

With both of the guests sedated, the crew of the *Star Venturer* assembled in the wardroom. As usual, the custodians preferred to stand while the humans relaxed around a table. One of the catbirds settled on Coestrand's shoulder, while the other remained with its master.

"Opinions?" Burret asked.

Coestrand snorted. "You know what that woman told me? She said Earth would not have been in such a mess if political and economic decisions were restricted to those qualified to make them."

"I am amazed she opened up to you at all. You are not exactly her kind of person."

Coestrand laughed aloud. "Not the right skin color, you mean? She did mumble something about yours truly being living proof there are exceptions to every rule, which I decided to accept as a backhanded compliment."

"You didn't tell her what happened to Earth, did you?"

"Of course not. The last thing I wanted was a smug 'I told you so'."

"What did she mean by 'qualified'?" Joan wondered.

"She expounded at length about that. According to her vision of an ideal society, universal suffrage is hogwash. Even the right to vote should be restricted to an educated elite."

Burret's mouth twisted in disgust. What was being exported to Genser's World horrified him, and his mind flooded with scenarios ranging from accepting the inevitable to destroying the *Mayflower II*. "What about Bessem?" he asked.

"You heard the man," Joan replied. "As far as he is concerned, servitude under the managers is a vast improvement over his former wretched existence. I suspect most of the others were selected because of similar hard luck stories. For the first few years anyway, I do not doubt the managers will have a docile labor pool at their disposal."

"What about afterwards?"

"If the managers are smart, and I do not doubt they are, they will select and train a team of well-rewarded overseers to protect the status quo. With an intelligent balance of carrot and stick, their obscene little technocracy will function just fine, thank you."

Coestrand shook her head. "You are describing an insular feudalism, Joan."

"So? If you don't think four-plus light years is far enough from..." Joan struck her forehead with the heel of her hand. "What am I thinking? *We* are there!"

"Damn right we are. And it worries me."

It also worried Burret. The people of Curtis would not take kindly to the presence of a totalitarian mini-state on Genser's World, even if it was thousands of kilometers removed. And what about the managers themselves? Would they be comfortable sharing a planet on which there was already a thriving community of free and equal citizens?

Uneasy tyrants had started wars for less.

Wars.

Burret snapped his fingers. "Gervaise!"

She appeared instantly. "I have been listening," the hologram said unnecessarily.

"Have your scans revealed anything more about that blank area in the asteroid?"

Konnenen shook her white head. "They have not."

"Could it be the result of deliberate shielding?"

A frown. "Possibly. But for what purpose?"

"Joan, please rouse our guests and bring them here."

His wife's eyes widened. "Both of them?"

"Oh yes." Burret's expression was grim. "Definitely both of them!"

Joan departed. A few minutes later she brought in Carmitia Davis, with Bessem trailing timidly behind.

Davis, who had been coldly ignoring 229, glanced at Konnenen's holographic image with only mild interest. But when she saw the custodians, she turned white. "Oh."

"We call them custodians," Burret told her pleasantly as he seated the two so they faced each other across the table. Yet the blonde continued to ignore Bessem in a manner which was clearly a practiced art. In contrast, the small man sat rigid as a post, his eyes downcast. "Like us," Burret continued, "they are also from Genser's World."

Davis licked her lips. "Do they work for you?"

"Not for us. With us."

"Is there a large population?"

"Large enough." Burret enjoyed her consternation.

The catbird on Coestrand's shoulder examined the blonde newcomer with huge-eyed curiosity, then decided to investigate closer. It launched itself across the room, but at the last second braked and alighted on the table in front of her.

"Nice pet," Davis said coldly. She apparently tolerated cuddly animals.

The toleration was not mutual. With a squawk of disgust, the catbird returned to Coestrand, then to its own master, who stroked the neck of his symbiot as he intoned solemnly,

"That one not think right."

"Not right," the other custodian agreed.

"What are they talking about?" Davis demanded.

"They don't like you," Coestrand replied. As if to emphasize the captain's point, the other catbird flew directly to Bessem's shoulder and settled there with a pleasant meow. Still maintaining his eyes-down posture, Bessem lifted a tentative hand to stroke the creature.

Coestrand said with relish, "But they do like you, Amjud."

Bessem lifted his head. "Are there others like this?" He seemed astonished at his own temerity.

"Oh yes. They get on well with people." Coestrand grinned at the blonde manager. "Most people anyway."

Davis was indifferent to the goad. "Why did you bring me here?"

Noting with disgust her self-centered 'me', Burret wondered if her thirty-seven colleagues were equally unpleasant. "There is a section of your ship which is opaque to our scans." He looked directly at 229. "Mr. Bessem, do you know anything about that?"

The little man swallowed, looked down again. "I have never seen the *Mayflower*, except in photographs they showed us at the recruiting station. They put us all to sleep before we were placed on board."

Burret was not surprised. If there were secrets to be kept, those who would supply the labor on the new world would hardly be the ones who prepared and loaded the ship.

"Ms. Davis?"

"Doctor Davis, if you don't mind," the woman said coldly.

"All right *Doctor* Davis, what can you tell us about that shielded section of your ship?"

Her face was an unreadable mask. "I am afraid I do not know what you are talking about."

The catbirds bristled.

✜ ✜ ✜

"What do you think is there?" Joan asked after the two guests were returned to their cabins.

"An armory," Coestrand replied without hesitation. "Most likely hand weapons to keep the rabble in line."

"Could be, I suppose." Joan bit her lip as she considered the logic of the possibility and its implications. She turned to her husband. "So Davis was lying when she told us she didn't know?"

"Of course she was lying. You saw how the catbirds reacted."

"My sweet, I am convinced that woman is as emotionless as a durasteel vault. The catbirds reacted because they could not read her!"

Coestrand asked, "Joan, aren't there drugs to make her talk?"

The psychologist shook her head. "Not on someone just out of stasis. There are residuals in her system which might trigger a fatal reaction."

"So what? If we are lucky, we will learn the truth. If not..." A graceful shrug. "She won't be missed."

"You don't really mean that, do you?"

The smaller woman considered. "I suppose not," she replied unconvincingly.

Burret was tempted to echo Coestrand's sentiments, but restrained the impulse when he saw his wife's face. Joan could forgive Coestrand, who certainly had reasons enough to regard racists as low on the evolutionary scale. But a husband is supposed to be supportive, especially when his wife has sworn an oath named after a long dead physician. He said, "So I suppose we have to find some way to get into that arm..."

Konnenen appeared. Although she was a computer-generated hologram of a dead scientist, she projected agitation. "Four armed men have appeared on the surface of the other ship and are headed in the direction of our airlock."

CHAPTER FIFTY-THREE

● ●

There was no point resisting. The space-armored men, each identified by a black number on his chest, carried handguns and laser rifles. At least they were polite.

"We are sorry for the imposition," #1 said woodenly as he and his companions flipped up their faceplates and revealed identical faces; ageless, sexless and expressionless. "Unfortunately it is necessary."

Cyborgs? Burret recalled a military research project run by an obscure general with the unlikely name of Montgomery Rommel Graham, supposedly terminated by a nervous administration during the fundamentalist decades. As he and the two women regarded the intruders with a nervousness just short of fear, he wondered if the general had sold out to people not so susceptible to public outrage. "Who are you?"

"We are called grahams," #2 replied. "Our stasis chambers are located in the high-security section of the *Mayflower*. We were automatically reactivated when you revived manager Davis. By the way, please bring her to us."

'Reactivated' sounded like someone had put a new battery in a gadget; hardly the image presented by stone-faced clones looking as if they were ready for participation in a war. That the clones were confronting three casually clad people in the control deck of a starship, seemed more the stuff of farce than reality.

"I will get her," Joan said, and disappeared down the access well.

"Do you know what ship this is?" Burret asked.

"We are aware this is the *Star Venturer*," #3 replied. They seemed to have an unspoken agreement they would speak in rotation.

"Then you must also be aware we are from Genser's World, which is your destination. We revived the manager only because the existence of the *Mayflower* was a complete surprise to us. I assure you Doctor Davis does not need rescuing. If she desires, we will even return her to stasis."

Joan reappeared, followed by Carmitia Davis. When the blonde woman saw the armored quartet, she did not seem surprised. "You took your time." With a dismissive wave of the hand, she added, "Never mind. Have you investigated all the decks?"

"Not yet," #4 said. "We came on board only a few minutes ago."

"Then if you see a white-haired woman, ignore her. She is a harmless computer-generated hologram. However, somewhere on this ship are two aliens. I suggest..."

"Aliens?"

It was not surprise. Burret suspected the oversized four were incapable of emotion. More likely it was a request for clarification.

"Please do not interrupt. Although the beings are not intrinsically violent, I believe it would be prudent to take basic precautions. So bring these people with us in case there is a confrontation."

"Then what?" Coestrand demanded as she angrily shrugged off a big hand which closed on her shoulder.

"Then we will see."

Burret and his wife stayed close together as they followed Davis, Coestrand and grahams #2 and #3 down from control to the deck which contained the living quarters. #1 and #4 clumped along behind. As they emerged from the access well, Davis ordered Coestrand shoved into the wardroom. Burret was pushed in after her.

"As soon as this ship is secured," the blonde woman said, "you will see your wife again. Until then, I am afraid you will have to make do with the less than adequate company of this..." Her lips curled. "Person."

Joan had barely enough time to cry out, "Don't worry dar..." before the door was slammed shut. After a moment Burret peered through the door's transparent panel and saw the bulk of #4 standing outside.

Frustrated, he clenched his fists. "Now what?"

Coestrand laid a light hand on his arm. "Richard, it is not in their interest to harm Joan. She is a hostage for your good behavior, after all."

Burret took a deep breath and let it out. "I know that. But what does that female have in mind for us afterward? Now we know what she and her friends have in mind, there is no way she can let us return to Genser's World!"

"Does she know the *Venturer* has an F.T.L. drive?"

"If she does, she hasn't let on. But when she has time to add two and two, she will figure it out."

"I am not so sure about that." Coestrand hesitated a moment, continued. "Davis is smart, but she is also a fanatic. My guess is she lacks the imagination to ask the right questions. But I agree she will not willingly send us on our way. Even with reasoning based on old fashioned physics, she knows *Star Venturer* will arrive at Genser's a quarter century before the monster she and her friends are riding."

"So it's kill us or keep us," Burret muttered grimly, realizing both alternatives were equally undesirable. "Pat, you know this ship better than anyone. Is it a good place for hide-and-seek?"

"John and Joe?"

Burret nodded. "I haven't seen them around since Konnenen announced we were being invaded."

Coestrand pursed her lips. "There are plenty of nooks and crannies within the various modules. What do you think they are up to?"

The man shrugged. "Trying to gain time, perhaps. If I knew how their minds work..."

Konnenen flicked into existence. The simulation had a no-nonsense look. The sweep of white hair was slightly disarrayed, the blue one-piece coverall not quite immaculate. It was a good effect, suggesting urgency. "There is not much time," she said crisply. "After I leave here, proceed to D18 where you will find the custodians waiting."

Coestrand gestured at the door. "What about the guard?"

"What guard?" Konnenen asked. As abruptly as she had appeared, she vanished. Burret ran to the door and cracked it open. #4 was gone. He opened the door wider just in time to see Carmitia Davis and the big graham disappear down the access well toward the lower decks.

Coestrand peered over his shoulder. "How...?"

Burret grinned. "Dollar to a donut, that Davis ain't Davis!" He grabbed his companion's arm, hauled her out of the wardroom, around the corner past the access well and the sound of voices a few decks down, to a heavy door marked MODULES A-B. He pulled open the door, revealing a short corridor with service hatches on either side and two more doors angled at the far end. "As I recall, there is an indirect route to section D through here. Right?"

She pointed. "That way." After Burret quietly pulled the door closed behind him, she opened one of the hatches on the right and squirmed through into a service tunnel. On his hands and knees he followed her about thirty meters to another hatch, which led into the cavernous interior of one of the cargo modules. Stooping low behind racks of storage palettes (still to be taken down to Genser's World as shuttles became available), Coestrand led the way to the end of the big cylinder and down through another hatch into an even narrower tunnel. "You'll get used to it," she panted as she crawled twenty meters to a further hatch and up into the next module. Burret followed her past more storage racks to a row of empty metal-walled compartments, one which was labeled 'D18'. With glad chirrups, two catbirds glided out of the darkness and landed on their shoulders. Their custodian masters were dark stick-figures barely distinguishable in the gloom. From behind them, a smaller figure emerged.

"Amjud! Who got you out?"

The little man looked embarrassed. "If I tell you, you won't believe it."

"Tell us anyway."

"It was..." Amjud took a deep breath and blurted, "A ghost!

✤ ✤ ✤

Joan felt like surplus baggage as she was manhandled down through the decks of the crew module, until they finally arrived at the morgue on the lowest deck. She watched as #2 checked each of the eight stasis chambers and announced, "They are empty, manager Davis."

"Obviously," the blonde woman said irritably. She turned to Joan. "Don't get your hopes up too high, Doctor Walsh. We will find your alien friends."

"If they don't find you first," Joan retorted, silently grateful Davis assumed such chambers were still necessary for interstellar travelers.

"I would welcome it. Those animated sticks are no threat to my plans."

As they returned to the access well, they heard the clatter of boots descending the narrow metal treads. #4 emerged from the well and said stolidly, "The man called Burret and the woman called Coestrand have escaped."

Despite her desperation, Joan wanted to cheer. Instead she controlled her leaping emotions as Davis inquired coldly, "Now how did they manage to do that?"

"It was when you called me away from my post. At least, I thought it was you, manager Davis."

For the first time, the woman looked as if she was about to lose control. She lost her elegance as she turned red and her face muscles twitched. "Me?"

"You came up the well and told me I was needed. So I followed you down two decks until..." The graham managed to look embarrassed. "Suddenly, you disappeared. I suspected a trick, so I immediately returned to my post and discovered the man and woman were gone."

Davis swung a furious face to Joan. "It is that damn computer of yours, isn't it?"

"Our harmless, computer-generated hologram?" Joan laughed aloud. "Quite probably."

"You are all getting to be somewhat of a nuisance," Davis said tonelessly. "However, I cannot afford further time for such irrelevancies." She turned to #1. "Do you know the codes for Storage A nine?"

"Yes manager."

"Good. Then go to A nine and bring one of the packages to me."

"Manager, the packages are restricted to..."

"Do it!"

"Yes manager," #1 said obediently, and clattered back up the well. The remaining three grahams shifted uneasily.

Seeing the look of satisfaction on Davis's face, Joan had a sinking feeling things were not going well. "What do you intend?"

"First I am taking you to the *Mayflower*. You will be a useful asset when we arrive at Genser's World, although for you it will be a generation too late. But because the descendants of your contemporaries will certainly know your name, perhaps even revere it, I suspect they will be more amenable if it is Joan Walsh Burret who briefs them on the new political order."

Joan remembered her history, and her heart sank another notch. "Order?"

"Ours will be a meticulously planned society which cannot tolerate disruptive influences from outside. Your colony must therefore become adjunct to New Acadia."

Adjunct meaning subservient, Joan thought bitterly. Davis and her friends certainly had the numbers for it. Also, as Richard had already suggested, the weapons.

"What about my husband and the others?"

"They will remain here of course. As I said, I have wasted enough time."

"What is the..." Joan licked her lips. "Package?"

"Oh that?" The blonde smiled broadly, although her slate-gray eyes remained cold. "Consider it a means to ensure the security of our operation. It is quite small really, a mere seven kilotons or so."

Joan gasped.

CHAPTER FIFTY-FOUR

●●●●●●●●●●●●●●●●●●●●●●●●●●●●●●

When Konnenen reappeared at D18 (despite Burret's careful explanation, Bessem remained convinced the white-haired simulation was a benign spirit), she announced brusquely, "Graham number one is returning to the aster-oid. At the instant he is subsurface, I will release the anchors and allow the *Star Venturer* to drift free. Before manager Davis realizes what is going on and attempts to reestablish capture, you must deal with her and the three remaining grahams."

Burret was doubtful. "With Joan as a hostage? You are asking a lot."

"You will have help," Konnenen told him, as the cus-todians flickered and disappeared.

"What the..." Astonished, Burret ran into the darkness of the compartment. Something brushed by him, causing him to swing around and bump into one of the side walls. With a brief flutter of wings, the catbirds vacated his and Coestrand's shoulders and disappeared as thoroughly as the custodians. "What is going on?"

Bessem said with awe, "The aliens are magicians. They willed themselves away from here!"

Konnenen shook her head. "They used normal locomo-tion. You did not see them because the custodians and their symbiots have the ability to blend into the background in a manner similar but superior to earthly chameleons."

"It's certainly the neatest disappearing trick I have seen," Coestrand admitted as she went into the compartment, groped around in the darkness and came out again. "All right, I give up. Where did they go?"

"They are on their way to disrupt the activities of manager Davis and the three remaining grahams." Konnenen pointed to storage racks further along in the gloom of the module. "There is a case of small arms in compartment D11. I suggest you equip yourselves and follow my directions toward..." She hesitated. "Just a moment please."

The floor shuddered slightly.

"We are now disconnected and drifting free. Please hurry, and follow my directions."

The weapons, which were narcotic-dart rifles designed for hunting game on the new world, were hardly a match for the hardware carried by the grahams. But the drug which tipped the darts was supposedly instantaneous, although Konnenen admitted she was unsure of its effect on a graham. In any case, with the more lethal needle pistols locked away in the crew module, there was not much choice. Bessem even refused outright to shoot at anyone, although he agreed to carry a spare rifle.

After Konnenen disappeared, Coestrand led the way through another service tunnel into a swelteringly hot sub-floor space below the life support section of the drive module. The egg-crate floor gratings cast a pattern of square shadows on their prone bodies.

"Gervaise told me the custodians will lead them here," the small woman whispered as they cramped against a rack of piping and listened. Yet all they could hear was the soft whir of pumps and fans.

Burret began to lift a section of grating and promptly lowered it again. "Someone's coming."

There was an approaching clatter of boots, followed by a toneless, "Where did it go?"

"There!" answered a second voice. There was the blinding flash of a laser discharge, followed by a crack of superheated air and a hiss of cooling metal.

"Did you hit it?"

"I am not sure. But I think so."

"Wait here. If it is still alive, it cannot get far." The footsteps retreated.

Again Burret lifted the grating. Graham #3 stood a few paces away, laser rifle at the ready. Burret took careful aim with his own weapon and squeezed the trigger. There was a sharp *crack*, the graham gasped, reached for the back of his neck, and toppled. Coestrand promptly emerged from below the floor and scampered over to retrieve the graham's dropped laser rifle. But as she reached for the weapon...

Coestrand jumped aside just as a searing shaft of light burned her right arm. Gasping with pain, she crumpled to the floor as Burret diverted the second graham's attention with a snap shot in which the dart bounced harmlessly off the cyborg's shoulder armor. Burret jumped up through the floor opening and dove for cover behind the prone bulk of narcotized #3 as a laser beam sliced into the big body, which jerked and gave off an odor of burned meat.

The bastard's killing his comrade to get at me! was Burret's shocked realization as another laser discharge blasted into already dying flesh. Hearing the deliberate tread of boots as the other graham approached, he braced himself for death. He heard Coestrand whisper, "Goodbye, Richard. It has been a good..."

There was an angry flutter of wings, a howl of fury and then a crash. Burret lifted his head in time to see graham #4 bounce off a bulkhead as he flailed at a catbird whose claws were firmly embedded in his face. The catbird screeched and flopped to the floor. Amjud Bessem appeared as if from nowhere, grabbed the laser rifle of the fallen graham and blasted #4's head into bloody ruin.

In the silence which followed the crash as the armored torso toppled to the floor, Burret pushed himself to his knees and looked with astonishment at 229. He wanted to say a lot of things. Instead, he said simply, "I owe you my life."

A look of repugnance on his face, the smaller man let the weapon clatter to the grating. "I will not kill again."

"Do not make promises you cannot keep, Amjud," Coestrand gasped as Burret knelt before her and examined her arm. Through pain-filled eyes, she looked up at Burret. "Will I live?"

"As long as you are prepared to put up with a permanent battle scar, of course you will." He reached out to help her up, but Coestrand resisted.

"You have to take care of Davis and the other Graham. Joan must be getting tired of their company by now. Anyway, I am comfortable where I am."

"Like hell you are," Burret retorted, wondering how he could take care of two enemies without harming his wife. As he got to his feet, he saw Bessem carefully pick up the injured catbird, carry it to Coestrand and lay the creature in the crook of her good arm. One wing hung at an ungainly angle and the large eyes were dull. With a barely perceptible *mew*, the small head nestled gratefully against her warmth.

Bessem said, "Mr. Burret."

Burret looked in the direction the smaller man pointed and saw a pair of skeletal limbs protruding from behind a fan casing. "Oh damn," he muttered as he ran over and found the body of a custodian. Although the chest of the alien was a mess of scorched bone and dark oozing blood, in some strange sense John (or Joe) seemed at peace. On his back, arms straight along his sides, head centered and eyes closed, he lay as if arranged for final immolation by his beloved Ship.

Was John a victim of his own carelessness, a brief but fatal relaxing of his chameleon mode during a critical moment? Or had it been a deliberate sacrifice, gaining vital seconds for the friends he sensed were close?

Burret looked back at Coestrand. "He's dead."

She nodded. "I know." She looked down at the catbird on her arm. "My friend just told me."

Bessem pushed a laser rifle into Burret's hand. "Time for us to go, Mr. Burret."

"*Us*, Amjud?"

229 retrieved the weapon of the other graham. "Us," the smaller man repeated. He looked embarrassed. "I know I am unimportant, and I know what I said about killing.

But if a being who is not human was willing to die for us, the least I can do is..." He flushed. "What must be done."

Burret looked at Bessem with a new respect. Although Amjud Bessem was a small man, it was in physical stature only. "Whatever else you are, my friend, you are certainly not unimportant." He wanted to express further encouragement, but was interrupted by the silky voice of Manager Carmitia Davis on the P.A.

"Listen to me Richard Burret, and listen carefully. You will come immediately to the control deck, alone, and instruct your computer to re-dock this ship to the Mayflower. *If you are not here within ten minutes, I cannot guarantee your wife will not have..."* There was the terrifying sound of a woman's cry of pain. *"An unfortunate accident."*

It was too much. Shaking with rage and fear, Burret wasted valuable seconds as he looked wildly around him for something to throw or break. Then, realizing he was wasting valuable time, he summoned an immense effort of will to fight back the waves of unreason.

"Gervaise!" he shouted. "Joe!"

No answer. Just Bessem, waiting patiently.

"Amjud, I am going to do precisely what the manager asked. Wait a couple of minutes and then follow quietly. When you get to the deck below control, conceal yourself and wait."

"What are you going to do?"

"I won't know until I get there. But whatever happens, I must get Joan out of harm's way before I attempt anything drastic. So wait, please, and listen."

"You can count on me, Mr. Burret."

Burret clasped the other's shoulder. "I know I can."

"Good luck," Coestrand whispered. She had raised her uninjured arm so she could gently caress the catbird. It turned its head and the large eyes, brighter now, regarded Burret solemnly. It transmitted something, he was not sure what.

Although, for just for a moment, Burret thought he saw himself doing unpleasant things to a graham.

✛ ✛ ✛

As Burret ascended the access well into the control deck, Davis and graham #2, who was holding Joan in a throat lock, watched him warily.

Burret restrained his fury. "Let her go."

"A little." Davis gestured, and the graham slackened his grip.

Joan took a deep, shuddering breath. "Richard..."

"Have they hurt you?"

She managed a wan smile as she replied hoarsely. "I have felt better." The arm tightened and she gasped.

As Burret seethed, the blonde woman said, "Just a reminder. By the way, where are Three and Four?"

"They are no use to you anymore."

"They are dead?"

Burret forced a grin. "Oh yes."

"I see." The woman seemed more puzzled than angry. "Later I must spare a moment so you can tell me how you accomplished that. However, first things first. Please instruct your computer to re-dock to the *Mayflower*."

Two monitor screens were illuminated. The first, a wide angle view, showed the converted asteroid drifting a few hundred meters from *Star Venturer*. The other was a high magnification image of a suited figure waiting patiently next to one of the air locks. It carried something.

"You are dying to tell him, aren't you Doctor Walsh?" Davis asked with a chill smile. "You can, you know."

Joan took a deep breath. "Richard, she intends to destroy our ship. The thing that graham is carrying is a nuclear warhead!"

Surprised that he did not feel surprised, Burret looked at his wife in the clutches of the graham and wondered what kind of life they could expect under the dictatorship of the managers. Perhaps it would not be quite as bad as Hell. On the other hand, he did not doubt it would be a very efficient purgatory.

"Richard!"

"I heard you dear," he said mildly. He turned to Davis. "If I do what you ask, then what?"

"Don't worry, both of you have become too valuable to leave you here to be vaporized. You will be stored in stasis until we arrive at Genser's World. What happens after we arrive will, of course, depend on you."

"What about the custodians?"

"Your alien friends will stay here, as will that silly little man you inexplicably chose to revive. By the way, what is their current state of health?"

"I have not the faintest idea," Burret lied.

A shrug of shapely shoulders. "No matter. Two-two-nine is undoubtedly quaking with fright in a dark corner somewhere, and your custodians look too frail to be much good for anything." Davis gestured. "Call up your tame computer, Mr. Burret."

"As you say." Burret raised his voice. "Gervaise!"

She materialized without fuss near the access well. "Yes, Richard." Konnenen seemed to be having trouble with the simulation. Her outline wavered and her features were indistinct.

"Is that what fooled number four?" Davis asked incredulously. "It is hardly better than an out-of-focus photograph!"

"Conditions vary," Burret told Davis vaguely as he turned to Konnenen. "Please show the simulation you used to distract the graham."

Konnenen shimmered and transformed into something vaguely resembling the manager, although the image was still indistinct.

Davis's thin lips twisted. "I am glad that muscle-bound idiot is where he can make no more stupid mistakes," she said contemptuously as the image reformed into the indistinct Konnenen. "Now you can instruct it to re-dock to the *Mayflower*."

Burret nodded, turned and looked at the screen which showed #1 and his deadly package. "Do as she asks, please."

Konnenen vanished. There was a slight trembling underfoot and the asteroid on the other screen slowly grew larger. The lumpy outline expanded beyond the rim of the screen, and a crosshair appeared at the point of contact. Suddenly the *Star Venturer*'s emergency thrusters roared into life and they were thrown off their feet as the ship surged forward and sideways and crunched against the asteroid. Burret had a split second glimpse of #1 flinging the package aside as it desperately tried to get out of the way, before the screen went dark and there was a terrible noise of rending metal.

Joan was flung sideways out of the graham's grasp. Burret stumbled toward her even as he realized he had little chance against the already pouncing graham. But even as he summoned his resources for a desperate spurt, there was a sizzling laser flash which ended at the graham's chest. The big body pitched forward and slammed into its frightened quarry.

The next few seconds were a moving snapshot indelibly recorded in Burret's memory. Joan, painfully pulling herself from under the dead graham. Manager Davis, chalk white and moaning with pain, crumpled against the corner of a control panel. And 229 Amjud Bessem, laser rifle still in his hand, emerging from the access well and walking across the deck to the body of graham #2.

After looking down at the body for a moment, Bessem gave the weapon to Burret. "This time I mean it. I will kill no more."

Burret nodded. "I believe you, Amjud, and I thank you." He assisted Joan to her feet, winced as she clutched him fiercely.

"I thank you, too," she said gratefully over her husband's shoulder.

Davis had pulled herself into an awkward sitting position. "Please help me. I believe my leg is broken."

"Consider yourself lucky," Burret said unsympathetically.

Konnenen appeared. The simulation was as crisp and faultless as her attire, which was a spotless blue tunic along with white slacks to match her meticulously coiffured sweep of hair.

"We are re-anchored to the *Mayflower*," she reported crisply. "Although there is some structural damage to Module C, all vital control and mechanical systems remain functional. Meanwhile, may I remind you there are two injured people who require medical attention?"

Bessem stepped forward. "Mr. Burret, I have some small knowledge of first aid. I will attend the manager while you and your lady look after Captain Coestrand."

"Pat?" Joan grabbed Burret's arm, asked urgently. "She's hurt?"

"Nothing you cannot fix, wife dear," Burret grinned as he picked up one of the deck's emergency medkits and urged his wife toward the access well. Just before they descended, he glanced back at Bessem. The small man was already kneeling by the side of Carmitia Davis, murmuring soothing words as he gently eased the ashen-faced manager into a more comfortable position on her back. Then Burret looked at the imperturbable image of Gervaise Konnenen. "Gervaise, although it is probably not my place to criticize your handling of the ship, I must tell you that was a bloody awful approach."

"I know," the computer said modestly. "I am truly sorry about that."

CHAPTER FIFTY-FIVE

• •

Dictated by Joan Walsh Burret aboard the *Star Venturer*, en route to Genser's World after a rendezvous with the asteroid-starship *Mayflower II*. Date: August 23, 2219 AD.

✢ ✢ ✢

Captain Coestrand and my husband returned to the May-flower *and confirmed our worst fears. The shielded section included an armory with enough hardware, including several nukes, to equip a small army.*

With the exception of a few hand weapons, they spaced it all.

The section also contained eighteen more grahams in stasis. They posed an ethical dilemma which we solved only after hours of agonizing debate. Were they human, or mere biological machines? According to information contained within our own database, Montgomery Graham's proposal was to literally 'hard-wire' human infants so they would grow to become (in his words) 'superior servants of the state'. Yet even as we deactivated life support to that section, we remained unsure if these particular grahams were indeed the monstrous progeny of Graham's work, or something less sinister. When I asked Carmitia Davis about the grahams, her reaction was a blank stare along with 'How would I know?'.

So I suppose it will be up to others to decide whether or not we are murderers. I do know my own conscience is clear, as is my husband's and that of the captain. Poor Amjud Bessem tried to dissuade us, even to the extent of becoming physically ill when I told him the deed was done. Amjud's only comfort comes from the catbird of the dead custodian. It is a remarkable relationship between a creature which will probably never fly again, and a confused human being who is trying to reconcile conscience and reality. I wish both of them well.

Carmitia Davis is another problem. There is no doubt it would have been easier to return her to stasis with the other managers, than attempt to persuade her there is a better way to run a society. But we finally decided she would be our test subject. If we can soften that heart of stone, then surely there is hope for her colleagues. Meanwhile the woman hobbles around the ship like a defanged tigress, refusing to talk to anyone and taking her meals alone in her cabin. I am tempted to tell her she eats with the rest of us or not at all. It may still come to that, especially after we get home. On the other hand, perhaps she will change when she sees with her own eyes what we have accomplished on Genser's World.

We shall see.

The surviving custodian and his catbird sensibly remained hidden until we finally separated from the Mayflower and engaged sideshift. Then, with a peculiar mixture of halting human words and empathic projection, he somehow communicated his role as repository of what both custodians experienced during the mission. Whether or not the knowledge contained within that round skull will help his people remains to be seen. At least the custodians will know that unlike them, we humans are a vastly varied species; even to the extent of sometimes being alien to each other. I hope they will learn to recognize and then accept that peculiarity of humankind.

It will be so good to get home...

CHAPTER FIFTY-SIX

• •

The return to Genser's world was a subdued event in which the travelers were welcomed with a mixture of warmth and tears. It would take time for the people of Curtis to come to terms with the fact that along with the Lunites and the few hundred in stasis aboard the *Mayflower II*, they were the only human beings left alive in the galaxy.

"Think of it as a new beginning," Eric Gerenson advised solemnly. A mixture of poet and pragmatist, he was already regarded as one of the stalwarts of the community, although like Richard Burret he stubbornly refused to run for the office of mayor or even as councilor.

"A new Eden?" Joan teased.

"Of course not. Unlike Adam and Eve, we do have the advantage of being able to learn from past mistakes."

"All of human history in the database, huh?"

"Why not? It is there to be used."

Carmitia Davis approached. Her leg had healed well, and her graceful walk drew more than one appreciative male eye. "May I join you?" she asked.

Burret pulled out a chair. "By all means." As the former manager sat down, he asked, "Have you come to a decision?"

The woman reached up and absently scratched the head of her catbird. The creature made contented noises. "When do you plan to return to the *Mayflower?*"

"Pretty soon. Probably within..." Burret did a rapid mental calculation. "A couple of months."

She nodded. "I will be ready."

Coestrand asked, "How many of your colleagues do you plan to revive?"

"This trip, only two."

"Is that all?"

"Believe me, I was a raving liberal compared to the others. In any case, what is the hurry? There will be more trips, especially after the other ships have received their sideshift modifications."

"How does Amjud feel about it?"

"He and I have discussed the matter, and he agrees with my approach. He intends to revive no more than five of his people."

"Out of nearly five hundred?"

A slight shrug. "It is a start."

Burret leaned back in his chair and regarded Davis thoughtfully. He was sure her transformation was genuine. Her adoption by a catbird was proof of that. But he suspected her revulsion at her past had swung the pendulum too far. Her problems were further complicated by the prospect of having to confront even two of her former colleagues and their dream of a new feudalism.

But he was forced to admit there was nothing wrong with the cautious approach. After all, they had the time and the resources. A few revivals each trip, with an evolving program of reeducation and integration stretched across the decades, until the *Mayflower* itself finally joined the other orbiting starships above Genser's World. By that time, Curtis would be more that just a huddle of buildings. It would be a thriving community with a proper school, a hospital, and the infrastructure to support continuous ground-to-orbit shuttle capability. With their five starships finally modified for sideshift, the people of Genser's World would already be searching for other habitable worlds among the stars while they maintained regular contact with the asteroid-ship.

It was even possible the two custodian ships would eventually be added to the fleet.

Someday, a ship jointly crewed by humans and custo-dians would set out to seek the original custodian home world. It would be a good partnership, especially if on the way they find, or are found, by other intelligent beings among the stars. The human-custodian-catbird alliance would be a clear demonstration that such a relationship is not only possible, but in evolutionary terms a desirable one.

Will there be a return to Luna? Burret wondered. *Or even to Earth?*

Tears came to his eyes as he remembered.

Earth doesn't live there anymore.

EPILOGUE

• •

This was not Earth, although it had been before the asteroid impact destroyed its biosphere. Now it was a new world, re-seeded, replenished, and literally re-terraformed by the inhabitants of its single large moon.

The beneficiaries of the decades-long project were not the Lunites themselves, who in any case were content to remain in their caverns. Yet the transformation of the dust-swirled sphere in their sky into something resembling (but not the same as) the blue planet of pre-impact memory, did at least assuage some of their guilt.

So perhaps it was only poetic justice that what was once known as 'Earth Allergy Syndrome' no longer had relevance to the colonists from Genser's World, as they emerged from their shuttle along with their catbirds, planted their first crops and began to assemble the prefabricated structures of their first settlement, which they named New Curtis.

But when the subject came up of choosing a name for their new world, it provoked a long and furious debate. By unanimous vote they rejected Earth, because that planet existed only in databases and a few scarred memories. Not quite so unanimous was the vote which rejected New Earth, because it was argued 'New' made no sense linked with what was long gone and best forgotten. Finally they reached back to more innocent times, to the name of the goddess who was the both the daughter of Chaos and mother of the Titans.

Gaea.

It seemed appropriate.

Our titles are available at major book stores and local independent resellers who support Science Fiction and Fantasy readers like you.

Alphanauts by J. Brian Clarke - (tp) - ISBN: 978-1-894063-14-2
Apparition Trail, The by Lisa Smedman - (tp) - ISBN:1-894063-22-8
Black Chalice by Marie Jakober - (hb) - ISBN:1-894063-00-7
Blue Apes by Phyllis Gotlieb (pb) - ISBN:1-895836-13-1
Blue Apes by Phyllis Gotlieb (hb) - ISBN:1-895836-14-X
Children of Atwar, The by Heather Spears (pb) - ISBN:0-888783-35-3
Claus Effect by David Nickle & Karl Schroeder, The (pb) - ISBN:1-895836-34-4
Claus Effect by David Nickle & Karl Schroeder, The (hb) - ISBN:1-895836-35-2
Courtesan Prince, The by Lynda Williams (tp) - 1-894063-28-7
Dark Earth Dreams by Candas Dorsey & Roger Deegan (comes with a CD)
   - ISBN:1-895836-05-0
Distant Signals by Andrew Weiner (tp) - ISBN:0-888782-84-5
Dreams of an Unseen Planet by Teresa Plowright (tp) - ISBN:0-888782-82-9
Dreams of the Sea by Élisabeth Vonarburg (tp) - ISBN:1-895836-96-4
Dreams of the Sea by Élisabeth Vonarburg (hb) - ISBN:1-895836-98-0
Eclipse by K. A. Bedford - (tp) - ISBN:978-1-894063-30-2
Even The Stones by Marie Jakober - (tp) - ISBN:1-894063-18-X
Fires of the Kindred by Robin Skelton (tp) - ISBN:0-888782-71-3
Forbidden Cargo by Rebecca Rowe - (tp) - ISBN: 978-1-894063-16-6
Game of Perfection, A by Élisabeth Vonarburg (tp) - ISBN:978-1-894063-32-6
Green Music by Ursula Pflug (tp) - ISBN:1-895836-75-1
Green Music by Ursula Pflug (hb) - ISBN:1895836-77-8
Healer, The by Amber Hayward (tp) - ISBN:1-895836-89-1
Healer, The by Amber Hayward (hb) - ISBN:1-895836-91-3
Jackal Bird by Michael Barley (pb) - ISBN:1-895836-07-7
Jackal Bird by Michael Barley (hb) - ISBN:1-895836-11-5
Keaen by Till Noever - (tp) - ISBN:1-894063-08-2
Land/Space edited by Candas Jane Dorsey and Judy McCrosky (tp)
   - ISBN:1-895836-90-5
Land/Space edited by Candas Jane Dorsey and Judy McCrosky (hb)
   - ISBN:1-895836-92-1
Lyskarion: The Song of the Wind by J.A. Cullum - (tp) - ISBN:1-894063-02-3
Machine Sex and other stories by Candas Jane Dorsey (tp) - ISBN:0-888782-78-0
Maërlande Chronicles, The by Élisabeth Vonarburg (pb) - ISBN:0-888782-94-2
Moonfall by Heather Spears (pb) - ISBN:0-888783-06-X
On Spec: The First Five Years edited by On Spec (pb) - ISBN:1-895836-08-5
On Spec: The First Five Years edited by On Spec (hb) - ISBN:1-895836-12-3
Orbital Burn by K. A. Bedford - (tp) - ISBN:1-894063-10-4
Orbital Burn by K. A. Bedford - (hb) - ISBN:1-894063-12-0
Pallahaxi Tide by Michael Coney (pb) - ISBN:0-888782-93-4
Passion Play by Sean Stewart (pb) - ISBN:0-888783-14-0
Plague Saint by Rita Donovan, The - (tp) - ISBN:1-895836-28-X
Plague Saint by Rita Donovan, The - (hb) - ISBN:1-895836-29-8
Reluctant Voyagers by Élisabeth Vonarburg (pb) - ISBN:1-895836-09-3
Reluctant Voyagers by Élisabeth Vonarburg (hb) - ISBN:1-895836-15-8

Resisting Adonis by Timothy J. Anderson (tp) - ISBN:1-895836-84-0
Resisting Adonis by Timothy J. Anderson (hb) - ISBN:1-895836-83-2
Silent City, The by Élisabeth Vonarburg (tp) - ISBN:0-888782-77-2
Slow Engines of Time, The by Élisabeth Vonarburg (tp) - ISBN:1-895836-30-1
Slow Engines of Time, The by Élisabeth Vonarburg (hb) - ISBN:1-895836-31-X
Stealing Magic (flipover edition) by Tanya Huff (tp) - ISBN:978-1-894063-34-0
Strange Attractors by Tom Henighan (pb) - ISBN:0-888783-12-4
Taming, The by Heather Spears (pb) - ISBN:1-895836-23-9
Taming, The by Heather Spears (hb) - ISBN:1-895836-24-7
Ten Monkeys, Ten Minutes by Peter Watts (tp) - ISBN:1-895836-74-3
Ten Monkeys, Ten Minutes by Peter Watts (hb) - ISBN:1-895836-76-X
Tesseracts 1 edited by Judith Merril (pb) - ISBN:0-888782-79-9
Tesseracts 2 edited by Phyllis Gotlieb & Douglas Barbour (pb) - ISBN:0-888782-70-5
Tesseracts 3 edited by Candas Jane Dorsey & Gerry Truscott (pb) - ISBN:0-888782-90-X
Tesseracts 4 edited by Lorna Toolis & Michael Skeet (pb) - ISBN:0-888783-22-1
Tesseracts 5 edited by Robert Runté & Yves Maynard (pb) - ISBN:1-895836-25-5
Tesseracts 5 edited by Robert Runté & Yves Maynard (hb) - ISBN:1-895836-26-3
Tesseracts 6 edited by Robert J. Sawyer & Carolyn Clink (pb) - ISBN:1-895836-32-8
Tesseracts 6 edited by Robert J. Sawyer & Carolyn Clink (hb) - ISBN:1-895836-33-6
Tesseracts 7 edited by Paula Johanson & Jean-Louis Trudel (tp) - ISBN:1-895836-58-1
Tesseracts 7 edited by Paula Johanson & Jean-Louis Trudel (hb) - ISBN:1-895836-59-X
Tesseracts 8 edited by John Clute & Candas Jane Dorsey (tp) - ISBN:1-895836-61-1
Tesseracts 8 edited by John Clute & Candas Jane Dorsey (hb) - ISBN:1-895836-62-X
Tesseracts 9 edited by Nalo Hopkinson and Geoff Ryman (tp) - ISBN:1-894063-26-0
TesseractsQ edited by Élisabeth Vonarburg & Jane Brierley (pb) - ISBN:1-895836-21-2
TesseractsQ edited by Élisabeth Vonarburg & Jane Brierley (hb) - ISBN:1-895836-22-0
Throne Price by Lynda Williams and Alison Sinclair - (tp) - ISBN:1-894063-06-6

EDGE Science Fiction and Fantasy Publishing
P. O. Box 1714, Calgary, AB, Canada, T2P 2L7
www.edgewebsite.com
403-254-0160 (voice)
403-254-0456 (fax)

WHAT SHOULD I READ NEXT?
Selected books published by EDGE . . .

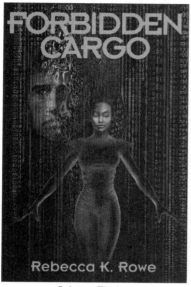

Science Fiction

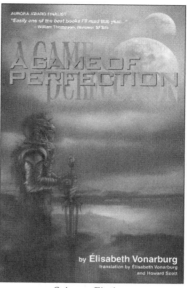

Science Fiction

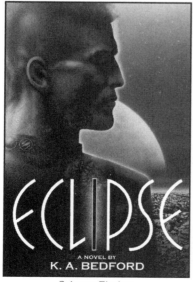

Science Fiction
Psychological Thriller

Fantasy Short
Story Collection